WICKED BLOOD

THE ROYALS: VAMPIRE COURT

MEGAN MONTERO

CHAPTER ONE

PIPER

The stench of damp earth filled my senses and sent a shiver over my skin. I tried to force my eyes open, but they refused to comply. There was nothing more disturbing than waging a war for consciousness and losing. My body was heavy and unresponsive, yet my mind began to fight. Each drop of awareness that came to me held an edge of panic that made me feel like I was drowning in a sea of darkness. Being trapped in limbo between conscious and unconscious where my mind woke and yet my body would not respond was my own kind of personal hell. I knew there'd been an attack and I'd been the unsuspecting target of an ambush.

Throbbing pain exploded behind my eyes, and I held in the groan burning in my throat. I knew I had to wake-up, I knew I was in mortal danger, I knew I had to be smart, and I knew I was truly and royally fucked. Helplessness was not something I was accustomed to. Yet here I was struggling to fight my way back and figure out where the hell I was and who the hell brought me here. Flashes of Marius and his followers danced in my thoughts. Would I die like this, drowning in a moment in which I was imprisoned in my own body?

My fingers were numb and hushed voices drifted through the walls toward me. Pain throbbed through my temples, around my head, and deep into my eyes. *Pain.* Pain was a good thing. If there was agony, then it would bring my senses to a quick, sharp focus. I tried to grab on to that pain and hold it. Memories of a pipe smashing into my face flashed in my head, and I knew these bastards had taken me by surprise. Rage warred with panic, and my blood was being boiled in my veins. I wanted the anger to take me. Anger was good, anger was fuel, anger would get me through whatever was about to happen next. Anger would hold off the fear long enough so I could think straight.

Ice-cold water splashed over my face and soaked my shirt. I sucked in a gasping breath, and my body swung back and forth before I put my feet down and steadied myself. My eyes flashed wide open and all at once everything came into focus. Agony, rage, and panic ran through me, sending adrenaline shooting through my body. My chest heaved as I tried to gain control of myself and size up my situation. When I took in my surroundings, there were two things I realized in this moment:

One, being woken up by being doused by ice water was only something a douche would do.

Two, I was absolutely screwed.

"Hello, Marius." *I give you the douche.*

I blew drops of water from my mouth onto the floor between us. The drops mixed with the blood trickling down the side of my face and fell to the floor. My hands were wrapped and bound. They were chained high above my head, and I hung there. I didn't know how long I'd been there, but my arms and fingers were completely numb. I couldn't open my fist with the bindings holding them shut. Power rolled in my stomach and up toward my fingers, but without my hands I couldn't let it loose. I couldn't rip him apart from the inside out. This bastard who had all the audacity and entitlement a person could have deserved my wrath.

He leaned against a table across from me with his arms crossed over his chest. An empty bucket sat next to him and a wide smirk spread across his face. "Hello, Piper."

"You'll never get away with this." I knew it sounded cliché, but I'd made friends in high places, and with Atlas now on my side, I knew I'd be hunted down soon enough . . . which meant he'd be more than dead soon enough. The thought of his death sent a thrill of pleasure through me. I just had to survive long enough until then.

"I already have." He shoved away from the table and began to prowl back and forth in front of me. I hated everything about him. I hated his long leather coat that wafted out around him for dramatic effect. I hated his attitude, and I hated the way others had fallen for his line of bullshit. Most of all, I hated that I couldn't kill him myself right here and now.

If Marius was about anything, he was all about the drama. "You're referring to your very powerful friends, I gather."

"Perhaps." I wasn't going to give anything away. "Or perhaps I plan on killing you myself."

He threw his head back and gave a humorless laugh. Dark strands of his hair fell back from his face, and he ran his hand through them, forcing them back into place around his face and down to his chin. "Your magic isn't powerful enough to take me."

"At least I have magic." *Low blow, Piper.* I knew it was stupid to poke the bear, but sometimes the bear really deserved it. Self-preservation should've won out, I shouldn't antagonize him, but I couldn't help myself. He had me chained here like an animal. It wasn't in my nature to cower or beg. Whatever he was going to do, I wanted to get it over with and done with. There was no use hanging here dreading what I knew would already be awful.

"Do not speak to me of magic!" he bellowed, and his voice carried and bounced off the rough, rocky walls. "After all that I have sacrificed! I deserve this."

I glanced around, trying to figure out where I was, but the best I got was *underground,* which meant that I could've been anywhere. My gut told me I was still in England, but even that could be wrong. He could've carried me through a mirror to anywhere in the world. I tried to make my voice sound bored.

"What the hell am I doing here, Marius?"

"Did you know magic resides in the blood? It's a life

force of its own." He moved in closer to me, so close our bodies were mere inches apart. He reached up and ran the backs of his fingers over my cheek. His skin was rough and scratchy. It was an unwelcome intrusion that made my skin crawl. When his dark eyes met mine, what I saw there made my stomach roll. They were full of covetous desire and intent. He was about to cross a line with me that he'd never be able to come back from. I braced myself knowing whatever he planned was going to be painful and there was nothing I could do about it . . . yet.

I threw my head back, jerking away from his touch. The chains rattled and jostled but had little give. Even my ankles were chained to the floor. Panic and fear rose in my stomach, but if life had taught me anything, it was to hide those emotions at all costs. Fear only encouraged bullies to do worse things. I'd learned that one too many times in the children's home. I glared at him and let my face fall into a mask of hate and venom. It wasn't difficult because I well and truly hated this vampire.

I cleared my throat, giving myself a minute to get it together. When dealing with a bully, there was only one thing to do . . . show no fear. "Your point being?"

"I wish to feel the sun on my skin again, the magic in my veins, the power at my fingertips. I had a life stolen from me. Now I want it back." He reached out and put his hands on my hips, taking a moment to press his fingers into the skin where my shirt had ridden up. His touch disgusted me. I ground my teeth together and my fangs started to lengthen.

"That doesn't answer my question. What am I doing here?" I had the sinking feeling he thought I would be the answer to all his magical desires.

Marius ran his fingers over his goatee. "Serving my purposes."

I threw my body around, struggling against the restraints. I wanted to use my strength to rip the chains from the walls and strangle him with them. Yet they didn't budge. Visions of how I would kill him and what it would feel like flooded my mind. He motioned to the chains. "They're magically reinforced. Your strength won't work here, nor will your magic. Amazing what you can get from a witch for the right price."

Greatttttt.

"Aw, you brought me presents. I'll be sure to strangle you with them later." I nearly smiled at the thought of wringing the life from his body with my bare hands. I wanted to call upon my power, but it was trapped within my fists. I narrowed my eyes at him. "I'll never serve you anything, let alone your purposes."

"I bet you taste delicious." He opened his mouth and extended his fangs, then leaned in so close his cheek brushed against mine as he sucked in a deep breath, running his nose over my skin, taking in my scent. His hot breath fanned over my ear, and I wanted to gag as he whispered, "I wasn't asking."

He leaned back and parted his lips, about to strike, and I braced for impact. I didn't close my eyes or flinch away from him. If he was going to bite me, I was going to make damn sure he saw me watching him do it. The door flew open with a loud bang and Marius drew back. He whirled around on the woman standing in the doorway. Her eyes widened as they darted from his fangs to me and back again. She had to know what was about to happen. As a vampire, taking blood from another vampire against their will was a violation. It could be beautiful and connecting like it was for Grayson and me. But this, this wasn't beautiful. This was done out of violence and greed.

"I am not to be disturbed!" Marius hissed at her.

"I beg your pardon, sir." She gave him a little bow, and I wanted to smack her for her loyalty to him.

"What is it, Kendra?" He hissed and turned to face her fully.

She was tiny with dark skin and a shaved head. Her bright, silvery makeup stood out in the inky blackness of this cave-like cell. Her makeup was like a mask over her face, fanning out from her eyes and back to her temples. Her lips pressed into a thin line, but still even they stood out with their shining red gloss. "The signal. We've got what you wanted."

She motioned to me, and I bared my fangs at her and hissed in her direction. "So, you wanna be the next to die. Noted."

"You hardly look like you're in a position to be dishing out threats." She winked at me.

Kendra just signed her death certificate.

"Enough." He took a step toward Kendra. "She is none

of your concern. You don't look at her. You do not speak to her. Do you understand me?"

Kendra lowered her gaze to the floor, and I snickered. "Good dog."

I was already at rock bottom. The least I could do was entertain myself and cause a little discord. When she began to lift her gaze toward me, he was in her face in moments. Marius wrapped his hand around her throat and jerked her closer to his body. "Send the bloody signal, and do not disturb me again."

He shoved her out the door and she stumbled back. When she regained her balance, she looked up at him from under her long lashes. She narrowed her eyes at him, but Marius hardly noticed. With a violent jerk he slammed the door shut in her face. Pebbles and dust rained down in the cave and scattered across the floor. The lone light at the center of the room swung back and forth, causing that single beam to draw a circle on the floor. He pressed his hands to the door and sucked in a deep breath.

I didn't know what signal they needed or wanted, but I knew that if I got him talking, he might just tell me. Not that I could help in my current situation. But any information could be used. "She's a real peach. Well trained."

"You lack the knowledge of what you are and what you could be." Undeterred, he darted across the room and pressed his body to mine. His hand wrapped around my throat and each of his fingers squeezed.

Though he was cutting off the air from my lungs, I

forced my eyes toward his and bit out, "And what is it you think I am?"

He leaned in and ran his nose over my cheek. "You smell of old blood magic."

He loosened his grip enough for me to suck in a gasping breath. Before I could even get a full breath, his tongue darted from his mouth and drifted over my skin, leaving a sloppy wet trail.

I made a gagging noise that he ignored. "When I get free, and I *will* get free, I'm going to cut your tongue from your head. And then I'm going to kill you."

He chuckled and shook his head as he ran his tongue up and over my other cheek, tasting the blood from the wound on my head. He lowered his voice to a whisper. "Your blood tastes of power. So rich and dark. It sings to me in the sweetest lullaby."

When he leaned back a little, I snapped my head forward. My forehead connected with the bridge of his nose. The sound of it cracking filled the silence in the room and he staggered back clutching his face. "Bitch!"

"That's original." I smirked at him.

He strode toward me with blood running from his nose down his face. I braced myself for impact a moment before his hand came up and he cracked the back of it across my face. My head snapped back against the wall, and for a moment I saw stars as black dots swarmed my vision. My chain rattled as I struggled to stop swinging. Blood filled my mouth, and I spat it on the floor at his feet. I sucked in a deep breath and met his eye. "How about you unchain me and we'll see what's what between us? This hardly seems sporting."

"I don't care if it's sporting. You have no power here. Nor will you ever. I'll drain you dry before that happens." He placed one of his hands on the side of my head and the other on my shoulder. He shoved my head to the side exposing my neck. "Your power will be mine."

I forced my eyes to stay open, I wouldn't give him the satisfaction of flinching or cowering away. He struck hard and fast, his fangs piercing my skin violently. It tore under his attack, and the blood seeped from my body. I jerked in his arms, trying to rip myself away. I shoved and pushed but the chains held fast, keeping me in place while he tried to steal everything from me. He dug his fangs in deeper and harder, so deep I knew he was doing it to inflict agony on me, but I refused to scream. I wouldn't give him the satisfaction. Visions of the different ways I would kill him filled my mind and I let them consume me. His death was imminent, and I would be the one to do it—of that, I was completely sure.

CHAPTER TWO

TITUS

"Fire!" I threw my arm forward, signaling for the catapults to launch flaming boulders into the dark forest surrounding the castle. Their mechanisms cracked and groaned as they let their flaming boulders fly. They gave a high-pitched whistle as they flew through the darkness, illuminating the sky with bright flames. Sunrise was only hours away, and for the first time in years, I could think of nothing better than daybreak. The Night Spawn would be forced to flee the rays of light or be burned to death . . . Unless their newly acquired power allowed them to walk in the morning light, which I prayed wasn't possible. Though the castle was well guarded, it wasn't ready for an assault of this magnitude.

I threw my arm forward once more, signaling for another volley of boulders. With each flaming rock we launched, trees crashed to the ground as they careened through the madness outside the walls of the castle. Their branches snapped and leaves rustled. Here I stood high above it all with the rebellious Night Spawn below. I failed to understand how things had gotten to this point. We'd been working with them for so long, yet their anger was apparent in this act of war. But I'd be damned if I let them continue to attack my home, my family. Rage flared within me and ran hot through my veins.

How dare they?

My own blood magic poured through me. A fine red mist swirled around my body and up my arms. It was like a velvet glove settling over my skin ready to be used at a moment's notice. I glanced down over the edge of the giant wall and watched as they moved like ants around the base of my castle. Their shadowy figures scurried in the night, making the ground appear to writhe. The moon barely shone down on them, but I knew where they all were, and I was more than ready for them. Their fire magic didn't reach me this high up, but when they exploded against the thick stone walls, the ground rumbled under my feet, and heat flowed over my body.

How had Marius gotten so many to support his way of thinking?

The walls were strong and fortuitous, I knew they would hold against any attack launched on The House of Shade, but still the castle shook with each blast of power hurled at us. Balls of fire launched up toward me. I didn't dare take a step back or show an ounce of fear. Their magic was unfamiliar. I had no idea when the Night Spawn got blood magic, but Marius did, and he'd been secretly recruiting.

My soldiers scrambled around the top of the wall, yelling orders to each other and firing back with their own blood magic. The fire was quickly followed by streams of water that knocked some of my men off the top of the wall to the ground below. Pebbles flew up toward us in a dark swarm, pelting at my soldiers. The elements were not in our favor tonight, yet the Night Spawn controlled them with ease. *How? Why?* The soldiers ran around swatting at the pebbles as though they were slapping away killer bees. I motioned toward two of my soldiers who I knew could combat this. They leapt into the swarming pebbles, and their power seeped from them in flowing red mist. The pebbles dropped to the ground but still vibrated there like they were trying to come back to life. The pebbles crunched under my feet as I marched around the walkways toward the other side of the castle. Night Spawn began to scale the walls like cockroaches. They climbed up, seeming to hold on to nothing but the stones.

Zinnia, the Siphon Witch Queen, hurried out from the castle. Her midnight hair fanned out around her, and her sharp sapphire eyes glowed with power. Silvery magic flowed around her in long streams that caught in her hair. She stopped just in front of me and looked me up and down. "Are you alright, your majesty?"

"As well as can be expected. Why are you looking at me like that?" She looked me over once more as though checking for injuries.

"One of the maids said you'd been attacked, that they were all here to take you." She glanced over the edge of the wall, spotting the vampires making their way to the top. She flicked her wrist and silver magic shot from her hand to knock away a ball of flames as though it were nothing more than swatting a fly. She flicked her wrist again and her magic acted like a whip, knocking the climbing vampires down. They fell off the wall and tumbled to the ground below.

Tuck, her soulmate and protector, was never far behind. He was just slightly shorter than me with dark-burgundy hair, and in the dark of night his eyes glowed like embers. He held his hand out and silvery light flashed in his palm as a blade began to form. The metal was a gleaming white with a sharp edge. The hilt was a polished gold mixed with black metal swirling around the grip. He wrapped his hand around it and held it at his side with all the ease and comfort of a soldier who knew his weapon well.

I motioned to myself. "As you can see, I'm quite well."

"Which begs the question, who isn't?" Tuck spun in a circle as another vampire leapt onto the wall behind him. He was trained well with skilled, lethal movements.

The vampire had a wild look in his dark eyes as he bared his teeth at Tuck and hissed. His clothing hung off his body and dirt smudged his face and hands. Clumps of hair jutted out from his head in all different directions. He held his sword up and the vampire leapt at him with a sword of his own, moving so quickly it made the world blur around him.

The Phoenix was impressive, easily keeping up and matching the vampire's speed strike for strike. Their swords clashed together, and the sound of metal scraping against metal filled the air. They sparred back and forth on the wall. At times it appeared Tuck would take the upper hand and at other times it was as though the vampire would. Tuck swung his arm out and knocked the sword loose from the vampire's hand. It clattered to the ground, but that didn't seem to stop him. He leapt forward with his hands curved like claws and went right for Tuck's throat. Flaming wings erupted from Tuck's shoulders, and with one flap he soared back out of the vampire's reach. But the vampire trudged forward, trying once more for his throat. Tuck spun around and knocked the Vampire off the side of the castle with his wings, setting him on fire in the process. His arms and legs flailed, and his fading scream wafted up toward us as he fell.

Another vampire scaled the wall and leapt in front of Zinnia. This one was nearly twice her size and covered in muscle. When he stood over her, he dwarfed her small size. A growl rumbled in his chest and then he gave a dark chuckle as he sauntered toward her. I took a step to intervene, but she gave a light wave of her hand and I hesitated. Zinnia pressed her lips into a hard line, and her silvery magic wrapped around the vampire. He fell to his knees before her, and she sauntered up to him as though holding him there was little more than an afterthought. Silvery power seeped over him, and I could see her magic growing brighter. It shined in her face and gave her skin an ethereal glow. His muscles strained as he tried to fight back to no avail. He was powerless under the weight of her magic.

On the other side of the castle opposite us, Tabitha, the Witch Queen of Elements, held her hands up high. Yellow streams of magic flowed from her hands down over the side of the castle like a waterfall. Her hair stood around her head in dark, wild curls. I could spot her a mile away even in the dark of night in her bright neon-green sweater and matching pants. The ground rumbled with her power and huge vines shot up on the side of the walls, knocking the Night Spawn away from the castle. The stalks were thicker than a car and rocked the castle as one after another shot high into the sky. Vampires clung to some of them while others fell to their deaths as the leaves swung and rustled violently.

Brax, their tiger shifter, prowled by her side in his hulking tiger form not letting anyone get close to her. He growled, baring his teeth over the wall. His shoulders rolled and he roared in her direction. Tabi didn't flinch. "You'll have your chance."

He turned away from her, continuing his slow lurk. A tiny pug wove between his paws as he moved back and forth. It nipped at his paws and jumped up, smashing its small body into his side. But the tiger didn't react. In fact, he seemed to enjoy it. Voices rose in a war cry to my left and I spun in that direction about to run toward that wall when I spotted Serrina, Queen of Desires, sauntering out toward the middle of it. She stood tall and confident in her black leather pants and jacket.

She smirked down at the vampires hurrying toward the wall as though she were having fun. They hurried forward in a thick wave of madness, yet she didn't flinch back. Red sparks danced from her fingertips and fell over the edge of the castle. The Night Spawn below began to retreat immediately. They collided with one another in confusion as they ran in any direction but near the castle. She threw her head back, cackling, and her long blonde hair drifted in the wind. As they scrambled away, Ashryn, the archer, stood by her side with her bow poised to shoot. Serrina blew them kisses and waved as they ran from her. "I know. I know the desire to leave really is a bitch to try and resist."

"Don't play with your food," Ashryn chided her.

Serrina shrugged. "They deserve it."

"Bloody hell." I ran my hand through my hair. I knew the Witch Queens were powerful. I didn't realize they were *this* powerful. Their magic just flowed so easily, and without the power to combat it they were a force.

Zinnia dropped her magic from the vampire she held, and he collapsed to the ground. My eyes widened. "Did you just . . ."

"No." She shook her head. "I'm not my father, King Titus. I don't siphon power for my own gain until someone is dead. But he will be unconscious for a few days."

"Well deserved." I stepped in closer to him and bent down over the vampire. I curled my hand into his shirt, ready to toss him over the edge of the wall.

"You might want to keep him for questioning." Zinnia shrugged. "Or you could throw him."

"Great minds think alike, Queen Zinnia." I picked him up and shoved him at two of my guards. "Lock him up and make sure he's bound. We don't know what kind of power he holds."

They staggered under his weight but still were able to drag him from the top of the wall. Zinnia spun away from me just as another vampire leapt over the wall toward her. A blue portal appeared in front of her and the vampire disappeared right into it. It opened over the forest below and dropped the vampire right on top of a tree. Beckett stood on the one remaining wall I hadn't checked. His smoky blue magic seeped around him like creeping tentacles, and suddenly another portal opened behind me, catching a leaping Night Spawn vampire off guard and depositing him at the top of a tree in the distance.

I nodded my thanks toward Beckett, and he gave me a single wink as he pushed his blond hair from his face. Astrid moved around him like water flowing between rocks. She ducked under his arm, so close to his body, and moved in front of him. He didn't hesitate to adjust the path of his own smoky power. It was as though they were so used to each other they didn't need to speak when working together. Gold magic flowed around him and out toward the forest. The trees sprang to life below, and her golden power blew her auburn hair back from her face. It clung to her body and forced nature to bend at her will. The trees began moving and throwing their limbs around, beating the piss out of the lot of them. I refrained from letting my jaw drop.

"Thanks, Beck." Zinnia gave him a little wave as he forced more vampires into his portals and away from the castle.

Beck winked at her with his bright ocean eye. "Wasn't me. Astrid is the one playing tennis with vampires and trees."

The redheaded Queen beside him shrugged. "Seemed the easiest thing to do."

Easy? I didn't think this would be easy at all, yet here I was with the Witch Queens of Evermore by my side protecting my castle. Another vampire leapt onto the wall in front of me and I held my hand out, letting my blood magic wash over him. It flowed like water around his body.

"You will halt." The vampire stopped in his tracks. "Why are you doing this?"

He pressed his lips together, trying to stop my influence. His dark eyes bulged, and he pressed his hands to the sides of his head, covering his ears. I let my power fully flow. "Answer me!"

His hands rose from his ears to his hair. He curled his fingers into the dark strands and pulled at them. His eyes widened and blood trickled from them. "I'm no one. I'm no one."

"What do you want here?" My voice was a low rumble deep in my chest.

Bloody tears streamed down his cheeks and ran from his ears. His voice rose to a yell. "I AM NO ONE!"

A deafening horn sounded, and my head snapped around trying to find its source. All at once, everything went quiet. The Night Spawn melted into the darkness, disappearing from view. They moved with a speed that didn't even rustle a leaf. The vampire before me looked at me one last time, then turned and ran for the edge of the wall. I held my hand out, trying to stop him, but that one distraction cost me a precious moment, a moment that was long enough for him to leap from the side of the castle. I hurried forward and watched as he landed on the ground and sprinted into the darkness.

Nothing. There was nothing left of the attack but the bodies of some of my soldiers. They'd dragged their own dead away, and the only evidence left behind were the pools of blood and destruction around the castle. I spun around. "What in the devil was that?"

Zinnia sucked in a deep breath and put her hands on her hips. She blew it out in a long, slow sigh. "That was too easy."

"You think they got scared when they saw us?" Tabi strolled over to us from her side of the castle.

Zinnia shook her head. "As much as I'd like to think so, I'm going with no."

"Then what the hell was that about?" Tucker's sword disappeared back into his palm, and he extinguished his wings, but he continued to let his flames flicker over his arms.

"I think it's more of *who* it was about." Zinnia looked to me with those uncanny sapphire eyes.

"Care to explain?" My power still simmered inside me, but as the moments ticked by, it receded into the calm pits of my stomach.

"It was too quick, too easy, and not particularly organized. Did you notice they were all just, like, doing whatever they wanted once they got here? It was as if it was meant to be a—"

"Distraction," I finished for her and my breath caught in my throat. There were only so many things, so many people, Marius would be interested in. Dread flooded my body. "Grayson? Moira?"

I ran past them toward the door that led into the castle. I pumped my arms and my heart thundered in my chest, pounding so hard it was deafening in my ears. There were no others that I cared about more than Moira and Grayson. If anything happened to them, I would rip the Night Spawn down until nothing but ash was left in my wake. I heard the others moving, but I was quicker, and they fell behind. As I hurried through the castle, the others followed in my wake. As we passed, more joined, and I didn't bother to stop to take note of who. I needed to get to Moira and Grayson now.

I hurried through the lab, passed the holding cells and technicians running around taking care of our wounded. Their eyes all snapped up as I sped past the carnage and shoved through the door into the dungeon area. The smell of damp earth filled the air along with something else.

Something familiar. I glanced to my side and relief washed over me at the sight of her long chocolate hair, deep eyes, and pale skin.

Moira ran to my side, and her dress billowed around her with each move she made. "What's happened?"

The relief at seeing her was short lived when I slid to a halt outside of Grayson's cell. I sucked in a sharp breath. My nephew was missing, and instead of an empty cell, it was full. Eight pairs of hulking black wings drew my eye first. They stood in a circle staring at the white line the witches had drawn around Grayson to keep him contained with their magic.

Moira grabbed on to my forearm, her fingers digging in at the sight of The Fallen. The others skidded to a halt behind me. They fanned out around us, each one giving the same reaction I had at seeing them standing there. The Fallen did not just show up . . . unless something was very, very wrong. The white line had been brushed aside in one place. That one move would've been enough to break the spell holding Grayson captive and set him free. And now he was loose in the world once more. A royal, feral vampire with more strength than anyone.

Matteaus, the leader of The Fallen, turned to face us all. The muscle in his jaw ticked and power rolled off him in waves. His eyes were so dark with anger they looked nearly the color of cobalt. He crossed his arms over his chest, and the muscles in his arms flexed and bulged. Two swords were strapped to his back between his wings. Knives were holstered on his hips and down his legs. I wasn't sure how many weapons he had in total, but I knew it would be virtually endless. In battle, I'd want no other by my side, but I would rather die than make an enemy of any of The Fallen. I'd never been on the bad side of The Fallen, but in this moment, based on the venomous looks we were getting, I might've been edging very close to it.

A light whimper escaped Moira's lips, and I placed my hand over hers, trying to reassure her that everything would be all right. I stood tall and squared my shoulders to face Matteaus. Before I could open my mouth to greet him, a low growl rumbled in his chest. "Who the fuck made a deal with the Devil?"

CHAPTER THREE

ZINNIA

No matter how many times I ran into The Fallen, I never found them any less terrifying. I held still, and even though I wanted to tamp down my magic, my nerves wouldn't let me. It flowed around my body in silvery, shimmering power. I wanted to pull it back, but I couldn't, so it hung in my hair and around my arms. My heart hammered in my chest, and there was a slight tremble in my hands. I'd faced all kinds of monsters, even my own father, but when it came to The Fallen, they rattled me. At times I found the angels helpful, at other times I'd seen them kill, injure, and maim without a second thought. Their punishments were swift and harsh. In Evermore, they had to be. Standing across from them now with only the cell bars between us was not a comfort.

Matteaus vibrated with rage, and I wanted to take a step back. Instead, I took a slight step to my side and let my shoulder touch Tuck's. His natural phoenix heat was always a comfort to me, so I leaned into him. He grew even warmer, and the scent of cinders filled me with ease. I swallowed and turned my attention toward them. Titus stood tall and proud before The Fallen, along with Moira who looked like she was about to fall apart at the sight of the empty cell. We'd only just gotten Grayson back, and now he was gone once more. Atlas was on the other side of Moira. With inky hair and the white stripes flowing from his temples, he reminded me of a deadly viper about to attack. His uncanny eyes were sharp and nearly glowed in this dank cell. His tattoos seemed to move over his skin as he stood there still as a statue. Yet every time those tattoos moved, I knew his emotions were swirling. The raven tattoo shot from his chest and soared over our heads in a slow circle. How had Grayson escaped with our magic keeping him bound? It should not have failed. None of this made any sense. Nor did it make any sense that they believed the actual Devil was here or that any of us would make a deal with him.

"How is that possible?" I muttered under my breath.

"You tell us!" Matteaus boomed in my direction. "The cell reeks of him. I want to know why, and I want to know why right now!"

"I can assure you none of us made a deal with the Devil." I glanced around at the others, feeling confident in my crew.

Matteaus glared at us but waved his hand forward. Aidenuli stepped up beside him. If Matteaus was huge, Aidenuli was impossibly bigger. His dark hair flowed down past his shoulders, and his amber eyes didn't miss a thing. When he arched his eyebrow at us, it made the scar going through his brow look that much deeper. He crossed his arms over his chest, and the muscles in his biceps bulged.

Matteaus motioned toward us. "Are they lying? Has one of them been in contact with Lucifer?"

I knew he was listening to all our thoughts one by one, checking to see if anyone was to blame. I tried to clear my thoughts and not think of Lucifer, of what he might look like, sound like, or even why he would be involved with Grayson. When he got to me, his power brushed through my mind like a caress on my cheek.

Don't think of the Devil. Don't think of the Devil.

The corner of Aidenuli's lip pulled up in a half-smirk and I held my breath. He waved a dismissive hand in our direction. "They're clean."

There was always a part of me that felt guilty even if I wasn't. Aidenuli took a step back as Tristen began to pace the cell. The moment he got closer to me, the smell of chocolate chip cookies wafted toward me and I leaned in closer. Tuck wrapped his hand around my wrist and gave me a side-eye glance. "Easy there."

"He smells like chocolate chip cookies," I whispered back.

"No, he smells like knives and leather." Ophelia sucked in a deep breath.

"No, it's flowers and sunshine." Tabi took a step closer.

"You're both wrong." Ashryn nudged Serrina. "He smells of the earth, right?"

"You all only smell what you're most attracted to." Serrina crossed her arms over her chest. "Or desire."

Tristan was The Fallen angel with the power over love, or so everyone believed. But the angel was intoxicating. He was tall and blond with piercing blue eyes. A thick necklace with a broken heart pendant hung just below the collar of his shirt, peeking out between the buttons.

Brax gave a dark chuckle. "No, he smells like animals. All of them."

I glanced at him, and he winked in my direction. "Mind yourselves and your desires."

Serrina shrugged. "I have no problem controlling mine."

Matteaus cleared his throat. "You think this is some kind of game?"

I shook my head. "Of course not."

"You have no idea the trouble you court," he growled, and I knew he was right.

Tristan ignored us all as he waved his hand over the circle and his eyes widened. "He was here."

"Impossible." Kadeion hissed under her breath. "He is trapped. We all know it."

She prowled back and forth in the cell with her curtain of dark hair swaying behind her with each step she took. Though she wore a black crop top and low-slung leather pants, the rest of her body was covered in weapons, much like Matteaus. The hilt of knives peeked out from the holsters around her torso. Her sage eyes were sharp and calculating. "If he'd gotten out, we'd know."

"Would we?" Matteaus pressed his lips into a hard line. "Then what the hell happened here? And who is having problems with Lucifer? Because his essence is all over this fucking cell."

"What have you gotten yourselves into?" Aidenuli moved to stand in the doorway to the cell.

"Because you have way overstepped your boundaries," Matteaus snapped.

"Do we really care so long as he's not out?" Collias grumbled and leaned against the wall.

"You could pretend to care about something other than yourself," Aidenuli grumbled.

"Enough," Matteaus snapped, and everyone fell silent for a moment.

"I have an idea." Ophelia took a step forward and ducked around Aidenuli. Sometimes I forgot how small she was until she did something like squeeze past a giant angel and his huge black wings.

"That's a good idea." Aidenuli nodded toward her.

"Want to fill in the rest of us who aren't mind readers?" Matteaus demanded.

Ophelia squatted down near the chalk circle and brushed her hand over the boundary. "I can't replay what happened, but I can make what Grayson heard available for all of us to hear. Not sure if that helps, but it might shed some light."

A growl rumbled deep in Matteaus' chest, but he took a

step back to give her some space. Ophelia reached into the pouch at her hip and fumbled around through her potion bottles. The sound of them clinking together was the only thing that filled the silence of the cell. She pulled a small vial with a white milky liquid from her pouch and gave it a little shake.

"Perfect." She rummaged around for more vials with her lips pursed.

"Matteaus, we need to move this along." Taliam shifted from one foot to the other. "If he is in fact loose, then we have bigger problems on our hands than one missing vampire."

A tiny lizard crawled out from the pocket of his jacket and ran up his arm to perch itself on his shoulder. A long sword hung from his hips and the hilt of a knife stuck out from his boot. Taliam was *just* shorter than Matteaus with silvery hair that was shaved on the sides and ran in a mohawk down the center of his head. He paused for a minute and tilted his head down toward the lizard as though listening.

He gave a small nod, then took a step back. "He says you need to proceed."

"I was totally planning on it." Ophelia held three more vials.

"Quickly," Matteaus demanded.

I wanted to jump in and help, but when it came to Ophelia and potions, there was no helping or interrupting. She opened the first vial with the milky white liquid and walked in a slow circle around the white marking on the floor. She let the liquid flow evenly until she completed the circle. It glowed a soft white, then she popped open another vial and dumped a pile of what looked like dust into her hand.

I'd never seen that before. "What is that?"

She shrugged. "Bone dust."

"Where'd you get the bone?"

She peeked up at me. "You don't want me to answer that."

No. No, I really didn't. I waved her on and she blew the dust over the floor. It whirled around in a small cloud that went from the floor up toward the ceiling. The wind whipped around the room, and she stood before it, studying the small whirling twister. She tilted her head to the side, then snapped her fingers. She turned from us and strolled over to a small puddle in the corner and bent down low over it. She pulled out an empty vial and collected some of the muddy water.

"Muddy water? Really?" Atlas scoffed.

Ophelia ignored him and tossed the vial into the twister. The water turned a brilliant blue and bubbles wound up the funnel. It glowed brighter, and now looked like a giant aquarium. Bubbles floated from the floor up toward the ceiling, bathing the room in that aqua glow. Ophelia dusted off her hands and held them out toward the swirling pool. Grey smoke seeped from her palms, and she closed her eyes.

"Cries of the visions speak unspoken.

Bound in lies and words as token.

Curse unsung and poison broken.

State this night the truth that's stolen."

At first the water just bubbled, but then a voice began to muddle through—a garbled voice that at first sounded like someone talking into a jar. Then it became clear as day.

"How pathetic you are." It was so smooth, almost soothing in a way, though the tone didn't match the words.

"Give me what I want. Bring her to me."

Matteaus stepped forward. "Bring who?"

"My guess is Dracinda." I muttered.

"What?" Tristan snapped and whirled around to look at me.

Matteaus held his hand out, stopping Tristen. The words continued from the spell giving us a peek into the words Grayson had been hearing this whole time. "You know what I want. Bring her to me and I'll kill you quickly. Your suffering will end, and your death will bring peace to the ones you love. Don't you want them to live in peace? But how can they with someone like you?"

Moira let out a light cry and Titus pressed his hand tighter over hers. I wanted to tell them we'd figure this out and Grayson would be fine. I wanted to offer them some comfort. But there was none to offer. That voice nearly had me convinced there was misery all around me, and he wasn't even speaking to me. The truth was I wasn't sure how Grayson had gone this long without killing someone else or himself. I didn't know if he'd be okay or if we could even save him. I wouldn't lie to them or give them false hope, but I would try like hell to bring him home.

Ophelia snapped her fingers, and the bubbles paused as though she were pausing a song. "I know that voice."

"So do we." Taliam's face paled. "Even after centuries, it's not something one forgets."

"My father used to speak to him. He'd use a looking glass spell." Ophelia shook her head. "It's Lucifer."

"Alataris had deals with the Devil?" My jaw dropped.

"Are you really surprised dear old dad was messing with evil?" She gave me a look that was more like *really, Zinn, come on.* "I mean if you're gonna do it, don't be so damn obvious."

"I'm going to pretend I didn't hear that." Matteaus groaned.

"Exactly." Ophelia nodded.

"What?" His brow furrowed.

"Exactly that too." She winked at him.

"Don't make me take a personal interest in you. You won't like the results."

"Oh, I already have a soulmate, sooo not interested." She shook her head at him.

"That is not what I was inferring to." He crossed his arms.

Her mouth dropped into a little O-shape and she lowered her voice. "Was it a threat?"

He rolled his eyes.

"You should be more obvious about that. I like to make it obvious. You know, really strike fear." She paused, thinking. "Though I prefer actions over words."

I needed to get this back on track before we ended up

in this cell next to Grayson for pissing off The Fallen. If this was the voice, then we were in deeper shit than even I thought. "Is this what Grayson has been hearing?"

"The only one who's heard the voice aside from Grayson is Piper," Astrid pointed out.

"Piper, is this the voice you heard when you went into Grayson's dreams?" I turned to look for her among the crowd.

"Piper?" Atlas took a step back and walked around us. "Where is she?"

"What if she was hurt during the attack?" Moira sucked in a sharp breath. "We have to find her. Now."

Atlas hissed in a low breath. "I'm on it."

"This is not over," Matteaus said, stopping us from going to search. "How did Lucifer get free?"

"I don't believe he is." Ophelia waved her hand, and the bubbles started once more. "If he was free, he'd have done much more than let Grayson out. I think this was just a projection of himself."

"What makes you think so?" Aidenuli crossed his arms.

She shrugged. "I can feel it."

He narrowed his eyes at her. "That's not good enough."

"When you've grown up around evil, you know when you're in the room with it." She pointed toward one of the angels at the back of the cell. "Ask him."

An angel I'd rarely seen and never heard speak slid from the shadows. He moved silently and bent down low next to the white markings on the floor. His hair was a bright blond cut close to his head. His eyes were a stormy grey with dark clouds moving through them. He pulled some kind of gadget I'd never seen from his pocket and waved it over the area. His eyes were riveted to the screen, and he pressed his lips into a hard line. I held my breath, waiting for his verdict, but Ophelia was already moving out of the cell and heading toward the door.

He pressed his lips into a thin line and shook his head. "The witch is right. It was a projection."

The Fallen seemed to take a deep, collective breath.

"Very well, get a leash on your vampire," Matteaus said. "The same rules apply. If he harms an innocent, you all know what will happen."

"I understand." I didn't want to answer for everyone, but the way that Titus and Moira looked, I knew they wouldn't agree. No matter what Grayson did, they'd always protect him. Before anyone could say another word, The Fallen were gone, leaving the cell completely empty. Ophelia's spell crashed to the ground, leaving a huge puddle of water behind. I stood there frozen for a moment, thinking about the things my sister must've seen living with Alataris, our father, for all those years. I was lucky enough to be hidden and raised by my mother, but Ophelia . . . she'd seen it all. She knew the voice of the Devil, and yet she stood beside us every day.

Ophelia paused at the door. "I know what you're thinking, and I don't like it."

"What? How? Are you psychic now too?"

She shook her head. "It's written all over your face. So, stop it and let's find Piper."

34

"I've got a bad feeling," Atlas muttered as he passed by me and headed into the lab.

I didn't want to admit it, but I did as well. There was no way Piper wouldn't have been in that cell with everything that'd happened with Grayson. She'd have to be hurt or . . . something else was very wrong.

"Meet you back here when you find her," I called out to the others as we all split up and began to search the castle.

CHAPTER FOUR

PIPER

The skin around my neck was raw as hell and ached all over from Marius' bites. Sweat slicked my body, and my own blood soaked my shirt. The rips in my jeans did nothing to protect my skin from the scrapes and bruises. His sickly scent clung to my clothing, and I wanted to gag. My arms had lost all feeling a long time ago as I hung there, the shackles cutting into my wrists, what little blood I had left in my body trickling down my arm.

The necklace dangled against my chest, glaring at me. The smooth pearl shape held a darker pink color, and I knew madness threatened to take over. It was ironic, really. Marius thought my blood would bring him power. I prayed it brought him my madness. He stood across from me waiting for something. His arm hung out to the sides, and he wiggled his fingers.

"When will I know it worked?"

I scoffed. "You're asking me when my blood will give you whatever abilities you're trying to get?"

At his direct gaze, I gave a humorless chuckle. "Even if I could help you. . . I wouldn't."

He made a sound of disgust in the back of his throat as he turned and began to pace. "Why do you not heal?"

I let my head lull to the side and rest on my arm. I peeked up at him, feeling all the blood loss and weakness in my body. I wasn't going to tell him I could only feed on Grayson's blood, and until I did feed, I would continue down this path. Going feral on him would be a blessing. I'd welcome it with open arms like an old friend and use it as an ally sent to kill an enemy.

Marius kicked the metal bucket across the floor. It hurled into the wall with a loud bang and crumpled under the force. "You are a vampire who can walk in the light, and yet you do not heal."

"Tired of seeing your handy work?" I forced a smirk. "Can't stand the sight of what you've done?"

He hissed in my direction. I didn't care. I was either going to die here or somehow escape. Either way, I wouldn't give him the satisfaction of seeing me break. Marius rushed up to me and his hot breath fanned across my face. He reached up and the chains loosened. My arms fell down to my sides, and the weight nearly took me to the ground. My knees went weak, and Marius yanked my chains toward him. I stumbled forward, and before I could collide with his chest, he shoved me upright.

I fought to hold my balance, but when I finally swung

to a halt. I held my chin up and the skin around my neck tore. New blood welled at my throat, and the warmth trickled down my neck. I didn't flinch, didn't look away. His lip rolled back from his fangs in revulsion.

"You disgust me."

"Aww, does it hurt your little feelings to know you're the monster who did this to me? You want to be like the Blood Borns, but even they would look at this and call *you* the monster."

He turned away and yanked my chains. I stumbled forward, and my toes dragged against the floor. Marius threw open the door, and for a moment I thought this was my chance to get away. My muscles tensed to run. I didn't know where I was or how I was going to get out of here, but I was going to bolt the first chance I got. That hope was short lived when all he did was drag me into another room.

Kendra stood there waiting for us, and when he dragged me into the room behind him, her eyes widened for a split second before she schooled her features. Marius wrenched the chains, and I fell to the ground in the center of the room. Kendra gazed down at me, yet she said nothing. The feeling began to return to my arms and fingers. I didn't know what was worse: not being able to feel them or the feeling returning too quickly. Pins and needles painfully shot up and down my arms. The ache was so acute I nearly cried out, but I wouldn't give either of them the satisfaction.

"I know. I look bad." I shrugged at her, "But now we match."

"You're getting what you deserve." She looked away from me and at Marius. "All preparations have been made."

Marius threw the long chain over a bar high above our heads that ran from one end of the room to the other. The chain scraped along the bar as he pulled it and jerked me to my feet. My arms shot above my head, and my weight hung from my wrists. I swung back and forth with my toes dragging on the ground. Marius secured the chain to a lock on the wall, and I glared at it, wishing my power was to set things on fire so I could burn this whole place to the ground. Unfortunately, my hands were still bound into little fists.

"Good. Leave us." He waved a dismissive hand at Kendra. When she didn't budge, he snarled in her direction. "I wish to be alone with her. Now."

Kendra caught my eye, and her lip quirked. "As you wish."

"You are not a girls' girl!" I shouted after her, but it was too late. The door slammed shut behind her and I was completely alone with this monster once more. I groaned and glanced around the room, noting only the slight difference between this one and the last. There was a small door on the ceiling with a string hanging down from it like an old attic with stairs that pulled down. If only it would be that easy, to just pull a string and get the hell out of here.

There was a small cooler in the middle of the room. Marius flipped the lid open. When he pulled out a bag of blood, my stomach rolled and I instinctively clamped my mouth shut. Marius strode up to me and held the bag to my lips. "Drink. Now."

I said nothing.

He shoved it against my face. "Drink and heal. Now."

I ground my teeth together.

A deep chuckle rumbled in his chest, and he held the bag to his lips. "If you won't drink, I'll force it down your throat. You're not going to die until I say so."

"Go fuck yourself."

His fangs extended and he bit the corner of the bag. The smell of the blood hit my nose, and my throat burned with thirst. I wanted nothing more than to drink my fill, and yet I knew the second that blood hit my stomach nothing would keep it there.

"You know you really do lack in so many ways." He hauled his hand back, and I braced for impact a second before his fist cracked across the side of my face. My jaw dropped open and black dots hovered behind my eyes. I blinked against the pain, but he was there right away, his fingers digging into my jaw and prying my mouth open. "When someone offers you a drink, you accept it."

He shoved the corner of the bag into my mouth and squeezed. Cool, tangy blood flooded my mouth. I wanted to fight not to swallow but my throat instinctively worked and the blood dropped into my stomach. When I spit the rest out at him, he took a small step back. Crimson drops covered his shirt and the lapels of his coat. His lip curled in disgust, and he scowled at me with pure malice.

"So, I'm just supposed to accept a drink from a random

psycho? Sounds like a quick way to die or get drugged." My stomach rolled and I knew I only had a moment before it came up.

"Drink. More." He held the bag to my lip, but it was too late.

My stomach heaved. That one large gulp shot up my throat and I vomited all over the floor. The breath burned in my lungs and every muscle in my body contorted painfully as it tried to get rid of any little thing I had in my stomach. Marius skittered back a few steps. He wrinkled his nose at the blood on the floor between us, then tossed the bag to the ground. "Fine, then rot."

If you keep this up, there will be nothing left to rot. I glanced down at the necklace once more and kept my dirty little secret to myself. Soon, I would go feral, and soon Marius would meet an even bigger monster.

CHAPTER FIVE

ATLAS

*R*age was becoming a close companion of mine as of late. The feeling was not unwelcome. Rage kept me sharp. Rage kept me in the moment. Rage gave me focus. I could see why Piper embraced the emotion at times. But now it was my turn, and I would live in it until my duty was fulfilled. Piper had protected Grayson against himself and against me. She was his soulmate, and as far as I was concerned, that meant she was now a part of The House of Shade, and I would serve the house loyally . . . until the day I died.

"Are you sure?" Zinnia leaned against the cell and crossed her arms over her chest.

"No, I've resided in this castle for the entirety of my long life, and when I searched it, I missed a spot." I narrowed my eyes at her. "She is not here, and the longer we stand here debating that fact, the longer she's missing along with Grayson. Who, may I remind you, is walking around with a bloody expiration date."

"I don't need reminding, thank you." Her voice was calm, calmer than I expected.

Titus, ever the diplomat, held his hands out and stepped in the center of us all. "That attack was no mistake. It was a diversion. Now, the question is, are Marius and Lucifer working together?"

"Nope," Ophelia chimed in quickly.

"I'm afraid to ask." We were taking too much time. "But how can you be so assured?"

"No offense, but Marius is small stuff compared to what Lucifer would be into." Ophelia shrugged. "He's not worth his time."

Titus nodded. "That's a fair assumption. So, Lucifer released my nephew and Marius has Piper."

"We'd be lacking in intelligence not to assume so." The smoke from my blood magic seeped around my body and the tattoos on my arms vibrated with the need to be used, to hunt.

"Either of them could be anywhere in the world at this point." Titus shook his head. "And we have no idea where."

"That has not stopped me before, your majesty. I will retrieve them forthwith."

"We aren't slouches at finding things either, *vampire*." Kylian scoffed and crossed his arms over his chest as he leaned back against the cell bars.

"If I light you on fire, will anyone in this room care? I could hardly muster the desire to bring you a glass of water should you start to burn." I glanced around and when no one responded, I met his eye. "Seems you're not important here, Dark Prince."

"This isn't helping" Zinnia stepped between us. "But he's got a point, Atlas. This room is full of magical people that can be used. Our spell worked on Grayson once before, and it should work again—despite Lucifer taking him."

"So, what you're saying is . . . you should be able to summon him back into the cell?" Titus held so still I could tell he had yet to breathe. No others in the room would be able to see this minute detail, yet I'd served him well these last years. Now Grayson, the son he never knew he had was missing, and I would be damned if it stayed that way. I would give the King the chance to know who his son was. And I would give him the chance tell Grayson who his real father was.

"In theory, yes." Ophelia tilted her head to face me. "But we'll need a stand-in for Piper, someone who's as powerful. Possibly two vampires will have to do."

"Done." Titus walked into the cell.

"Perhaps I should, your majesty." I didn't know what that kind of power would do to the King, nor did I want to find out.

"I don't recall asking," he snapped and glanced at the others. "Well, what are we waiting for? Get my nephew back here. Now."

Ophelia sauntered back into the cell. "We need another.

No offense, Vamp King, but you alone are not strong enough."

"Then I will." Moira joined him in the cell, and the two of them next to each other fighting for their son twisted something in me. They would have their family one way or another. I'd see to it.

Ophelia rubbed her hands together. "Let's get this party started. One vampire coming right up. Queens, join me in the cell, would you? Beckett and Tuck, just outside the cell. You know, just in case it works too well and he goes all crazy on us. . . again. Maze, Tilly, Kylian, Brax, Logan, Ash, and Adreinne, can you all wait outside the door. And Atlas—"

"I'll stay right here." This spell had once pulled Grayson through space and time, right into this cell. I could only pray it would work once more.

She gave me a shark-like smile. "Excellent. We need a killer in here. Well, besides me."

The others all joined her in the cell, forming a loose circle. Tuck slid the door shut, and the clang echoed in the silence of the room. "Love doing this for a second time. Do you still want me to melt the door to the frame?"

"Seeing how Lucifer busted it wide open, I think we can leave it this time." Zinnia shrugged. "If he tries to run, Beckett can stick him in a portal loop so he just runs in and out of the cell."

Beckett looked through the bars into the cell and nodded. "Simple enough. I'm ready."

"We'll be right outside if you need us." Logan held the

door open for the others as they all filtered out of the cell leaving only Beckett, Tucker, and me to handle anything that might go wrong.

"One triquetra coming up." Ophelia reached into her potion pouch on her hip and pulled out a vial of white powder. She shook it up and let the dust fall into her palm. She closed her eyes and cupped her hands together, holding it close to her mouth. Grey smoke swirled around her hands, and when she held her palms up, the white powder glowed. She held it up to her lips and blew on it. The powder soared up into the air and mixed with her grey smoke. It spun around in a whirling circle and started to drift toward the floor in slow motion. The tiny particles landed in a perfect circle. She waved her hand, and more lines ran through the middle of it.

She glanced at Moira. "We need some of his blood. Your blood. Just make sure it drops onto the circle."

"Yes, of course." Moira pulled the sleeve of her dress up to her elbow and held her wrist to her lips. The bite was so delicate it was almost invisible, but when she held her arm over the circle, her blood fell onto the markings.

The ground rumbled and dust rained down from the rocky walls. Zinnia's eyes darted and she nodded to the others. "You all know what to do. Titus, Moira, just open up your power and let it flow. We'll do the rest."

Zinnia began to read from the book at her feet. The wind kicked up around the cell and their magic flowed together in an array of colors. There were bright yellow streams, silvery glitter, red ribbons, golden sparkles, and red blood magic. Power flooded the room, and I could feel it pulsing against my skin. I sucked in a sharp breath. "Bloody hell."

"I know, right?" Beckett shook his head. "They're impressive."

"Indeed." Light flashed in the circle and a faded version of Grayson appeared there in the center. He threw his head back, cackling, then gave a salute to Titus and faded from the circle once more. The magic abruptly stopped, and the Queens all stood there staring at one another.

"Well, he's a cocky shit, isn't he?" Ophelia sighed. "But fighting the pull of power is a great way to stay out of jail. Can't blame him for that."

"Really, O?" Zinnia put her hands on her hips and gazed at me through the cell bars. "He knows it's coming, so now he's fighting it."

"And if he doesn't get the chance to fight it, will it work?" Moira wrung her hands in front of her as she shifted from one foot to the other.

"In theory, it'll work," Zinnia said with all the confidence in the world.

I could only think of one way to get Grayson back, and it was one way that could possibly get us both killed. "So, we need to distract him long enough for the spell to take hold?"

Zinnia shrugged, "Again, in theory, that'd work."

"Lovely, I'll be the distraction." I was tired of standing here watching anyways. I needed to do something, to hunt and get my hands dirty.

Ophelia dropped down onto the dirty floor and pulled a knife from her boot, then started examining it as if this whole situation was boring to her. "He might kill you."

I gave a humorless chuckle. "I'd like to see him try. If I'm holding on to him, will that spell bring both of us back here?"

Zinnia, "I mean, it should. But it's strong and unpredictable."

"Good enough for me. Just be ready for my sign." I started toward the doors when there was a sharp whistle.

Just as I turned back, an oval-shaped rock soared at my head. I caught it and held it in my palm. Ophelia still didn't glance up at me, but somehow I knew the stone came from her. "Crush this and it'll let us know to start the spell."

I gave her a nod and turned for the door once more. "I won't be long."

"I hope not. We need to find Piper, and we can't just sit here waiting." Zinnia called out after me.

"Like I said, I shan't be more than a moment."

"We'll be waiting."

CHAPTER SIX

SANCHITA

"The mirror is up ahead." I pointed down the hall.

"I hope we laid low long enough." Jester held the little vampire who called herself No One in his arms.

"I think we have." Prisha glanced over her shoulder, looking for anyone who might be lurking. "They've been looking for her, but I don't think we can wait much longer to get her to a doctor."

This deep in the Night Spawn headquarters, we didn't know who could be trusted besides the three of us. My heart hammered in my chest and my hands shook with nerves, yet I wouldn't change what we'd done for anything. Stealing her and bringing her back to the castle was the right thing to do, and when the King saw her, he'd agree. He wanted to know what was going on in the Night Spawn headquarters. This was the proof he needed.

Jester hiked her up in his arms and her head lulled back.

A few hours ago, she'd fallen silent, and I didn't know if that was a good thing or bad thing. All I knew was that I had to get her back to the castle to the doctors there and to Titus. The King needed to know this wasn't a sickness at all that was hurting the Night Spawn. It was all Marius. We hurried toward the mirror, and I stopped just in front of it. Jester held No One with one hand and pressed his other to the mirror. The surface rippled under his touch, and he motioned toward it.

"You lot through first."

"Come on." I reached back and grabbed onto Prisha's hand to pull her forward with me.

She tugged her hand free. "I'm not coming."

I whirled around to face her. "What do you mean?"

Prisha lowered her voice and her brow furrowed. "We need to know what happened to her, what happened to them all. If I leave now, it'll be for nothing."

"Then I'll stay with you." I wasn't about to leave my sister here in this danger with no one to trust.

"You can't." She shook her head, sending her long, straight locks flying around her face.

"Are you bloody daft staying here? You have no one to watch your back down here." The Night Spawn headquarters was full of traitors. None of us knew who friend or foe was down here.

"You need to tell the King what's happened, and it has to come from one of *us*. He put us on the council for a reason, and I intend to take my job seriously." She grabbed my hands. "You have to go."

"Me? You bloody well go." I shoved her hands away. "I'm not leaving you here."

"Sanchita, you must." She got that stubborn look about her that I hated. The one where her lips pressed together in a hard line and she narrowed her eyes at me. "You and Jester can do this, and I know I can help here and get more information."

"I hate to break up this little argument," Jester hissed at us. "But someone is coming, and we need to move now."

I paused, listening to see if I heard what he heard. In the distance there were voices and light footsteps heading in our direction. I turned with wide eyes toward Prisha. "Please. We can come back together."

She took a step back from me. "You need to trust me, Sister."

"We will come back as soon as we can." Jester's words were laced with urgency, and he motioned to the mirror. "But we have to go now."

"Go." Prisha turned away from me and started running down the hall away from us.

"Sanchita. Now," he hissed.

I hesitated a moment before my sister sped out of sight. Being separated from her was so wrong, and yet I forced myself to take a step toward the mirror . . . and then another. My stomach twisted in knots and nausea rolled through me. This was wrong, so very wrong.

"We will come back. I swear it," Jester gritted out.

I turned just as he stepped through the mirror. Sadness ran through me along with deep-seated doubt. I hated this plan, hated leaving her, but I had to get No One back to the castle and tell Titus what happened to her, to them all. I stepped forward into the mirror. It was cool and sticky against my skin, and once I moved forward, it slowly peeled back from my skin and I stepped into a long white hallway.

Jester stood there waiting for me. Even though I'd found his looks harsh at first, I was warming to the way the muscles in his square jaw flexed when he was concerned for me or how his dark eyes seemed to turn a shade lighter when he glanced my way. "We won't leave her for long."

"Certainly not." I marched down the hall toward the glimmering light at the end and didn't stop until I reached it and pushed my way through. The sooner we got this done, the sooner we could go back for my sister.

I didn't know I was going to walk right into chaotic hell. The lab was in shambles with soldiers lying everywhere. Lab workers scurried around tending to their wounds. I took a step back and bumped right into Jester. He gave me a small nudge forward and moved to stand beside me. "What the hell happened here?"

No One began to mumble, and he jostled her in his arms to reposition her. I glanced around at the carnage and knew this would be another vision I couldn't scrub from my mind. Soldiers lay all over the place, some on cots and others on the tables spread throughout the lab. Blood coated the white sheets of the cots and ran over the sides of the tables. The lab workers' pristine white coats were covered in crimson, medical supplies were strewn about, and they all yelled orders to each other as they worked to bandage injuries and sew the royal soldiers back together. They were immortal but vampires could be injured and even killed under the right circumstances. Whatever happened here was more than the right circumstances. Their cries filled the lab, and I wanted nothing more than to leave this place.

"I'm No One," she mumbled, and her head began to thrash in Jester's arms.

"We need some help over here!" Jester bellowed over the chaos.

A slim lab assistant hurried to us. He looked no older than twenty, with light blond hair and dark eyes. His skin was pale and slicked with sweat. "How can I assist?"

Jester took one look at him and shook his head. "No offense, but we need a grown-up."

The smaller vampire blew a hard breath out. "I am two hundred years old."

"Infant." Jester looked over his head. "We prefer an adult."

"What is the meaning of this?" Titus threw the doors to the dungeon wide open and stormed right up to us.

I never got over the sheer size of Titus and the way a room seemed to revolve around him. He was huge, with dark blond hair that flowed past his shoulders. His velvet coat nearly brushed the floor as he walked up to us. Jester held No One out toward him.

"We've brought her back here, Your Highness. She needs medical attention . . . now."

Moira hurried in next to Titus and looked down at her. "What's happened? Is it the sickness."

I sucked in a deep breath. "I don't think there is a sickness going around. I think Marius is doing this to other vampires."

Titus' eyebrows shot up. "He did what? How?"

"I'm not sure how or what exactly is done to them. But there are a lot of vampires in her state, and he's been keeping them locked up to be used."

"Or worse," Jester added.

Moira leaned over No One and her face fell. "She's so young, delicate even."

Moira wasn't wrong. She was small and delicate. Her features were almost elven with a small pert nose, full lips, and eyes that were a touch too big for her face. Though she was pale, and her dark hair was matted to her head, I could see she was beautiful. If only I knew who the hell she was. "I think she's dying."

"What's her name?" Titus glanced down at her.

"I'm No One," she mumbled and began to thrash more violently. Her voice rose, "I'M NO ONE!"

Her body began to convulse, and Jester dropped to the ground, holding her there. His legs spread out under her, and he wrapped his arms around her. His whole body shook with the effort to keep her still. "Help over here!"

Moira held her hands over No One's face and let her blood magic flow. Pink mist slowly drifted down to her pale skin. "Shhh, be at ease."

"Moira, don't." Titus placed his hand on her shoulder, but it was too late.

The blood magic rebounded off of No One and knocked Moira off her feet. She shot back into Titus' chest as he wrapped his arms around her and they both fell back onto the floor. My eyes widened. "Moira!"

Her hands shook and her skin turned an angry red as though she'd burned her hands. She shook in Titus' arms. "Moira? My god."

"I'm okay." She looked so slight in his arms. Tears stung the backs of her eyes, and she swiped at them as she tried to rise to her feet.

"I'M NO ONE!" No One's voice rose above the cries of the soldiers being treated, so loud everyone else fell silent. Her back bowed and black smoke shot from her mouth and wrapped around her and Jester.

"No!" I reached forward and grabbed onto the back of his neck and yanked as hard as I could. The smoke burned my hand like touching ice and holding on to it. I screamed and ripped him back, throwing him against the table behind us. Right before I pulled him out, he dropped his arms and let No One fall to the floor. His skin was an ashy blue and his lips were nearly purple. Tremors racked his body, and he seemed to be stuck in a sitting position with his hands frozen into claws in front of him.

Titus wrapped an arm around Moira and spun away, jerking her behind him. Smoke shot up toward the ceiling and spun around in a dark cloud. The doors at the back of the lab flew wide open and two witches with dark hair stormed into the room. One had long flowing midnight hair, sapphire eyes, and silver magic, and the other had her hair braided into pigtails and wore leather shorts and a crop top. Weapons covered her from head to toe and grey smoke poured from her hands.

"O! Get them out of here." The one with the flowing hair threw her hands up and her power shot straight toward the ceiling. It covered the black smoke as though holding it in place.

More people poured into the lab, people I didn't recognize. They started pulling injured soldiers out of the lab, along with the techs. People scrambled away, now screaming for a different reason. From the corner of my eye, I spied Theon stumbling out of a room off to the side. Restraints hung from wrists and his eyes widened the second he spotted No One. He glanced around and spotted a needle. He ran toward it and grabbed it up, then ran right at No One. I tried to get to her before he did but I wasn't fast enough.

Theon slid across the floor and wrapped his arm around her. He shoved the needle into her neck and pushed the plunger. Her body went limp, and the smoke stopped flowing from her lips. I stepped up to him and cracked my hand right across his face. "What did you do?"

He snapped back to look at me with an angry red handprint on his face. "Saved her."

"You're a traitor!" I screamed.

"So they tell me!" he growled back.

No One sucked in a deep, relieved breath and let it go.

The lab went still and I bent over her, checking to see if she was okay. Her eyes fluttered up in a sleepy daze. They were a shockingly pale gold. She turned and gazed at Theon. "I am No One."

He held her in his arms and shook his head, holding her close. "No, you're not. I know exactly who you are."

CHAPTER SEVEN

MARTIN

"I didn't realize you were so . . . well off." I stared up at the carved columns in Eloura's foyer. Everything around me was beyond lavish. It was simple and clean with warm lighting and soft colored walls. The floors were a sparkling white marble, with golden mosaic flowers inlaid at the center of the foyer. It was a tastefully done focal point. Many of the Blood Borns had a tendancy to go overboard. But not Eloura, her home was the epitome of taste.

Eloura followed my gaze with a light smirk on her face. Even in this situation, she was the picture of elegance. She wore a pale-blue dress that was cut tight to her body with lacing up the back. The dress fell in loose shimmering material from her hips down to the floor. A small top hat sat perched on her head while her dark hair was pinned back from her face. She took a few steps toward the epic staircase, and her cane made a tapping sound with each move. "One does not age for so long without learning how to play the market. And how do the kids say it? Oh yes, treat yourself."

I chuckled. "Indeed."

The staircase was large and imposing and swept up to the second floor. Plush white carpeting covered the stairs, and when she stepped onto the staircase, I followed suit and nearly melted at the feel of it under my shoe. "I feel the need to remove my shoes."

"Hardly, we shall see what our little rats are up to, and I do look forward to it."

I hiked my leather computer satchel up on my shoulder. "I must admit I am too. The overly privileged of the Blood Borns do grate on my nerves with their ungrateful demands. I mean, is it really that difficult to order your own blood supply? Plus, if they can't see where their loyalty should lie, then perhaps a wake-up call is needed."

"I quite agree." She kept on walking until she reached the second floor, and I followed.

We turned down a long hallway with high ceilings and more marble flooring. The walls were painted a cream color with flecks of gold in them that reflected the warm light coming off the chandeliers that hung every few feet in the hall. Double doors lined each side of the hallway, and I had no idea how many rooms there were or where the doors led, but I just followed Eloura. She turned and pushed through one set of double doors.

They flew wide open, revealing an office with a French-style white desk with gold filigree inlaid into the desktop.

Three monitors were there with two ergonomic chairs set up behind them. I glanced down and smirked at the chair. "Gaming chair?"

"Functional and comfortable." She dropped down into one of the chairs and motioned to the other. "Please."

"With pleasure." I sat down next to her and put my bag on the desk in front of the monitors.

"Did you bring it?" Her eyes lit with interest.

I reached into my bag and pulled out a small box the size of a ring box and placed it on the table. "Of course. I'm good at getting things, particularly things I want."

I opened the box and showed her a drone the size of a small fly. "Now you're sure you heard what you heard?"

She pursed her lips at me and arched her eyebrow. "Are you questioning my knowledge?"

I chuckled and shook my head. "Of course not."

"Calm down, Martin." She patted my arm. "I am quite sure this will give us the information we need. Clive did meet with a vampire at that ridiculous ball he threw, and I heard enough to know he's in deep. I just couldn't see who that conversation was with. I'm hoping tonight we will get a name or see a face, because whoever is dealing with Clive is giving him the means to keep himself afloat."

"This ought to be interesting." I placed the tiny drone on the table and pulled my iPad from my satchel along with my laptop. Once I plugged the laptop into the monitors and images of the room we stood in came to life on the screens.

"Won't it just." She leaned back in the chair. "Now, let's

get me that name so that the double-crosser will know what it really means to play the game. I was glad you got the invitations and all the information."

"Well, it helps when you're the one sending out said invitations." It was easy to know who would be there, where it was going to take place, and how long any of this would take when I did all the work. "Planning the party, the menu, and getting all the RSVPs."

"I do believe the upper crest underestimates those who assist our way of living. You all see everything, hear everything, and know everything." She leaned back in her chair.

"Yes, they would all do well to remember that." I hit the keys in rapid succession and our little drone took off. "I'll just input the address, and we'll see just how quickly it gets there."

Eloura glanced at the clock on the wall. "I'd say by now they've had their dinner and traditional snobbery—complete with brown-nosing, which I'm sure Clive has enjoyed."

"And yet I'm still surprised you did not attend. I know I sent you an invitation." This drone wasn't something that just anyone could get. It was so small and quick, even top government agencies would pay heavily to have this technology.

"And forgo attending our little meeting?" She shook her head. "I wouldn't dream of it."

"It pays to spend time with the lowly." I chuckled.

"I hardly think of you or anyone else as lowly."

Eloura was what all Blood Borns should aspire to be: kind, loyal, and saw everyone as worthy of respect.

"Part of what I like about you," I said.

"Do you really like anyone, Martin?" She narrowed her eyes at me, studying me.

I thought about her question for a moment while we waited for our little spy drone to arrive. When I glanced at the screen, I saw Clive's gaudy property come into view. There were twelve-foot topiaries all around the property, all covered in snow. There was a difference between classy wealth and decorating things in poor taste, which was a waste of money. Clive was exactly that: tasteless. The drone flew in through a small, cracked window. My eyes widened at the decor.

Eloura snickered. "You can see why I declined the invitation. I would leave with a headache from all of . . . that."

She wasn't wrong. The walls were painted a light cream, which wasn't awful. It was everything else that was the problem. Bright paintings that matched absolutely nothing lined the walls, and each piece of furniture was a different color, but all looked incredibly uncomfortable, like they were made to look at and not sit in. Gold patterns were sewn into the fabric of the legs and the arms of each chair were always painted gold. Weird nicknacks were spread through each of the rooms. Nothing went together aside from the fact they were random and cluttered and came from all over the world.

Clive sauntered into the room, and I landed the drone on one of the tables next to him. He waved his arm, motioning to everyone. "If you all would adjourn to the study."

Eloura rolled her eyes. "I'm sure this will be a show."

"You have a lovely . . . home." Waldon Fredrickson glanced around the room as he walked in and sat stiffly on a small settee. He was a taller vampire, with sickly pale skin, a small round head, and a gangly body. His sunken eyes were small and beady, and his long straight nose protruded boldly from his face.

"Indeed, did you see my recent acquisition?" He oozed with pride, exuding so much of it that it nearly matched his slicked back hair.

"No, I haven't." Waldon pulled a cigarette box from the inside pocket of his suit coat. He offered one to Clive. When Clive declined, he reached into a drawer of a small end table that was beyond gaudy with little cherubs carved into it. He pulled a pipe of his own and perched it on his lips. "That table is from the home of a Tibetan monk along with that gold tea set on the other side of the room."

Eloura snickered. "Pompous ass."

"Monks own no worldly possessions." I rolled my eyes and turned the drone as more people filtered into the study. When half a dozen others took uncomfortable seats, the doors closed behind them.

"Precisely." She glared at the screen. "Pompous ass. No one in their right mind cares where he got those ridiculous things. As though possessions bring prestige . . ."

"And don't forget this carpet," Clive continued on, "I

ordered it from halfway around the world. But they did give me a considerable discount."

Lordess, a prim and proper vampire who had tied herself to Waldon long ago, sat down just across from them. She was slightly chubby with short brown hair and dark brown eyes. They suited each other, both very plain looking and both with their own social ambitions. She plastered a smile on her face. "And how did you come about that?"

"Privileges of being an English Blood Born vampire." He winked.

Lordess and Waldon both gave him those posh fake laughs, which Clive joined in on. Lordess held up her glass toward him. "You'll have to give me the number. I'd love a new carpet as fine as this."

"Oh please, darling, we both know your taste leaves something to be desired." Waldon chuckled and the others in the room gave polite, uncomfortable laughs.

"Yes, because she likes my carpeting, so I suppose it could be your taste that's lacking." Clive directed his snide comment toward Waldon.

"I joke, my friend." Waldon lit his cigarette and the smoke billowed around him. "It's a lovely idea to collect things from around the world."

"A steady reminder of the ability to possess whatever one wants." He too lit a match and placed it on the end of his pipe. He sucked in a few pulls and more smoke filled the room.

"Yet another reason I despise these gatherings." Eloura wrinkled her nose. "The smoke. The smell is wretched."

"I couldn't agree more." I nodded.

"Even so, this life comes at a price." Clive's words drew our attention back to the screen.

The room fell silent, and Clive strolled into the middle of it as thought he was holding court. He placed one hand on his hip while he held his pipe with the other as he strolled in a small circle gathering everyone's attention.

A king playing a fake court.

Waldon sat back and watched him with an intent gaze. "Come now, we all know what you're going to say. Titus holds the wealth and uses it or takes it."

"Would I be wrong?" Clive countered. "He's building an entire city for the Night Spawn trash, while we—"

"Purchase carpets from halfway around the world." Lordess gave a light chuckle but no one else followed, and when Clive's face fell, she covered it with a polite cough.

Waldon blew a puff of smoke across the room. "We all have a deal, we all have things to do, and we all have lives to manage. Responsibilities. Wives to take care of. Perhaps your idea has more merit than I first thought. It's true The House of Shade does boast an extreme amount of wealth, and they do lord over us. I can't say I like being under their thumb. Freedom is our right if you ask me."

"Lord over them?" I rose to my seat. "I'll give him a good flogging."

Eloura wrapped her hand around my wrist and pulled me back into my seat. "Yes, but Waldon is a liar through and through. He will agree, he will say he will do whatever it takes, and he will reassure Clive until he's blue in the face. But there's one thing that's great about liars."

My brow furrowed. "There is nothing great about liars."

When I sat down, she slid her hand from my arm. "I beg to differ, young one. When you're as old as I am, you learn the best thing about liars is they are predictable. A liar will always lie just like a cheater will always cheat. It's never a matter of if it'll happen, but always a matter of when."

"I'll give you that. But these vampires are distasteful with their wastes and wants."

"Everyone wants the good life. But if they don't work for it, they don't deserve it." She shrugged. "I'm sure Clive could do without all those self-portraits he commissions."

I chuckled. "They are rather ridiculous lining his hallways like he was some great regent to be remembered, when all I'd like to do is forget him completely."

"Here, here," a vampire called from across the room, and I spun back to the screen.

"All I'm saying is perhaps we should offer Titus a partnership?" Waldon gave a sneaky smile as he took another drag of his cigarette and blew the smoke from his nose like a dragon.

"And what would a partnership get us?" Clive put one hand in his pocket while he motioned toward Waldon with his pipe.

"An inside look of course." Lordess preened and glanced around the room at the others. "Waldon *is* brilliant, you know."

"Please, do impress us with your brilliance, Waldon." Clive narrowed his eyes at him. "Considering I've been the Blood Born Ambassador with privileges beyond all others within the castle."

"Yes, but in a professional capacity." Waldon snubbed his cigarette out in a huge glass gaudy ashtray on the table beside him and blew out the last puff. "Perhaps what they need is a friend."

"Perhaps." Clive shrugged. "And then what?"

"I think what Waldon is trying to say is that we use the means we've been given or happen upon to purchase well . . . an army." Lordess shrugged. "There are plenty of monsters for hire."

"You want to purchase an army to go against Titus? Using his own wealth against him?" Clive pretended to be calm and only slightly interested but I could tell from the tight set of his shoulders he was more than interested.

"Now, now, would I do such a thing?" Waldon snickered. "I happen to think it's justified. I mean, are we not under thumb and not taken care of? In truth, I feel the Blood Borns are neglected in their current state. It would only be right to relieve him of his duties and wealth. If he thinks he can play with the big boys, then really we'd only be teaching him a lesson for his future."

Clive's eyebrows shot up and he looked around the room at the others perched so prettily on their ugly stiffly cushioned chairs. "You're talking about treason."

"I'm talking about handling all our problems in one shot." He pursed his lips and motioned to the others.

"Really, it's the price of just doing business and making friends. You can't blame me for playing the game better. Plus, tying up a few loose ends would take the pressure off of most of us."

"Ah, you mean Lorenzo." At Clive's mention of that name, they all stiffened. The room went deadly silent as they shot nervous gazes at one another. "Oh yes, we all have been known to make a deal or two."

"That does include yourself, Clive." Waldon crossed his ankle over his knee then rested his arm on the high side of the settee.

"I'm well aware."

"Then you're aware that he's also a problem." He glanced at Lordess. "We are all feeling the strain from him and none of us want to afford the time or resources it would take to satisfy any debts with him."

Clive gave a humorless chuckle. "Hence this meeting. I've thought of all the things you've brought to light here. But the real question is, who is with me?"

Waldon lifted his hand ever so slightly. "I'm happy to join you."

"See? He lies." Eloura sneered. "He'll be loyal to whatever lines his pockets fast enough. Right now it's Clive. Tomorrow it'll be Titus."

"Then he's a weak link and can be used," I pointed out.

"And what of Lorenzo?" Lordess spoke over the hum of people agreeing to take Clive's side.

"Well, who would dare defy a King?" Clive's lips pulled up into a wide smile.

"To you, my friend." Waldon held his glass up to Clive. "Future King of the Vampires."

"With a brand-new army." Clive held his pipe to his lips and took a deeper puff. He let out a cloud of smoke, then he started chuckling and the others all joined in.

"How easily they all speak of treason over cocktails and ugly homes." I let the disgust drip from my voice. "I will assure they get pigs' blood for their next party."

Eloura chuckled. "Don't let their little talk shake you. Fools and liars belong together."

"I couldn't agree more." I began to steer the drone out of the house and back toward us. "But what is next?"

"Can you dig into all their financial histories?"

I gave her a sideways glance. I could get their entire family history in moments if I chose to. "Easily."

"Good. Then that will give us a list of potential traitors." She sat back in the chair. "Then we need to find out who this Lorenzo is and if his allegiance can be swayed."

I raised my eyebrows at her. Eloura was quite the surprise. A most welcome surprise. "I like the way you think."

"Then stick with me, young one, and we will see if I can teach you a thing or two more."

"It would be my extreme pleasure."

CHAPTER EIGHT

ATLAS

"Fly with a swiftness. Take me to him, lest we lose him and the house for good." I motioned for Poe, my raven, to fly ahead of me and I quickened my pace to follow. He was a piece of me, the piece that I used to hunt my prey, and yet he was more like a favorite pet.

Poe soared down the hall of the castle toward the mirrors. His pace didn't stop as he pumped his wings and flew straight into one of them. The mirror only rippled after Poe flew through. I knew I said it with haste, but I did loath jumping into a mirror with such vigor. It tended to sting. I would add this to the list of things Grayson owed me for. I ran for the mirror and leapt into it. The surface held for a moment, like running into a trampoline. I thought I'd be stuck but then it gave way and the mirror melted across my skin, letting me pass. I landed in the long hallway and took off running. Poe was already farther than I anticipated, and I wouldn't slow him down.

He disappeared into the light at the end, and I pumped my arms harder to catch up. I dove for the light and shoved my way through. When I came out the other side, I crashed into a large man dressed in dark clothing with heavy makeup around his eyes. He shoved both his hands into my shoulders and tried to push me back.

I glared at him and didn't move.

He froze for a minute, then threw his body into some sort of spasm with his arms flying up and his eyes rolling around in his head. He threw his body back and crashed with another guy dressed much the same. They collided with each other in ridiculous fits and then it hit me: I was standing in the middle of a mosh pit. Screaming music blared and bright lights flashed. Men and women all threw themselves into each other, and I rolled my eyes.

Bloody fantastic. Here? How could he be here?

Poe circled high above, going unnoticed in the chaos of this club. Toward the front of the room a band stood on stage blaring that asinine excuse for music. All the bloody screaming and crashing into one another. The smell of alcohol, sweat, and . . . blood tinged my nose. I spun around, looking for the source, but it came at me from all directions. The people in the mosh pit reeked of blood, then I saw it. They all had a nick here, a cut there, or tiny punctures on their bodies. Grayson was close. I knew it.

I glanced up and Poe made a smaller circle at the center of the pit, focusing his attention on one spot. "Perfect."

I shoved my way forward as the patrons all slammed into me as though I were a wall. There, in the center of it all, stood Grayson. He too was unmoved, but his eyes glowed under the flashing strobes. A dangerous smile spread over his face, and he locked eyes with me. They were bottomless black depths. Veins forked out from his eyes and drops of blood trickled from the corner of his mouth. He was snacking on these fools, and they hadn't noticed. He held his hand up toward me and crooked his finger.

I rolled my shoulders and held my arms loose at my sides. My blood magic sizzled in my veins and it sprang to life. A fine dark mist swirled up my arms, and if I'd been under bright lights, perhaps the humans would have seen it. But in this dark club, no one was the wiser as to what either of us was doing or about to do. The weight of the stone Ophelia gave me was heavy in my pocket, and I knew I had to bring him back as unscathed as I possibly could. He made a show of running his thumb over the blood on his mouth and then sucking it between his lips.

I took a step toward him and Grayson grabbed a bottle from a patron and smashed the end of it over his knee. The guy took one look at Gray and ran the other way. Grayson's skin tore in a deep jagged cut, but he didn't seem to notice as the blood flowed down his leg. I pressed my finger to my forearm and my blade sprang from my skin. I held onto it as another mosher jumped into me. I shoved my shoulder into him and knocked him into three other men, and they fell to the ground like bowling pins.

Grayson leapt over them and shoved his body into mine. He swung his bottle and it cut across my ribs, ripping my shirt and slicing my skin. Sharp pain shot through my side. I twisted away from him and threw my elbow back, striking his face. Grayson stumbled back and crashed into two guys who shoved him back in my direction. He turned and hissed at them, and I took the opportunity. I kicked out the back of his knee and he dropped to the floor.

He spun to the side and popped to his feet, throwing two more people off to the side. The pit of people seemed to close in around us, and I wanted to shove them all away. I wanted to compel them to move the way Grayson and Titus could, yet I couldn't do anything to move them out of harm's way. If he killed any of them, The Fallen would descend upon this place and wipe him off the face of the earth. I rushed forward and wrapped my arms around him, tackling him to the ground. He hauled his hand back, about to stab me with the bottle, but I flipped him onto his back and shoved his hands to the ground. The bottle smashed in his hand, cutting his palm and wrist.

"Hey, buddy. Too far." A human tried to wrap his arm around my neck and pull me off Grayson. I threw my arm out, knocking him away like a fly and he flew across the room crashing into the wall. The band paused for a second but then the room broke out into cheers, and they started again, playing with more vigor than before, which stirred the mosh pit into more spasming fits.

Grayson snarled up at me as he twisted his body and threw me off him. I rolled to the side and three people fell on top of me, pinning me to the ground. I kicked out and shoved my way to my feet. Grayson stood across from me with his arm wrapped around a woman's neck. He stood behind her with his fangs fully extended. His eyes met mine, and I knew he was going to kill her. He leaned over her neck and ran a fang over her skin. Blood welled and he ran his tongue over the side of her neck, licking it off. She quaked in his arms and tears ran down her cheeks. Yet the others flopping around to the music didn't seem to notice. I reached into my pocket and pulled the stone out.

"Enough of this." I dropped it to the ground and stomped on it. A small puff of grey magic drifted up from under my boot.

I called out for Poe with my blood magic and my raven dove down and smacked right into Grayson's face, scratching at his eyes with his claws. His thick black wings flapped and feathers dropped from them. Grayson bellowed as Poe scratched around his eyes. I took that moment to charge forward and dive right for Grayson. I tackled them both to the ground and shoved the woman away from him. She skidded across the floor and smacked into a barstool that toppled over on top of her. I held Grayson down as he snarled and rolled. I wrapped my arm around his neck and his fangs dug into my forearm as he bit down.

White, magical light surrounded us, and Grayson flailed in my arms. His fangs dug deeper and pain shot through my body, but I wouldn't let go. I wrapped my legs around his, trying to stop him from getting free. Blood flowed from my arm down Grayson's face and onto the floor. It pooled beneath us. People stopped throwing themselves around and backed away from us. Power rose up within that white light and it dug into me like hooks in my insides. They pulled at me. None of the witches warned me this would be agony, and yet my body was going to be ripped from the inside out. Grayson snarled and growled against my arm but I wouldn't let go.

"Good. Hold on, you bastard." I squeezed his neck harder and the world around us began to fade.

My insides were being ripped out and twisted around. I was pulled, twisted, and forced through the universe. I was shattered into a million different pieces that scattered in the wind and then formed back together in a burning mess. I didn't feel Grayson's fangs in my arm or the cuts on my body. I was nothing and everything at the same time. My body began to reform, and the cool of the cell seeped into my skin. The familiar smell of damp earth and blood surrounded me. My body crashed to the ground beside Grayson and pain burned me to my core. Grayson writhed on the floor beside me within the confines of the circle. Fire burned through my veins, and I threw my head back and bellowed. Like a shot, my body was thrown from the circle and I slammed into the wall.

I fell to the ground as the Queens, along with Titus and Moira, hovered off the ground around Gray. The wind flowed around them, and the build-up of power was thick all around us. Grayson released his blood magic and shot to his feet, roaring at the top of his lungs. But his magic was met with an invisible wall. The build-up of power was palpable, and I knew it would come to a head. I sprang to my feet and darted to the side. The power exploded outward, and I got myself behind Moira just in time for her tiny frame to slam into mine. I wrapped my arms around her and smacked into the cell bars.

They clanged with the impact from my back, and it stung like I'd been beaten with a metal pipe. When I fell to the ground, I managed to keep her on top of me and take the impact on my side. I groaned and blinked against the pain. The others all lay on the cell around me, each of us in a stunned state of pain.

Tucker rushed to the bars. "Zinnia!"

She lifted her arm weakly and grumbled, "Present."

The nervous planes of his face seemed to relax. "Anything broken?"

"Not yet." She slowly rose to her feet and sucked in a deep breath.

They all slowly began to stand, and when I let Moira up, she looked like she was about to fall over. She held on to my arm for a moment while she steadied herself. "Thank you, Atlas."

"Of course." She was the mother I'd never had. I would give and be much more whenever she needed, even if it required using my body as a shield.

Titus strolled up beside me and clapped me on the shoulder. "Thank you."

His gratitude made me feel uncomfortable and all I could muster was a simple nod. A blue light opened in the cell, and Beckett walked through and hurried right toward Astrid. He looked her up and down and she gave a slight smile. Without a word they linked hands and walked through the portal. The others all followed them out, and I hesitated in front of it. I'd been ripped apart and put back together by bloody witches' magic enough for one day.

Ophelia moved to stand beside me. "It'll be fine."

"And you've come by this knowledge how?"

She shrugged and motioned toward Beckett. "He takes his happy wife, happy life bullshit seriously. If she's happy, he's happy. That portal will be like sitting in a bath."

"Enough said." I stepped through and she was right. It was like moving through a warm bath. One moment I was in the cell and the next I was on the other side standing with the others.

Moira approached me. "You're hurt."

"Don't think of it." I glanced down at my forearm. It was torn to shreds from Grayson's fangs and the slash across my ribs still seeped dark blood.

She held her hand over my wound and Titus pressed his hand to her shoulder. "Should you? After what just happened?"

"What happened?" I looked past them toward the lab where the sounds of chaos seemed to be dying down.

"I'm stronger than I look." Her blood magic flowed from her hand over my arm and instant relief washed over me. As she moved it to my side, my skin knit back together. When she dropped her hand, it itched like hell, but I was grateful for the bleeding to come to an end.

"Oh, look, Mother's favorite," Grayson growled from within his circle. His dark eyes locked on the two of us. "I used to be the favorite one. And what, they take to an orphan now? Pity the orphan by choice."

I didn't bother to look at him. I just ground my teeth together to keep silent. This version of Grayson had no idea what choices I'd made and why. I turned back to Zinnia. "You'll be sure to watch him?"

"I'll stay," Tabi volunteered. "I'll watch him."

"Me too." Serrina stepped up. "He's one of us, after all."

"Dah, me too." Brax, that huge tiger, moved next to them. "He is like brother."

I know the feeling.

"Very well, then I will go." I turned to the others and gave a deep sigh. "One down, one to go."

Zinnia's eyebrows shot up. "You're going after Piper?"

"The House of Shade is not complete, and I will see it done." It was that simple. Where the hunter was needed, I would go.

"You're not the only one with gifts." Kylian shrugged.

"And I find your gifts so unremarkable I forget the need to even inquire about them, Dark Prince." I'd heard enough about Kylian to know that I didn't want to work with him. Trust was not a currency he dealt in. "Besides, I'm well aware if there's nothing in it for you, then you are what I would call *hardly reliable.*"

"I have my reasons. None of which concern you."

I took a step toward him, wanting to give him a good

thrashing. "I know exactly where you can stick your concern, you daft prick."

Zinnia stepped between us. "Put the rulers away, boys. We will all do this."

"I won't," Ophelia muttered under her breath.

"What? O?" Zinnia wrinkled her nose. "Come on."

She shrugged and gazed at the two of us with that uncanny dark look. "They'll have it done soon enough. I have more interesting things to do."

"The witch is not wrong." I didn't turn away from Kylian.

"No, she's not." He arched his eyebrow at me.

"Then what do you propose?" Zinnia crossed her arms over her chest.

The only thing that'd be possible. "Divide and conquer."

"Perfect." Kylian snickered. "May the best man win."

"And that's your first mistake." I turned to walk away. "This is no game to me."

CHAPTER NINE

PIPER

Just a little bit more.

My time as myself was about to expire. I could feel it coming on now, as opposed to before when I couldn't feel it at all and it would take me by surprise. Hunger pains knotted my stomach so badly it made me want to vomit . . . again. The chains rattled as I shifted my weight back to relieve some of the strain on my arms. I'd counted to one hundred and twenty and then shifted. It gave me some sense of time, not that I knew how much time had passed, or what day it was, or what time of day it was. Pain turned time into an infinite number that was nearly impossible to track.

The hatch at the top of the cell sat open and a stream of sunlight shined down, giving the dim cell just enough light that I could see everything perfectly. Marius sat there staring at the light for long moments. He bent and flexed his fingers, coming a little closer to the light each time.

I scoffed. "Coward."

His head snapped up and he narrowed his eyes in my direction. "What a sad, pathetic thing you are. Hanging there."

"Says the dude who's afraid of a little sunshine." I let my head fall back and hang there for a moment. The muscles in my neck and shoulders released before they bunched and strained again.

"I will drain you dry if you don't shut your mouth," he snapped.

I glanced down at my necklace. It was very close to turning red. I chuckled. "I think we're getting close to that, so why don't you just stop talking shit and just do it."

"You'd like that, wouldn't you?" He rose to his feet. "For me to just end it all?"

I didn't want to die. I had so much more life to live, an infinite one if I didn't get myself killed. If I could spend that time with Grayson, then it would be well worth it. But being stuck here like this had a way of making me give up hope. I knew the others would come for me, but I had no idea if they knew where I was. Hell, *I* didn't even know. Judging by how dark my necklace was getting, it seemed like time was not something I had.

"Or stop this stupidity." I glanced at the ray of light. "You're not even brave enough to see if what you're doing works, which means you just like torturing young women, you fucking psychopath."

He cackled. "Oh, I'm far from a psychopath. You think I

was born like this? No, this is what I was made to be, what the crown turned me into."

"Oh, pardon me, narcissistic sociopath then." I rattled my chains to make my point.

"Difficult to be helpless, isn't it?" He strolled around the ray of light. "To feel so out of control of your own body."

"If you're looking for pity, you'll find none here." I knew what it was like to be out of control, to be changed into this monster and then try to figure out how to survive in this world, which I clearly was not doing very well, considering I was chained up in a dungeon feeling like death and madness was at my doorstep.

"I don't need your pity." He bared his fangs at me, and I gave him a bored look.

I might die here but I wouldn't die cowering before the likes of him. If I was gonna go out, I'd talk shit to the end. "Well, that solves that problem then, doesn't it?"

He strode over to me and I locked down my muscles, bracing for the hit I knew would come. He was becoming predictable in his abuse. His hand cracked across the side of my face and pain exploded there. I sucked in a deep breath as my vision dimmed around the edges. I swung back and forth for a second and forced myself to meet his eye.

"*Cow-ard.*" I spit blood on the floor. "When I hit you back, I promise it won't tickle."

He turned away from me and went to stand in front of the light once more. He reached his hand forward and the ray touched his palm. He held it there for a minute and I sucked in a sharp breath, waiting. Seconds ticked by and still nothing.

Oh fuck. If this worked, I'd be Marius' personal blood bag for the rest of my life.

Then a thin plume of smoke drifted up toward the opening in the ceiling. Marius' hand shook and the muscles strained. He wrapped his other hand around his wrist, and he began to scream. Fire sparked in his palm, and he stumbled back from the light. He waved his hand around trying to put the flames out. He smacked it on his pants and flailed about.

I chuckled. "Burn, bitch. Burn."

CHAPTER TEN

MARIUS

*2*00 **years ago**

Darkness surrounded me, yet I could see every grain of the wooden box I lay in. It was hard against my back, and the walls appeared thin and flimsy. I shoved my fist forward and the box splintered around it. A strength I didn't know I had flowed through my veins and thrummed in every muscle. I knew if I wanted to shatter this box, I could without a second thought. I'd only punched through that one hole, but if I wanted to do more damage, somehow I knew I could, even if it didn't make any sense. Dirt poured in from the hole, and the ground moved all around me. The earth closed in so tight I could feel the cool grains against my skin. I tasted it on my tongue, and it settled deep in my lungs.

Cold assailed my body and I began to quake in the darkness. Panic like I'd never known overcame me, forcing my breath to come in quick, panicked puffs. I'd been buried alive. I tried to scream but the dirt was stuck in my throat. I coughed, trying to dislodge it, but all it did was make me choke more. My throat closed and my lungs struggled for air. I pulled my knees into my body and pressed them up. The lid to my box splintered wide open, the ground caved in, and I knew I would suffocate here, drowning in a sea of damp muck. Yet I had to fight, to try to survive this. I clawed with my finger, searching for the surface while pulling myself up. My nails grew brittle with each moment I continued to dig. They splintered and broke off, yet I had to continue. No one was coming for me, no one would help me get out of this grave. The sweet smell of blood assailed my senses, and my stomach tightened for a taste. I didn't have time to think about what that meant or why it was now happening to me. The surface was out of reach and every muscle in my body burned to reach it.

I crawled upward. Dirt and gravel scraped against my skin. When my hand broke the surface, it was met with cool, misty air. Soaking grass stuck to my skin, and I dug my hand down to pull myself up. A thick pool of mud or quicksand surrounded me as I attempted to tug free. It suctioned in tight to me, trying to hold me in the ground. But I fought with all my might to pull myself up. My bloodied fingers sank into the earth as I shoved and clawed my way from this early grave. I pulled my knees up and crawled the rest of the way out. When I reached the surface, I stayed on all fours, coughing up the dirt from my stomach and throat. Racking gags assailed my body, and every muscle cried out in pain from the retching. Confusion and fear filled my mind. *How did I get here? And why would any of my friends bury me? Was I just left for dead in this flimsy box or was I well and truly dead? If I was dead, then why would they just bury me here out in the forest like something to be ashamed of?* I had a family estate, a place where I could be laid to rest beside my parents. They would've known, my friends would have known to bury me there, not in some random field.

I stayed there on my hands and knees, just sucking in deep breath with my mind wondering how I could be abandoned so poorly by the ones I loved and trusted. Once I could catch my breath, I flopped over onto my back, sucking in deep breaths. I stared up at the sky, wanting to see that infinite darkness covered in sparkling stars. But none could be seen. Even the moon dared not make an appearance. Heavy clouds blocked it all out, and even though I was well above my heavy grave, I was still trapped. Misty rain fell over my face and clung to my filthy clothing, causing the specks of soil to turn into mud.

"Marius?" A delicate voice whispered my name, yet I heard it as if she were shouting from right beside me. I flinched at how loud it was.

Before I could finish the thought of getting to my feet, I was already standing. The motion brought on a spell of dizziness and sharp pains in my stomach. When I turned to her, I drew in a sharp breath. "Moira?"

There standing before me was Moira, Queen of The House of Shade. She looked worn and troubled. Dark circles hung under her round chocolate eyes. She wasn't dressed in her normal formal gown and crown. Instead, she wore a plain black dress that cut in tight to her body and flowed from her hips down to her ankles. Puffy black sleeves covered her from her shoulders down to her wrists. I'd never known Moira to wear such colors . . . unless . . . unless she was in mourning.

"Did I fail?" They'd called me here to help save the King from himself, from the curse. The memories were foggy but slowly coming into light.

Her eyes widened. "Beg your pardon?"

I took a step toward her. "Did I fail? Did I not save the King?"

She drew in a sharp breath. "You remember?"

"I was summoned here." My words were halted as I tried to recall the events that brought me to this moment. "But alas the memories are foggy at best and now this."

I held my arms out, motioning to myself. I was dressed in a white burial shift and covered in muck I still tasted on my tongue. Moira held a small bundle in her arms that jostled and gave a small cry. She held him close and swayed in a calming way. "Are you well? I didn't think . . ."

Her words trailed off, and when she couldn't look at me, a sense of dread sat heavy in the pit of my stomach.

"Didn't think what?"

"When you didn't rise on time, I thought I'd lost you." Her voice was so low it was nearly a whisper. "You were so late. I'd nearly given up hope."

"Rise?" I glanced down at the hole I just climbed out of. "What happened?"

When she didn't answer, I found my ire rising. "Moira, what happened?"

She looked up at me with those wide round eyes. They were so full of sadness and a desperation I'd never seen in them before. A single tear trickled down her cheek and she quickly swiped it away. "When we tried to save Titus, there were problems."

My whole body thrummed with how overwhelming everything was. I could see every blade of grass, feel every drop of mist, smell the many scents wafting from the castle in the distance. We were out in the forest beyond the walls of the castle. It looked like a normal sized home this far away, not the imposing castle I knew it to be. I glanced back at her. "Problems? What's happened to me?"

"Oh, Marius." She sucked in a breath and let it go on a shutter. "Something went horribly wrong. I'm not even sure what happened. But Graymont . . . He's dead. Titus still sleeps, and you, well, you were as close to death as I've ever seen someone. Had I waited for a moment longer, you wouldn't be standing here, so I had to save you. I just couldn't let you go."

"Save me?" Confusion and fear riddled my mind. "How did you save me? I've been buried alive."

"Marius, you weren't alive . . . You still aren't." She shifted her weight. "I changed you."

No, this couldn't be. I was a powerful warlock. I thrived with my magic. I'd hidden here from Alataris for years among my vampire friends and now they . . . changed me into one. I shook my head and took a step back from her. "No, this can't be. You couldn't have."

"I didn't want to let you die after all you've done for the crown."

My fangs descended in my mouth for the first time, jabbing my lip. Blood dripped into my mouth and the flavor hitting my tongue was bliss. I hated it. "After all I've done for the crown, you should have let me die."

"This life can be a blessed one, Marius. You are our friend. I had to save you." She looked up at me with those pleading eyes. It was difficult to bear any ill will toward Moira. She was so gentle, so pure, she wanted only goodness for everyone around her, and yet she'd turned me into this . . . monster. I opened my hand to call on my magic but there was nothing there. That well deep in the pit of my body was gone. In its place there was an emptiness I'd never known. Only hunger and sadness.

I'd lost everything I was, the person I was. My magic was me and I was my magic. I'd never known a time when I couldn't call on it. I hung my head and fought against the ball in my throat that threatened to overwhelm me. "I understand your intentions."

"I intended to give you a life. Yours was cut short helping *us* after all."

It was cut short helping them. I'd lost who I was because of them. "Oh, Moira, I wish you'd just let me go."

"No." Her words were laced with a tone of finality. "I couldn't lose another one who was close to me."

"And Graymont? How did we lose him? I remember using my power to try and filter the curse from Titus." I shook my head. "It's all so foggy."

"I can't be sure how exactly it all went wrong or how the magic backfired." The baby gurgled in her arms, and she continued to bounce him.

"My magic backfired? Impossible." I'd carefully planned out the whole thing, how to save Titus from the curse and keep them all happy and alive.

"It's quite possible, I can assure you. You and Graymont died . . . and Titus," she glanced back at the castle, "he's yet to wake, if he ever does wake."

The pain in her eyes nearly stole my breath. She'd lost her whole family to a powerful curse I could not break. Hubris had gotten me into that cell with Titus, but her decision had made me this thing I never dreamt of becoming. "I didn't ask for this."

"No, but I gave you the chance to live a full life now." She took a step toward me, but I didn't want to get closer. I took a step back.

A life with no magic was no life at all. "Kill me."

"What?" She shook her head. "I will not."

"I don't want this, Moira." I looked down at my muddy hands. "I don't want any of this."

"Give it time." Her words were soft and pleading. "I promise we will see you well."

"I can't live like this. My magic . . ." I couldn't even bring myself to say it was gone now. That most precious part of me was no longer here. "Please just end this for me."

"I can't. As my progeny, I care about you. Enough that I cannot bring myself to harm you."

A maid from the castle hurried to her side and we both fell silent. She was slightly chubby with dark hair and brown eyes. She looked me over but said nothing. Instead, she turned toward Moira. "Duchess, the King is awake."

My brow furrowed. *Duchess?*

"Oh, what good news. I will come now." Her face lit with a small smile. "Just give me one moment . . . alone."

The instant her maid was out of earshot, I couldn't hold my questions in. "Duchess? But you're the Queen."

"No one remembers that, Marius. They all think I'm now the widow of Graymont and that Grayson is his son. I don't know how the magic backfired and spread to cover the kingdom, but it is all of them who believe this."

"But they are wrong! You are Queen! I stood as witness to your marriage." How had this all gone so awry?

She was by my side in an instant, and her eyes locked on mine. The connection sizzled between us. I her progeny and her my sire. I was locked there under her command. "No one remembers, but there is this."

She pulled up her sleeve to reveal that her soulmate mark had faded. It was nearly invisible. "This only happens when the soulmate bond is broken."

"Oh, Moira, I'm so sorry." I didn't want that for her or for their son.

"I've had time to think on this. More days than I care to admit. If that mark is faded, that means that Titus and I are no longer soulmates, which means that he would no longer be cursed. In a way, I believe you held off the curse from taking him."

"But this isn't right. To fool a whole kingdom and the King himself?" I shook my head. "I won't do it."

She reached out and grabbed on to my arm and pulled me closer to her. "You will do it. As your sire, I am telling you, you will do this. You will keep this secret and never speak of it. The King will live, and I will tolerate this burden to keep him alive. I cannot stand to lose him, not again. Nor can this kingdom."

Her words melted into my body and something in me needed to comply to keep the secret. "What have you done to me?"

"It is our bond as a sire and progeny. I will command this of you—"

"Please don't." I didn't want to keep this secret. Titus should know. The kingdom should know.

"This is the last thing I will ever command of you. I swear it." The honesty in her words rang true, and something inside me unlocked like I was free. Yet the hold on that secret remained. I would never be able to speak of it to anyone.

I glared at her. "How could you?"

"You will have a life, a grand one. I will see to it. But I will protect my family, and you will keep this with you just as I will." She held the baby close to her chest and turned away from me. "Titus wakes, and by the grace of the Creator . . . if he was made to forget, then that is the life we are all meant to lead. He will be safe."

"And what of Graymont?" I pleaded.

"Graymont is dead, and I will not have his loss be in vain. He will be as they all say he is. He will be known as Grayson's father and my husband."

"Moira, no." How could she possibly think this was the way? "The King, he should know."

"The King will still be with his son, and I will take solace in that, as will you, even if he will only be known as his uncle." She turned back to the castle. "Now I will see to Titus and then I will see you well taken care of."

"But Moira—"

"Enough," she snapped. "We will bear this together . . . forever."

CHAPTER ELEVEN

THEON

The rhythmic sound of her heart beating gave me only a short-lived reprieve from the stress of my current situation. I watched the steady rise and fall of her chest, and with each breath she took, I found comfort in that small feat. My body had barely begun to heal from my encounter with Marius, yet somehow I found the strength to sit by her bedside, a strength that she gave me. The room they'd put her in was more like one of the holding cells for the Night Spawn who were riddled with the sickness. I imagined it was more to keep me in than it was to keep her in.

A tiny witch named Ophelia sat outside the cell just staring at us. If the rumors I'd heard about her were true, then I would stay in this cell. Because as much as the cell kept me in . . . it kept her out. Her huge black eyes were unnerving in the way she watched *everything*. Her sister Zinnia placed a magical barrier over the door and the single glass window, which I was not going to test. Through the window, I could easily see the others huddled together talking and glancing toward the cell. I was in a precarious position within the walls of this castle. Marius was a known traitor now, and I was his progeny. If I were them, I wouldn't trust me either. Somehow, I managed to remain alive.

"I am . . ." Even unconscious, her brow furrowed, and she moved in the bed, fitfully kicking out with her legs. "No One."

I placed my hand over hers and her fingers instinctively wrapped around mine. "You are not No One."

I lowered my voice. "I should've never stayed away from you for so long."

A knock at the door brought my eyes up from her and I held my breath. There, taking up the whole doorway, was Titus. He was imposing as ever, and I could feel his blood magic at the ready. "I see you've recovered from your incident."

"If you mean when Marius snapped my neck," I ran my hand over the back of it, "yes. I've recovered enough. My thanks to your doctors."

"Difficult to know if it was worth it." He stepped farther into the room, but he wasn't alone. Sanchita and Jester were right behind him while Zinnia remained by the door.

"I can assure you it will be." I didn't want any part of what Marius was doing to the vampires. To betray my sire was blasphemy, but here I was being the son who needed to stop his father. If the stories were true, then the witches who walked the halls of this castle knew something about that.

"You must leave this room, and we will see what you do and do not know." He motioned to the door.

I wanted to go with him, yet she needed me here, and something in me could not leave her side. "My apologies, Your Highness, but I cannot leave."

"You dare defy my wishes?" He arched his eyebrows at me, and I nearly caved at the look he gave me. I found myself looking back down to her for the strength I needed to stay.

"I'll gladly drag him out of here for you, my King." Jester cracked his knuckles and took a step toward me.

The King held his hand up, stopping Jester from moving forward. "I'm sure Theon is well aware that my wish is his command."

His blood magic seeped from his fingers and spun around his hand. I let go of a breath I didn't know I was holding. "Please, Your Majesty. I can't leave her. Have you ever felt like you couldn't leave someone even if you wished it? It's my fault she's here."

The King gave a small grunt but said nothing. Sanchita moved forward and her hand curled into a fist. I didn't bother moving away or trying to block the hit I knew would come. She believed I deserved it, and in her eyes maybe I did, but I knew better and soon they would too. Jester grabbed her wrist and pulled her back.

She yanked her hand free from him and narrowed her eyes at him. "You heard him. It's his fault she's here." She shot me a killing look. "What the hell did you do to her? And to the rest of them?"

"I would never do this to her or any other vampire." Even in her sleep, her hand tightened around mine and I moved in closer. "If I hadn't left her alone and ignored her for so long, this wouldn't have happened."

Sanchita marched to the other side of her bed right across from me. "Why did you?"

I didn't even want to admit what I was about to say to myself. "I didn't want to draw any attention to her. If Marius had seen . . . I didn't know what he'd do to her."

"Well, congratulations on being completely useless." Sanchita motioned to her. "He got to her anyways."

"What are you talking about? This is the sickness." How could it be anything else? I'd seen how it affected the Night Spawn, the toll it took on them all. I knew the crown was trying to find a cure for whatever had riddled them. This sickness drove vampires to madness and made awful things happen to them physically. Some of them were stored in the lab here and I could see them in the other holding cells. One woman played with her own blood while muttering to herself. Another burst into a puddle of water and reformed every few minutes. I couldn't imagine the pain or insanity, but this couldn't be Marius.

"No." Sanchita shook her head, sending those wild waves flying around her face. "Marius did this. He's making them sick. All of them."

"What?" I rose to my feet. "How?"

"Don't play dumb," she snarled. "The right hand of

Marius had no idea what the left hand was doing? Oh please."

"I swear, if I had known anything about this, I would have come to you." I turned to the King. "I swear it."

"And you're to believe this?" Sanchita looked from the King to me and back again. "He's lying."

"You're starting to get on my nerves," I growled. "I haven't lied to you or anyone else."

"Watch your tongue or I'll cut it out," Jester hissed as he palmed the hilt of a knife he had in a holster at his hip. He moved to stand beside Sanchita.

"Silence." The King waved his hand and his magic shot across the room and wrapped around me. It took over my body, and I was no longer in charge. Though he let me stay standing where I was, I knew if he commanded me to leave the room, I would. He strolled around the hospital bed. "Tell me the truth. I've no time for games."

His words sent the command through me.

"Ask me."

"Are you working for Marius?"

"No." Every muscle in my body knotted painfully.

"Do you know what he's doing to the Night Spawn?"

"No."

"Would you help him if he asked you?" His questions came rapid-fire.

"No." *I'd rather die.*

"Do you know what the sickness is?"

"No, I would tell you if I did."

Titus waved his hand and his hold dropped on me. I

sucked in a sharp breath and slouched closer to the bed. The King stopped and stared at me. "He's clean. Now, let's see if he's useful. If Marius is in fact poisoning the Night Spawn, it would explain their newfound abilities and their sickness. If what he's doing to them is backfiring and causing all of this, then we've been looking for solutions in the wrong places."

"He's experimenting on them, and this," she waved to the cells in the lab, "doesn't even come close to the consequences of his actions."

"She's right, Your Majesty." Jester pressed his lips into a hard line, which gave his already severe features a harder look. "There were more rooms than I could count. We were lucky to get her out alive."

"We cannot allow that to continue." The King paced back and forth. "We will need more proof, locations of holding cells. We will need everything."

"I'm going back," Sanchita announced. "I must."

"It's not going to be safe for you there," the King countered.

"My sister is there. She needs me." Sanchita didn't even sound like she was asking for permission. Determination covered her face and she stood tall and still. "She's already looking for all you require. I will help her."

"As will I," Jester vowed, and I could've sworn he moved in whatever direction Sanchita moved. It was unconscious, like the push and pull of magnets.

"I want to believe that my old friend is not capable of such atrocities, but I will take your words for truth." He turned to me. "You know him best. I expect you to prove yourself useful."

Horrified was the only word I could use to describe what I was feeling. How could Marius do something like this? I thought he was trying to make a better life for us all, but instead he was poisoning us for his own gains. I gave a heavy sigh. I knew Marius better than he knew himself. I would be more than useful to King Titus. "I wouldn't expect to be accountable for anything less."

"Let's start with something easy then, shall we?" He motioned to the bed. "What's her name?"

"She's not No One. She could never be No One." I looked down at her dark hair and soft features. "Claire. Her name is Claire."

CHAPTER TWELVE

ELOURA

"Steady there, young master." Martin fidgeted by my side as we walked the halls of the castle. I always loved the dark, gothic look of the castle. It was a stark contrast to the light, bright decor of my own home. Dark stone flooring and walls gave that old world feel. Wooden beams arched from the ground upward where they met in intricate carvings that ran over the ceiling. Warm candlelight lit the way to the throne room. It was all so familiar at times. I felt that the castle was a second home to me.

Martin brushed the lapels of his suit, picking at a speck that was not there. "I find my level of agitation is not conducive to being steady."

I lowered my voice. "I too share your sentiments; however, when playing the long game, you must remind yourself who you are surrounded by and what your goals are."

I tilted my head in the direction of two courtiers strolling down the hallway about to pass by us. I placed a wide smile on my lips. "Lady Mathis, Lady Kline, how lovely to see you out and about the castle."

Lady Mathis was a smaller vampire with a round body and a round, innocent face. "I have to say it has been quite the ruckus lately. I have half a mind to leave the castle."

The courtiers all held rooms within the castle and came and went as they pleased so long as they pleased the King. It was an overly privileged position, but such was the way of how things were done in England. "I'm sure the danger has passed. No one is as strong or reliable as the King."

"Indeed." Lady Kline looked both up and down with a pinched-looking face. "Let us hope this unrest is dealt with soon."

"I have no doubts it will be." I gave them a little bow. "Martin, we must excuse ourselves, we have much business to attend to."

"Of course." Martin bobbed his head in a small bow, and they too did the same. We began to stroll farther down the hall, and once they were out of earshot, Martin gave a heavy sigh. "The castle has been attacked and all they can think about is themselves."

"My dear Martin, you've worked with us for many years now. This shouldn't surprise you. But don't be mistaken, those two ladies and their husbands have been loyal to the King for his entire reign, so we tolerate them. Not only have they supported him, they've invested in the King's plans for the Night Spawn."

"Perhaps they are a bit more forward thinking than I originally thought." We turned down another hallway that led to the throne room and Martin grew quiet.

"Penny for your thoughts." Nothing about the game we now played was easy. There were blurred lines between who we could and could not trust. There were those who pretended to support the King and those who did not. Then there were those who just didn't like the King, which was their prerogative so long as they didn't move against him.

"It is disheartening to be in the position of having to tell the King of how others are plotting against him. I wish they would see things our way."

We paused in front of the throne room doors. "That's all part of this world. If we all agree all of the time, then you'd only have zealots with no thought for themselves. It is our differences that make us stronger, for the correct answer usually lies somewhere in the middle."

"You make a fair point. There must be differences to keep things balanced." He sucked in a deep breath and blew it out in a long, slow sigh. "Are you ready?"

"Don't take it all too seriously. After all, we're on the winning side." I winked at him, then turned toward the two guards stationed outside the throne room. They each had their hand on the large handles. I waved toward them, motioning for them to open the door.

The doors were at least twenty feet tall and made of thick wood. When the soldiers pulled them open, it was like a choreographed dance. They creaked with a deep groaning, making them sound as ancient as they were. Usually the throne room was full of courtiers lingering around to get a moment with the King, now it was only Titus and Moira who stood in the middle of the room talking. When I entered, they both turned to face us, and I could tell from the deep set of their mouths and how their eyebrows drew low over their eyes that they were troubled.

The throne room was the centerpiece of the castle, with thirty-foot ceilings, wide open space, and warm wooden beams going in all different directions. A single throne sat on top of a dais at the head of the room. Two flags hung on the wall behind it, both bearing the symbol for The House of Shade: a single silver sword, with deep red roses winding around it, sitting on a black shield. The same symbol was made of stained-glass, and as the sunlight shined through, it projected on the floor in front of Titus and Moira as they stood waiting.

Moira rarely fidgeted, yet now she seemed unable to hold herself still. She wrang her hands in front of her and there were two worry lines in between her eyebrows. Titus straightened his shoulders and held his chin a bit higher. We stopped just before them, and I gave them each a deep curtsy. Martin too bowed beside me, and I was struck by how quiet it was in the throne room.

"Your Majesties, always a pleasure." I rose from my curtsy and met Titus' eyes. "I trust all is well after recent events?"

"If you mean have things calmed since the attack, I'd say

yes and no." He ran his hand over his hair, a nervous gesture I rarely ever saw from him. "The castle is slowly coming back to normal and the injured are being cared for."

"It seems you are on track." I wanted to point out the positive before I hit him with any new negative.

"Piper is missing, and we know not who or what might have her." Moira wrang her hands even more. "I hate to think of what is happening to her."

Martin's jaw dropped. "Is there anything I can do to help find her? She and I have become friends, and I'd like to help in any way I can."

"You already are." The King pointed out. "You're helping me make the castle a safe place for her to return to once she is found."

"The Witch Queens, along with Atlas and Kylian, all have it well in hand. There are none who are stronger in Evermore. We can't ask for more than that." Moira turned to face the stained-glass windows, and her voice dropped to a whisper, "All we can do now is pray to the Creator for her safe return."

I didn't want to ask the next question, but I felt I had to. "And what of the Prince?"

She turned back toward Titus and her shoulders hunched slightly as she dropped her gaze to the floor. "The Prince remains . . . unwell."

"Oh, Moira, I'm so sorry." I wanted to pull her into a hug and tell her everything would be all right, but the truth was I didn't know if I truly thought it *would* all turn out well.

"Never you mind." She squared her shoulders and forced her chin higher. "What have you brought for us?"

"It's not the best news, Your Majesty." Martin pulled his tablet from the satchel he wore on his shoulder and flipped the cover open. His fingers ghosted over the screen, and in a moment he had the video from the drone up and ready to play. He handed it over to the King. "If you'll just hit play, I'm sure you'll find the whole exchange intriguing."

Titus pressed play and the video came to life. "This should be enlightening."

"Indeed." I pressed my lips together, waiting for the whole thing to play.

I watched as Titus' face went from eyebrow-raising surprise to downright angry. "Is that Waldon and Lordess Fredrickson?"

Moira went up on her toes and peeked over his forearm to view the screen. "It is, but are we surprised? They've always been an advantageous family willing to play both sides of the coin."

"That was my thought." I inclined my head toward her. "Their loyalty is easily bought and paid for."

Titus paused the video and handed the tablet back to Martin. He crossed his arms over his barrel chest, pulling the fabric of his coat tight across his biceps. "And the other families, they're all in agreement with Clive?"

"They are indeed, Your Majesty." I motioned for Martin to bring up the list of names we'd collected. Martin handed him the tablet once more, and Titus' eyebrows raised as he read them. "I found the Maricks, Peterson, and Blackstone names particularly surprising."

"As do I." He turned from us and started pacing in front of the dais. "I thought their loyalty was to the crown."

"If it makes you feel any better, it seems they all have gotten themselves into some deep debts and now they are going against you in the hopes that Clive will restore their coffers."

Martin scoffed. "And yet he's the worst off out of the entire lot."

"But hiring an army?" Titus ran his hand over the whiskers surrounding his mouth. "Do we know how far they've gotten in this little . . . task?"

Moira's hands curled into fists at her sides. "It's treason, no matter what their reasoning is."

I took the tablet back and handed it to Martin. "As far as we can tell, this was a newly hatched plan."

"And this Lorenzo, he's some kind of loan shark?" Titus continued walking back and forth.

For some reason, I liked the idea of Lorenzo. He had half the Blood Borns in his debt and yet we were only now hearing of him. That to me spoke of his intelligence. "He is. Martin and I have located him. Martin has drawn his financials, and he's more of an entrepreneur than I thought."

The King paused to face me. "Do tell."

Martin cleared his throat. "He's rich, Your Majesty. Not just slightly rich, he's filthy rich. His holdings include multiple human businesses: plumbing, construction, carpentry. You name it, he's got his finger in it. And now he's got the aristocracy in his debt. From my understanding, he doesn't take well to unpaid debts."

"Political ambitions?" Moira stepped closer to us. I could understand why she'd ask. A vampire with that much money and influence would usually keep moving forward to gain more power and influence.

"I can see why you might think that, but as far as our research tells us, he's not into getting involved in vampire politics. In all honesty, it seems he's more influential in the human world than ours." I also found *that* intriguing about Lorenzo.

The King raised his eyebrows at that. "Then perhaps we need a meeting with this Lorenzo."

I was hoping he'd suggest a meeting. "Of course, Your Highness."

"In the meantime, I will alert the rest of the council to be vigilant and to look for any hint of where Clive might hire an army." He shook his head and a sound of disgust rumbled in his chest. "We're surrounded by traitors."

Moira vibrated with anger. I didn't think I'd ever seen her so put out before, with her lips pressed into a line and her brow drawn low. There was a red flush to her cheeks and a light-pink mist drifted from her hands. "All of which will be dealt with accordingly. Isn't that right?"

"Of course," Martin and I answered at the same time.

Titus motioned toward the doors. "You have my every confidence."

"Thank you." I gave him another curtsy. "I will see it handled."

I turned with Martin and headed toward the door when Titus called after us. "Eloura, it would do well to remind the vampires of Evermore how we deal with traitors."

As we moved through the door, Martin lowered his voice and whispered, "What does he mean by that?"

I smirked up at him. "There will be blood to pay."

CHAPTER THIRTEEN

PIPER

"You bitch! Give me what I require!" He threw me away from him. My legs had long since given out and I hung here just from my wrists.

Marius put his hand into the ray of light once more, then yanked it back out. I wanted to laugh, to snicker at him and his stupidity. Instead, I would die knowing I could walk in the sun and he never would, so I hung here waiting for the moment this would all be over. The shackles cut into me, but my blood had dried up and there was nothing left for me to bleed. Marius had drank me nearly dry. The fact was, I didn't know how I was still breathing. The metal just continued to rub my wounds, making them deeper. Pain had become my companion, and I just lived in it now. My necklace had turned a deep, dark red, but with no blood or life force and no madness to take over, I remained semi-sane. I was a husk of myself, and I knew I would die here like this.

My only regret was I never had the time I deserved with Grayson.

I would've finally known what it was like to have someone to love and rely on. Now even that was so far out of reach. I prayed that Ophelia would keep taking care of Dice after I was gone. They were the only two I left behind. It was funny to think that what I considered my family was only two people, but they were. A dull ache had begun in my chest. It was an ache of loss, of sadness. I'd already begun to mourn *us*.

"I don't know why I thought you were so special." Marius paced around me. "You are weak. You'll die from your inability to take any nourishment. And you're a bloody vampire!"

His voice rose with annoyance. Scorch marks covered his arms and face. His clothing was singed in places, and yet we'd been at this for hours . . . or days, I wasn't sure. He'd stand under the light and burn, then return to me, thinking my blood would somehow fix him. But there was no healing for him, no walking in the sun. Hell, if anything, he'd weakened himself with this little experiment.

"And you're a prick." I wanted to laugh to myself, but I didn't have the energy. Though my words were cutting, my voice sounded weak.

He marched over to the wall where my chains were bound and holding me up. He grabbed them off the hook there and yanked them free. My own weight dragged me to the ground, and the chains rattled as they slipped over the pipe overhead. New pain exploded in my knees and side when I hit the floor. But I was too weak to move or even groan. Everything hurt and exhaustion had a death grip on me. I lay there in the position I'd fallen in, with my arms bent at weird angles and my legs folded over each other. When I got a look at the cuffs and my wrists, I nearly gagged. But there was nothing left in my stomach to be rid of. My wrists were raw, and I could see into the deep wounds. The shackles were covered in my dried blood and had a dark rusted color over the silvery metal. I closed my eyes for a split second, letting the cool floor soothe my body. I let my bruised face mush against it, and I sucked in a reedy breath.

I fought an internal battle with myself. Part of me wanted to continue to fight and the other part of me wanted to give up and let this be over. I hated to admit even to myself that the giving up and letting go part was winning me over. What good would I be to Grayson and the others broken and beaten like this? My muscles went limp, and I began to slip away from this place to another. Blackness threatened and I welcomed it.

The sound of his footsteps dragged me back from the edge. My eyes flashed wide open before his hand landed on my shoulder. He jerked me to the side and I flopped over onto my back. My arms fell over my head, yet my legs were still twisted to the side. I looked up at the rocky ceiling and Marius' face filled my vision. He sneered down at me, then wrapped his hand in my shirt and dragged me toward the light peeking through that small hatch. He flung me into the light, and I just lay there with the sun on my skin. The warm rays covered my stomach, and the only thing I could think was how I would miss the feel of it on my face on a summer day.

A sharp kick stung my side, and the sound of my ribs cracking stabbed at my ears. More pain, so much more pain, it blended in with the rest of the agony covering my body. It became harder to catch my breath, and I knew he'd punctured one of my lungs. Marius wound up to kick me again and I coughed. Fine drops of blood sprayed from my lips. "Jealous."

He placed his hand in the light once more and instant blisters formed over his skin. The smell of rotting flesh wafted from him and more smoke drifted from him up toward the opening. I could still enjoy the rays of light and he couldn't. There was an irony in the fact that my death would bring him nothing. For all his efforts, his torture, his biting, he would get nothing from me.

He bellowed and pulled his hand away. "I will kill you for this."

I'm already dying. There was something strange about accepting my own death. It was a mix of relief and sorrow that all the fighting, stress, and hurt would now be over. The sorrow struck me hardest, knowing the life I could've had with Grayson would've been a beautiful one. I could almost picture it perfectly, even see our children with their thick chocolate hair and cocky smiles. I wanted it all. I wanted that life, those children, and the family I knew we could make together. I knew the witches would save Gray and I saw myself there when it happened. I wanted my face to be the first sight he saw when he came back to us. Now it was his face I would picture as my last sight.

Marius pulled what looked like a hunting knife from his waistband. He held it high over his head and I locked eyes with him. When he looked back on this moment, I wanted him to remember he never broke me. I wanted him to remember that I never feared him, I never respected him, and when Grayson killed him for this, I wanted it to be my face he saw, knowing that his own actions brought his demise. Because my death would surely bring that about and in that I found myself smirking up at him.

"He's going to kill you for this."

He paused, holding the knife there high above his head. His muscles shook and his face turned a deep crimson. I knew he would do it. I knew I would die in moments, so I let my mind drift back to the first time I'd been alone with Grayson. A thousand images flashed through my mind. The night he slept next to me, the stolen moments when we were alone wrapped up in each other, the way his lips pressed against mine, and how his flavor would linger on my lips for hours afterward. I licked my lips, trying to hold that close to my mind.

Marius bellowed and the blade plunged down toward my chest. The jagged metal cut through my skin and so much deeper. The breath caught in my throat, and when I let it out, I couldn't catch another. My muscles went limp and there was nothing. I let my eyes slide shut. I didn't want my last vision to be of Marius. There was nothing left for me here. Death would be peaceful, and I would wait for Grayson on the other side. I sent a thought out to him as the last shutter of my heartbeat filled my chest. There was only one thing he needed to hear from me.

. . . *Goodbye, my love.*

CHAPTER FOURTEEN

MARIUS

$\mathcal{I}$ turned away from the mess on the floor and walked over to the table at the back of the room. "Kendra!"

Ever the devoted soldier, she was through the door in less than a second. "Yes, my lor—"

Her words trailed off at the sight of Piper on the floor with a knife through her chest. She was a bit of a sight. Her legs were at odd angles and her arms were bound above her head. Blood matted her midnight hair and covered the side of her face and down her neck. I thought the pool of blood under her would've been bigger but that was just another disappointment when it came to dealing with the likes of Piper. I motioned to her dead body. "Clean this mess up."

I'd wasted days on Piper. Her blood tasted of untapped magic, yet her weaknesses far outweighed that power. All I desired was the sunlight and she failed to provide that to me. I wanted to breathe the warm air and walk in the summer with the butterflies and blooming flowers. Memories of those gentle springs riddled my mind. To be relegated to existing in the darkness and shadows like some kind of skulking monster was far beneath me. I deserved the light, I deserved the crown, I deserved everything that was taken from me by *them*.

"As you wish." Kendra bent over the body and wrapped her hand around the hilt of my knife, trying to pull it free. The muscles in her arms bulged and strained with the effort to yank it out.

I grabbed a towel from the table and wiped the blood from my hands. The dark stains didn't wipe away, and I tossed the towel back onto the table. "What a waste."

I'd driven the dagger clean through her heart and embedded it into the rocky floor beneath her. She deserved it. That foul mouth and the way she carried herself begged to be taught a lesson. Her lesson was death. I listened for any sign of life. But there was none—no breath left her lips, her heart did not beat, and her eyes remained closed. She was well and truly gone. A sense of accomplishment ran through my chest. It wasn't every day that a member of the royal house fell at my hands. Piper was the first, but she wouldn't be the last.

One less Shade to kill.

I wanted Piper's blood to give me the ability to do what I wished, to bring back some of my magic, yet all it'd done was weaken me. I needed fresh blood to replenish myself and ready for the next steps in my plan. But there were matters that needed my attention. One could not rule all vampires if one was weighed down with distractions like her. The world was better off without another useless vampire. Kendra yanked once more but still couldn't dislodge the blade.

I strode over to her and wrapped my hand around the hilt, then yanked it up. It pulled free of Piper with a sticky wet sound. Her chest rose with the motion but as soon as I freed my knife, her body fell back onto the floor like a wet sack. I paused, staring down at the delicate features of her face. "She is rather pretty to look at though."

"Yes, but there are many other pretty ones without that tongue." Kendra crossed her arms and stared down at her. "Do you think perhaps you—"

"Perhaps I what?" I narrowed my eyes at her and my annoyance rose.

She swallowed and didn't meet my gaze. "Perhaps you went a bit too far? Perhaps you shouldn't have killed her. When The House of Shade finds out, they will—"

"They will what?" I cut her words off. "We're at war now. They know it and we know it. Death happens in war. She was a casualty."

"They will be bitter about losing a beloved pet. The Prince in particular will be horribly put out."

"The Prince is lost to madness. I would've kept her as my own pet. She was entertaining really. Breaking her would've brought me great pleasure. There really is nothing like bringing an untamed beast to heal. But she would've died anyways. She couldn't take blood."

"Then how has she lived for this long?" Her brow furrowed in confusion as though she was trying to reason it all out.

"What does it matter? She was a waste of our time and resources." I sighed. "And we've given the Blood Borns a taste of the power we wield, which would have been worth it had it paid off. But alas, I gained nothing from her, so it has not proved fruitful and now they are aware of the magics we wield."

"Can it be that important to walk in the sunlight?" She grabbed Piper's limp body and started dragging it toward the door. A trail of blood streaked the floor in her wake.

"You've lost your memory of what it was to feel the warmth on your skin. There really is no other bliss to compare." I held my hand out toward the beam of light, but I didn't touch it. "Now I will have to find my powers in other ways."

"Very well." Kendra picked Piper off the floor and threw her over her shoulder. "I'll be rid of this."

"Be sure to bury her where no one will ever find her." I motioned for her to leave.

"As you wish." She turned and walked out the door with Piper draped over her shoulder. Her long dark hair hung down, nearly dragging over the floor.

"What a disappointment." I wanted nothing more than to leave the dissatisfaction behind. I left the cell and turned to the right to walk down the long hall. The lights were spread out sporadically down the hall, which meant there were spaces of darkness between them. Much to my annoyance, I was forever in the darkness.

When I reached the end of the tunnel, I turned and opened a thick metal door. The moment I entered, screams sounded even louder. Their pained cries brought a smile to my face. My pets had worked themselves into a frenzy on this day. The large space was lined with cells on each side. Thick metal bars were shoved deep into the rocky earth, which made them nearly impossible to break. But I'd had them magically reinforced like all my holding cells and shackles. My pets hurried to the bars and reached out toward me. They shouted and cried out for release. But they just hadn't been properly tamed . . . yet.

This was my collection: Night Spawn vampires from all over the world. They were harvested with perfect precision and kept here for the taking. I waved and smiled at them as I passed, even if they *were* filthy and whining. But I didn't stop to inspect them as I normally did. Usually I took my time to view my inventory, lavishing in the variety of vampires I'd collected, but right now I needed to pay a visit to my most trusted subject.

I moved through a door at the back of the room, and when it fell shut behind me, the cries of my pets were silenced. I pressed my back to the door and allowed my eyes to adjust to the darkness. The room was small, but I'd taken my time to assure there was every comfort provided. Plush fluffy carpets covered the hard-packed earth completely. A small fireplace sat at the back of the room where a few lingering embers still flickered in the dimness.

Pillows were strewn about the room, and there was light classical music playing in the background. It was the perfect ambiance to serve my purposes.

I strode over to the fire and quickly stoked it, bringing the flames back to life and bathing the room in warm light. I glanced above me and there she lingered, a black hazy cloud high above my head. I lifted my hand toward the cloud.

"There you are, lovely thing."

The cloud swooped down from the ceiling and circled around my arm for an instant, then drifted back away from me. "Come now, you're being shy with me? Since when?"

I turned and dropped down onto one of the pillows and spread out in front of the fire. When she took shape in front of me, I dared not move or startle her. Though she was mostly dark, smoky fog, at times she could force the inky cloud into the beauty she used to be. Her face was small with full lips and a pert nose. When I tried to look into her eyes, there was nothing but cloudy black depths. Her hair remained dark and smoky, as did the rest of her body. Tiny silvery sparks twirled within the smoke each time she moved.

"Ah, there you are." I gave her the warmest smile I could muster, and she made the only sound she was capable of. It was a light hum with a happy tone as if she were greeting me. "Yes, it has been some time."

She shot away from me, reforming near the ceiling. I made a show of sticking my lip out and pouting at her. "Come now. Don't be cross with me. We've work to do and I'm afraid my project was not as successful as I hoped."

She made a little *hmm* and I leaned back onto one of the pillows and rested on my elbow.

"I know. I'm disappointed as well. I believed that mutant had the power to let me walk in the day and see the sun once more. If I want the entire vampire world to fear me, to follow me, then I need this. To be viewed to be just as good as the Blood Borns. If I had my magic . . ."

She made another little sound, and I lay back. "I know you can help, but our tests are not yet complete. Once we know how to unlock the power within me safely, then I will trust only you to do this."

The cloud spun around above me and sank to the pillow across from me. Again, her soft face appeared, and I looked into the hollow depths that would've been her eyes. "Yes, and then we will find a way to restore you. Of course we will."

I held my hand out toward her, and I hesitated, staring down at the blood stains there. I groaned. *Such a waste.* "I swear it, my darling. All will be yours soon enough. Once our experiments are complete and my army is fully built, we shall find the answers to your . . . plight. Soon, darling, soon you will be free of this."

CHAPTER FIFTEEN

ZINNIA

"*D*ance monkey, dance!" Grayson roared from his cell.

I rolled my eyes with a groan. I missed the old Grayson, the one who always had a witty word to say. Sure, he was cocky, but he wasn't a straight up psycho ass. "Will you shut up for two seconds?"

He turned away from me, giving me his back, then he dropped down onto the floor and lay there. He put his hands behind his head and crossed his legs at the ankles. He went silent for a moment before he started yelling out once more. "Let me out, Zinnia! Zinnia, let me out! Come on, Zin!"

It went on and on and I was starting to get sick of my own name. I turned away from the cell and began to pace the length of the hall between the bars on either side of me. I didn't know why we'd all set up in the dungeon as a base of operation, but it was right to be this close to Gray because even in his state of insanity it seemed necessary. Not to mention we could all keep an eye on him. We knew Lucifer wanted him, which meant that out of everything walking this Earth, Grayson could possibly be one of the most dangerous. There was no telling what Lucifer might come at us with next. He'd already freed Grayson simply by astral projecting. I couldn't imagine what he'd do if he got free of Hell.

So, we'd made ourselves as comfortable as possible. Tabi had taken up residence in the cell across from Grayson, changing the dank, drab cell into what could only be described as a jungle-themed flower shop. Bright-green foliage covered the bars and spread over the floor. A dazzling array of flowers bloomed over the full green leaves. They wove up the walls and over the ceiling and began to spread down the ceiling into the hall.

In another cell, Ophelia had begun collecting weapons. I wasn't sure where she was stealing them from inside the castle, but somehow she'd managed to get herself a battle axe, a cannon ball, some kind of spiked chain, countless knives, a few bows and arrows, and some random apparatus that looked like it'd rip someone limb from limb. It was made of two thick wooden beams in the shape of an X, and leather straps looped from each of the four posts. Ophelia hung from one side of the X, then jumped to another like it was a jungle gym.

Serrina sat across from Maze at a small wooden table with four chairs. The other two chairs were occupied by Tilly and Ashryn. A map of the world was spread out in front of them, and Maze sat there staring down at the map while his cards circled above his head. His eyes glowed an intense milky-white. A card dropped to the table in front of him and he picked it up. When he looked at it, his eyes widened for an instant, and he shook his head. "No."

He threw the card back above his head where the others swirled around. Tilly placed her hand over his. "The cards don't lie."

Maze pulled his hand from hers and slammed his fist down on the table. "They are this time."

Odin hopped up on the table and dropped some kind of puffy pastry in front of Maze. He shoved it toward him with his little paw, and Maze grabbed it up and shoved it in his mouth.

He gave the cat a single nod, then reached into his pocket and pulled out a bag of hot Cheetos. He flipped them over onto the table and held one up. "One for you. One for me." Odin hissed at him and knocked half the Cheetos onto the floor. Maze growled at him. "Don't be greedy."

Odin jumped from the table, and all I could hear were his tiny crunching bites. Tuck walked in from the lab and strolled around their table, dodging the mess on the floor. He reached out and wrapped his hand around my wrist, pulling me closer. The heat from his touch spread over my body and instantly calmed me. "What's going on in here?"

"Serrina and Ashryn are trying to figure out where Piper is being held by following the trail of Marius's desires."

"Any luck with that?" He turned and glanced down at the map.

"His greed knows no bounds." Serrina ran her hand through her hair and tossed the strands over her shoulder with a frustrated jerk. She motioned to the map and little red lines were spread all over the country in a random crisscross pattern. Her magic kept jumping from one location to the next with no rhyme or reason. "Which means it's everywhere."

Tuck turned to Maze. "And what about you?"

Maze shot him a glare, his eyes turning from milky-white to neon-green and back again. He picked up a handful of Cheetos and shoved them in his mouth. "As the Brits would say, piss off."

I lowered my voice and leaned into Tuck. "I think whatever he's seeing, or the cards are telling him, it isn't good. Tell me, how are things out there? What's going on around the castle?"

Tuck shook his head. "It's calming down but still chaotic. Titus has his guards searching the country for Piper, the lab is starting to get back to normal after yesterday's attack, Beckett and Astrid went to some vampire clubs in town to see if there was any loose-lipped Night Spawn hanging around, and Brax is keeping watch on the castle walls. Logan is up there with him. That guy doesn't say much. For a charmer, he's certainly quiet, in a creepy kind of way."

"If you'd been tortured by an unseelie general for months in another world, I'd think you'd have some things on your mind too," Maze grumbled. "He'll be fine . . . eventually . . . maybe . . . if all the factors align. Possibly. Damn it, Tuck, stop distracting me."

"I wasn't talking to you soooooo . . ." Tuck let his words trail off.

"Fair enough." Maze went back to the map and more cards fluttered down from above him. He growled at them and threw them back into the swirling mess.

"That's not good," Tuck muttered to me.

"Yeah, that's been going on for a minute." I turned away from him and began pacing once more. "No word from Atlas or Kylian either. What about the others?"

"I have them spread around the castle just keeping watch. I don't really know who we can trust besides our own people."

I completely agreed. "Good idea. This war is messy. We don't know who to trust or not trust. Both sides are in disarray from what I've been hearing around the castle. Titus has his hands full, and really all I want is to find Piper and save Grayson."

"You and me both. Somehow, I think we all need him." I hated seeing Grayson like this, with no control over himself. He was always so calm and suave in any situation. I might've taken the way he kept us all balanced for granted.

"I've got it!" Ophelia swung from the top corner of her stolen apparatus. She threw her legs out, then let go and propelled herself through the door of her cell and landed in the hallway. She ran over to the table where Serrina and

Maze sat and yanked the map off the table, sending Maze's cards flying and other supplies they had spread out flying in different directions, including the Cheetos. Odin pounced on them as they fell to the ground but so did Maze. "Gluttonous demon feline! We need to work on your ability to share!"

"Hey, O!" Serrina called as Ophelia ran away from them and pressed the map to the wall just outside Grayson's cell. She pulled four daggers the size of toothpicks from her hair and shoved one in each corner of the map to hold it to the wall.

"Are those dagger bobby pins?" Ophelia looked at Serrina over her shoulder. "You know for all that perfect hair to conceal weapons and after all this time with me you've learned nothing from me. *Anything* can be a weapon or conceal one."

"What I'm wondering is how those tiny little things can dig into solid rock?" They were so small I expected them to bend the second she tried to jab them into that thick wall.

Her eyebrows pinched together. "You think I would have flimsy daggers? They're magically reinforced, duhh-hhh. These bad boys can cut through a human in seconds. Puncture wounds kill, Zin. Remember that."

"Of course."

She winked. "You all should be taking notes on this stuff. I can't just keep spitting out solid gold only for it to be lost on you."

I chuckled. "Right. Noted."

"That's the problem. I don't see any of you noting

anything." She gave a heavy sigh. "You'll learn eventually. Until then, here you go."

She pulled another dagger from behind her back and tossed it to me. My magic shot from my hand and wrapped around the knife before it got to me. I let it hover in the air and gently drift down to my palm. "What am I supposed to do with this?"

"Throw it at the map and it'll tell us where Piper is." She stepped back from the map.

"How is that even possible?" I glanced down at the dagger in my hand. It didn't look special in any way. It had a simple leather-wrapped hilt and a long silver blade.

"Oh right. I forgot." She reached into the potion satchel and pulled out a bottle full of glowing neon-pink liquid. Then she hurried up to me and poured it all over the blade. "That should do it. You just have to throw the blade with the intention of finding Piper, then it'll land wherever she is."

"Why don't you do it?" I extended the blade out toward her, trying to hand it over.

She shook her head and backed away. "Oh no, it'll just land on whatever intention goes through my mind in that second, and we do not want to take that chance. Could, you know, stab Serrina . . . or something."

"Hey, what'd I do to you?" She crossed her arms over her chest.

"You really haven't been paying attention." Ophelia made a little sound of frustration in the back of her throat. "I've given you a list."

"Watch yourself, O. You never know, I could make you fall in love with a toaster . . . and a bathtub." She snapped her fingers, and her little red streams of magic bounced on the floor in front of her. "Just like that."

"The best assassins always make it look self-inflicted or like an accident. I approve of your methods and no longer feel the desire to stab you."

Serrina muttered, "Lucky me."

"Sometimes I worry about her," Tuck whispered from my other side, "But she's kept her impulses in check."

"So far," Ophelia whispered loud enough for all of us to hear. "Okay, give it your best shot."

I really needed this to work. Our little group needed a win today—more of a win than just swatting away a few stray vampires making some noise outside the castle. We needed Grayson back, we needed to find Piper, and we needed to break this damn curse. Something in my gut made me believe that we needed Piper to do all of that. I knew the extent of her power and I saw the way Grayson loved her. I had to believe that in this war and things to come, she was more than just powerful, she was necessary.

I lifted my arm and flicked the knife at the map. It flew end over end right at the map and then suddenly veered to the left. My breath caught in my throat as the damn thing curved like a boomerang and sailed through the cell bars right at Grayson. He leapt to his feet just as the knife embedded right in his thigh.

"Shit!" I ran into the cell just as Gray pulled the blade

from his leg. He held the blade to his face, then licked the metal, tasting his own blood.

"Bit of fun, is it?" Gray tossed the blade up and caught it. A crazed light danced in his eyes as he locked his gaze on me.

"O, what happened?" I held my hands out and let my power flow around the room.

"Her location must be protected by some kind of dark, higher magic." She hurried into the cell to stand beside me.

Grayson smirked in my direction and threw the knife right at me. The world slowed and I saw it sailing end over end toward my chest. There was a flash of fire in front of me and then his arms were warm and unyielding as they wrapped around my body. We fell to the side and the distinct sound of a *thunk* of the blade sinking into him filled my ears. His body jerked and I wanted to scream as we hit the floor.

"Holy shit, Tuck." I scrambled to get out from under him and crawled to his side. I pulled him into my lap while forcing my power to surround us in a protective wall.

His face fell into a deep grimace and sweat soaked his body. He tried to suck in a breath but couldn't. Flames lingered over his arms and steam rose from his body. I rolled him onto his stomach. The blade was embedded in his ribs on his right side. Dark blood seeped from the wound, and I didn't dare pull it out. "We need some help over here!"

Ashryn hurried into the cell and loosed two arrows. "Don't you dare move."

Grayson gave her a wild laugh. "I'm surrounded, remember? I can't move."

Dark-red blood magic shot across the floor and wrapped around Ashryn's arms. With the flick of his wrist he forced her to let the arrows fly. Both arrows shot toward him, and he caught one in each hand. He clicked his tongue at her and shook his head. Her arms were bound with his power. He threw one arrow and it plunged right into Ashryn's stomach. She staggered back and hit the wall. Serrina screamed as Ash dropped to the ground and pressed her hands around the wound. Blood seeped between her fingers, and she curled in on herself. Before Serrina could get to her, Grayson threw the other arrow and it hit Serrina so hard that she flew back and the arrow went through her shoulder and pinned her to the wall.

"Over here, fangy fangs." Ophelia jumped to the side, drawing Grayson's attention.

Grayson turned to face her and bared his fangs. He tried to step out of the circle but was thrown back into the center of it. "Why don't you come in here and play?"

"I'd love nothing more." She smirked at him with that deadly smile.

"We can't kill him, O!" I tried to drag Tuck toward the door.

From out of nowhere, a dagger flew across the room and right toward Ophelia.

Maze appeared at her side and caught the knife before it got even close. "Enough of that." His milky-white eyes saw right through Grayson. "NO!"

Grayson dropped to his knees and clutched his head. All at once the chaos stopped and his power abruptly diminished. He rocked back and forth, bellowing so loud it hurt my own ears. "No! Nooo!"

I glanced toward Maze. "What's happening? What are you doing to him?"

"Nothing." Tilly walked by me. The cards all swirled above her now. That neon-green smoke drifted from Maze's hands to Tilly and then above her. Her voice was almost hypnotic. "He did nothing to him. It's something else. Something is gravely wrong."

Grayson toppled over onto his side. "She's gone! Noooo!"

"Will someone tell me what the hell is going on?" Tuck groaned in my arms.

I had to get him to the clinic where they could help him. The door flew open, and Titus marched into the dungeon. He took one look at Tuck and then bent down and wrapped his arms around him, lifting Tuck as though he weighed no more than a feather. It was impressive considering Tuck was over six feet tall and well-muscled.

The King took him toward the lab. I wanted to follow, but I had to know what was happening.

Maze turned toward me, and at the same time, the face of one card flew forward between us.

Tilly swallowed hard and whispered, "We're too late. We're all too late!"

My eyes locked on the card and my stomach dropped. *Death.*

CHAPTER SIXTEEN

DICE

Frustration ate at me every minute of every day. It'd been a while since Ophelia left me here trapped in her castle. Sure, the floating island was beautiful. It was full of tropical plants and animals and hidden waterfalls. The ocean around the island was a bright blue and the warm sea breeze was more relaxing than I'd ever thought possible. Even the dark, gothic castle was an interesting place to live. I was beginning to love my room and the way the wind whipping through the hallways sounded like a ghost in the night. I even loved the quiet when the wind stopped and everything seemed to just relax. There was no one here besides Cross and me, which made for an interesting dynamic. Though he was quiet and only spoke to me when we trained, I found his presence comforting in a way. Over the days, I'd grown to feel completely safe around him.

Yet with all this good, I still couldn't shake the feeling that something was terribly wrong with Piper. This world that she'd fallen into, a world full of witches and magic, was dark and dangerous most times. The things I'd seen Ophelia do with a bit of potion and some words were astounding. I'd seen her walk through portals that took her from one room to another. I'd seen her grow huge plants from nothing. I'd even seen her turn all of Cross's black clothing to bright-pink when he refused to spar with her for the eleventh time in a day. She lived and breathed this world, and as a human, I found it all so fascinating . . . terrifying but fascinating.

At first I was petrified, but now I secretly loved it. I wanted to be in this world with Piper. It was the first time I truly felt at home. Even though technically I was a prisoner. But Ophelia and Cross were tight-lipped about what'd happened to Piper and where she was. So, I waited and I trained. I'd always been fit, but even I could tell how much stronger my body was. The muscles in my arms and legs were well defined, and I could hit with a force that would sometimes take Cross by surprise.

Even now he stood below me as I jumped from one hanging log to another. I was about fifteen feet off the ground, but I found the height soothing, like up here nothing could touch me. I loved being above him where I could see the full training area and even some of the island.

When I jumped to the next log, it swung wildly and I bobbled my next step.

He groaned in frustration. "Pay attention to what you're doing."

"I am," I snapped back as I held on to one of the wires holding the log to keep my balance.

"Clearly not. You're swinging around like a rookie. You're no rookie, Dice. Get it together." He crossed his arms. "Now do it the right way."

"Pushy."

"Better to push you than for you to be dead. Ophelia would be very upset if something happened to you." He walked along as I leapt to another log. "Which might upset me."

Might? Thanks? Up ahead was a rock-climbing wall, or that's what O called it. In reality, what it was, was a sheer rock face with jagged stones sticking out of it. I'd cut my hand on them on more than one occasion. "Always with the death."

"That's pretty much how it goes." He shrugged, then pointed ahead of me. "Watch out for that—"

"I see the vine." There was a thick green vine hanging down in front of my path and I grabbed on to it and yanked it, trying to pull myself forward. It fell free of the tree and coiled around my hand. "Holy shit! Not a vine!"

The damn thing hissed in my direction and began to slither up my wrist. Panic ran through my chest, and I did the first thing I could think of: I threw it toward Cross, who caught it with one hand and held it away from his body.

"Why the hell did you throw it at me?"

"Reflex?" I took a calming breath, then reached for the rope ladder and began to climb down. Before now this would've taken me a long time to get down. Between the swinging and shaking, I'd twist around and have a death grip on the stupid thing. But now I just flowed with it and made it down to the bottom quickly.

Cross pursed his lips and strolled over to where the tropical jungle grew denser. He bent down low and let the snake go into the plush foliage. "Maybe next time you'll listen to me instead of cutting me off."

"Hey, I thought I had it. I'm getting pretty good at that obstacle course." I smiled up at him.

"For a human," he clarified.

I couldn't believe that only days ago I was terrified of Cross. Sure, he was tall and muscular with dark hair down to his chin and honey eyes that seemed to almost glow— not to mention his dark-red magic or the way he looked like he could kill anyone at a moment's notice and enjoy it. The all-black clothing and weapons freaked me out at first, now I found it all so familiar. Even his grouchy surliness was part of my normal day. At any instant we could be attacked, and I knew Cross would have my back. Even though he and Ophelia undoubtedly had bodies buried in a basement somewhere, I was sure whoever was in that basement probably deserved to end up in there.

"Oh, come on. I'm kicking ass at this stuff." I tried to sound convincing.

"Yeah, keep telling yourself that." He strolled away from me and into a clearing that was all sand and surrounded by palm trees and lush bushes. Birds sang happily in the background, and a light breeze sent the leaves rustling and my hair flowing back from my face. He walked over to a table full of weapons, boxing gloves, and targets. He picked up the gloves and tossed them to me.

"It's all good if you can run fast but vampires are faster."

My eyes widened. "I still can't believe vampires are real."

"Keep up, blondie. Everything exists." He pulled on a pair of gloves, but these had pads on the palms.

I couldn't stop myself from asking. "Does Medusa exist?"

He paused. "Yes, and she oddly loves to set up dating profiles for Athena."

I shoved my hand into one glove. "Wait, what?"

"Don't ask," he muttered.

"What about elves? Like Lord of the Rings style." I took my stance holding my hands up and spreading my legs.

"You've already met one." He held his hand up. "Now, jab, jab, duck."

I threw my first few out in rapid succession, hitting the pad on his hand and then ducking when he swung his arm. We circled each other and the sand shuffled under my feet. "I have?"

"You know him as Kylian." He swung his arm out and caught me on the side of my head. The hit wasn't hard, but it knocked me sideways. "My, my, aren't we distracted today."

"Kylian is an ass. And I'm not distracted."

"Good. Distractions get you—"

"Killed. I know." I swung out, connecting with the pad in his hand with two quick jabs, then ducking before he could hit me.

"Add the kick." He clapped his hands together and the pads on his gloves made a smacking sound. "Come on. Focus."

Sweat covered my body, and the humidity of the island was thick as I sucked in deep breaths. I jabbed twice, then shifted my weight and kicked his hand. He wacked me in the side of the head again. "Drop that hand and you drop your guard. Sloppy."

I groaned and did it again, being sure to keep my hand up when I kicked out. Each time I hit the pad it made that satisfying tapping sound. *Tap, tap, kick. Tap, tap, kick.* Each hit was more satisfying than the next.

He moved faster. "Shift your body and keep up."

I moved faster. Heat flooded me. *Tap, tap, kick.* I worked the frustration out of my body and thought about the things that pissed me off, like the distance between me and Piper, my worry for her, my worry about getting off this island, and how I knew my life would never be normal again. I was in a place where I didn't know what happened next. *Tap, Tap, kick.*

The sound of a phone ringing brought Cross up short, and when he didn't block the last kick, my shin connected with the side of his head. He stumbled back and clutched his face. "Fuck."

"Keep up." I winked at him and took a step back to catch my breath.

He glared at me as he pulled the glove off and took the phone from his pocket. He held it to his ear. "Yeah."

I smirked at him as I took a bottle of water from the table and chugged it.

His face paled and his grip tightened on the phone. "Well, that's rather inconvenient, don't you think?"

The hair on the back of my neck tingled. "What?"

He glanced at me and sucked in a deep breath before he looked away. He ducked his head and ran his hand through his hair. "Yeah, I'll take care of it."

"Take care of what?" I whispered. Somehow, I knew this was about me—or even worse: about Piper. Cross rarely showed such annoyance and it was usually only when it came to having to deal with other people's emotions.

He hung up the phone and slid it back into his pocket. "Look, there's no easy way to say this . . ."

I slammed the water bottle down on the table a little too hard and water splashed from the top over my hand. I shook it out, sending drops to the ground. "Just spit it out."

"They think Piper is dead." He shifted from one foot to the other, looking at me like I was a bomb about to go off. "I'm sorry."

If there was one thing I'd learned on this island, it was that O and Cross weren't the touchy feely type. No one was going to console me through this, and frankly, I didn't want to be babied or have my hand held. Panic threatened to settle in my stomach, but I fought it back. I ripped my gloves off and threw them to the ground. Piper was dead? It couldn't be. I would've sensed it, known it somehow. She was a sister to me, and I'd have known if she left this world.

I refused to believe it. Not this time, not when I was so close to seeing her again. "What do you mean they think?"

"Maze—"

I cut him off. "Freaky psychic dude with the white eyes?"

Cross pressed his lips together. "Yeah. Him."

"So your psychic thinks Piper is dead." No, I refused to trust it. "This isn't the first time he's led me to believe she died and don't forget I heard her voice on the phone before I got here. I know damn well she's alive."

Cross looked away. "Look, he's not usually wrong."

"You'll forgive me if I refuse to take his word for anything." I shook my head, and my hair fell around my face. Tears threatened but I refused to cry, not this time. I swallowed past the ball in my throat.

"Dice, I'm so—"

I held my hand up. "Don't you dare say you're sorry. You take me to her."

His eyebrows drew together. "What?"

"If she's dead, then take me to her. I wanna see her freaking body."

"I don't even know if that's possible." He shifted uncomfortably. "Where she'd be at is . . . well, it's war on all fronts."

"Then I guess we're going to war."

He threw his hands up and let them smack back onto his legs. "Humans. For being such a fragile species, you're awfully violent. Do you know that? You have no idea what you're walking into."

"If there's anything I've learned, it's that anything is possible in this world." I met his eye and held it. I wasn't going to take no for an answer. "Get me to her. Now."

CHAPTER SEVENTEEN

PRISHA

I sucked in a deep breath and blew it out in a slow exhale in an effort to calm the adrenaline pumping through my body. My hands shook and beads of sweat gathered in the small of my back. I'd never done anything like this before, but deep down I knew it had to be done. I pressed myself against the wall, trying to hide as best I could. Deep in the tunnels under London, or at least I thought it was London, I scurried like the vermin around my feet. I wasn't even sure if the King knew these secret chambers existed. But I'd followed Marius's little helper, whose name I recently learned was Kendra, here after spotting her reentering the headquarters. She'd just come back covered in dirt but seeming pleased with whatever task she'd just accomplished. She dusted off her hands and ran them over her jeans with a self-satisfied smirk.

I followed her deep underground where light dared not

touch any bit of this darkness. My sight adjusted quickly, and I kept my footsteps light as I moved behind her at a distance. A flash of red mist popped up next to my face with a white note hovering in it. My name was written in strong scrolling letters. I snatched it from the air, and it crumpled in my fist. I froze and looked up just as Kendra tilted her head to the side, listening. I jumped back into the darkness and held my breath. I didn't know how long she stood like that, just listening, but I didn't dare move. When she started walking once more, I let her get ahead of me before I tore into the note.

I knew the King had vampires with the ability to send messages to whomever they thought of. I just never thought I'd see it in person. I read it. Then I read it once more, not believing what I was seeing. *An army? Clive was going to try to hire an army to kill the King?* I was overwhelmed by the thought of what it must feel like to be the King and have the world closing in on all fronts. I quickly shoved it back into my pocket and glanced down the hall. I'd nearly lost Kendra but there was only so much I could do. I had to take this one thing at a time. If I heard anything about Clive or an army, I would be sure to let them know. But I also had a duty to find out what the hell Marius was up to, so I hurried my steps catching up to Kendra and following along.

We walked for a while just going deeper and deeper into the Earth. When I thought we could go no farther, sporadic lights with shoddy wiring appeared on the cave ceiling. They were few and far between, and I found it easy to step around the beams of light and keep to the darkness.

As we got closer, I noticed smaller tunnels shooting off of the main one. Random voices cried out in painful wails, and it sent a chill down my spine. I didn't know what they were doing here, and I wasn't sure I wanted to know. But I was in this now, and if I was going to help other vampires, whatever happened here had to be stopped. The smell of filth and sickness permeated the dank air, and I pressed the back of my hand to my nose to try and block it out. When she turned down one of these tunnels, I followed behind. Cells lined both sides of the walls. The bars were driven into the hard rock with doors that vampires would have to crawl through to get in . . . or be dragged through. The cells reminded me of hovels, and I couldn't imagine anything besides little critters living in them, yet when I passed by, reflective vampire eyes watched my every move.

Some reached out to me, and I wanted to go to them, to get them out of these chambers, but I had to find out what Marius was doing to them here. Saving one or two would only alert Marius and his crew that we were on to them, and judging by the number of units, I knew we would need the element of surprise. The door at the end of the tunnel flew open and I jumped to the side, pressing myself against the wall between two different cells. A vampire reached through the bars and grabbed my ankle. The fingers dug into my skin, pinching so hard I nearly cried out from the pain. I was yanked off my feet and hit the floor so hard there would be bruises on my hip and shoulder later. I pressed my lips tightly and fought not to scream. I kicked my leg out, trying to get away, but the vampire dragged me closer to those thick bars.

I dragged over the dirt and gravel and my jeans tore up my thigh. My skin scraped over the ground and the side of my body slammed into the bars. I sucked in a sharp breath as I tried to make out the face of my attacker. "Mark!?"

We'd just ran into Mark and Jessica the night of Marius's little gathering. They were so excited to hear what he had to say. This *was* Mark, but it also wasn't. His body was sickly thin, I could see his ribs through the rips in his filthy shirt. His jeans were shredded and hung around his legs. They too were covered in scratches and deep cuts. At the back of the cell, two more eyes peered at me and a feral hiss came in my direction.

"Jessica?" She was huddled in the back corner of the cells. Her eyes flashed from blue to black and back again. She rushed to the bars and reached out, wrapping her hand in my shirt and keeping me trapped against the bars. I wrapped my hand around her wrist and tried to pull free, but she was strong—impossibly stronger than I was.

"What the devil is going on back there?" I knew that voice. It sent a shiver down my spine and a cold lump sank in the pit of my chest.

Marius.

Jessica and Mark dropped their hold on me and scurried back from the bars to huddle together at the back of the chamber. I glanced over my shoulder to where Marius stood with Kendra. They were far enough away that I was protected in the shadows, but when they started to stroll toward me, I had to move. Just above the cells at the top of the cave was a small hole. I didn't know if I would fit there, but if I ran they'd catch me. I jumped up and grabbed on to a rock protruding from the wall. The muscles in my arms burned as I pulled myself up and grabbed on to the next one.

When I reached the small hole, I swung my leg up and shoved myself into it. I shuffle back from the edge and lay there holding my breath. Bugs crawled over my skin and scratched at my neck. Something larger nibbled on the ripped strands of my jeans, but I didn't dare look. Marius stopped just outside Jessica and Mark's cell, and I held my breath, afraid he'd hear my chest heaving.

"What have we here?" He bent down and looked through the bars. "Causing a ruckus, are we?"

Kendra dropped to one knee beside him, and they studied them like they were looking at a group of puppies and trying to pick their favorite. "Getting stronger by the day."

"Yes, but not strong enough yet." He rose to his feet and started strolling up and down the tunnel. "They're all not strong enough."

"I agree. The Queens slapped them down fairly easily." Kendra fell into step beside him. Each time they passed a cell, the vampire within fell silent and crawled into the back corner to hide, though the cries and shouts didn't stop. I heard them all begging to be let out or going crazy with madness. There wasn't one healthy vampire among the lot of them.

"So I've been told." He gave her a sideways look. "And what do we have planned to remedy that?"

Kendra made a little *hmm* sound in the back of her throat. "Perhaps another round?"

"I've yet to test the theory of a second round of exposure." He tapped his finger on his chin as though he was thinking about it. "It could be intriguing."

"If we want more powerful vampires, then it would stand to reason more exposure would work."

Marius raised his eyebrows at her. "More could also kill them faster."

"From what our previous tests have shown, only the humans-turned-vampires would die." She pointed to a cell that was eerily quiet. "They don't take to the infusion of power. They just kind of suffer and die."

They talked about the death of vampires so casually, as if it wasn't their fault. Hatred for these two flooded my chest, hatred for what Marius's ambition had done to the vampires and hatred for how easily he'd hurt the innocent. My body vibrated with it, and I wanted nothing more than to see him die the death he deserved.

"It's better to be rid of the waste." He waved his hand as though those poor humans-turned-vampires were nothing more than Sunday's trash. "What of the others? The witches or warlocks-turned-vampire?"

"Their survival rate is higher, though there is no sign of their original powers returning to them after the test." Kendra folded her hands in front of her. "But their physical attributes have improved greatly. Super strength is proving to be one of the things they gain."

Marius made a sound of annoyance in the back of his throat. "All vampires are strong."

"Yes, but these are more so. Some are faster, smarter, they can hear things from farther away. Some even show promise with moving things with their minds."

"Interesting twist." He smirked. "What of the elves-turned-vampire?"

Her smile broadened. "Now *those* are more interesting. They seem to get some elemental powers . . . you know, your fire throwers, earth movers. They have a bit of a problem with water."

"What's the problem?"

She paused. "Well, they keep exploding into puddles . . . but they re-form nicely."

He chuckled. "How comical."

Comical? Was he serious? He was experimenting on us and he found their pain funny?

"I thought so too." She joined in his round of laughter, and it made me sick.

"Well, perhaps if we give them a second dose, they'll stop exploding into puddles." She shrugged. "Or maybe not."

They spoke of all this so casually, like killing vampires was an everyday occurrence. It seemed for them it was. While I was terrified to be here, just hearing these two ensured my belief that I was doing the right thing. Now I knew I was. Taking down Marius was now my number one priority. I couldn't tolerate this for a second longer. These vampires were innocent and in pain all because of Marius.

"Only one way to find out." He shrugged and turned to Kendra. "Perhaps you should leave . . . unless you want to try your second dose."

She gave her head a frantic shake. "I'd rather not."

Without another word, she turned around and took off running like she was on fire, sprinting away so fast I nearly lost sight of her. When Marius turned back to the doorway he'd come through, he waved his hand, beckoning something or someone. "Oh, darling."

Darling? I thought this was some kind of test or experiment. When a black cloud shot from the doorway like a raging tornado, I shuffled farther back into the hole. Light flashed within the cloud like a storm that could not be contained. Whatever critter was trapped in the hole with me squeaked in protest at being squished, but I dared not move. Marius stood in the middle of the cells as the prisoners wailed with terror. The cloud jumped from cell to cell, covering the vampires. It flowed into their eyes and mouths, taking over their bodies completely. It was a violent act of invasion.

Tears streaked down my face and I placed my hand over my mouth to stop from crying out. *How? How could he do this?* Their wails of pain filled my ears. The terror, the sadness, the desperation echoed in their calls. Yet that cloud continued moving from one cell to the next while Marius stood among it all with his arms spread wide and his head thrown back. A smile spread across his face, and he closed his eyes, relishing the moment . . . relishing their screams.

CHAPTER EIGHTEEN

PIPER

*D*arkness was peaceful. Darkness was cool to the touch. With darkness there was no more pain. Was this death? Peaceful? My body was floating in a weightless sleep that I never wanted to wake from. There was nothing but quiet here. The world pressed down on me, yet I didn't feel any panic or the need to move. I forced my eyes open, hoping I would be in a place full of soft white light and warmth. Perhaps I'd find myself in a field full of dogs playing in the sun. But no, it was dark and cold.

Am I in hell?

I closed my eyes once more against the dark grit filling them. I melted into the peace and let it take me. *If I was in hell, I was supposed to burn . . . right?* Or would I be tortured by demons? But who really knew what hell was like? I reveled in the darkness. There was nothing. I was nothing. I didn't know how long I lay in this place, just floating in the cold without a care in the world. I could exist in this space for eternity.

Something stirred above me, yet I couldn't find the will to move or even attempt it. But the sound of something scraping around drew me back from the abyss that threatened to overtake me. I tried to blink my eyes and more dirt fell into them. I wanted to shake my head and brush it away, but my body wouldn't respond. All I could muster was closing them once more. The scratching above became quicker, like a rapid thumping, yet there wasn't an ounce of panic or concern. This was what I'd become . . . nothing. A dim light pierced the darkness, and I closed my eyes tighter, holding on to the darkness.

Soft, fluffy things began hitting me all over my body. It was like being batted at with cotton balls. When they started patting my face, I wrinkled my nose and forced my eyes to peek open once more. Everything was blurry and yet those little cotton balls kept brushing over me. It wasn't unpleasant or torturous, it was kind of nice. Just when I let my eyes slip back shut and fall back into the abyss, a deep voice broke the silence.

"Enough."

His words forced me to try and see around the grime in my eyes. A large man stood over me. He was tall with a thick beard and shocking sage-colored eyes that looked like stars in the darkness. Huge deer antlers protruded from his head and stood like tall branches. I blinked my eyes, trying to get them to focus, but it was still difficult. Tiny creatures I thought might be rabbits hopped all around my body. As he looked down at me, I realized I was lying in a deep hole surrounded by earth.

"Is this hell?" My voice was barely a whisper.

He reached into the hole, and his warm hands wrapped around my arms. He slowly lifted me from the ground and placed me on the back of something warm and fuzzy. When I got a better look at him, I realized he wore no shirt but seemed to have a fur cape on his shoulders, fur gloves that went up his forearms, and fur pants. The muscles of his upper body bulged as he walked next to whatever I'd been laid out on. The thing I was on began to rock back and forth and suddenly the pain I thought had left my body came rushing back. I squeezed my eyes shut and whimpered. That one sound was answered with a rumbling growl from below me.

Pain. So much pain.

It ripped through my chest, across my face, down my neck, and through my legs. I wanted to cry but I had no tears to give. I tried to lift my arm, but my body refused. *Why wouldn't death just take me?* When the thing swayed and moved upward, sharp agony ripped through my chest, and I swore I was being stabbed all over again. Each breath I took was labored like I was drowning. I couldn't stop the air from hissing through my teeth. The giant man placed his warm hand on my shoulder. "Be at ease."

At ease? I couldn't possibly be at ease with anything. The longer I lay here the more I gathered about my surroundings. I was a prisoner in my own body, helpless to defend myself. I hated the feeling of helplessness. Yet here I was broken beyond repair and being carried to some far-off place by a deer-beast. As far as I could tell, I was deep in a forest somewhere. Tall trees loomed over me. Their bare branches were dark shadows over the evening sky. Tiny snowflakes drifted down and touched my skin, sending cool chills over me. The red mist seeping from me mixed with them, turning them into red and white-splashed flakes.

The enormous deer-beast stared at them as he walked. He opened his hand to catch one. "Fascinating."

The forest teemed with movement. So many things skittered around us I didn't know if it was the wind rustling the trees or animals. The longer I gazed up at the bright round moon, the more little critters I saw running across the branches to keep up with our lumbering pace. There were squirrels hopping about with raccoons hurrying to keep up with them. The howl of coyotes came from just beside me. Even birds fluttered along with the others. It was like having Disney princess status, if said princess was half-dead and being held by a beast. If I had been able to move, I would have run as fast as my legs would carry me. But I was helpless and completely at the mercy of the deer-beast and his animal friends.

Perhaps I was about to become their dinner. It wouldn't have been the first time I'd been bitten by an animal. I moaned, trying to plead for him not to eat me, but unable to speak out loud. The deer-beast grumbled, "You are not food."

Had he heard my thoughts? I sucked in a breath and my

body began to relax or shut down, I didn't know which. But the snowflakes and cool air soothed my aching wounds. I existed in the space between life and death, between pain and numbness. I wanted to die. *Just let me die.*

"The wild in you will not allow it."

I didn't realize I'd spoken out loud, but deep down, I meant every word.

Just let me die.

CHAPTER NINETEEN

ATLAS

*H*ours ticked by. The tedium of worry was comparable to getting stabbed by a needle repeatedly in the face with each passing second. A constant twitch had started above my eye, and the tension of not finding my prey, Piper, was getting to me. Poe flew in wide, lazy circles high above as he too searched for any sign of her. It was only hours ago that I could hardly see him against the night sky. Now the early morning rays of light peeked over the hills in the countryside, and he looked like a shadow against the rising sun. Hues of pink, orange, and blue grew brighter, which meant it had been days since we last saw Piper. Days where anything could've happened to her. I knew the horrific things the supernaturals of this world were capable of. Hell, I was one of them. Dark-grey clouds drifted in front of the sun, sending shadows across the land and almost mimicking the mood I'd fallen into.

My breath fogged as I hurried my steps, and a thin layer of snow crunched under my feet. Above, Poe cawed and curved his flight, pivoting into a tight circle to signal he'd found a lead. I broke into a run, pumping my arms to move faster. Something tingled my senses ahead, and I hoped it was her power calling to me. I ran right into some kind of invisible barrier. It suctioned around my body, catching me mid-step. The air shimmered around me, and for a split second I was frozen there. Then the barrier snapped back into place, and I was flung backwards. I flew through the air, twisting in all different directions. I tried to right myself so I wouldn't land on my head. I turned just as I crashed to the ground a few yards back from the barrier. Snow and dirt flew up around me and soaked my clothing. I slid onto my knee and placed my hand on the ground, stopping myself from going any farther.

"What the devil . . ." I rose to my feet and glanced up at Poe.

I thought he was circling before, but no, he was trying to fly forward, and he too was being propelled back into the air by the barrier. I marched forward with my hand extended out in front of me. There was nothing but open field before me. Yet my blood magic sang in my veins, telling me there was something more than the eye could see. When I reached the barrier once more, I pressed my hand forward. It was like being stopped by a thick layer of plastic over a body of water. It moved only so much, then rippled and stopped. It shoved my hand away, and I stood there trying to figure out why I couldn't pass.

"Bloody magic." Piper was behind whatever the hell this was, and I needed a way in. I'd be damned if I let her stay missing any longer. I pulled my cell from my pocket and called a number I never thought I would. It rang once before she answered. "Umm, hello?"

"I beg your pardon, Siphon Queen, but I believe your assistance is required."

"Atlas? How did you get my number?" She sounded out of breath, and her voice was laced with worry.

I sighed and closed my eyes. "I have the ability to acquire all things when time is of the essence."

There was a long pause. "Is this some kind of rich, tech-savvy, vampire-privilege thing?"

"Precisely." I tried for patience to give her a moment to think this through. "But in this situation, I fear I am out of my depth where magic is involved."

She held the phone away from her face as she spoke to someone else. "As long as he's no longer bleeding."

"Zin, I'm okay." Tucker's voice sounded strained in the background. "If they need you, go."

Yes, do go. I cleared my throat, calling her attention back to me. "What can I help you with?"

"I believe I've located Piper."

"That's great."

"But I cannot get to her." I pressed my hand to the barrier. "She's behind some kind of magical wall."

"Yeah, okay. Send me your location." She held the phone away from her mouth again. "Don't you freaking move. None of you. We've got this."

As much as I wanted to know what was going on at the castle, my single-minded focus had one objective: Piper. I quickly typed in my coordinates. "Sent."

"Is this longitude and latitude?" She made a sound of frustration in the back of her throat. "Never mind. Beckett, you got this?"

He mumbled something in the background and a blue portal opened right next to me. Queen Zinnia didn't even say goodbye, she just hung up. I shoved my phone back into my pocket just as Zinnia stepped through the portal. She was dressed in a black sweater and black jeans, and the smell of blood lingered on her, though I couldn't see any stains. Her hair was a tangled mess, and her usual air of confidence seemed worn.

"I sense something's happened."

She held her hand out, stopping me from speaking, and sucked in a deep breath. "First of all, Grayson happened—"

My heart froze in my chest. "What of the Prince?"

"He stabbed a couple of people." She shrugged. "It was a bit of a shock."

Ophelia popped through the portal next to stand beside Zinnia. "I give it a seven out of ten. With a touch more effort, he could've gotten more of us."

"O." Zinnia rolled her eyes. "Tuck is in the lab getting stitched up as we speak."

"Shifters." I scoffed. "They lack in healing abilities."

Ophelia chuckled. "I could've healed him faster, but the last time he got stabbed he didn't trust me to heal him."

"Because you were the one who stabbed him!" Zinnia snapped.

"I was only trying to get him to move faster so he didn't get stabbed in the future. Because, you know," Ophelia motioned to me, "they don't heal as fast as vampires."

"Not helping." Zinnia ground her teeth together, then faced me. "Second of all, stop calling me Queen anything. My name is Zinnia. Let's just go with that, shall we?"

Why were we standing here debating this? Names were of little importance. "If you wish it so."

We didn't have time to decide names. Piper was here and I knew it. She wouldn't have stayed away from Grayson for so long unless she was injured or held against her will or both. Astrid came through the portal next along with Beckett and Tabi. Tabi turned right toward the barrier and began running her hand over it. She stood out in her bright-orange jumpsuit that was like a beckon against the pristine snow. Becket looked up toward the sky and gave a long, low whistle. "Would you look at that? What a piece of magic that is."

The portal closed behind them and Astrid glanced around. "Oh, I see the problem."

Zinnia turned to face the same direction. "Oh, yeah. There it is."

"There what is? Have I missed something?" There was nothing beyond the shimmering barrier. It was an open field covered in snow. At least that was my perception of the situation.

Beckett groaned, "Is that what I think it is?"

Tabi glanced over her shoulder at him. "It definitely is."

"Is what?" I tried not to pull my knife on one of them to force them to speak clearly.

Ophelia went up on her tiptoes beside me and whispered, "*Psst.* I know what you're thinking. But like, if you try it, then I'm gonna have to kill you and make it look like an accident. Actually, that feels like a lot of work. I'll just kill you."

"You're all bloody daft." I took a step back from Ophelia. I didn't feel any fear toward her, but I also believed she would indeed try to kill me. She'd have to wait in line for that honor.

"Um, my guy. Or should I say, my vampire?" Ophelia shook her head. "No, imma go with my guy. You're clearly not as powerful as you think because you can't see the big freaking mountain covered in magic."

"There are no mountains in this area of the country. I'm sure of it." Witches were proving to be the current bane of my existence. Perhaps tomorrow that would lessen, but for this matter I was about throttling a few of them, or all of them, if they didn't get their shit together.

"Oh, you poor sweet vampire." Ophelia winked up at me. "Can I have your fangs when you die from being so obtuse? You know, for a necklace or earrings."

"Am I to greet the Grim Reaper now?" I spun around in a circle. "None of you speaks with sense, and I grow weary of it."

Ophelia jabbed a finger in my face. "Listen here, Mr. McShakespearian pants, I always make perfect sense."

"We need to get to Piper—" I paused as a light tinkering started to play.

Beckett pulled his phone from his pocket. There was a moment of pause, then he pinched the bridge of his nose. "Yeah, we're already here."

"Oi." They all spun toward me. "Will you all pull it together and get me through that bloody wall? Now."

Beckett held a finger up at me. "Yeah, just a second."

He opened his hand and smoky blue magic flowed from him. It formed a swirling whirlpool that glowed and twisted. A dark figure sauntered through and stepped out a few feet in front of me. I growled at him. *Great. Just what I needed. Another imbecile to add to this party.* "Oh, piss off."

"That any way to greet me?" Kylian snickered and ran his hand through his hair.

"Right." I pressed my finger to the sword on my forearm and black smoke seeped from me. My sword slid into my hand, and I pointed it at Kylian while I faced Ophelia. "Now him I can kill?"

She pulled a dagger from her hip and offered it to him. "Yep, go ahead."

"So much hostility." Kylian knelt down and placed his hand on the ground. His power seeped under his fingertips. When he rose to his feet, he held a dagger made of ice. "But if you must."

"You're a daft prick." I didn't know why I hated him, but it seemed to be ingrained in every fiber of my being.

"Enough." Astrid stepped between the two of us, and suddenly I was wrapped in golden magic, frozen in place.

"If you want to kill each other, do it later. We have things to do."

"That's what I've been bloody well saying." I struggled against her hold on me, but for the first time, I was stuck here, powerless.

"Good. Now, Tabi, you see anything interesting over there?" She twisted her hand, forcing us to look at Tabi.

Tabi opened her hand and yellow ribbons of her power bounced around the outside of the barrier. The dirt around the edge erupted and probing vines shot up and crawled over it. The vines seemed to climb on forever. "Yeah, it's old wild magic."

Astrid dropped her hold on us. "For those of us in the class who don't know, what do you mean *old wild magic*?"

"Not as old as The Fallen but way older than us. It could be a creature, or Greek, or anything really. But definitely not a witch."

I rolled my shoulders, trying not to be unnerved by Astrid's power. "Excellent, can you lot blast me through or get me around it?"

"There is no *around* it. I was on the other side when Beckett portaled me here." Kylian motioned to the dome. "It's expansive."

"Are you saying we can't get through?" That was not an answer I was willing to accept.

Tabi rolled her eyes. "Of course we can. We are us. But we'll need something as old as the elements, a bond that will get you through to guide you to her. It's kind of like fighting fire with fire. If the bond is bone-deep, then it's almost as strong as this old ass magic. Is there anyone besides Grayson who Piper is attached to? A mother? Father?"

I shook my head. "As far as I know, she's an orphan."

Tabi pursed her lips. "Okay, what about a best friend?"

"Everyone needs a best friend," Ophelia chimed in.

I had to think back to the sassy blonde who was so close to Piper, the one who'd caught my attention for a time. But she was human and being a human in this world was like a death sentence. "She has a best friend named Dice. But she's human, and I'm not sure how she'd handle this world. Plus, we'd have to locate her, and I'm not even sure she remains in Salem, which is where I last saw her."

Kylian coughed into his fist, then looked directly at Ophelia. We all followed his gaze.

Zinnia arched her eyebrows at Ophelia. "Why is he looking at you like that?"

Ophelia shrugged. "No idea."

Kylian crossed his arms over his chest. "Don't turn me into a rat. I loathe rats."

"Yes, I would think self-loathing is a problem of yours." He flipped me off and I chuckled. "Is that the first appendage you want to lose . . . noted."

"O, what aren't you telling us?" Zinnia put her hands on her hips. "Spill. Now."

Ophelia held her hands up in surrender, "Okay, fine. I might have her trapped on the island in my castle."

"WHAT?" we all yelled at the same time.

Ophelia pointed to Kylian. "He gave her to me."

"I take it back. The finger will be the last appendage you own." I was going to kill him. How dare he bring a human into this and give her over to a psychopath.

"Everyone just calm down." Ophelia held her hands out as if she were a teacher telling her class to settle down. "It's not like I stabby-stabbed her or anything . . . Well, I might've once. But I swear I fixed it."

"I am surrounded by chaos, and I find the burden thoroughly unenjoyable at this juncture in time."

CHAPTER TWENTY

PIPER

a blinding light burned my eyes and I squeezed them shut, holding them tighter, not wanting to wake. I blinked against the offending rays and tried to move my head to get them out of my vision. But there was no reprieve. I couldn't move so I was stuck there, keeping me in a bright hell. The sound of rustling leaves and branches surrounded me. Fresh flowers must've bloomed somewhere close by because their smell permeated the air. I wanted to get up and run back to the castle, back to Grayson, but my body wouldn't comply. I'd been beaten and fed on for far too long. I was a shredded mess— bruised, bloody, and broken. I'd found peace in the ground. It was a deathless sleep that I'd embraced. I didn't want to give up on living, but everyone had their breaking point, and I thought I'd reached mine. But lying here trying to blink out the sun, I supposed I was still fighting to live.

"Oh, there we are," a deep familiar voice rumbled from nearby. There was a rustling of branches, and the light suddenly dimmed. I was able to blink away the bright dots in my vision and let the world slowly come into view.

When my sight cleared, I found myself lying on some kind of bed. It wasn't a standard mattress or anything as luxurious. Instead, it was piled high with thick hay and then covered with huge green leaves that were cool against my body. It wasn't the softest, but it was far cozier than where I'd been held captive and buried. A small fire flickered a few feet away and the warm scent of burning wood drifted to me. There was something heartening about the crackle of the fire and the warmth filling the space around me. When I peeked at the ceiling, I realized I was in some kind of thatched hut. Branches were woven together to let in bits of light through the leaves but keep the other elements out. Though I was almost certain there was snow before, now it looked like springtime outside, or perhaps I was hallucinating. I didn't care so long as I was away from Marius and his torture.

Tiny critters quietly scampered around me. Their little movements were almost reassuring compared to the silence of the cave-like dungeon I was held in. This place was full of life and warmth. Several warm little animals were draped over my legs and beside my body. I didn't know what kind of animals they were, and I didn't care. It was soothing having their soft, furry bodies next to me.

"Where am I?"

"Close to death." He crouched down next to the fire, and from where I lay, he still looked like he would be taller than me even while crouched. The antlers nearly brushed the roof of the hut as he moved, but somehow he managed not to get them snagged on any of the little branches or leaves.

"Are you going to kill me?" My throat was dry like sandpaper as I spoke.

"If I wanted you dead, I'd have left you for it in that hole of yours." He tilted his head to the side, studying me.

"Fair," I croaked out, and my throat was more like fire now.

"Water," he ordered, and a tiny raccoon hopped off my bed and ran across the hut. He grabbed a leather pouch with his little hands, hurried toward me like he'd stolen it, then hopped up on the bed next to me.

I tried to turn my face away from the raccoon, but the best I got was a small twitch. My stomach couldn't take another round of vomiting. "No."

"You will," the deer beast man demanded.

When I pressed my lips together, he sighed and held his hand out toward me. Swirling sage magic drifted between the two of us and hovered over me. It grew brighter and then fell over my entire body. I froze, locking my muscles in place, expecting pain to follow, but there was none. Instead, a warmth spread through my stomach and up my throat. It was the first sign of relief I'd had in days. I held still, hoping the feeling wouldn't end, yet when I moved my hand the discomfort doubled in the rest of my body. A groan escaped my lips, and I tried to hold it in.

"Drink." It wasn't a request, it was an order.

I didn't have the energy to fight him. When it came back up, he'd have his own regrets to clean. I tried to open my mouth to drink, but my jaw was too swollen to open wide enough. The deer-beast waved his hand, and the raccoon placed the tip of the leather pouch between my lips, pouring drops of water in my mouth. It seeped through my teeth, and I took one greedy swallow. The dry rubbing in my throat immediately eased.

The raccoon moved away from me, taking the cool water with him. I wanted more, I wanted to chug it all down, but even I knew if I did that it would only hurt me more in the end. My stomach would only accept Grayson's blood. When I licked my lips, they too were dry and cracked. I coughed through my teeth.

"Why are you helping me?"

He paused, then stared at me with glowing vivid eyes. "I sense the wild in you."

I didn't know what that meant or why he dug me up from a grave I was content to stay in, but I would take it. I didn't know how long I'd been here or how long I would remain, but my will to live had returned tenfold and now I wanted nothing more than to get back to my life and help Grayson. Once he was better, I would take my revenge on Marius, and it would be a sweet thing. Something unlocked in the pit of my stomach and warmth spread through the palm of my hand. A fine red mist drifted up from where my hands lay on my stomach, and I exhaled with relief.

"Yes, that's been happening." He picked a wooden bowl off the floor and threw some flowery contents that looked like potpourri into it, then began to mush it together with a stick.

"Good."

"Not good enough." He crouched and started moving toward me like a wild animal. His rough, chiseled face filled my vision, and I found something familiar in his looks, though I couldn't put my finger on it. "You will die. Your injuries are too grave."

"No." I hadn't come this far to die now. I'd accepted my fate in that hole, but he dug me up and I'd be damned if I accepted it now. Death would have to wait.

"Then we must unleash your wild." He placed his hand over one of mine and that soothing warmth spread through me once more. Our magic mixed together and drifted toward the roof in a twist of burgundy and sage sparkles.

"What is . . ." I sucked in a pained, sharp breath, ". . . my wild?"

"It is the part of you that exceeds your vampire side. The part of you suppressed when you were born to a human. The part of you that is me."

I didn't quite understand his words, but I was desperate to live. I didn't want to mourn the life I could have had. I wanted to embrace it. "Do it."

He didn't look away from me, he just continued to hold my gaze. "It will be painful."

What's new? "Will I live?"

"Most do not live through the awakening process."

"But if we don't . . . release my wild, I will die?" I asked, appreciating his honesty.

He looked over me and I knew he was seeing all my injuries. "Soon."

I didn't have to look in the mirror to know how gruesome they were. I had broken bones in my chest and face, it was difficult to breathe, and I knew the stab wound was grave enough to kill me. It was shocking it already hadn't. There was little blood left in my body and my breath was reedy. Even now I could taste the copper flavor of my own blood in my throat. He was right: death and I were about to be very well acquainted.

I swallowed and squeezed my eyes shut, trying to find the courage for what was to come. "Do it. I want to live."

"I truly hope you survive this." He took his hand away and the loss of his soothing touch sent shivers over my body. He reached into the bowl and grabbed whatever he'd been mixing. It was now a thick paste, and he spread it over the stab wound in my chest, shoving the paste into my torn skin. It burned like acid, but I locked my jaw shut even as tears leaked from my eyes. He let his hand trail up to the ripped skin at my neck and rubbed the thick paste over the countless bite marks.

More burning and fire filled my body, traveled up to my head, and settled there. The animals in the hut scurried off my bed but gathered in a circle around it. I could feel them all around me. The deer-beast raised his hands over his head and began chanting words I didn't understand. Bright, sage-colored magic gathered between his palms as a glowing ball of power that I could almost feel pulsing within me. With a bellow, he shoved the ball of magic down toward me and it slammed into my chest.

I thought I knew pain . . . I did not. It burned through me, turning my every cell into dust. Parts of me were forming and re-forming only to burn to nothing all over again. All I wanted was to explode with energy and melt to nothing at the same time. The light grew so bright that I wanted to close my eyes and pretend I was somewhere else, but the pain was so acute I couldn't lose myself in my mind. I could only lie there taking the onslaught of it all. When I thought there would be no more, he lifted his hands again and formed another ball of power. This one burned hotter and smelled of rain. Bolts of electricity shot from it, igniting little fires all over the hut. I wanted to tell him no, not to do this, but there was no going back now. He shoved his arms down and the ball of power entered my body with so much force I thought I was going to explode from the inside out. Power and energy filled me to the brim. One by one my bones broke and shattered, only to be pulled back together and shattered again. I tried to suck in a breath my lungs burned for, but my chest was too tight.

This was all too much—the burning, the breaking.

Shuttering spasms racked my body and I shook my head. "No more."

"More!" he bellowed, and more of his power entered me. I glowed so bright I didn't know where my skin started and his power stopped. He twisted his hand and something pulled deep inside me. Past my well of vampire power, past the human Piper I used to be. It was hidden away like a small drop of hope in this dark hut. His magic wrapped around it and pulled, stretching my insides. I thought he'd ripped me open from my throat down to my hips. My insides must've been ripped from my body. Visions of magical animals made of my red blood magic and his sparkling sage danced above my head. How could they be so happy frolicking around while every cell in my body burned and ripped apart?

The hut vibrated with power, and I didn't know how the branches stayed in place or why the animals remained by my bedside. But when he placed his hands over my chest and stomach, his touch was like a brand against my skin. When he lifted them up, my body levitated off the bed and I floated there with my arms and legs dangling limply. He lifted his hands off me, and when he did, he pulled my magic with his touch. Inch by inch he forced it to move like pulling a million needles with thread at the same time. My insides expanded and twisted in ways I didn't think possible. And not for the first time in the last few days, I prayed for death.

"Scream if you must," his voice boomed over the pounding in my ears, "for I will not stop."

The last bit of control I held faltered with his words. I became the pain and the burning. I was no longer me, I was only this moment of being ripped apart from the inside out. My head fell back and I let the screams I'd been holding tear up my throat. I wanted to give in and let death take me. It so clearly wanted me. But I would endure, I would survive, I would unleash my wild.

CHAPTER TWENTY-ONE

DICE

"*A*re you sure you're ready for this?" Cross looked down at me as he slid a dagger into the holster at his hip.

"This is what I've been waiting for." I didn't want to tell him I was nervous as hell to confront the people who'd been keeping my bestie from me. But this was a *fake it till I make it* moment. "Besides, I think I'm ready."

I did everything Ophelia told me too when preparing for a fight: my hair was pulled back from my face and tied back, I wore a thick leather vest with a tank under it so it wouldn't chafe, along with matching leather pants, my belt held a dagger on each of my hips, and I wrapped a holster around my thigh as well. I slid my arms into a loose-fitting jacket to hide the knives I had strapped to my forearms. I put my hand in my pocket, checking to make sure my dice were there. When I wrapped my fingers around them, their reassuring warmth spread over my skin and I knew I could do this. To finish out the whole outfit, I shoved my feet into a pair of Ophelia's steel-toed boots. It was a good thing we were nearly the same size, otherwise I might've been short on clothing. How anyone could possibly need this many weapons was beyond me. But I wasn't going to argue the *always be prepared* logic that Ophelia spit at me for days on end.

"You might have as many weapons as O does." Cross snickered.

I shrugged. "As the only human in this situation, I feel like it's my job to protect myself however I can."

"Good point." He pulled his cell from his pocket and hit one number. He held it to his ear and said one word, "Ready."

A second later, a bright blue portal opened in front of us and Cross moved toward it. I'd never walked through a portal intentionally before. I knew Kylian had dragged me through one, but this was the first time I knew what it was and what I was doing. Was it crazy? Yes. Was I still going to do it? Hell yes. I would walk through fire and back for Piper.

Cross stepped into it. I sucked in a deep breath, then followed behind him. The portal swirled all around me like walking through a tornado. Yet it wasn't turbulent or windy. It was more like gliding through a warm pool of water. I wanted to linger here to watch the magic move around me. I'd never seen anything so beautiful in my life. Cross and Ophelia did small magical things around me, like potions or decorating trees or playing with weapons, but it was nothing like the all-encompassing power of something like this.

Cross stepped out first, and I paused glancing around for a moment, just trying to remember what portaling was like. I stepped out of it and into a dank cell. It was cooler here, much colder than being at Ophelia's castle. I was grateful that Cross threw the coat at me and told me to put it on. I glanced around at the faces staring back at me. I found Ophelia giving me a huge shark-like smile from a cell to my right. While the door was open, she swung from a huge wooden apparatus shaped like an X. She gave me a little wave and I returned it.

Farther back from her cell was another cell covered in all kinds of vines and wildflowers. Their smell almost masked the damp scent of earth in the dungeon. If it wasn't for those flowers, this place would be miserable. The walls were this dugout rock and the cell bars had been driven deep into the ceiling and floor. No one said a word, they all just stared as I took in my surroundings.

When I glanced to my left, I had to do a double take. Grayson was trapped within some kind of white circle of magic that was inside a jail cell. He was somehow bigger than I remembered, with bulging muscles. Gone was the suave cocky bastard who'd tempted my friend to this life, and in his place was this half-naked monster. His shirt was gone, leaving his chest completely bare, where I could see the dark black veins spread over his forearms and down his neck. His pants were torn to shreds, and when I met his eye, I didn't see any flicker of recognition. He had no idea who I was.

His eyes were pitch-black with red veins forking through them. He hissed in my direction, and I raised my eyebrows at him. I could see why Piper wouldn't want me to see her strung out boyfriend. Even so, I hated to admit it, there was still something striking about him. He was the kind of red flag she'd see and want to play with. "Well, fuck. That's kind of hot. I'm thinking Piper would love that."

Cross chuckled at the others. "I told you she'd be fine."

"I'm always fine." It was my thing: no matter what rolled my way, I would always be fine . . . eventually. I turned back to Grayson. "So, what's wrong with him?"

"He's cursed," a woman with wild dark hair and bright blue eyes answered quickly. I instantly recognized her from the pictures Ophelia made me study. It was like a bible of who's who and what they can do. According to Ophelia, I needed to know their strengths so I could learn how to avoid them while at the same time exploit their weaknesses.

I gave Ophelia a side-eye. "Your doing?"

She chuckled. "I wish. It's a nasty piece of work. Generational curse. Come to think of it, it'd be cool to curse a whole bloodline. Note to self: give cursing a try."

"Don't even think about it," the one with the wild hair snapped. She pressed her hand to her chest. "I'm—"

"Zinnia," I finished for her. "I know who you are. I know who you all are. Ophelia quizzed me so I wouldn't be behind. You're Zinnia, the High Queen of the Witch Court. Also, the most powerful siphon to walk the Earth. Your soulmate is Tuck, a Phoenix shifter, though I don't see him here."

Zinnia groaned. "He got stabbed."

I glanced back at O. "By you?"

She tapped her lip. "Fair question, but no. By him." She pointed toward Grayson who snarled at me.

"Come now, pretty bird. Come closer to my cage so I can just . . . snap your neck." He chuckled, then turned to the side as if looking at someone who wasn't there. "I will get you what you want. *Shhhh*, stop yelling."

He grabbed his ears and hunched over screaming, then dropped to his knees. "Dead, dead, dead!"

"He does that." A guy with dark hair and neon eyes stepped forward. "And I'm—"

"Maze. Yeah, I remember. It wasn't the best entrance or meeting." I just remember him showing up and telling me I was trapped on that island because there was blood on the streets in London. And now I was in the middle of it all.

"And you're Astrid." I pointed to the redhead and continued to the others. "Beckett, Tabi . . . your pictures do not do you justice. You're hot. Brax, can you really turn into a tiger?"

Black strips spread over his skin. "Da."

"Cool." I moved to a woman with ebony skin and long braids flowing back from her face. "Adrienne, daughter of Athena, I still find it hard to believe in Greeks. It seems far-fetched to me."

"I wish it was sometimes," a guy with blond messy hair and a five o'clock shadow muttered.

I lowered my voice. "Logan, I'm so sorry about—"

He held his hand up, cutting me off. "Don't mention it."

I turned to greet Tilly. "We've already met."

"Good to see you again." She winked.

"Seems our circumstances haven't changed much." Here I was about to go looking for my bestie who they all thought might be dead. It was familiar territory that I didn't relish visiting again.

I locked eyes with Kylian and glared at him. "Ass face."

There was a collective chuckle, and I wanted to get to know them all even more. Though I could see a few faces were missing, like Serrina and Ashryn, I knew we needed to get moving. I wasn't here for a meet and greet, I was here to find Piper. I'd gone long enough without her, and I wouldn't stop until I found her. "Alright, what is going on? Where's Piper?"

Zinnia gave a heavy sigh. "That's the thing. We need your help to find her, if she's still alive."

"She's still alive." I let the determination in my voice shine. If she was dead, then I'd know. "You want my help? You tell me everything."

Zinnia crossed her arms over her chest. "I hardly think you're in a position to demand things."

"It's fair to assume the human is powerless in this situation. I can assure you I'm not." I pointed toward Ophelia, "You wanna try me? She trained me."

"You did what?" Zinnia's voice rose and she narrowed her eyes at Ophelia.

Ophelia sauntered to the cell door and leaned against the frame while crossing her arms. "I told you. I only stabbed her once."

I pulled the sleeve of the coat back, showing them the scar that ran along my forearm where I had the knife strapped. "More than once."

"Oh, I don't count how many people I stab or how many times." She held her own arm. "We'd be here all day long. Besides, you got me a few times too."

Beckett nudged Cross with his elbow and gave him a look that said *how could you keep this away from me you bastard.* "This is where you've been the whole time?"

Cross shrugged. "At first I couldn't let O kill her, but then I had to make sure they didn't kill each other." A shot of pride went through me. It wasn't every day the killer complimented the trainee.

"Why are you looking at him like he kept some kind of big secret?" I pointed to Kylian, "He dropped me there. And he," I pointed at Maze, "facilitated it."

Maze held his hands up in surrender. "Hey, I don't need to explain why I do what I do."

Tarot cards shot from the side pocket of his cargo pants and swirled above him. Neon smoke seeped from his hand and mixed with the cards. My eyes widened, and I couldn't stop staring at the show of power. He didn't move, didn't need a potion or spell the way that O did. It just happened so easily.

Tilly jumped up and grabbed a card. Her blonde curls bounced with the movement, and she smiled at me. "I understand something about besties, so I will totally explain."

All at once the cards flew back into his pocket, and he wrapped his hand around Tilly's mouth and pulled her back against his chest. "We're not at liberty to say."

I tried to play it cool, like I wasn't standing in a freaking castle dungeon surrounded by magical beings with super-powers and flying tarot cards. "Well, there's a reason why I'm here. So, spill."

Astrid stepped forward. "I've got this."

Zinnia motioned for her to continue. "Please do."

"Look, I know it's a lot but here goes: Grayson turned your bestie into a vampire. Apparently she was going to die, and he tried to save her."

That drew me up short. "She what?"

"She got hit by a car and was going to die and he couldn't bear for her to die, so he changed her and now she's an immortal vampire."

Holy shit. "Like blood-sucking, coffin-sleeping, fang-having vampire?"

"Well, all of that is accurate," a smooth voice came from behind the group, and they parted for him. My breath caught in my throat. He was as beautiful as I remembered with his dark hair and crazy-colored eyes. Flashes of his tattoos peeked out from the V-neck of his shirt. "Except the coffin part. We tend to sleep in beds. Huge, comfort-able beds."

My eyes locked on him, and I couldn't hide my smile. "Atlas."

"Hello, trouble." When his lips pulled up in a sexy smirk, I didn't want to look away.

"Well, you'll just have to make me a vampire too." The words were out of my mouth before I could stop them.

"I beg your pardon." His brow creased and he shook his head in disbelief.

"Hey, if she's a bird, then I'm a bird." I shrugged. "It's bestie code."

Tilly and Astrid nodded at the same time. "It's true."

They chuckled and Astrid cleared her throat. "We'll deal with that later."

"Sounds good." I glanced at her while keeping Atlas in my peripheral vision. "Please go on."

"Well," Astrid continued, "turns out Grayson fell for her—"

"Naturally. She's amazing."

Astrid frowned. "Which triggered the curse in him and his current state of madness. We all tried to get together to help. But the vampires are in turmoil, and while we were trying to help him, the castle was attacked. While we were fighting and distracted, Piper went missing and we're not sure who or what has her. But we have an idea of where she is, and we need your help to get to her. We want her back, and if we're ever going to make Grayson better, we also need her for that. We just want our family back together."

"How can I help?" I found it hard to believe that with all

this magic packed into one room they needed the human's help. But if they already considered her part of their family, then I would make damn sure to do anything I could, because she was my only family too.

"She's trapped behind some kind of magical barrier, and we need someone she holds dear and is deeply bonded with to help guide us through to her." Atlas said, stepping in closer to me and sending a thrill of excitement through my body. "And I believe that is you."

I gazed up at him and instantly knew he wouldn't let anything happen to me. He wanted Piper back just as much as I did, and that was all that I needed. "Okay."

"Let's go get our girl, shall we?" He offered me his hand, and I took it.

CHAPTER TWENTY-TWO

DICE

$\mathcal{I}$ didn't think I would ever get used to how cool it was to be able to portal. It was amazing. I wanted to be somewhere and *boom* I was just there. If only I had this in my everyday life, I'd be in London to walk around, New York to shop, and Italy for breakfast, lunch, and dinner. The world would be my oyster. As it was now, I was going to follow a group of magical people through a portal to break some kind of barrier-spell to find my bestie. It made me feel good to be doing *something*. I'd been trapped and feeling helpless for so long, and now I would find her. I just knew it in my gut.

When we stepped out on the other side of the portal, I was in an open field covered in snow. Patches of grass peeled out from the snow, breaking up the pure white that covered the distance. Grey clouds filled the sky above, and flurries drifted around me. Fog blew from my mouth with each breath I took. A shiver rolled over my body, and I curled my hands into the sleeves of my leather jacket. Had I known I'd be going from Ophelia's summer castle straight into winter, I would've taken one of her many sweaters.

Atlas moved next to me, then quickly pulled his sweater over his head and offered it to me without a word. I shook my head. He only stood there in a T-shirt with more of his tattoos showing than before. "Won't you be cold?"

"I find watching you be cold makes the temperature seem harsher." He waved it at me.

"Yeah, blondie, we wouldn't want to make the vamp any moodier than he already is." Kylian moved to stand on the other side of me. He crossed his arm and glared at Atlas.

"And what's your mood?" I pulled my jacket off and handed it to Atlas while I pulled his sweater over my head. "Constant asshole?"

"Aww, and here I thought our time together was more special than that." He pressed his hand to his chest. "Just because I'm not a little bitch about things doesn't make me an asshole."

I took my jacket back from Atlas and slipped my arms back in the sleeves. The sweater went down to my knees and bunched under my jacket but at least I was warm. "No, throwing me through a portal and leaving me there does."

"You survived."

"You suck."

"Don't you have some place to be, Dark Prince?" Atlas hissed over my head toward him. "There's nothing here for you to profit from."

"Maybe you're not well equipped enough to handle this, and that's where I come in. You need me." Kylian crossed his arms over his chest.

I had to admit it was kind of hot standing here watching these two argue. Atlas scoffed. "Historically speaking, you're bloody useless."

"You're a Prince?" I asked, finding it interesting that someone like Kylian was royalty. "Prince of what?"

"Prince of pure fucking about." Atlas motioned toward where the rest of the group began to gather. "Shall we? I know you're eager to find Piper."

I fell into step with Atlas, but Kylian remained on my other side. "I don't fuck about."

"Could've fooled me." He tricked me into trusting him and following him all based on the fact he was going to get me to Piper. Then he threw me through a portal right into the arms of Ophelia and Cross. I was good with them now, but those two were terrifying killers and he knew it. "Let's not forget you just left me there with O and Cross. So yeah, fucking about seems to be the right description."

He pressed his lips into a thin line but said nothing as we got closer to the group. Ophelia strolled over to me and stuck her hand in the sleeves of my jacket and pulled the extra fabric out, then took her knife and chopped it off. She ducked under my arm and slashed a slit down each side of the sweater to make it easier for me to move and then put her knife away and glanced at Atlas. "Hope you weren't attached to that."

He shrugged. "I have few worldly attachments."

"Cold bastard," Kylian muttered.

"Piss off," Atlas snapped back.

"If you two are finished," Zinnia cleared her throat, "we're going to try and get through now."

"Who is holding Piper? Like, what are we up against? And where is this barrier thing?" As far as I could see, there was nothing around us for miles.

"We thought it was Marius, an enemy of Grayson's. His army attacked the castle, and we thought he took her in the chaos." Zinnia swallowed. "But now we're not sure who has her. We have theories but nothing concrete."

"Right. Great." I swallowed the nervous ball in my throat. "So, we'll be walking in blind?"

Tabi waved her hand and huge vines shot from the ground behind her and slithered over some kind of round, invisible dome. "This kind of power is beyond anything that Marius can do. It's old magic. Very old. So we think there's what human mythology would call a Greek God in there, and it's holding on to Piper."

"Before I go down the rabbit hole of Greek Gods, I'm just going to ask, what makes you so sure she's there?" I couldn't take my eyes off the vines and how they just kept climbing.

"When I hunt, I'm never wrong," Atlas said simply, with no evident ego. It was just truth. "And my hunt brought me here. I know she's there. I can almost feel it."

"Right. Okay then."

"This guy, am I right?" Kylian hiked his thumb in Atlas's direction, then mimicked his stance and British accent.

"When I hunt, I'm never wrong. Slow your ego there, buddy."

"We are not friends." Atlas' voice was emotionless. "If you were on fire, I would bathe in a bucket of water before I gave you a drop of it."

Kylian arched his eyebrows. "I'm not afraid of a little fire."

"Take it off. Take it off. Take it off," Ophelia chanted. We all turned to look at her. "What? I thought we were about to have some mud wrestling. It would've been better with their shirts off."

"Anyways." Zinnia drew our attention back to the task at hand. "Tabi, Ophelia, Becket, Astrid, and I are going to do the spell that will turn you into a kind of radar for Piper. You're the one who's connected to her the most, and she connected with you. Then we'll use our magic to make an opening in the dome for you to go through."

"By myself?"

"No," Kylian and Atlas snapped at the same time.

My head whipped back and forth as I looked from one to the other and back again. "Okayyyy."

"Umm, yeah, we were going to send Atlas in there with you. The rest of us have to stay out here to make sure that when you come back, we will be able to open the dome so you can get out." Zinnia's brow furrowed when she looked at Kylian. "I didn't realize you were going."

"I'm going."

Zinnia shrugged. "It couldn't hurt."

"Yes, it could." Atlas seethed with power, and red mist drifted up from his arms.

Kylian narrowed his eyes at him. "No one asked you, leech."

A burst of laughter bubbled up my throat and they all stared at me. I pressed my hand over my mouth. "Leech, because he's a vampire . . . who drinks blood."

When no one reacted, I pressed my lips together. "Sorry. I'm new here."

"It couldn't hurt to have more muscle." Zinnia looked at the two of them. "If you two could get it together."

"Yeah, it's not about you," Astrid snapped, "so get it together for Piper and Dice. She's a human and is going to need protection."

"Fine." Atlas ground his teeth together.

"Great." Kylian rolled his eyes.

"Grow up." Beckett shook his head and joined the Queens as they began to form a circle.

Ophelia waved me over to her. "Give me your dice."

"What?" My hand automatically went to cover them in my pocket.

"I'm not going to steal them." She held her hand out to me with her palm open.

I didn't like letting other people touch my dice. They were the only thing I owned since childhood. It wasn't easy for me to let anyone near them. I'd even gotten in fights over them in the group home. I curled my fingers around them and let their warmth seep into my fingers, then I took them from my pocket and handed them over.

Ophelia was surprisingly gentle with them as she cupped them in her palm. Grey smoke drifted from her skin to wrap around my dice, and I almost snatched them back out of her hand. She raised them to her face and whispered over them.

"A bond so strong must never be broken.

Heart's desire shown in light awoken.

Bound in blood a connection of souls.

Follow the line and reverse the rolls.

Magic for Magic through space and time.

Pull the body through desire of the mind."

The stone glowed a bright blue, then went out just as quickly. She handed them back to me. "What'd you do?"

"You have to find Piper as quickly as possible and bring her back. These will help. Well, if she's not dead already." She shrugged and joined the others in the circle.

My stomach sank at the thought of losing her. It must've been plain on my face because Atlas walked up to me and stood close without touching me. "We will find her."

"Right. Yeah." I wrapped my hand around the dice and put them back in my pocket.

The Queens all took a few steps back, turning the circle into a half-moon. They all faced the barrier. Zinnia was the first to let her power flow. Sparkling silver magic shot from her hands and wound across the snow before hitting the barrier like a sledgehammer. The hair on the back of my neck stood on edge like a storm was coming. Even as a human I could feel the power rolling off of her. She focused her magic on a single spot on the barrier and suddenly I could see it. It was like a piece of old glass, completely see through but wavy in places.

Atlas bent down low to whisper. "She's going to try to siphon off the power in that one spot to weaken the barrier and create a hole."

The silvery magic in her hair turned a dark green and tiny leaves started to fall all around her as if she were standing under a tree but there was none. Next, Astrid opened her power and golden magic shot at it, joining Zinnia's beam of power. A gold circle began to form in the glass, and smoke drifted up in a thick plume.

"She's trying to burn through the weak point," Atlas continued to explain. If he didn't tell me what was happening, I'd have no idea what each of them was thinking.

Ophelia was next, and her power wasn't as subtle as the others. Balls of grey smoke shot from her one after the other as if she were shooting a cannon at the one spot. Each one collided with the barrier with an earth-shattering *thump*. When Beckett joined in, also firing blue balls of magic, the ground began to shake under my feet.

Atlas chuckled. "Brute force magic. Not gentle but very effective."

The barrier cracked where their magic was focused, and the fissures forked out from that one spot. Tabi stepped up next. "Get ready."

Atlas wrapped his hand around mine and his body tensed. Tabi let her yellow ribbons flow from her body across the space between her and the barrier. A huge leaf spread over the one spot and the sides unfurled with sharp vines that looked more like spider legs. They dug into the barrier and fell forward onto the other side.

"NOW!" Tabi screamed, and I was flung forward. I pumped my legs trying to keep up with Atlas's pace but I couldn't.

My feet were swept out from under me, and I flew up into the air. Two strong arms caught me and wrapped around my body, holding me close. We moved with a blinding speed and dove through the hole. I was twisted and tumbled across the ground, then suddenly I was upright and still in his arms.

"Thank—" The words died in my throat when I glanced up. I expected it to be Atlas who carried me through but I was tucked in tight against Kylian's chest. This close I was surrounded by his deep woodsy scent and warm embrace.

He placed me on my feet. "You're welcome."

Atlas was standing there waiting. "Shall we add reckless to your resume?"

"I'm not the one who was dragging the human behind me at vampire speed. Or would you prefer to dislocate her shoulder in the process?"

"Apologies." Atlas gave me a light bow of his head. "I forgot the delicate nature of humans."

I gave him a little pat on his chest. "You'll make it up to me later."

"Hey, I'm the one who got you through the damn hole before it closed." Kylian pointed back to the point where we'd entered. It was indeed closed back up and the Queens along with Beckett were only shadowy figures on the other side.

"Yeah, somehow I still feel like I owe you nothing." I turned away from him to start walking and stopped short.

None of this was visible from the other side of the barrier. I sucked in a shocked breath. There was no field and no snow. Instead, a huge mountain rose up in front of us. It was no wonder Tabi's vines just kept climbing upwards. A canopy of trees covered the mountain and the ground was covered with leaves, rocks, branches, and moss. Birds sang happy tunes in all different directions and streams of light peeked through the very green leaves. It was as though we stepped out of winter and right into a springtime forest. It was still cool but there was life all around us.

Kylian groaned. "Oh no."

"What?"

"Anything powerful enough to create all this and keep it hidden isn't going to be happy about our arrival."

"For once we are in agreement." Atlas pressed his finger to his forearm and the tattoo on his arm sprang to life. It leapt off his skin and slid into his hand.

Kylian bent down low next to him and pressed his hand to the ground. His dark-crimson smoke seeped into the ground. A wicked-looking knife with a curved blade made of stone appeared in his hand. The hilt wound around his wrist and hand. He rose to his feet and stepped beside me. "Lead the way."

"I hope this works." I pulled the dice from my pocket

and shook them until their familiar burning warmed my skin. I bent down low and threw them across the ground. They all tumbled out into a straight line. One by one they burst into tiny blue flames as though I was an airplane trying to follow a runway of blue lights. I pointed in the direction they went. "That way."

That way was straight up the mountain. I picked up my dice, and the moment they hit my palm, the little fires went out.

Atlas glanced down at them. "They don't burn you?"

"Not at all." It was a question I'd gotten all my life. People were always curious as to why I only felt slight warmth when I held the dice but they burned others. I didn't have an answer for them or myself.

He motioned for me to go ahead. "By all means."

Kylian stepped in front of me. "Maybe we don't let the human walk first into what could possibly be a trap."

"Since when do you care?" I stepped around him and began climbing in the direction the dice told us to.

He stepped in front of me, taking the lead. "You have no idea."

Atlas fell into step behind me, and I was stuck in between these two hunters who apparently loathed each other. We fell into silence as we began to hike up the mountain. I tried to make myself not sound out of breath, though I was clearly struggling to keep up. These two had barely broken a sweat yet the climbing was time consuming and difficult. Kylian pointed to rocks in my path as though I'd trip and die on them. Or he'd hold a branch up for me to walk under only to let it go to smack Atlas in the face. When we came upon a downed tree trunk, he turned and placed his hands under my arms and lifted me over it as though I weighed nothing. Before I could smack his hands away, he placed me on my feet and kept on walking.

I didn't know what to make of his behavior or why he was so intent on coming with me when he had no interest in helping me before. He paused when we got to a sheer rock face that went straight up. "Let's give those dice a roll and see if we have to go straight up?"

Sweat covered my body, and I took that moment to take my jacket off and remove Atlas's sweater. Without a word he took it back and tucked it into the waistband of his pants. I slid my arms back into the jacket. As much as I wanted to take it off, it'd saved me from the scrapes that would come with a hike like this. I put my hand in the pocket to pull the dice out and paused. The hairs on the back of my neck stood on edge and I glanced around.

"What?" Atlas followed my gaze.

"I feel like we're being watched," I whispered to him. I knew it sounded crazy, or in this world perhaps not so crazy, but there was something out there in the forest.

"We are," Kylian said so simply as though it wasn't creepy as hell. He pointed to our left. "Over there is a bear."

I tried to see what he saw but there was nothing there but rusting leaves. He pointed behind us. "In that direction are a couple wolves."

My heart started to hammer in my chest, and he pointed to the other side. "And over there is a large group of mountain lions."

"We don't have those animals in England." Atlas shook his head.

Kylian gave him a pitying look. "You've been around long enough to know when it comes to magic that doesn't matter."

The muscles in Atlas's jaw ticked and he shot daggers with his eyes at Kylian. "Then we better keep moving."

"What if they attack us?" I couldn't keep the worry from my voice.

"There are some things in the forest that are more dangerous. We aren't prey, Dice. We're predators and they know that." Atlas extended his fangs to emphasize his point.

"Fang boy is right." He made a little circle with his knife. "They know we'd kill them easily. They're just watching."

I didn't want to sit here and tempt them to try. I shook the dice and again they fell into that straight line and lit with little blue flames. They went straight up the mountain, and I groaned. I didn't know how I was going to climb that sheer rock face. No matter how much training O gave me, mountain climbing wasn't part of it.

Kylian dropped his knife, and it exploded into tiny pebbles returning back to its original state. "I can carry you up so we can make it faster."

It wasn't that I wanted him to carry me, but he had a point. If I tried to climb that, it would take me hours, and we need to get to Piper. If they thought she was dead, then there was a chance she was in bad shape. We didn't have time for the human to slow them all down.

Atlas stepped closer. "And why are *you* carrying her?"

"Because you can scout ahead and behind us faster." Kylian swept my knees out from under me and lifted me up into his arms. Once again I was cradled against the warmth of his chest and surrounded in his intoxicating scent. He held me so tight, but it was gentle. "As much as I hate to admit it, vampire speed is to our advantage."

"You're right. I am better than you." Atlas took off running up the mountain, easily jumping from one rock shelf to the other.

Kylian smiled down at me. "Ready?"

"No."

He bent his knees and leapt up into the air. My stomach dropped into my toes and the wind whipped by my face. He bounded from one spot to another, and my stomach twisted like I was on a rollercoaster. We went up and down and from side to side. If I'd eaten breakfast, he'd be wearing it. I wrapped my hands in his shirt and held on tighter to him. I pressed my face into his chest and closed my eyes. When we finally stopped, I just stayed there trying to breathe so I didn't throw up.

"You daft prick. You broke her," Atlas snapped.

Kylian chuckled and placed my feet on the ground. "She's fine."

Was I? I staggered away from the two of them and pulled my dice out once more. I threw them and they pointed to the side, down a dark and winding trail. I gave a sigh of relief and wobbled in that direction on unsteady feet. Atlas stepped in front of me, silently letting me have my moment to regain my senses while Kylian walked behind me.

"I'd be happy to carry you again," Kylian's deep voice rumbled.

"I think I'd rather set myself on fire and jump off this mountain." My stomach was still trying to decide if it was going to evacuate in the worst way or if we were just going to suffer like this for the foreseeable future, so I focused on keeping my head down and walking the path.

The forest grew denser, and I could hardly see through the trees. The movement around us got louder, and it seemed we were surrounded by animals. The path opened up to a clearing just ahead and a thatched hut sat at the center of it. A scream ripped through the silence, and I knew it was Piper. I sprinted forward, wanting to get to her. Kylian bellowed from behind me, and I skidded to a halt. The branches had closed around Atlas and me, effectively blocking Kylian from entering the clearing.

Kylian growled his frustration. "Whatever is in there wants me to go no farther."

"I have to—"

He cut me off. "I know. If anything happens to her, it's your head, leech."

Atlas didn't say anything in return, he simply wrapped his hand in mine and pulled me toward the hut. When we reached the door, he took a step back like he was going to kick it down, but there was something telling me not to just barge in there. Whoever or whatever was in there was powerful. We had no idea how powerful. I squeezed his hand and he halted.

He growled. "She's in there. I can feel it."

"I know, but let's not go in fighting. We don't know what's behind that door."

I motioned to the door. "Let's knock."

He arched his eyebrows at me. "You want me to knock?"

"I can feel the power, which means that you can too." I took a step toward the door and gave three light raps. "You can kill whatever is in there if they don't answer."

"Agreed." His muscles strained with the need to move, but he held still.

There was a silent pause and then a deep, rumbling voice came from behind the door. "Enter."

CHAPTER TWENTY-THREE

SANCHITA

$\mathcal{I}$ stood outside of Claire's holding room, wondering what the hell kind of magic could've turned her into this mess. Odd things were starting to happen in her room. The medical tools had levitated off the tray about an hour ago and still hadn't come down. But she had yet to wake. Theon stayed by her side, which I found surprising. In all the years that I'd seen him by Marius's side, I'd never seen him take interest in any specific vampire. Now he was practically glued to Claire.

"I don't trust it," I whispered to Jester.

His gaze followed mine and he gave me a nod. "I agree. Any man who turns so quickly against his sire can't be trusted. I also question why he remains. Did he show interest in her prior to this?"

I shook my head. "No, I honestly don't even remember seeing her before all this. But headquarters is a large place. Any vampire could easily get lost in the shuffle there."

"So he could've been spending time with her and no one would've been the wiser?" Jester ran his hand over the scruff on his chin.

"I theory, yes." I didn't take my eyes away from Theon as he looked up and poked a pair of scissors levitating next to him. It spun away from him and drifted to the other side of the room.

"I still don't like it." Jester turned his back to the cell and faced the rest of the lab. He was still close enough that our shoulders nearly touched, and I could feel the heat coming off of him.

I wanted to lean into him, but I held myself still. "I don't either."

"Someone has to stop all this." He wasn't wrong.

I turned to face the lab. The staff seemed to be slowly coming back from being shell-shocked by the vicious attacks of late, but I didn't want the vampire world to be in turmoil any longer. Marius and Clive had their own agendas against The House of Shade. They lavished under their protection while Alataris wreaked havoc among the witches and all of Evermore. But as soon as he was dead, these two came to fight for their own aspirations. It was almost sickening.

Even now there were still soldiers on cots, and the holding cells were filled with Night Spawn vampires suffering whatever sickness this was. Moira moved from one cot to the next, taking her time to use her blood magic to heal the soldiers. If she wasn't careful, she'd exhaust herself. I thought she might've already. Though she still wore her proper dress, she'd ripped the high neck off of it and used the strap of fabric to tie her long chestnut hair off to the side. Dark circles hung under her eyes, and her skin was a sickly pale. She was going to work herself ragged. But rumor had it that Grayson was in the worst shape of all, and there was nothing she could do about it. If I were a mother in that situation, I would keep myself busy so I too wouldn't go mad with worry.

I wished things had been simpler and more peaceful, but I didn't see that happening any time soon. "It's all too much."

"I couldn't agree more." King Titus appeared next to me, and I jumped at his silent appearance.

I gave him a light bow. "Your Majesty."

Jester too gave him a bow. "My King."

King Titus turned toward the lab and motioned with a sweep of his hand. "We need to get things under control and soon. There are too many unknown variables at play."

"I plan on returning to my sister now." Her absence was a constant pain in my chest. Without her by my side, I didn't feel complete. "And we will get to the bottom of this."

"I think I might be able to help with that." Doctor Stanbourn hurried from a room at the back of the lab. He looked exhausted and completely disheveled. His white lab coat was dotted with specks of blood, his glasses were slightly crooked on his nose, and his salt and pepper hair stood on end.

"What do you have for us, Doctor?" The King stood a bit taller and straightened his shoulders.

"If you'll please follow me." The doctor motioned for us to follow behind him.

I didn't know if it was our place to go, but I found myself moving along with the King and Jester. When we walked into a small lab, the doctor slid the door shut behind us. The hustle and bustle of the lab silenced behind the closed door, and it was only the four of us.

The doctor pulled his glasses off and pinched the bridge of his nose. "I've been looking at blood samples of different groups of vampires for the past few hours."

The King glanced toward the microscope on the counter. "And what have you found?"

The doctor lowered his voice, "Blood Born vampires have specific cells. They tend to be perfect in formation with an additional component in them that interacts with other tasks of their own DNA. These interactions are what give the Blood Borns blood magic. It's a seamless addition to our bodies at a cellular level. Now, I should mention it cannot be replicated."

"Yes." Jester shifted from one foot to the other. "I know some biologists and witches tried long ago but the alterations never took. Essentially a Blood Born vampire would naturally heal whatever changes were made and revert back to their natural state of being."

I shot him a sideways look. "How do you know that?"

"It was a voluntary program supervised by the doctor

here to see if we could enhance some of our abilities." He shrugged as though being experimented on was a normal thing. "Nothing worked. We just kept healing and no one got hurt."

"That's right." The doctor sighed. "But I've been looking at the sick vampires and the ones that were captured during the attack, and this is where it gets interesting. The sick Night Spawn Vampires are having a complete breakdown on a cellular level. Their blood cells are literally exploding and re-forming at a tremendous rate. But instead of the body healing itself and expelling whatever was done to them, it's trying to repeat the process of change."

"So this foreign, let's call it infection, this foreign infection tries to reinfect the cells when they start to form once more," the King said. "Then why are some of them surviving, some of them holding on to the power, and some dying?"

"From what I can tell, it all comes down to the Night Spawn's origin at creation. If they were human before they were turned, then the infection will take over their body and they will die a horrible death."

My breath caught. Prisha and I were only human when we were turned to vampires. If either of us were infected, then we'd be screwed. "And what about the others? Like Claire for example?"

"Ah the patient who calls herself No One. She's slowly mending. From what I can tell, she used to be a witch, was driven into hiding by Alataris, and was somehow changed into a vampire. When she first arrived, her body was in a state of destruction where the cells just kept re-forming and dying, but I'm seeing them starting to slowly accept the infection and awaken some recessive abilities hidden deep in her genes. When she was turned, the vampire infection took over and essentially forced anything she was—"

"Like a magical witch?" the King asked quickly.

The doctor nodded at him. "Exactly, the vampire infection is strong and took over, forcing all her abilities as a witch to become dormant. The same for any other supernatural species. Fae, witch, shifter, the vampire infection dominates and turns them vampire, forcing them to lose any and all abilities."

This was all crazy. It was one thing to know we were all turned vampire, it was another to start to understand it at a cellular level. "So, what's the new infection doing?"

"That's just it. It's trying to bond the vampire infection with old and new abilities . . . or I should say a different cellular infection. It is most violent and invasive. Which is why the humans and some of the others die. It's very unstable, and there's no telling how it will manifest each time it's used."

The King groaned. "This is a dangerous infection, and there's no telling what it is? Bacterial? Viral? An infection in the blood they're consuming?"

"That's just it, Your Majesty. It's not biological." The doctor swallowed. "It's magical."

My jaw dropped. "What?"

"Something is doing this to the vampires. Most intentionally. It's not spread like a human cold or flu. It's forced into them with purpose." The doctor swallowed. "And rather painfully, I'm afraid."

I didn't want to ask this next question, but I had to. "Can it kill Blood Born Vampires?"

The doctor looked utterly exhausted. "In theory, I have no doubts that it can."

"Bollocks," Jester snapped under his breath.

"My sentiments exactly, Jester." The doctor ran his hand through his hair. "It is very disheartening."

"Damn Marius to hell." The words were out of my mouth before I could stop them. He should be damned to hell for what he was doing to us.

"Indeed," the King agreed, but there was a hint of sadness behind his eyes. Almost like he didn't want to believe all that was transpiring. But the evidence was overwhelming now.

Panic started to flow into my chest. "My sister, she's in the Night Spawn headquarters. We have to leave now."

"I can't send you there now knowing what you might face." The King placed his hand on my shoulder. "It would be too dangerous."

"Your Majesty, I beg your pardon, but I must go. I will not leave her there alone, and you still need to know what Marius is doing to them to even be remotely effective in trying to combat it."

"We now have the Witch Queens on our side. I'm sure

they will be able to assist in these matters." He didn't drop his hand. "They are powerful."

"May I speak freely?" I didn't want to offend the King if it wasn't my place to speak.

"I have put you on my council for good reason. Please do."

"We don't want to put the Queens in unnecessary danger. If they are walking into something as deadly as this, they should know exactly what it is. Saying it's magic is not enough. Nor is it enough to go after Marius based on so little. He has a number of supporters in the Night Spawn Headquarters who have no idea what is happening. Don't turn him into a martyr and give them a reason to make him one. Give me the chance to get the information so this can be dealt with swiftly."

"And me, Your Majesty," Jester jumped in. "Send me with her, and I will keep her safe."

Even though we'd only been in each other's company for a matter of days, I knew he meant what he said, and I trusted him. "As part of the council, allow my sister and I to do this for you."

The King dropped his hand from my shoulder and let his head hang. "Very well. But take every precaution."

"We will." I turned for the door, ready to jump through the first mirror I saw that would take me back to the Night Spawn Headquarters.

Jester was at my side with his hand on my elbow in an instant. He bent down lower to whisper in my ear. "And where are you going?"

"You heard me. I'm going to find my sister, then I'm going to figure out what the hell kind of magic this is." I pulled my elbow free from him.

He wrapped his hand around my wrist and pulled me to whirl around to face him. "I also listened when you said it's entirely possible to get lost in the headquarters. You know your sister, if she stayed to spy on Marius, where would she be?"

I tried to fight for calm when I just wanted to get moving and leave. "She would be following him."

"And who would know exactly where he might be? Work smarter not harder, love." He tapped on his temple, and I couldn't help but smile up at him.

He wasn't handsome by anyone's standard, but this close, with him smiling at me, I couldn't help but find him compelling. With his square jaw and deep eyes, I couldn't help but move closer. "I like the way you think."

I didn't know what gave me the courage to do it, but I went up on my tiptoes and pressed a kiss to his cheek. Before he could say anything, I left him standing there slack-jawed and marched into Claire's room. Theon sat up straighter when I came closer to the bed. I didn't sugar coat my words. "I don't like you."

"I'm aware."

"I don't trust you." Jester moved to stand behind me.

"Also aware of that." He leaned back in the chair. "Anything else?"

"Yes." I cleared my throat. "You want to change that?"

He cleared his throat and ran his hand through his hair.

"Let's say I did want to change your opinion of me . . . What would it take to do that?"

With that one answer, I knew I had him hook, line, and sinker. My lips pulled up in a small victorious smile. "All the information you've got on Marius, including where the hell he might be."

Theon sat forward and his gaze locked on mine. "Deal."

CHAPTER TWENTY-FOUR

ATLAS

*T*he door creaked open, and I made sure I was the one to step through first. I kept Dice close behind me as I crept forward. The hut was relatively small and made of sticks that'd been thatched together. Across from the door, Piper lay on a pile of dried hay and leaves. A brown threadbare wool blanket was draped over her, covering her from her chest down. A cloud of dark sage magic floated over her. It mixed with her own blood magic, which seemed to be seeping from every orifice of her body.

The scent of her own blood was heavy in the hut, and I wanted to rush to her side to check her over, but there was something in this dank hut with us. Something I didn't recognize. Dice tensed and hesitated to go to her. I placed my hand on her arm and gave it a squeeze, telling her to stay put. My eyes quickly adjusted to the darkness, and I knew she couldn't see what I did. The floor teemed with smaller critters of all shapes and sizes. Rabbits surrounded her and were huddled close by.

A single fire burned in the center of the hut, and a small plume of smoke drifted up from it. I tried to find who had taken her here and whose magic was surrounding her. That's when I spotted him. I took a step to the side and he turned his head, tracking our movement. Dice sucked in a sharp breath, and her hand gripped the back of my shirt.

The man would've been huge if he wasn't crouched down like a beast about to attack. His eyes glowed green and reflected the light of the fire the way an animal's would. His face was all sharp angles and chiseled features, and his chest was bare, but fur covered his shoulders, forearms, and legs. Huge antlers stuck out from the sides of his head.

"Are you here to retrieve her?" he asked.

"Yes." I kept my tone deep and firm.

I looked back down at Piper. It *was* Piper but she looked different than the last time I saw her. Tiny dark roses were spread through her wild hair. What looked like an ivy-vine tattoo covered one side of her forehead and ran down her temple where it circled her neck and flowed lower to the center of her chest. The leaves were spread flat, but there was a glittery green glow to them.

"What have you done to her?" I took a step toward Piper and the animals all froze, staring at me.

"Um, Atlas?" Dice pulled me back. "Maybe don't piss off *all* the animals surrounding us?"

"Trust me, I'm trying not to. I don't fancy being

attacked any more than you do." I kept my voice calm and even to not provoke the deer-man or his animals.

"I've saved her." The man's voice was a low, deep rumble.

It hit me all at once. The animals, the wild forest surrounding the hut, the antlers. "I beg your pardon, but are you Pan?"

"It is one of my names." He gave a single nod and a sparrow flew from the branches of the hut and landed on one of his antlers.

"Why take her?" It made no sense that the god Pan would take Piper from the castle. He was a known recluse and was rarely seen by anyone.

He tilted his head to the side and the bird flapped his wings, trying to keep its perch on the antlers. "Take her? I found her discarded, like trash. Buried in the earth."

My brow furrowed. "Buried? That cannot be."

"You dare question me?" The world rumbled and the animals all began to cry out in panic.

More birds flew around the hut, and I had to duck my head from getting hit by one. Dice too ducked down behind me.

"What'd we say about pissing off Pan?" She poked me in the back.

"The human speaks sense." He placed his hands on the ground and pulled himself toward Piper, moving in a creepy gorilla-like manner. He stopped when he got closer to her head and her blood magic shot from her body, mixing with the sage power. It didn't expand outward, like there was something holding it all in place over her.

"My apologies." I swallowed and tried for calm. I was a hair's breadth away from retrieving exactly what I'd set out to do. The House of Shade would be pieced back together with the return of Piper.

Dice stepped out from behind me and stared at her best friend. I couldn't imagine what it was like to see her in such a state. Her fangs peeked out from her lips, dirt covered her from head to toe, and dried blood was smudged into her skin. That would be enough to unnerve anyone, especially considering the flowers in her hair, tattoo-like magic on her skin, and that freaky mix of magic. Instead, here she stood. She was a brave human.

"God Pan—" she began.

"Pan is acceptable," he interrupted her.

"Pan," she corrected herself. "Perhaps you could help us understand. We don't know how or why she ended up here."

A rumble vibrated in his chest, and he gave her a nod. "She was tortured. Close to death when her wild called to me."

"Her wild?" Dice took another step toward Piper and the animals allowed it. A little blue bird even flew toward her and landed on her shoulder. Dice didn't flinch, just smiled at the bird and ran her finger under its chin.

Pan spread his arms wide, and that sage green magic flowed from him, filling the hut and glowing bright. "The spark that ties her to all things, including me."

I started to take a step toward Piper, but a bobcat hissed at me and I moved back. "You felt her?"

"I felt her spark dying." He glared at me. "Your kind did this. Her body lay broken and bloody, with bite marks riddling her skin and a deep, deadly wound to her chest."

We knew she was taken during the attack and there was only one explanation for it . . . *Marius*. He was as good as dead. "I will make them pay."

"Good."

Piper began to thrash on the bed, and a scream ripped from her throat. Dice hurried forward but Pan was in front of her in a flash. "You, human, are no match for her now."

This time I wouldn't be stopped from moving. I stepped behind Dice and placed my hands on her shoulders. "She will kill you."

"In this state, she will not hesitate," Pan agreed. "I feel the love you share. It is much like our wild, untamed and unending. With you she will be cared for."

Dice leaned back into me. "Why do you keep saying *your wild*?"

"The wild is as old as time and is as unpredictable. It is the magic that seeps into the earth. She is of the wild and of death. Now she walks the line between both." He turned toward Piper. "I have healed her wild and her body. Now *you* must heal the side of her that walks with death."

My heart dropped, and when she thrashed again, I knew the familiar sharp movements. Piper was held here in a state of feral. "Is she starved?"

Pan tilted his head in an animal-like manner as he studied her. "I believe it is so."

"We need to get her out of here. Now." A feral vampire was a dangerous thing. A feral vampire would kill the first chance it got.

"Will she survive this?" Dice swallowed hard, and I knew our thoughts were mirrors of each other. She'd come so far and didn't want to lose her now.

Pan shrugged and a small mouse popped out of the fur on his shoulder. "There is no telling. The spring of my wild often do not survive the depth of power. But this one has survived the worst."

Spring of his wild? No, it couldn't be. "Are you saying—"

"I am saying take her now and be off with you." He waved toward the door. "The elf will help you. Though I prefer to avoid his presence, I will allow him entry."

"Yeah, we're not that fond of him either," Dice muttered, trying to lighten the situation but the tension around her eyes and concern in her voice made her words fall flat.

"The elves faun over me and their worship of the wild." Pan shook his head. "And I don't like questions."

Pan was known for disappearing for decades, even centuries at a time. It was a wonder we spoke to him now. He preferred his animals and nature to any company, just as I preferred Poe and my armchair to any others. "We understand."

"You must take hold." He rose to his feet and his antlers ripped through the roof of the hut. The branches began to fall down around Piper and light from the sky above shined through the hole. He opened his hand, and that little dome of power holding her down started to dissipate.

Her eyes flashed wide open. I wrapped my arm around Dice and threw her behind me. The hut came crashing down around us, and the animals all scurried from the wreckage. The world quaked and Piper shot to her feet. I dove forward, wrapping my arms around her and tackling her to the ground. The animals ran over us to get out of the way and the birds flew off in a thick swarm. The hut was gone, and we were surrounded by the forest. When I tried to ask Pan what he was to her and why his magic lingered on her, he was gone without a trace.

Piper's arms shot out and she fought my hold. Her head snapped back, and at the last second, I turned my face away before she broke my nose. "Kylian!"

Now free from the wild magic, Kylian charged in. "What the hell happened?"

"Pan," I growled as Piper kicked her legs. "Grab her."

Kylian wrapped his arms around her legs, and we both struggled to our feet. Dice moved in closer. "Piper?"

"NO!" Kylian and I bellowed at the same time.

Blood magic mixed with the wild sage power pouring from her and her power started to seep into my skin. It was taking over. Sweat broke out over Kylian's body and he met my eye. "Feel that?"

"Bloody hell." Before Piper could take us down, I forced Poe from my chest. He shot up into the air and circled above us, cawing so loud it was nearly deafening. Pain exploded through my arms and legs and I fought the sudden desire to let her go. The desire must have been from her. I threw my head back and bellowed, "ZINNIA!"

The portal opened up a few feet away and she came charging through. "Holy fuck."

Kylian's body shook but he didn't let go. "HELP! NOW!"

Silver magic exploded from her and wrapped around Piper. Zinnia sucked in a sharp breath and her shoulders hunched over. She staggered to the side and crimson flower petals rained down from her magic. The others hurried through and surrounded us. Piper hissed and screamed at them while kicking her legs and flailing in my arms. Beckett dove forward and wrapped his arms around her hips.

"What do we do!" Dice screamed as she backed away. "What does she need to stop this?"

I held on tighter even though I could feel Piper's blood magic in my own veins. My body would not be my own soon, and no one would stand a change once she got free. She would hunt and she would kill. If a feral vampire was dangerous, then a feral vampire with powers of the wild would be catastrophic. There would be no stopping her.

"BLOOD!" My body shook and I ground my teeth together, fighting to keep a hold of her. "SHE NEEDS BLOOD!"

CHAPTER TWENTY-FIVE

DICE

"*H*old her down!" Atlas ordered as she slammed Piper down on an exam table while Kylian climbed on top of her to pin her shoulders down.

She bucked wildly, kicking her legs out, and sent Kylian flying into the wall next to her. He knocked all the medical equipment off the wall and crashed to the counter, cracking it. He fell to the floor, taking more trays of tools with him. Vampires in lab coats rushed into the room with bags of blood. When they approached the table, Atlas snarled at them.

"Are you daft? Piss off!" They dropped the blood on a tray on the other side of the room and scurried out the door. "Take her with you."

He gestured in my direction, and I glared at him. "I'm staying right here!"

Zinnia kept her power flowing over Piper, but the

crimson rose petals were turning to dust. Blood-red sweat covered her body, and she looked like she was about to fall over. Tucker ran into the room. He wore only a pair of low-slung jeans and a thick bandage was wrapped around his chest and back.

"Astrid!" he yelled after taking one look at her.

The fiery redhead marched into the room and stood beside him. He glanced down at her. "You've got this?"

Beckett hurried to her other side. "We got this."

"In three. Two. One." Tuck leapt forward and wrapped his arms around Zinnia, jerking her away from Piper and breaking their connection. Her silvery magic dropped and she collapsed in his arms. Astrid and Beckett fired their magic at the same time. Beckett's blue smoke wrapped around her wrists and ankles, pinning them to the table while Astrid's golden power pressed into her chest and hips.

Zinnia hunched over and vomited blood onto the floor beside Tuck. She sucked in deep gasping breaths, trying to stop from heaving. "Strong. So strong. We fought for control."

Tuck brushed her hair out of her face and scooped her up. More flowers fell from her hair onto the floor. He pulled her from the room. "You're going to smell like roses for weeks."

Ophelia marched in and pulled two knives from her holsters. She twirled them in her hands and took a step toward Piper.

I didn't know what came over me, but I jumped in front of her. "No!"

"She won't die. I'm just gonna stab her to the table." Her gaze locked on Piper. "Like a thumbtack."

I pulled my own knife. "You . . . you have to go through me first."

She arched her eyebrows at me. "That's cute."

"If you're not helping, fuck right off!" Atlas bellowed. "Titus!"

"We need help in here." Astrid's entire body shook, and Piper snarled at her.

"Come on, bitch." She bared her fangs at Astrid. "Let me go."

Astrid's magic faltered for a moment, and she shook herself. Piper threw her head back, screaming and thrashing on the table. Kylian jumped back up and threw his body over her, holding her legs down. Beckett joined him and pinned her hips to the table with his own body. Atlas glanced at me. "Give me the blood!"

I ran to the tray where the lab techs left the bags and threw one at him. He caught it and shoved it right to Piper's mouth, using her own fangs to pierce the bag. For a moment everything slowed as she sucked down greedy pulls. The bag was gone in seconds and her thrashing doubled. Red mist shot from her body, mixed with that sage magic. Atlas, Kylian, and Beckett all flew off her and slammed into the walls, their bodies tossed like rag dolls.

Astrid dropped to her knees and screamed. Piper swung her legs over the side of the table and gave her a devilish smile. Her body tensed to attack, and I tried to get to Astrid before she did. Ophelia wrapped her hand around my wrist and yanked me back. "Out of the way, human."

Cross was right behind her, and the two of them tackled Piper to the ground. They fell from the table and dented the hard, rocky wall. Shards of rock fell down on the three of them.

Ophelia wrapped her arm around Piper's neck and held her in a choke hold as Cross pinned the rest of her. "Go to sleep, psycho vamp."

Piper lifted her hand and raked her claw-like nails down Ophelia's leg, tearing her leather pants and gouging deep furrows in her skin.

Ophelia squeezed her neck tighter. "You scratched me! GIRL FIGHT!"

Astrid staggered closer, trying to keep a hold on Piper, but I could see her magic was faltering. A huge shadow marched into the room, and I sucked in a deep breath. King Titus. He was huge and imposing, taking up most of the space. He took one look at Piper and the people on the floor. He opened his hands and red mist shot from him to wrap around Piper completely.

"Still." His voice was deep and commanding, and she went still.

Atlas staggered to his feet and hunched over, sucking in deep breaths. "My gratitude is yours, Your Majesty."

"Speak for yourself. I almost had her." Ophelia dropped her hold on Piper and popped to her feet. Blood ran from the deep cuts on her leg and pooled on the floor around her. "I've always wanted to take on a feral vamp. You ruined it."

Piper vibrated with power, and I could see her own magic fighting against the King's in the space between them. Kylian also rose to his feet and deep bruises appeared down his arms and across the side of his face. He too was covered in sweat and sucked in deep breaths. He and Atlas exchanged a look, then the two of them walked over to Piper and picked her up and put her back on the table.

King Titus never dropped his hold on her, though I could see this too took a lot of effort on his part. "What the devil happened to her?"

Atlas backed away from her, and I could see where she'd cut his arms and the side of his face. "Marius kidnapped her, tortured her, and staked her . . . in the heart."

The King did a double take. "He did what?"

"It's true." I don't know what gave me the audacity to speak to the Vampire King, but here I was.

He gave me a sideways glance. "Why is there a human in my castle?"

"Long story, Your Majesty." Atlas grabbed another bag of blood from the tray, walked over to Piper, and shoved it into her mouth.

She sucked down the blood, her chest heaving with deep breaths between gulps. That's when I noticed her necklace. There was a small pearl in the center of it, and it was a deep crimson. "Where'd she get that necklace?"

Ophelia pointed toward it. "Ohhh, righttt. Grayson got that for her. It's kind of like a warning system. The darker red it is, the closer she is to being feral. It kind of tells her when she needs to feed."

"She's already had two bags of blood. How many more will she need until she gets better?" I wanted my best friend back, not this monster with magical powers who threw fully-grown supernaturals like they were nothing.

Atlas didn't meet my eye. "As many as it takes."

I rolled up my sleeve. "Okay, I'll donate. Take some of mine."

"As much as I admire your willingness to give her your blood, there is only one person's blood she can take without getting sick." Atlas swiped at the blood on his arm.

Beckett moved next to Astrid and wrapped his arm around her shoulder. "You okay?"

"Just tired." Her knees gave out and he caught her before she hit the floor. He picked her up and glanced toward Titus. "Have you got this?"

"For now." The King's hands vibrated with the effort to keep Piper still. "This is more than blood magic. It's like nothing I've experienced before."

"Pan said something about unleashing the wild in her," I blurted out. "But none of that matters right now unless we can get her back to normal, so whose vein do we have to tap to do that?"

Atlas grabbed the last bag of blood from the tray and

placed it over her mouth once more. He turned and met my eye. "Grayson's."

"Batshit crazy Grayson?" How could this be happening? They were both mad for different reasons. "Can you people even get close enough to get blood from him?"

"What do you think?" Atlas tossed the empty blood bag away.

"Great. Just great." I ran my hands through my hair.

"Could be interesting." Ophelia chuckled. "Like a cage match. We could see who comes out on top. My money is on wild vamp Piper."

I looked to the King. "Could that work? If you let her go in that cage with him, would she bite him?"

"Without question." Atlas sighed. "Feral vampires are going to hunt whatever is closest."

"I will not endanger my nephew like that." Titus took a step back, and Piper's power started to fill the room. Her arms vibrated like she was going to break free, and she snarled at the King.

"Your Majesty, I don't think we have a choice here." Atlas shook his head. "We need her to help him, and she needs him to help her."

The King hung his head and gave a heavy sigh. "Very well. Carry her to the cell and I will hold her as much as possible."

"As you wish." Atlas motioned to Kylian who was eerily silent this whole time. He seemed to understand the unspoken request. Atlas slid his arms under hers and wrapped them around her chest while Kylian took her legs.

I followed them as they carried her through the lab while others stared with wide eyes at her show of power. Ophelia limped beside me, and I glanced down at the trail of blood she left in her wake. "Don't you think you should get bandaged up?"

"And miss this?" She shook her head. "It's like a death match."

"Comforting. Real comforting."

"There's no stopping her," Cross muttered. "Just go with it. And O, take the damn potion. You're getting blood on the floor."

"Oh, right." She reached into her pouch and pulled out a potion I was very familiar with and chugged it down.

Zinnia and Astrid sat in chairs next to each other, and when they saw us head to the dungeon, they both rose to their unsteady feet and followed. The moment we entered the dungeon, Grayson's incoherent words rose to a yell.

"I'll kill her! She's yours! Just stop!"

When we got to his cell, he stood there pressing his hands to his ears and shaking his head.

Piper's body thrummed with tension and Titus's steps faltered. "She's so strong. It's hard to fight her pull."

"It's like a war for control over your own body," Zinnia agreed with him.

"And magic." Astrid added. "I've never known anything like it."

Beckett pulled the cell door open, allowing Atlas and

Kylian to walk in with Piper. They placed her on the ground across from Grayson. His screaming stopped and his eyes locked on her. His fangs lengthened and his eyes went full black.

I cleared my throat. "You sure this is a good idea?"

"No." Ophelia shook her head. "But it's a fun one."

They backed out of the cell, and Beckett slammed the door shut behind them.

Titus stood just outside the bars, holding her in his power. "I'm going to drop my hold now. Prepare yourself for anything."

He dropped his magic, and she jumped to her feet so fast I didn't even see the movement.

The dungeon opened and a woman who shared features with Grayson hurried in. "I heard you found her. Is she well?"

She went to the cell, and the King reached out and pulled her back. "No, Moira. She is far from well."

Kylian strolled up beside me. "You okay?"

"How could I be? My best friend is a monster." I lowered my voice to a whisper, "And there's nothing I can do."

"You've done all you can. You're the reason we found her." His tone was low and soft.

I shook my head and tears threatened to spill over. "Not soon enough."

"Don't do that to yourself. You were trapped."

"Thanks to you." I took a small step away from him. "Good reminder."

He ground his teeth together but said nothing else. We all held our breaths as she turned to face Grayson. His yells halted and his eyes locked her the second she took a step toward him. Piper lifted her nose and took in a deep breath. Her fangs extended and a dark mist mixed with green seeped from her toward him.

"Does it remind anyone else of Christmas?" Ophelia clapped her hands together. "Blood and sage, it's like presents all the time."

Piper leapt toward Grayson, and he braced his legs, taking the impact and catching her. She raked her nails down the side of his face and across his neck. Grayson bellowed and wrapped his hand around her neck, squeezing so tight I could see where his nails dug into her skin. Tiny rivets of blood trickled from them. They snarled and snapped at each other and my heart dropped.

"They're going to kill each other."

"She's right!" Atlas moved toward the cell door, about to go in, when Titus stepped in front of him.

"If it is to be like this, then it is to be. They are soulmates and cannot be parted." He pulled Atlas back. "It will be life or death."

Piper leapt up and wrapped her legs around his hips, locking herself onto him. She shoved his hand away from her throat. In one swift motion, she tilted her head to the side and struck hard. Grayson growled deep in his throat and tried to shove her off, but she wouldn't stop. She took deep, greedy pulls, and with each one, those black veins receded from his body. His eyes slowly cleared, and his skin turned from a sickly blue to a smooth pale. His hand crept up the back of her head and wrapped in her hair, holding her closer. Her legs slid down his body and she leaned into him, her pulls growing more delicate as she did.

"The pearl," Ophelia whispered, and my eyes went right to it. It turned from dark-red to a lighter pink, then to a blush, and then pure white.

Piper pulled her fangs back and tipped her head up toward him. Her voice broke. "Grayson?"

"It's me, little creature." Their eyes locked, and for a moment I was witnessing an intimate exchange I shouldn't have.

He pressed his hand over the pink healing line on her chest and over the marks on her neck. "Did I?"

"No." She shook her head. She rested her forehead to his, then went up on her toes and pressed a kiss to his lips.

I let go of a breath I didn't know I was holding. It was her, my bestie, the sister I never asked for but found when I needed her most. She was a monster, her boyfriend was worse, and yet I was here for her. She was back and in the arms of a killer vampire.

I shook my head and an involuntary laugh escaped me. I didn't know if I was losing it or if the stress of the last few weeks was finally broken. "Whoa, you are into some kinky shit."

Her head whipped around toward me and her gaze locked on mine. "Dice?"

CHAPTER TWENTY-SIX

PIPER

*I*t couldn't be her, but that voice was so familiar. My blood raced in my veins and my eyes widened. "Dice?"

There she was, standing in this dark cell surrounded by powerful supernaturals. I wanted to run to her, to protect her from them. She was so fragile, a human in a world of killers. Grayson's body started to shudder in my arms, and it drew my attention back to him. Those red lines forked out over his eyes and his hands went from holding me to pressing into my shoulders. I held him tighter. I wanted just one more second with him, the vampire I loved.

He squeezed his eyes shut and a growl rumbled in his chest. When they flashed back open, he shoved me away. He shot Atlas a deadly look. "Keep your word."

Atlas's jaw dropped and his shoulders hunched for an instant before he yanked the cell door open and marched in toward me. He wrapped his arm around my waist and began dragging me back.

I didn't want to leave his side. I reached out for him. "No, don't leave me. Fight this."

His head whipped from side to side as black veins began to cover his arms. He became impossibly bigger as the muscles in his body tensed. He sprang toward us to attack but slammed his body into an invisible barrier. The fight left my body all at once, and I let Atlas drag me out of the cell. The door slammed shut behind us with a clang of finality, and I tried to keep it together, but the events of the last few days all came crashing down on me.

The kidnapping, the torture, and the weird deer-beast doing something to me. Something that made me feel different down to my core. My body shook and magic began to pour from me.

Atlas loosened his grip on me but didn't let me go. "You need to calm yourself."

"Hasn't anyone told you to never tell a woman to calm down?" Dice snapped, and suddenly she was standing in front of me.

I wanted to run to her, to wrap my arms around her and hold her tight. I needed someone to lean on and she had always been that for me. But I was different now, so much stronger than she was. If I wasn't careful, I could hurt or even kill her. She stopped in front of me and looked me up and down.

"So, this is where you've been hiding? Gotta say, never saw the vampire castle thing coming." She gave me a nervous half-smile as she waited for me to fall into our comfortable banter.

I swallowed around the ball in my throat and ran my hand over my knotted hair. "Go big or go home."

"But like *royalty*? And you're a vampire now." She put her hands on her hips. "Your broken picker has led down some interesting paths but none as interesting as this."

"I'm so sorry." My breath caught in my throat.

"No, don't you dare." Unshed tears glistened in her eyes. She took a step toward me and threw her arms around me, pulling me to her. "I've decided we aren't blaming ourselves for giving people the chance to be good people. It's their own problems if they turn into dicks. So maybe your picker isn't so broken after all."

"Yea, I think you're right." At first I didn't move and just let her hug me. The others all moved in closer, tensing in case I did something to the fragile human, but I could never hurt her. I wrapped my arms around her and sucked in a deep breath. "I really needed you."

"Well, I'm here now." She pulled back and brushed my hair out of my face. "So catch me up? What happened?"

I blew out a long breath and glanced around at all the people watching us. The King and Moira stood there with wide eyes looking from me to Grayson and back again. The King cleared his throat "Perhaps we should give you a moment."

I gave him a tight-lipped nod of appreciation, and he escorted Moira from the dungeon. The others started to back away and go in different directions. Atlas didn't move and I narrowed my eyes at him. "You can go too."

He shook his head. "You've just regained your senses. I would think you'd want me close by to protect your friend as a precaution."

I groaned. "Very well."

"What he said." Kylian crossed his arms over his chest and stared at Dice.

My brow furrowed and I muttered to Dice, "What's up with that?"

She rolled her eyes. "Apparently they hate each other."

"Yeah, but like, why are they hovering over you like you're their favorite toy?" I wasn't sure I was comfortable with two guys as deadly as Atlas and Kylian taking an interest in my very human bestie. She was so much more delicate than them. Well, she used to be. Her appearance had changed since I saw her last. Her muscles were more well defined, and she held herself with more confidence, like she knew she could hold her own. Her hair was pulled back from her face and weapons were strapped all over her.

She shrugged. "Men, am I right?"

"You have a point." I pointed at the two of them. "Back off or I'll turn you inside out."

They both took a half step back but didn't move any farther.

Zinnia cleared her throat. "I'm sorry but some of us must stay as well. We can't leave Grayson unguarded."

I nodded and pulled Dice farther away from his cell. "What happened to you?"

"Well, after you got ass face over there to dump me with Ophelia, I've kind of been in boot camp this whole time." She lowered her voice. "I didn't know there were so many ways to kill a person."

"We've only gotten through the first quarter," Ophelia called over to us. "Really, we need like another year to get you all caught up. Want to give her to me?"

My eyebrows shot up. "No, I don't think I want to give you my best friend."

All this time something had been missing and now I knew it was Dice. I missed her so fiercely that it was a constant sadness I carried around. Dice gave me a little smile. "I missed you too."

"I can't believe you came here." I pulled her in for another hug.

She held me tighter. "Someone had to find you."

"I had no idea where I was or what was happening." I tried to remember everything, but it was a bit foggy. Pain mixed with power and the desire to live were the most prominent memories. "I still don't really know what happened."

"Well, according to everyone, you got hit by a car and nearly died, and that's why Grayson turned you. To save you. And I guess I have to thank him for that because I'd take you as any creature really, even a vampire, over not having you at all. Then they said you got taken by some dude named Marius—"

A hiss escaped my lips and my fangs lengthened. "Marius has death coming."

Atlas and Kylian moved in closer as if they were ready to step between me and Dice. She turned and shoved them back and they actually let her. When she faced me, she smirked. "This whole *I am powerful, I will kill you* thing that you have going on is freaky as shit but I kind of love it."

I closed my eyes and tried to find calm, but when I opened them, we were surrounded by my blood magic and something else, some kind of glittering green power mixed in with it. "What the hell is that?"

"I believe it's your wild." Atlas cleared his throat. "At least that's what Pan told us."

Kylian's face fell. "You met Pan?"

"Not important." Atlas waved a dismissive hand toward him. "What is of importance is your lineage, Piper. What do you know about your parents?"

I hadn't thought about them in years. As a kid I dreamed that they'd show up one day and want me. That they'd realized they'd made a mistake by giving me up and letting me live my life in a broken system. "I, um, I don't know anything really. Why do you ask?"

He hesitated and that one hesitation got the attention of Zinnia, Ophelia, Tabi, and Astrid who had all stayed behind to keep an eye on Grayson. They fell silent and their gazes were locked on our conversation. So much for privacy.

Dice cleared her throat. "Atlas, what are you saying?"

He sighed and shook his head. "I believe you are a child of Pan."

"Impossible," Kylian snapped. "They can't survive the wild power within themselves. They rarely even make it past the birthing process. The wild . . . well, it's too much for any human."

"In most if not all cases." Atlas motioned toward me. "I believe we're looking at the exception. If she remained human, I believe the wild would've lay dormant, but when she was turned, it awakened in her. And when Marius—"

"Tried to kill me." I was going to hurt him in ways not even that twisted bastard could think of.

"I think he might have killed you, Piper. No other vampire could withstand the things he did to you." His voice was low and full of sorrow. "I am sorry I wasn't there to protect you."

The others all let their gazes drop to the floor, and I knew those looks well. It was pity, and I hated pity.

Dice smacked my arm. "Yeah, and my girl survived that fucker and came back swinging harder. I pity his stupid ass."

My lip pulled up in a half-smile. "That's right."

Zinnia moved in closer to me and held her hand up. Her silvery magic ran over my body and probed me but not in an invasive way. "That's what I felt? The old wild magic of Pan?"

Atlas nodded. "I believe it's what kept her alive when Marius surely did his best to try and kill her. It's what called to Pan to find you."

"Unbelievable," Kylian muttered.

"Cool." Ophelia got closer to me, as if she was studying me with those big black eyes of hers. "So, what can you do with the wild? Is it like Tabi and you can go all jolly green giant on people, or is it like Beastmaster status?"

I opened my mouth and closed it again. "I, um, I don't know. I haven't even processed the fact he might be my father."

"It makes sense." Astrid waved her hand to the magic seeping around me. "The magic is something else."

"A demigod vampire." Tabi shook her head. "Now I've seen everything."

"Dude, you're a demigod." Dice chuckled. "Of all the scenarios we could've thought of, like who our parents could be, never did I suspect for one second a Greek God."

It was unbelievable. "Somehow I don't think he's going to want daddy-daughter visitation."

I wanted to feel some kind of connection to Pan. But I didn't. He was this wild thing that appeared and disappeared just as quickly. Somehow never knowing who I was kind of made me okay with not knowing and accepting me for me.

Dice chuckled. "I met that guy. There's no way he's going to pop in for a visit."

"So I finally met my father." The words were hollow sounding even to me. "I guess he came through when it counted. He saved me . . ."

Kylian ran his hand through his hair and tugged at the dark strands. "I can't believe I missed it. My people would bow down to her now. They search for him eternally. And he blocked me from entering that hut. Wait till I tell Ashryn."

"I think she's nearly recovered," Tabi chimed in. "But perhaps give her a few more days."

"Recovered from what?" I glanced at the others. I knew I'd been away for days but what could've happened in that time? "What did I miss?"

Astrid held her hands out. "I got this covered. During the attack when you were taken, Grayson got free."

My eyes widened and my breath caught in my throat. I remembered The Fallen being very specific. If he hurt anyone, then he would be annihilated. I opened my mouth to ask a million questions, but Astrid held her hand out to stop me.

"I'm getting there," she said. "Essentially an astral projection of Lucifer let him free. Apparently, that's the voice that Grayson has been hearing."

"The one telling him to give him Dracinda?" The one I heard when I walked through his dreams with Morpheus.

She nodded. "Yep. So we know that Lucifer is involved in this curse, but we have no idea who Dracinda is or why he wants her. But what we do know is that if he gets her, it'd be a very, very bad thing. We were on our way to figuring out who she was when you were taken."

"Great, let's go do that." I pointed toward the dungeon doors.

"Um, Piper." Dice pressed her hand to my arm. "You

might need a second to, I don't know, shower? You're kind of terrifying-looking right now."

"She makes a valid point," Atlas agreed.

"Since when do you give a fuck about my well-being?" Before this he'd barely spared me a glance and told me to stay away from Grayson. Now he was suddenly concerned.

Dice's voice went gentle. "Piper, since he was the one to find you and bring you home."

"That's a new development. He only did that for his best friend. Not for me." Anger rose in my stomach. We had to get moving. I'd been missing for days and that left Grayson here cursed for days longer than he needed to be.

"I mean, she's not wrong." Kylian snickered.

"Shut up," Dice snapped at him.

Atlas shrugged at both of us, "I'm an ever-changing evolution of what I used to be, which means I'll keep you safe from here on out."

Not that I didn't want him on my side. Atlas was the best kind of ally to have and the worst kind of enemy. "Why? Because Grayson asked you to? Thanks, but no thanks, I don't need your pity protection."

Atlas scoffed. "You of all people should know I have no pity for anyone. You are of The House of Shade now, and I protect The House of Shade."

Again with this poetic nonsense. "Whatever that means."

"It means that he learned to care about you." Dice reached out and pulled a lock of my hair in front of my face. It was full of tiny crimson roses. "And he's right too.

No one is telling you not to get going. All we're saying is maybe shower first and change your clothes."

I looked down at myself. They were right. My clothes were torn to an indecent degree. There were few straps of fabric covering my chest and even less covering my legs. "Very well. Once I'm cleaned up, then we need to get going."

As if on cue, Grayson bellowed from his cell, and it was like a shot to my heart. Despite the things I'd endured the last few days, I knew this madness was worse. I would rest when he was by my side once again. I turned toward Zinnia, "What's the next move?"

"We know that Dracinda cursed The House of Shade a thousand years ago. But she's supposedly dead, so we need to talk to someone who was around a thousand years ago and who might have some insight into this."

I met her eye. "We need to talk to Titus."

She gave me a single nod. "It's time we met with the King."

CHAPTER TWENTY-SEVEN

SANCHITA

"I'll rip his throat from his body if he lied to us," Jester growled under his breath.

"I do believe you'll have to get in line for that honor." I glanced over my shoulder, looking for any sign of life.

Theon's information led us deep underground. We were well past the last stop on the tram that ran up and down the main spiral of the headquarters. Here there was a layer of dust that gathered in the corners of the hallway. Rats and other manner of vermin scurried in the darkness. Much like the other hallways, these were dug deep into the earth and the walls were rough to the touch. But there was something older about these tunnels. The stale air told me they hadn't been used in centuries. It'd taken us hours to wind our way down here, and now there was a labyrinth of turns to get us to the single door we sought.

There, hidden in the side of a wall, was a single metal door. I placed my hand on the knob. "Just like Theon said."

"But why would he live this far down?" Jester peered up and down the empty hall. "These housing units haven't been used in decades. All the Night Spawn have been moved to updated quarters."

I turned the knob and the door creaked as I pushed it open. I could only hope that Theon was right when he said Marius wouldn't hear the exterior door to his apartments. It was only when we got deeper into his rooms that he would know. I stepped into a small foyer room. There were two doors on either side of us. They were closets and neither would lead us any closer to him. I pointed straight ahead toward an archway, and we crept forward into a sitting room with two leather chairs pulled in front of an iron stove with a small fire flickering within. It warmed the damp room and took the chill out of the air.

We kept going. According to Theon, when we exited this room, there would be another hall that ran to the right or left. We were to go right and follow that to another room where Marius spent most of his time. Directly beside that room was another where the walls were thin enough to hear every word he spoke. It was more of a storeroom than anything else. There we would sit and wait for any information we received.

We got to the intersection of the hallway, and just as I turned right, a hand shot out from the darkness and wrapped around my mouth, yanking me into a room across from us. My body collided with the one holding me and I staggered back. Jester was there in an instant and the hand disappeared. When I turned, he had my sister pressed against the wall with a knife to her neck.

"You've got to be out of your senses to grab her like that." Jester took the knife from her throat and stepped back. "And even more daft to be in here."

Prisha threw her arms around my neck and jerked me to her. "Thank goodness you're all right."

I pulled back and eyed her closely. She was covered from head to toe in dirt, so filthy I could hardly make out her features. Her eyes were wide with shock. "What are you doing here?"

"Us? What are you doing here alone?" This was stupid even for her. Prisha was daring in so many ways, but this was beyond her.

"I had to." Her words came out in a rush. "Marius, he's keeping hundreds of vampires locked up in cells. He's poisoning them, or attacking them, I'm not even sure what I saw. But it was powerful and dangerous. I need to know what it is so I can tell the King."

"I knew you'd be here." I knew we were in danger and Marius could be lingering anywhere, but I couldn't help myself.

Prisha reached out and squeezed my hand. "I knew you'd find me, Sister."

"I hate to break up this reunion, but we need to get moving." Jester motioned to the door. "Now."

He turned and didn't wait for us to follow. I fell into step behind him and the three of us moved silently down the hall toward the storage closet. It was a miracle that no one spotted us.

We hurried into the room and Jester eased the door closed behind us. "Theon said Marius was the only one here and only takes meetings in that one room."

I lowered my voice. "If there's anything to find out, we'll hear it here."

Prisha pursed her lips and moved closer to the wall, then sat on the floor with her back to it. She crisscrossed her legs and rested her arms on her thighs. I didn't think I'd ever seen her so shell-shocked in her life. She just sat there taking deep measured breaths. Jester pulled a blood bottle from one of the pockets of his cargo pants and handed it over to her. She took it and quickly chugged it down. I knew she would open up more about what happened but Prisha was the type who always needed time to process her thoughts, so I sat down on the floor next to her, silently keeping her company.

Jester strolled around the room, looking at the mismatched assortment of things stuffed in it. He moved a few things away from the wall, then bent down low and crooked his finger at me. "Look at this."

There, toward the back of the storage room, were two tiny peepholes that peered right into Marius's meeting space. I bent down low and closed one eye to peer through the hole with the other. A full-length mirror stood in the middle of the room. It had a thick gold frame and even wider legs holding it up. Two wall sconces were dimly lit with flickering flames soaking the room in gentle lighting.

A thick purple carpet sat under the mirror and filled the whole room. Off to the side were two leather armchairs with a single table between them.

I glanced up at Jester. "Have I told you lately that you're bloody brilliant."

"I'll take my compliments later." He winked and joined me on the floor, peeking in through the other peephole.

I didn't know how long we stayed like that, taking turns watching an empty room, but the silence surrounding us was deafening. My skin started to crawl, and my legs were riddled with restlessness. Just when I thought we were going to sleep on the floor of this hovel, Jester patted my arm and pointed toward the hole.

I ducked my head and peered through. The mirror began to ripple and my adrenaline kicked in. Marius stepped into the room through the mirror and dusted his arms off. His hair was freshly washed and slicked back from his face. Though his jacket looked to be stained with blood, the shirt he wore under it was a crisp white. He sauntered over to the table and grabbed the crystal decanter there and poured himself a glass of blood. Then he dropped down into one of the chairs and fixed his gaze on the mirror as though he were waiting for someone.

The mirror rippled a few moments later and another man stepped through. I sucked in a sharp breath, then pressed my hand over my mouth. I'd recognize that oily, slicked-back hair and old-school suit coat from a mile away . . . Clive Christiano. These two hated each other. One was of the highest Blood Born family, and the other from the lowest Night Spawn. What the hell were they doing together?

Clive's gaze roamed over the small room and his lips curled with disdain. "Night Spawn."

Marius gave a dark, humorless chuckle. "Clive."

"Aren't you going to invite me to join you in a drink?" He put one hand on his hip and held the other loosely at his side.

Marius made a show of taking a deep sip from the expensive crystal. "I think I'd rather not."

"The indecency of it," Clive snapped. "You Night Spawn are all the same. Lowly creatures—"

"You requested this meeting," Marius cut him off. "Perhaps you'd like to get to the point of it before I grow tiresome with all your . . . posturing."

Clive straightened his sleeves and ran his hands over the lapel of his jacket. "Very well."

Marius leaned back in the chair, crossed his ankle over his knee, and let his arms rest on the sides of the chair. He motioned for Clive to continue. "By all means, impress me."

Clive hissed and bared his fangs. "Careful, pup. I've walked this Earth for much longer than you, and I have been known to slay a Night Spawn or two."

"Save your idle threats for someone who might show you a touch of fear." He placed his glass on the table. "If you have nothing of value to say, then you should see yourself out and I will attend to my business."

"You and I have a common enemy," Clive snapped. "We both know it."

Marius raised an eyebrow at him. "And you believe . . . *what* will happen here? The enemy of my enemy is my friend?"

"Of a sort." Clive cleared his throat. "I believe we can eliminate this threat together."

"Interesting, and what are you offering in return for my assistance?" Marius took another sip, then swirled the blood around the glass.

"I am in want of an army, and I believe you have one." He locked eyes with Marius, and for tense moments they stared at each other. "Would be willing to compensate you heavily."

When Marius chuckled, Clive flinched as though he'd been slapped. "Let's just say I do indeed have an army. You think I would just hand an army over to you? A vampire who stands against the advancement of the Night Spawn?"

"We would take the throne, I would replace Titus as King of the Vampires, and you would be afforded all the privileges of the court."

The smile dropped from Marius's lips. "I am already afforded all those privileges. Perhaps you should give me the backing of the Blood Borns and I shall be King with my own army."

"Absurd." Clive shook his head. "The likes of you shall never sit on the throne."

"Do keep telling yourself that, for when I do take the throne, your head will be the first I chop off."

"I came here tonight—"

"You came here tonight to make a fool's offer, thinking I am a fool." Marius rose to his feet. "What you forget is I am no fool. I don't need you or your aristocracy to take the throne."

Clive's face grew a deep red. "Then why take this meeting?"

"Curiosity." He turned for the door. "Now I know how desperate you are and how little I'll need you."

"How dare you—"

Marius waved him away as though he were a gnat. "See yourself out."

Without another word he turned for the door and left Clive standing there like a fool. Part of me appreciated the way he told Clive to piss right off. The other part of me hated that enemies were piling up all around The House of Shade.

CHAPTER TWENTY-EIGHT

PIPER

"*I* gotta say, the perks of being a vampire princess are kind of astounding," Dice called to me from just outside the bathroom door. "Have you seen this closet?"

Warm steam billowed around me, turning the bathroom into a sauna. I'd spent longer than I cared to scrubbing my own dried blood from my body. Flashes of being bitten over and over again shot through my mind like an assault on my senses. I wanted nothing more than to keep moving forward and restore Grayson back to his cocky self, but it was difficult not to linger on the last few days.

I swiped my hand over the mirror, brushing away the fog, and just stared at myself. Ivy-like vine covered the side of my face down to my neck and across my chest. I looked like an insane half-vampire, half-wood nymph. And Pan was my father? The freaking God of the Wild was my father? How the hell was I supposed to unpack that bit of knowledge? And what did it mean to unlock the wild in me? I was still myself . . . kind of. But I didn't really look like myself anymore. Those little red roses were a bitch to get out of my hair. I tried washing them out, but even now as I stared at myself, they began to appear one by one in the damp waves.

The bathroom door slid open, and Dice leaned against the door frame. She crossed her arms. "Are we freaking out?"

"Just a bit." I turned my head to the side and pointed toward the vines. "I mean, what even is this?"

She tilted her head and gave a shrug. "It's pretty bad ass. You have a permanent tat without the needles and pain of getting one."

"Oh, there was pain. Trust me." I closed my eyes and saw the flashes of sage magic being forced into me.

Dice moved into the bathroom and turned her back to the mirror while leaning against the vanity. "You made it through though. Next stop, fixing your boy."

"Don't you think all this is weird? Like, you were practically thrown into all this because of me. Aren't you the least bit annoyed?" I watched her profile in the mirror for any hint that she was pissed I'd brought her into this.

She shrugged. "I mean, at first it was terrifying. Kylian literally threw me at the feet of O and Cross. And if you don't know those two, they are literally disturbing."

I hung my head and focused on the drops of condensation around the sink. "I am so sorry about that. I just didn't know how else to get you to me. Grayson told me a human couldn't survive in this world, and to keep you safe it was better off if you thought I was dead. I'm not so sure he was wrong."

"He's an overprotective ass. Of course he was wrong." She gave a chuckle. "These last few weeks have been the most terrifying of my life, but they've also, I don't know, unlocked a side of myself I didn't know I had. Even if I am a puny human, I kind of feel like this is where I belong. With you."

"I know what you mean." I lifted my gaze to meet her eyes. "It's been a roller coaster ride, but I don't think I've ever felt more like me."

"You mean all-powerful, wild vampire, bad ass bitch?" She gave a playful scoff. "Yeah, I bet you feel like yourself."

I chuckled and shook my head. "It is crazy to think about. But I'm glad you're here. I need a little bestie approval."

"Are you kidding? I totally saved your ass." Her lips pulled up into a smile. "You know, with the help of an insane vampire and supposedly a Dark Prince."

Just talking to her cheered me up and made all the drama and pain of the last few days go away. "But what is up with that? Those two are hovering around you like bees to pollen."

She rolled her eyes. "I just think they hate each other and I'm their little toy to fight over. Neither one of them is actually interested. Why would they be? I'm only human and they're both immortal warriors. Now, come on, we've got a meeting with a king . . . in a castle."

When she said it like that, it did all sound so far-fetched, especially given where we started. "You're right."

"Besides, you have to save your boy so you can come back and turn me into a vampire." She wagged her eyebrows at me. "There's no way I'm leaving you to live like this forever without me."

I didn't know how I felt about killing my best friend just to keep her with me. It seemed wrong somehow. "Don't you want a chance at a normal life?"

"Oh please." She shoved away from the sink and walked out the door. "What has normal ever gotten us?"

"Touche." I sucked in a deep breath and followed her out into the room. "Just give me some time to think about it. I don't even know if I can make another vampire. I'm kind of a mix of fucked-up freak over here."

She pulled a pair of jeans and a red long-sleeved V-neck T-shirt from a dresser drawer, then handed them to me. "Well, don't think about it too long or I'll just get Atlas to do it. Somehow I think he'd be willing to do it if I asked."

I pulled on some undergarments, then shoved my legs into the jeans she handed me. "So, your plan has a backup plan?"

She shrugged and grabbed a pair of combat boots from my closet and dropped them at my feet along with a pair of thick socks. "Don't I always?"

"I feel like we're gonna have to have a serious talk about this." I pulled the shirt over my head and started to tuck my feet into the socks. "But not now. One crisis at a time."

"I don't see it as a crisis, but sure we'll table it . . . for now." Her tone indicated that she'd already made up her mind and our chat was just a formality to convince me she was right, which she usually was. She walked over to my closet, then pulled out two leather jackets. She looked at them both and opted for the looser fitting one. She tossed it to me, then spun around in a circle, looking for something more. "Weapons?"

"What?" I raised my eyebrows at her as I slid my arms into the jacket.

"Seriously? You need some weapons. Where are you daggers? Whips? Chains? Axes?" She put her hands on her hips.

"Who the hell are you and what have you done with my bestie?" I turned for the door. "I don't usually carry weapons."

"First of all, you need to start. Second of all, you never know when someone deserves to get stabbed." She unstrapped the dagger on her thigh and then walked over and fastened it to my leg. Then she pulled another out of her boot and shoved it into mine.

"Remind me to never leave you with Ophelia again." I checked that they were strapped into place.

She turned for the door and yanked it open. "It wasn't that bad, surprisingly enough."

I walked out the door and she fell into step with me. It was hard to believe I was back at court within the walls of The House of Shade. So much had happened, yet now I was more in control than ever.

Atlas melted from the shadows and fell into step with us. "You're looking well."

"You mean not covered in my own blood and fully clothed." Just the thought of the state I was in sent a shot of annoyance through my body. A chorus of howls sounded from outside the castle. They were so loud they rattled the windows. I froze mid-step. "What was that?"

Atlas cleared his throat. "That has been happening for some time now."

"How am I just hearing this?"

"You were riddled with bloodlust and in a feral state." He glanced up at the stained-glass windows lining the hallway that led to the throne room. "Since you've come back to your senses, they've calmed some."

I turned and started walking once more. I didn't know what to make of that . . . or anything else, though I did know my powers had grown and there was going to be a big learning curve that I didn't have time for. "Yep, okay."

"I should probably also note there are a flock of crows that have taken up residence on the castle walls, as well as a bear that has been testing the strength of the doors." He said this all like it was of no matter, like he was reporting on the weather.

"What am I supposed to do about it?"

"I happen to think there is nothing you can do about it. Where you go, the wild will follow. It seems only a matter of time before we are overrun." He shrugged. "I'm of the opinion it will liven things up around here."

Dice chuckled. "Can I have a pet red panda?"

"What?" We arrived just outside the towering double doors of the throne room.

"A red panda. I really want one. So, if you could make that happen, that'd be great." She chuckled. "I'd settle for a raccoon, but like, a red panda would be cool."

I shook my head and chuckled. "At least you think this is cool."

"Oh, I'm all for it." Dice glanced up just as the Queens strolled up to us. "Now *they* are intimidating as hell."

She wasn't lying. It seemed all of them had taken the time to clean up as well. Zinnia was at the center of them with her long midnight hair flowing down her back and bright sapphire eyes. Silver magic swirled around her, and red flower petals dropped to the floor as she walked. She blew one out of her face and groaned. Astrid was on her other side with her golden power making her skin practically glow. She flicked her wrist and her hair braided itself down the side of her head.

Tabi was on Zinnia's other side, and she winked at me. "I'm loving the vines."

I self-consciously ran my hand over my neck. "I didn't really have much of a choice."

Zinnia blew a rose petal toward me. "Tell me about it."

"That's what you get for taking power from a demigod vampire," Ophelia teased. "We should see if you can hang out with those wild wolves outside."

"You want to give me to a pack of wolves?" Zinnia scoffed at her. "And here I thought we were getting this whole sister thing down."

"I didn't say I was going to chop you up and feed you to them. I just said we should see if they'll bite you." Ophelia groaned. "So dramatic."

Serrina tossed her hair over her shoulder and gave O a sideways glance. "Careful or I'll make you fall in love with the bear."

"*Pshh*, little do you know me, I'd choose the bear every time." Ophelia motioned to the doors. "Are we going in or are we standing out here all day?"

"If all of you are up here, then who's watching Grayson?" It wasn't that I didn't trust the palace guards, but I didn't think they were powerful enough to keep him contained.

Zinnia gave me a reassuring smile. "We left all our guardians with him. Beckett, Tuck, Brax, and Ashryn, and for some reason, Kylian insists on hanging around."

"And the warlock heirs—Logan, Cross, Maze, and of course Tilly. He should be very well protected."

"Change of plans." Tuck's deep velvety voice came from a few feet away.

My heart dropped at the sight of him. He was supposed to be with Gray. "Has something happened? Do we need to get back to him?"

"I happened." Maze moved to the front of the group, and even now the sight of him sent a chill down my spine. He was tall and brooding with inky hair and those freaky eyes that went from milky-white to neon-green and back again. Sometimes I didn't know if he was in the present or seeing all of our futures. He glanced at me and spoke out loud. "Both at the same time." He moved past us and walked up to the guards at the doors. "Open them."

Without hesitation, they scurried to open the double doors.

Tuck lowered his voice. "He insisted on coming up here and bringing me and Beckett along. The others are still watching Gray."

The doors opened to the throne room and King Titus. He sat perched on the edge of his throne. His face was a mask of worry, with deep lines between his eyebrows and around his eyes.

When we entered, his eyes widened for a split second before he leaned forward, watching us. "I supposed you've come here for a reason?"

Moira, ever by his side, placed a calming hand on his shoulder. "They are only here to help us."

"I know." He pinched the bridge of his nose, and it was the first time I'd ever seen Titus show any sign of stress. But with the mounting war, Grayson's curse, and a castle full of magical beings, I could see how this would trouble anyone, even the mightiest of kings. He motioned for us to stand before him.

Maze cleared his throat. "Tell them."

"Can you be more specific?" The King sighed. "I've a lot on my mind as of late."

I stepped up next to Maze. We needed to make this as quick as possible, and I wanted my Grayson back. "We need to know everything there is to know about Dracinda —the witch who cursed you."

He leaned back in his throne and a heavy sigh heaved in his chest. "She was the most powerful witch to ever walk the Earth. More powerful than even Alataris. On the night of my curse, she summoned us all to a clearing in a forest. And by us all, I mean even The Fallen were pulled toward her."

We all sucked in a breath. To summon The Fallen would take a great amount of power. More power than the Queens held now. "But why would she take that risk?"

"The one person she loved was dying, and no amount of magic could save her: her most beloved sister, Danna. Death had a strong hold on her and we all knew it." Titus rose to his feet and walked over to the sideboard where there was a crystal decanter of blood laced with whisky. He poured himself a generous glass. "But none of us would save her."

"Why?" The question was out of my mouth before I could stop myself.

He took a deep sip. "Because Dracinda and her sister were a plague on the world. They did terrible things to all of Evermore."

Zinnia shifted her weight and plucked a petal from her hair. "There's one thing I don't understand. Why only curse The House of Shade? Why not The Fallen as well, or whoever else was summoned there?"

"Because no magic could save her."

The answer came to me almost immediately. "She wanted you to turn her sister into a vampire?"

"Precisely." He raised his glass to me. "When I refused,

she died only moments later in front of all of us. And in her grief, she cursed The House of Shade." He sucked in a breath and continued,

"Mark these words, avenge thy crime,
Bound by blood in space and time.
From kin to kin one wretched vine,
A wicked curse seals a shaded line.
What was denied shall now be taken,
For when thee love thee turn forsaken.
Deep in thee veins thy soul will burn,
Forever more thy thirst shall yearn.
Breath by breath thy mind unwound,
To madness now thy life is drowned.
And if fate shall deem thy love requited,
Don't speak the words or curse the blighted.
For if on the wrist thy souls entwined,
Death shall call and forever find."

They sent a shiver down my spine, and I could feel their power here in this room. "Then what happened?"

He strolled back to the throne and dropped down into the seat. "She was gone before any of us could find her, and once we did, she was heavily protected and nearly impossible to get to."

"How could you not keep trying?" Maze piped in. "How could you not kill her?"

"Don't you think I bloody well tried?" Titus snapped at him.

Maze groaned and the one-eyed cat who was usually perched on his shoulder popped from the side pocket of his cargo pants. He hissed at Titus but didn't move any closer. "It's difficult to believe that a vampire with someone like Atlas couldn't get to her."

"Maze, why are you pushing?" Astrid chided him. "I would think the King would go to any length to stop this."

A growl rumbled in Titus' chest. "She was protected by a powerful warlock family who always saw us coming. I believe you yourself are familiar with them. They were after all your family and the Circus of Freaks. And then news came that she was dead, and I thought the curse would be broken with her death."

They all sucked in shocked breaths and glanced back and forth between each other. Zinnia stepped forward with wide eyes. "Are you saying—"

"I am saying I believe the witch you seek, the dead one, is known to you all as the Crone."

CHAPTER TWENTY-NINE

MARIUS

200 Years Ago

"*N*o, I beg of you. Don't leave me in this place." I held on to Moira's wrist for dear life.

She'd brought me to the Night Spawn headquarters in London, which was little more than a hovel compared to the life I'd led before this. It was a vile place where the stench of human was equally bad as the horse-drawn carriages. The streets writhed with humans scurrying about like cockroaches. Moira stepped around them and glided easily through the throng, but I found it over-whelming.

My vampire senses were difficult to adjust to, and each cry from an alley or argument was equivalent to a horn being blown directly into my ear. And the foul odor they exuded . . . I pressed a handkerchief over my mouth. "Moira, please, I much prefer the country."

"Oh, my dear Marius." She took my arm, curling her tiny hand into the crook of my elbow. "Our laws are in place for a reason. You must register yourself with the Night Spawn. They will be able to help you get settled."

"I cannot understand why I can't take up residence in the castle with you. I am your progeny." I wanted so badly to stay with my friends. I didn't understand a life without magic, and I needed their support through all of this.

"We are lucky no one has taken me to task over that. A royal family member doesn't often make a progeny. I feel their grief over Graymont has distracted them from what I've done." She gave my arm a little squeeze. "Let us not draw attention to it. Besides, you will visit as often as you like."

It was as though I was a flea-riddled dog being put out of the house. It wounded me deep within my soul to be turned out by ones I considered family. I hated to admit my feelings to Moira, but there was something I couldn't resist about her. "You wound me, Moira."

She pulled me off the road and into a small alley between two brick buildings. "It is never my intention to wound you in any way."

Looking into her wide chocolate eyes, I nearly melted on the spot. She was full of charm and so much sorrow. I nearly felt selfish in my wish to stay within The House of Shade. But she turned me into this, wasn't there some responsibility there? "I know you don't, but I can't help but feel I'm being shuffled away into a dark hole where I do not wish to be."

"Oh, Marius, no one is putting you in a hole. We've spent the last few weeks getting you accustomed to being a vampire." She lowered her voice so the passersby couldn't hear, "How to hunt without being detected, how to get by as human, and all the laws that come along with being a vampire. Perhaps you would do well to spread your wings and fly just a bit."

I took a step out of the alley and kept her hand tucked into the crook of my arm. "You think me afraid?"

She shook her head, and her chocolatey waves of hair fell around her face. "I think this is unknown to all of us. With the loss of the King's brother and your transition into the vampire world, who wouldn't be . . . apprehensive. Plus, I have a child of my own now to think on, and I have not paid him the attention he deserves."

Moira's words were gentle, but I would be remiss not to notice the distance growing between us. "I do understand all that, and I'm happy you've grown into your role at court."

I left the rest of the sorted drama unspoken, mostly because my words were bound by her and the power she used over me as my sire. True to her word, she never did it again, but I was still bound in silence, never to mention the fact that she was actually the Queen and Titus's true wife. I was forced to go along with this lie that she was married to Graymont and Grayson was his.

The last bit of magic I'd ever done had concocted a lie

that everyone in the kingdom believed to be true, a lie that we would both live with for eternity.

She gave me a heavy sigh. "I have and so should you. Titus has gotten you a place as the assistant to the Night Spawn Ambassador. It is a chance to make a real difference in the world. Not to mention the ability to grow in wealth and social standing."

"Yes, but never to rise to levels such as yourself or any other Blood Born for that matter. I must admit, when I was a warlock, I never thought on such things as vampire politics. I just thought of your laws as *the* law and that it is. Now having been relegated to the Night Spawn headquarters, I can see flaws in the way things are."

We turned down another street, this one much darker than the main road, and it reminded me how I would never stroll the streets during the day anymore. I would never see the street vendors or the women gossiping on corners. I was stuck with the seedy views of the night and the dredges of society that came with it.

Moira didn't seem bothered by the night in the slightest. "This is something Titus had always wished to work on. He's making great strides. Perhaps when he is fully recovered, you might work together. Two old friends making the world better for us all."

Old friends? Did old friends leave each other alone in a strange place? "If you say so."

Moira pulled us to a stop in front of a small shop that looked closed. The lights were dim and the windows were covered over by thick curtains. No one came in or out of the door, and there weren't signs of life. "Here we are."

The entrance was at the back of a dark alley surrounded by brick walls. It was nothing compared to the castles in the countryside.

I wrinkled my nose. "Here?"

"You can't expect them to be out in the open. We're vampires, Marius. Discretion is key to our survival. We do not draw attention to ourselves." She took a step back from me and motioned to the door. "This is where I leave you. They're expecting you."

"You're not coming in?" I motioned to the door.

She shook her head and gave me a warm smile. "You can do this, darling. It is close to Grayson's feeding time, so I must attend to him. I will see you at luncheon tomorrow."

"Tomorrow then." I watched as she walked away, leaving me there in the alley alone.

A huge human strolled up and stopped her in her tracks. He peered down at her with a sinister smile. "Join me for the night."

Moira tilted her head back, looking up at him. "No thank you, human."

The man chuckled and grabbed her arm so hard I thought she would surely have bruises. I was about to hurry to her side when she reached up and wrapped her hand around his throat. She went up on her tiptoes and extended her arm high above her head. His toes barely scraped the ground. "I *said*, no thank you." She tossed him into the brick wall headfirst, and he landed in a dazed heap. She stepped in front of him and bent down, getting inches from his face. "When a lady says no, she means it." Then she called back to me. "Do tell them there's a bit of a mess out here, will you?"

"Um, of course." I'd never seen her manhandle someone like that before, but I noted it for my future reference.

"Men," she huffed as she marched out of the alley, and her little heels clicked on the cobblestones.

I turned back to the door and drew myself up as much as I could. I'd been abandoned and I was alone to face a world I knew nothing about. Being a Night Spawn was clearly different than the world my friends lived in. It was difficult knowing I would never be on their level or be seen as their equal when in the past I was so clearly part of them. Now the space between us was far more detectable, and the farther it got, the more I realized I was on my own for eternity . . .

I think I'd rather be dead.

CHAPTER THIRTY

PIPER

"I'm sorry WHAT?" Zinnia was the first to speak, and the others started to go crazy around her.

"This is bad. This is really bad."

"Could be interesting. I've been wanting to take a trip back to the Underworld."

"How is that possible?"

"No. I take it back. Hell no."

"Well, fuck."

I raised my voice over them all. "Someone explain to me who the Crone is and how are we all so familiar with her?"

They fell silent, and for a moment I thought no one was going to speak. Maze cleared his throat. "The Crone is a powerful witch who traded immortality for her soul. She did things that not even the evilest witch would dare do."

"Like my father," Zinnia cut in. "From what we know, even he gave her a wide berth."

Maze pointed toward her. "Precisely, she used to feed off of other's soulmate marks or I should say the ancient magic that formed them. It kept her alive for centuries and very dangerous. There wasn't anyone I knew who didn't fear her."

"Okay so what does she have to do with Lucifer?" None of this made sense. If she was powerful in her own right then why did Lucifer want her?"

"My guess is she was probably doing a lot of that magic and taking power from others and giving it to him." Ophelia shrugged and march toward the throne.

Titus cleared his throat. "Don't even think about it."

"Can't fault a girl for trying." She turned and started heading back toward us. "If I were the crone and I wanted to live forever, I'd make a deal with the Devil. If you think about it, it's mutually beneficial. She gets to live forever and do whatever the hell she wants on Earth, and he gets a piece of the power she takes."

"I don't know what's worse: the fact that you thought of that so quickly or what you might be tempted to do." Zinnia ran her hand through her hair and tugged at the strands with a frustrated yank. "I have concerns, O. I have concerns."

"And we call those back up plans, Sis."

I held my hand out, stopping them all from talking. "So, let me get this straight, this bitch cursed the House of Shade's entire bloodline, she reports to Lucifer, and to top it all off, she's dead and there's nothing we can do about it. So where does that leave us?"

Maze shifted from one foot to the other and gave a *meh* sound. "I mean, technically she's not dead, she's just trapped."

"This is unbelievable." Titus rose from the throne and moved closer to our group.

"You've known about this for a thousand years and you did nothing?" I wanted to keep the accusation out of my voice, but I failed miserably. "How could this have gone on for so long?"

"I really thought that her being in Tartarus was going to be enough to end the curse. And yet only days after she was trapped in there Grayson fell to the curse. Not even in death was the curse broken," Titus hung his head.

"Technically not dead." Maze held his finger up. "Just want to make that clear. Not dead, just trapped . . . forever."

The air grew hazy with red mist around Titus, and he puffed his chest out. "For a thousand years, I have tried to break this curse in every way possible. I have hired more witches and warlocks than I can count. I have hunted Dracinda to the ends of the Earth and back again. You think I wanted this for my nephew? You think I wanted this for myself? Never to love or have children of my own for fear of what could happen to them?"

I had to force myself not to look at Moira, knowing she was his love and Grayson was his son. "I know this has been difficult, but—"

"Difficult is an understatement," he cut me off. "This has been a personal kind of torture watching my own family die because I refused to help her. If I had saved Danna, her sister, in that moment, then none of this would've happened. But I did what I felt was right and I've been paying for it ever since. For years after she cursed us I hunted her. Every soldier I lost in pursuit of Dracinda were all a price paid to the curse and that single night. I've seen her kill so many beings without consequence and survive longer than us all, only to be stopped in the last fifty years. She'd been heavily protected by magic the vampires just don't have. I couldn't turn to Alataris, there was no viable way to get to her."

"And let's not forget Lucifer," I pointed out. "That was a layer to this puzzle that you didn't know about either."

Maze groaned and squeezed his eyes shut. "And my parents made a deal to protect her in order to protect me."

Titus deflated a little. "Who do you think they were protecting her from?"

Ophelia snickered. "Kind of funny though."

"There's nothing funny about this, O." I wanted to see the humor in what she saw, but I just couldn't. Titus had lost his whole family to this curse and even himself. He lost things he hadn't even known he lost, which made it that much worse. I wanted nothing more than to end this not just for Grayson and myself but for Titus and Moira.

"Come on, think about it," Ophelia chided. "What a tangled web. Titus won't save Danna, so he gets cursed. Titus hunts Dracinda who then needs the protection of

Alataris and Lucifer. I mean, really, if you think about it, Titus should be proud of himself. It took a warlock king, the Devil, and an entire circus of freaks to keep her safe from him. Kind of impressive really."

Titus raised his eyebrows at her. "And that to you is funny?"

"Hey, if someone needed that much protection from me, then I would find it hilarious." The other Queens all shook their heads and sighed while the darker ones like Maze, Cross, Logan, and Beckett all chuckled in agreement.

Titus continued on, choosing to ignore her. "As I said before, when the lot of you sent her to Tartarus, I thought the curse would break, but the moment I saw Grayson and Piper together, I knew it had not. That's why I wanted to keep them apart. But nothing can stop the curse once it's started."

Moira made a little whimper in the back of her throat. "Damn this curse, and damn that witch."

Before anyone could respond, she stormed from the room, and I could understand why. She'd already lost her love and life to the curse, and now she was potentially going to lose a son to it. No one would be able to stay so tightly controlled over their emotions in her situation. Titus gazed after her, staring at the doors long after she disappeared. He strolled back to the throne and dropped down into it.

The first time I saw him sitting in that throne, he seemed to take up the whole thing. Now he just seemed exhausted by the burden of being royal. *Heavy hangs the head who wears the crown.* I faced the others and sucked in a deep breath. "Okay, I don't know much about magic or how it works for witches, but now that we know who and where the Crone is, how do we break this curse? Like, what do we have to do? Do we make the deal with Lucifer?"

"NO!" they all yelled at the same time.

Astrid held her hand out. Her golden magic wrapped around her fingers and a bag of plantain chips appeared. She tossed it to Maze. "You look nervous."

He wrinkled his nose. "Healthy garbage."

"Then give it back." She held her hand out, waiting, but he didn't return it. "You see how I made those chips?"

I nodded. "Yeah?"

"For the sake of explaining the curse, let's say I'm the only one in here who can make those. I can make them and unmake them. But no one else can. So if we want to break this curse, she's going to have to be the one to do it." Astrid shrugged. "Zinnia could siphon my power and probably do it, but she can't siphon that dark magic. O could probably buy him a bit more time. But in the end, none of us can break a generational curse that's older than all of us."

"So you're saying it's hopeless?" I refused to give up on Grayson and his family. Hopelessness would never take hold with me.

"Oh, hell no." Astrid smiled. "We're the Queens. We will make this happen, even if *she's* the only one who can break it."

Dice raised her hand like we were back in school, and I understood why. She was a human playing in a super-human game. "What if she dies for real for real? Will that break it?"

Ophelia pointed toward her chest. "I like the way you think! Let's just go down there and shank the bitch."

Titus shook his head. "If Dracinda dies, she won't go to the Underworld like the rest of us supernaturals do. She paid her soul to Lucifer, so if she dies, Lucifer gets her and he's getting exactly what he wants. That is not an option unless you want to answer to Matteaus, and you won't survive that."

"I take it back. Let's unshank the bitch," Ophelia grumbled. "They never let me have any fun anymore. We cannot set the Crone loose in the world."

We were running into brick walls at every turn. We needed a plan, something smart that would actually work. "So, we have to break the curse without killing her or her soul will be sent to Lucifer and he gets exactly what he wants . . . and then we all get killed by The Fallen for doing so. So how the hell do we do this?"

"You have to make a deal with her." Tarot cards flew from Maze's pocket and circled over his head. Without a word, two of them floated into the middle of us all. Two of swords and wheel of fortune. Maze motioned to them. "The two of swords is *decisions to be made*. We're going to have to present her with a choice, a deal—options she'll be interested in. The wheel will make her see this as an opportunity. That's how she works, so that's what we need to do. Trades and prices, just like Lucifer."

Titus groaned. "The only thing she'll want is Danna."

Tabi shrugged. "If I were her, I might want out of Tartarus. That's a brand-new angle to work with."

"We can't let her out." I shook my head. "She'll just run to Lucifer for protection."

"I didn't say we have to let her out. We only have to make her think that we will." Tabi winked at me.

My lips pulled up in a smile. "I like the way you think."

"Trick the evilest witch ever." Maze grabbed his cards and shoved them back into his pocket. "Why the hell not?"

"We're going to need a plan. A very specific plan." I didn't want to leave anything to chance this time. I wanted this damn curse broken, and I wanted it now.

Titus nodded. "And a way to get to the Crone."

"We've got that covered." She chuckled, "We have a connection in the Underworld."

I wanted nothing more than to stand here and figure this all out—every little detail. If we were going to go in swinging, then I'd swing to knock her out on the first hit. The throne room doors flew open, and Prisha, Sanchita, and Jester rushed in. Any excitement I began to feel instantly vanished. Prisha was filthy, her long curtain of hair flew out from her head in all different directions. Sanchita mimicked her air of worry as she too hurried toward Titus. Jester ghosted behind them, taking a moment to glance over his shoulder looking for something or someone. They were all wide-eyed and disheveled.

Sanchita rushed up to me and pulled me into a quick hug. "Oh, thank the Creator you're alright, Piper."

I pulled back. "I'm all right, but are you?"

Prisha shook her head and turned to the King. "Your Majesty, a moment of your time, if you please."

"It's in regard to that note we all received," Sanchita added while glancing around the room at the witches watching her. She swallowed. "It's important."

The King took one look at them, and I knew they were all on high alert. He motioned for them to move closer. "Come. We will speak of this."

Zinnia cleared her throat. "And on that note, I believe we have a Crone to kill. Excuse us, King Titus."

I wanted to stay and listen to what Prisha and Sanchita had to say. They were my friends and I wanted to help them, but I knew the best way to help them all was to get their Prince back. The King motioned for the three of them to follow him to a room off to the side of the room and they followed him. When Sanchita glanced back, she gave me a small wave, and I mouthed the words *good luck* to her, hoping that would be enough.

Zinnia clapped her hands together, getting our attention. "It's time for us to plan a trip that might only be one way."

My brow furrowed. "Why only one way?"

"Because the last time we went into the Underworld, we all died . . . and Nova is trapped there . . . forever."

CHAPTER THIRTY-ONE

ELOURA

"What an interesting choice of location." Martin craned his head back to look at the red, green, and white awning that hung above the entrance to the mozzarella shop.

"I rather like it." The shopfront was completely unassuming from the outside. The building was slightly run down but in good working order. The exterior was a dark red brick while the window facing into the shop took up most of the wall.

Inside, a deli counter ran the entire length of the store and was full of meats to slice. Behind the counter, I spotted two men standing over bowls of mozzarella with milky-white water. "I do believe those are humans."

Martin sucked in a breath through his nose. "Yes, the smell of it."

"How intriguing, and you're sure this is his base of operations?"

Martin nodded his chin toward the two vampires sitting at a table all the way in the back of the shop. To the human eye, they would appear like two bodyguards outside of the entrance to the back room, which from here looked like a simple doorway with a plain, dark wood frame. "Those are not humans."

It was true they had the air of immortality about them in the way they sat so still that they even might startle a human. They each wore a dark-colored suit and a button-down shirt that was open at the neck. I spotted the distinct bump of guns under their jackets. Not many vampires carried weapons that were so . . . human. "Indeed, they are not."

"It's good that we have dressed for the occasion." He smirked at me, and I knew what he was thinking.

I'd traded in my normal regal dress for a black pantsuit and tightly fitted vest that dipped into a low V in the front. I might've been an older vampire, but I looked no older than the age of thirty. The suit was a deep burgundy color that complimented my dark skin. Though Martin tried to get me to give up my walking stick, I refused. I felt safe when keeping my weapon on my person. "Yes, well, dress the part is a saying for a reason, young one."

"I happen to think you look fabulous." Martin motioned to the door. "Shall we go?"

"Perhaps I will take this meeting alone." There were things that I knew had to be done. Things I wasn't sure Martin was ready to face, and if I could save him from this, I would.

He inclined his head toward me. "As you wish. But I will be right here if you need me."

I gave him a light pat on the arm. "I know you will."

Without another word, I pushed through the door to the shop. As the bell above the door gave a little tinkering sound, the guy behind the counter moved to face me. "Hey, what can I get ya?"

I loved the heavy Staten Island accent, though I was pretty sure I was in New Jersey. I glanced over the meats and cheeses offered and gave my head a little shake. "I'm here for other business."

He looked me up and down. "Oh, you're one of those, aren't ya? Should've known from the get-up."

He knocked on the countertop and called out to the two men at the back of the shop. "Yo, Berto, Michale, you got another one."

"Appreciated." I gave him a little nod and turned toward the two vampires as they rose from their seats and lumbered in my direction.

"Yeah, we'll see if ya do or not after this." He walked away from me and went back to sticking his hands in the mozzarella bowls.

When I faced Berto and Michale, I realized they towered over me by at least a foot. They were monster-sized vampires with barrel chests and hulking arms. The one on the right spoke to me first. "What can I do ya for, lady?"

"I'm here to speak with your boss." I held my chin up,

though I had little choice. If I wanted to look them in the eye, I had to tip my head back.

The one on the right, I decided he was Michale, crossed his arms blocking the door. "Boss ain't here. Can I give him a message for ya?"

Everything in me told me that Lorenzo was sitting in that darkened room right through the doorway. The faint smell of a cigar drifted on the air mixing with the smell of the food. I tapped my cane on the floor. "I do believe he will want to hear what I have to say. My proposal is most advantageous for him."

"Michale," a deep voice came from the back room, "let her through."

Michale stepped to the side, then waved me through. "Apparently the boss is in."

"I thought as much." I didn't hesitate to walk through the door. With each step I took, my cane made a little clicking sound on the tiles before I stepped onto a dark brown carpet.

A large mahogany desk took up most of the room, with two chairs right across from it. Lorenzo sat behind the desk, leaning back in his leather armchair. He wasn't at all what I expected. I thought perhaps he'd be an older vampire who'd frozen into his immortality at an older human age. I expected a slightly rounded belly with some hair loss. What I got was a young-looking vampire with warm olive skin and curly light-brown hair cut neatly to his head. His eyes were a deep honey color with flecks of yellow in them.

While his bodyguards wore suits, Lorenzo opted for a black button-down shirt, charcoal grey pants, and matching black belt and shoes. The shirt fit him like a glove, showing off a sleek muscular physique. He rose to his feet as I entered, and he blew a stream of smoke toward the ceiling. As I moved closer, he slid one hand into his pocket and held the cigar with the other. He licked his lips, and when his eyes lingered on me, I paused.

"If you keep looking at me like that Mr. Romano, then our business will have to wait, and if you are the businessman I think you are, then you wouldn't want that."

A smile played on his lips, and he motioned for me to take the seat across from him. "I'm not sure what a lady like you would want to do with me. But consider me interested."

"Then I'd say we're off to a good start, wouldn't you?" I dropped down into the chair and crossed my legs, leaning back against the plush leather.

"I'd say we were off to a good start when you walked through the door. Anything else is just a bonus as far as I'm concerned." He extinguished the cigar in the glass ashtray on his desk, then leaned back in his chair. "What can I do for you, Miss . . ."

"Danrich. Eloura Danrich."

He raised his eyebrows at me. "The Eloura Danrich? The high-born broad who hangs with the Vampire King?"

I inclined my head toward him. "The one and only."

"I can't say I ever expected one of your kind to be

sitting in the chair across from me." He steepled his fingers.

I tried not to snicker. "My kind?"

"High-born Blood Born vampires don't hang out in Jersey if you know what I mean. But I shouldn't be surprised, judging by the accent."

I rested both my hands on top of my cane. "Oh, come now, Mr. Romano—"

He held his hand up, cutting me off. "Lorenzo, please. A woman as beautiful as yourself should be on a first name basis with me."

"Lorenzo then. Well, Lorenzo, we both know that's not true. I have it on good authority you have many contacts among the Blood Borns of England." I glanced around the office at the detailed woodwork and expensive crystal decanter sitting on a handcrafted tray.

"Oh yeah? Who says so?" He sat forward and folded his hands on the desk.

"I say so." Somehow I'd gotten myself into this banter, and I had no idea how. I expected an old mob boss, and what I got was a handsome loan shark who was much older than his looks gave away.

"And what makes you say so?"

"Let's just say I'm very good at what I do. And currently it's my job to know things about everything." Being a part of the council only gave me more permission to do what I was already good at . . . knowing things.

He chuckled. "Yeah, I'm good at my job too."

"So I heard. As a matter of fact, I hear you own most of the debt accrued by high society."

"I dabble." He shrugged. "It's easy to make acquaintances when you dabble."

We could go round and round all night. As much as I was enjoying the word play there, it had to come to a point. "Shall we speak plainly?"

He waved his hand over his desk. "I love it when people get honest."

"The honest truth is you've collected debts from many traitors to the crown." I paused, waiting to see how he'd respond.

"I don't get involved in politics." He leaned back once more. "They came to me for loans, and I was more than happy to grant it to them."

"Even if that money is being used to purchase an army to unseat a king?" I sucked in a breath. "No, not just a king, but a great king."

"It's only my business when it comes to how they pay me back."

I pursed my lips. "And how is that looking for you?"

He scoffed. "I'm about to own my first estate in England. Go figure."

"Yet you have no political aspirations?" I found it hard to believe that a vampire who, according to Martin's intel, was turned in the late 1920s and accrued this much wealth in such a short time wouldn't have aspirations.

"Look, I like my business. I like what I do. I don't need

the needs of a nation on my back." He waved his hand from side to side. "I enjoy the babble."

"Right, a little of this and that?" I gave him the side-eye.

"Exactly." His accent seemed even harsher now that we were getting to the meat of the problem.

"The debts you collect buy you no loyalty."

He gave me a small shrug. "What do I need their loyalty for?"

"Your future," I offered, hoping my words let him see the future possibilities he had here.

He pressed his hand to his chest. "I didn't realize the King was so concerned about my future. He might want to worry more about his own."

I froze, feeling ice run through my veins, and was on my feet before I knew it. "Is that a threat?"

"Don't get your panties in a twist." He motioned for me to take a seat. "I ain't stupid enough to threaten the King, even if your Blood Borns are. Though they're sneaky about it. I think a guy should know when you're gunning for him. The anticipation of my arrival might kill 'em before I do, you know?"

I sat down, slowly ready to draw the thin sword from my cane and slice his throat if need be. "I can assure you the King and I are aware of Clive's attempts to acquire an army."

"Oh, yeah, me too." Lorenzo folded his hands on the desk. "So, what does the King want with me?"

"I think it could be an advantageous friendship. The

King can assure your businesses thrive. There are many, we know."

"I mean, I'm already thriving." He wasn't wrong. According to Martin he was richer than rich. "If I do this, what does he have to offer me?"

"Ah, your age is starting to show now. And you had me fooled for a moment." I shook my head and chuckled. "The young ones never see the bigger picture."

"I'm not that young, Eloura. I can call you Eloura, right?"

"Seeing how we're such fast friends, of course you can."

That brought a smile to his lips. "I was turned into a vampire in the twenties. I'd hardly call myself young. And I've been in this game a long time. Longer than that Capone character. I mean, who gets clipped on taxes? Waste of talent. But even now I have to know before walking into a deal what is in it for me and my guys."

I rose to my feet. "What younger vampires such as yourself forget is that instant gratification doesn't last, and us older vampires prefer gratification over and over again for ages to come. You, my new friend, are seeing only instant gratification and not the long-term prospects."

He paused for a moment, thinking over my words. "I can see your point. A long-term relationship with a king is better than a short term one with an idiot."

"Ah, he *is* brilliant." I winked at him. "Perhaps you should ask yourself what you can do for your King. There is a difference between aligning yourself with a cockroach and a king.

Lorenzo sighed. "I'm not usually a political man. I like to do what I do."

"It appears that you've somehow gotten dragged into this line. Now you have to decide which side of it you're on." I reached into my pocket and pulled out a small white card and dropped it on the desk in front of him. "When you figure that out, there's how to reach me."

"And if I only want to reach you?" He picked the card up and turned it over in his hand.

"Oh, Lorenzo, I'm not sure you're ready for the games I play." I had yet to find a man who could keep up with me mentally, and I wasn't sure Lorenzo was it, but I did enjoy the harsh accent and attitude. Even now while staring me down, he owned every inch of space in this room, and it was palpable.

He snickered. "I look forward to the games you play."

Without another word, I turned and headed out the door. It was now in his hands, but I had no doubts he'd be in touch . . . soon.

CHAPTER THIRTY-TWO

MARIUS

$\mathcal{I}$ took a step closer to Kendra and she took a half-step back. "I must admit the results are rather impressive."

"I was rather surprised myself, sir." Kendra, ever the loyal soldier, stood by my side. The first time I'd had the smoke unlock her power, I was almost disappointed. She didn't possess the outward abilities of others. Instead, she became influential with them. They listened to her like soldiers following a general, and she was all mine. When she spoke, there was power in her voice. It ran across my skin and resonated deep within my body. She was nowhere near as powerful as Titus or Grayson though. The royals controlled things down to their very blood. With Kendra it was more of a suggestion they wanted to follow. But for some unexplained reason, her abilities didn't have an effect on me. If they had, I would have killed her.

We strolled in a large cavern with our newly made

soldiers lining one side of the cavern. Kendra split them into groups based upon ability and set up stations around the cavern. It was roughly the size of a football field, with the dirt packed down hard at our feet and the walls and ceiling rough and dome-like. Torches lined the walls, and their flames flickered high, sending their light in all directions.

"Didn't get the electricity, I see?" I preferred the modern amenities and the luxuries they had to offer.

"We only just had the earth-movers create this space. The other holding cells and training rooms are full, and I prefer to get the soldiers ready in an orderly fashion.

"Then I'll allow it. See that it's updated soon though. We no longer live in medieval times, and as such, our living arrangements shall reflect our status." We strolled all along the smolders as they readied themselves.

Each group had a multitude of targets set up across from them. Kendra broke them down by elemental abilities. The fire-throwers wore red, the water-movers wore blue, the earth-movers wore brown, and of course the air-movers wore grey. It wasn't rocket science, but the simple organization made it possible to tell them all apart. At the other end of the cavern stood another group of vampires who were able to pick up and move boulders that would've crushed even the strongest vampire. There were more vampires crawling up the walls like cockroaches. They didn't need to dig their fingers in or leap from ledge to ledge, they simply climbed like spiders on a wall.

"Ready!" Kendra's voice boomed over the light hum in

the room, and they all fell silent. She held her hand up. "Aim! Fire!"

I jumped back as a group of vampires with fire abilities turned their targets into ash. The heat from the power burned my face and singed the hair on my eyebrows. "Marvelous." Even with the Witch Queens aligning themselves with The House of Shade, we would put up more than a good fight. A few feet farther down, the earth split open and large rocks jutted from the ground like spears. Dust and pebbles filled the air, and I found it difficult to breathe. I clapped my hands together. "This is very promising."

Elation filled my chest. After years of tests and practice and plotting, my dreams were finally coming to fruition. A smile tugged at my lips, and I fought the desire to let it show. Kendra walked with her hands clasped behind her back, studying each of the vampires like they were a prized horse. When she reached the water-movers, she stood before one who looked like he'd seen better days. He was sweating literal buckets of water, and his skin was a sickly blue. He looked too thin, too frail to be of any use.

"Problem, soldier?" She stopped right next to him.

His body quaked as he shook his head. "No, ma'am."

Yet the longer she stood there, the more nervous he grew. He pressed his hands to the sides of his head and a scream ripped up his throat. It was drowned out by a gurgle sound as though he were being forced down into a pool. His body turned from solid to translucent liquid.

Kendra took a step back just as the man exploded into a puddle of water.

She called over her shoulder. "Mop!"

"How often does that occur?" I stepped over the puddle and followed her as she moved closer to the wind-movers.

"One out of five who show water abilities tend to explode into puddles. Some of them re-form but mostly they just turn to water. I'm assuming they die." She glanced back at the puddle on the floor. "Would be a certain kind of hell if they were still alive when we mopped them up."

"I'd hoped we'd gotten past the exploding by now. But I see it's proving more difficult." I wanted each of my soldiers to be an unstoppable machine, not falling apart. "How disappointing."

"Like all armies, some recruits don't make it. We weed out the weak ones from our ranks to make them the strongest." She chuckled and brushed it off with a shrug. "It happens."

"I suppose you have a point." Human armies also weeded out their weakest links. I followed as she stopped in front of the air-movers.

They were the first lively bunch that I'd witnessed, and they all stood there laughing as they created a tornado at the center of their little group. A girl with bright eyes and wild, spiky hair ran right at the tornado and jumped into the wind. It caught her body, and she spun around with it. Laughter bubbled up her throat as she floated higher and higher, all the while holding her arms wide and letting the wind carry her up the funnel.

She popped out of the top and went sailing across the room. I thought she would surely smack into the wall and be crushed, but she threw her hands out, a gust fired from her palms, and she easily directed herself to a gentle landing. The others in the air-movers group all threw their hands up cheering for her. She clapped her hands together. "Woooo! Who's next?"

Another guy ran at the funnel and leapt right into it. I raised my eyebrows at Kendra. "Spirited, aren't they?"

"It seems to be a side effect, sir. The wind-movers are our daredevils, for lack of a better word. They have no fear, they just are."

"Difficult to control?" I didn't need liabilities, I needed results.

"For some perhaps." Her ruby lips pulled up in a wide smile. "But not for me, sir."

I didn't like having to rely on her powers to direct my army. Once I assumed the throne, I would have to reassess her usefulness. Kendra was loyal to a fault, but at one time so was I. I didn't need to make an enemy of someone whom the troops responded to. As if she could read my mind, the smile dropped from her face, and she smoothed her features.

I didn't want her to suspect my thoughts or intentions, so I placed a reassuring smile on my face. "You should be proud of the organization we have here."

The organization that I developed and directed.

"Yes, sir." She didn't return my smile. "I'm only following your plans."

At least she acknowledged my prowess. I would let her live . . . for now. "Of course, and what plans we shall make."

"The crown will be yours, and we will finally take our rightful place under your rule." She gave me a light bow. "Your Majesty."

"I quite like the sound of that." I watched as they all continued their training and found myself filling with pride. I had brought this about and now the crown was only days away from being mine. Our army was larger than I ever expected and more powerful after their second exposure to the smoke.

Kendra didn't rise from her bow. "You should get used to it."

"Yes." The others all began to follow suit and drop down to one knee, bowing to me. The entire room lowered themselves to me, and in this moment, I knew beyond a doubt I would be king.

CHAPTER THIRTY-THREE

PIPER

*a*s I walked back toward the dungeon with the other Queens, I wanted to have complete faith this would all work out. But a lifetime of disappointments told me otherwise. It wasn't that I was a pessimist, but things had been rough to say the least. Now my blood magic was all kinds of weird because of the wild—the wild power I got from a father I'd never met and probably would never see again. I still didn't know how to feel about that revelation. Not to mention there were three tiny mice who'd been following me since we left the throne room. Their little legs scurried as quickly as possible to keep up and I almost offered them my hand to give them a lift. The number of steps from the throne room to the dungeon must've seemed huge to them.

Dice bumped my shoulder with hers, drawing my attention to her as we walked. "Nervous?"

"A lot is riding on what happens next." I wanted

Grayson free so badly I could almost taste it. But she was right. I was nervous. There was so much happening so quickly it was overwhelming. But what other choice did I have but to keep on going?

The courtiers hurried out of the hallways as we walked in a massive group. The Queens were a sight to see with their powers swirling around them constantly. It wasn't that they did it on purpose, I'd learned that they just contained that much magic that it seeped from them at any given point—especially Zinnia, who still had flower petals falling around her because she tried to help me.

I paused and turned to the little mice. I crouched down and put my hand on the floor. "Come on. That's too much work for you guys."

Ophelia cackled. "I love when they scurry out of the way like cockroaches about to get stepped on."

"They're just mice." I had no idea why I needed to carry them but here we were. Normally I'd jump away from them, but now I somehow was as connected to them as they were to me.

"Oh, I wasn't talking about the mice." She chuckled. "They're cute. I was talking about the prissy vampires."

"They're not all bad." I'd met Martin, Eloura, and Moira among these courtiers. I knew they weren't all awful. Hell, I thought most of them were just scared of the unknown and change. The Witch Queens, Dice, and I were very unknown to them, and they were vampires who were very set in their ways.

"I didn't say they were bad. I said I liked when they

moved out of my way." She wagged her finger at me. "It's rough being short and not allowed to hurt people to make them move. I mean, it takes extra effort to duck and move."

"Oh right, yes. I could see that." Dice snickered beside me and shook her head. "You get used to her."

I didn't think I would ever get used to Ophelia. It was hard enough getting used to being a vampire and hanging out with witches. We were in the middle of an impending war and trying to break a curse. It was enough to drive anyone mad. My insides were tied into knots, and adrenaline had consistently pumped through my body since I'd returned. If we messed any of this up, then everything would be lost. Grayson would have to be killed to save others, Moira would never get over the loss, Titus wouldn't either, and I would never forgive myself. I couldn't imagine living without him, not now . . . not ever. We were so close to finding a solution.

I glanced at Dice. "I might be nervous."

"It's understandable. I mean, you're going into the Underworld." She lowered her voice, "Without actually dying."

My eyebrows drew low over my eyes, and I snorted. "Technically, I am kind of dead. Pretty sure I've been buried twice."

"Yeah, but it didn't take." She followed me through the lab, and even though I knew she wanted to walk around and explore the castle, she stuck with me. I was impressed how well she was taking all of this. I missed her all this time. Now I was finally with her again, but I barely had a moment to just regroup and check in.

"No, it really didn't." I scoffed and motioned to all the things surrounding us. "We never saw this coming."

"Not in a million years," She hooked her arm through mine and lowered her voice, "But I kind of feel at home in this world. Is that weird?"

"You're a human," Kylian snapped at her. "Of course it's weird. You don't belong here."

"Then I guess you should leave and stop worrying about me." Dice was so fast to retort I couldn't stifle the laugh that bubbled up my throat. Even the little mice in my other hand gave an entertained squeak.

Atlas melted from the shadows and moved to walk behind us. "We could only be so lucky."

Kylian stepped in front and pushed the door to the dungeon open for us. "I think I'll stick around. I have a feeling things are about to get intriguing."

"You mean profitable." Dice rolled her eyes at him as she tugged me past him.

We moved down the familiar walkway between the cells. Thick metal bars lined each side, and most of the cells were empty. If they did have a prisoner, they huddled into a dark corner hoping not to draw our attention in any way. I couldn't blame them. If I wasn't friends with the Queens, I'd find them terrifying as well. When we reached Grayson's cell, I stopped and placed my little mice friends on the floor, letting them roam free. When I rose to stand, my eyes locked on Grayson, and I couldn't stop myself from staring at him. He was so beautiful yet so fucked up. In the back of my mind, I wondered if he would ever be himself again. I shook my head, trying to push those away. This had to work . . . It just had to.

Zinnia cleared her throat, getting our attention, and turned to the guardians who stayed behind to keep watch over Grayson. "So, we have to return to the underworld for the Crone."

"Fuuuuuuucccckkkkkkkk." Tucker kicked at the ground, then ran his hand through his hair. "Sounds like a bad idea."

"A really bad idea." Ashryn didn't rise from her chair, where she sat resting her hand over her abdomen. Thick bandages were wrapped around her stomach and shoulder. She winced and tried to sit forward only to lean back in the chair.

Cross strolled up next to Ophelia. "So the Underworld again?"

"I'll bring you back a souvenir." She went up on her toes and pressed a kiss to his cheek.

Cross wrapped his arm around her waist and pulled her tight against him. "I believe we've been separated long enough."

O gave a little giggle and leaned into him. "Yeah, we have."

"Ew, no." Astrid wrinkled her nose at them. "Listen, some of us are going to have to go, but some of us are going to have to stay behind to keep an eye on Gray and the castle."

My mind cried out. *No, absolutely not.* "We can't leave him here."

"What? Why not?" Zinnia glanced around the cell. "He's trapped in here with guards."

"No offense." I glanced at all of them. "But he's gotten out before, and we have no idea if Lucifer is going to return for him again or not."

Zinnia bit her bottom lip and nodded. "I mean, good point. What do you suggest?"

I hurried down the hall and rushed into a cell to pick up a pair of vampire handcuffs. I handed them over to Ophelia. "Can you reinforce these?"

She shrugged. "Easily."

I handed them over, and she hurried into her own cell across from Grayson. Bright flashes of magic flooded the dark cell and spilled out into the hallway. Grayson howled from his spot on the floor, and I turned to face him. I opened my hand and thought with intention. I had to be sure what I was doing when I pulled my blood magic from that well of power deep in the pit of my stomach. The moment my blood magic began to flow around me, wolves howled all around the outside of the castle and something large hit the doors, rattling the castle.

Beckett's eyes widened as they darted over the walls and ceiling. "Here we go."

My mist flowed over the floor and right at Grayson. It touched the white chalk perimeter and drifted up and over it. He popped to his feet and took a step back away from it, but he was trapped. When his back pressed to the magical border, he growled in my direction. But I couldn't stop, I let my power crawl up his body and wrap around his shoulders. It danced along his skin up to his full lips. The magic seeped into him, and I could almost feel every part of him. The real Grayson, the one that was pushed down so far he was being crushed by this curse, lingered there just out of my reach. I forced my power up to his mouth and moved in closer to the bars. He narrowed his eyes at me, but I refused to look away.

"No biting." I kept a hold over him and knew my words had an effect. It wasn't a request but a command he had to follow. "Ophelia, are we ready?"

Ophelia hurried out of the cell and handed the cuffs over to Astrid. "Do your thing."

"No, wait." I ran into the cell and moved closer to Grayson. "Cuff him to me."

"You have really gotten into some kinky shit." Dice chuckled.

"He is not leaving my side. Astrid, go ahead and do it." I gave her a reassuring nod. "I'm strong enough now."

She held the cuffs out in front of her and wrapped them in her golden magic. They disappeared from her hands and appeared around our wrists. I thought they'd be uncomfortable, but Astrid added padding around the cuff and more length to the chain so I could move more easily. Grayson's eyes dipped to where we were connected, and a menacing smirk spread across his face. "Mine now."

I jerked him toward me until he hit the magical circle holding him in. "Mine."

"Yeah, so hot," Dice teased from outside the cell.

Ophelia sauntered into the cell and brushed a line through the circle surrounding Grayson. The second he was free, he tried to bolt for the door. I yanked him back and we both stumbled and collided. A growl rumbled deep in his chest, and I held my hand up. "You're stuck with me."

"Whole new level of stalking for you," Dice teased.

I stifled a chuckle and turned to the others. "Okay, I'm ready. Let's get us to the underworld."

Grayson tensed by my side, but when I let my power flow over him, he calmed.

Zinnia motioned to Tabi. "Can you please draw the symbol?"

"On it." Tabi hovered over the hard-packed floor and waved her hand over the dirt. Yellow bands of her magic hopped on the floor in a pattern I couldn't make out. The ground split ever so slightly and a shape began to take form. First a complete circle, then a half-moon shape under that. She finished it off with a X over the whole thing. She rose to her feet and dusted off her hands. "That should do it."

The shape glowed a bright white color and then we all stood there waiting. Nothing happened.

Zinnia shifted uncomfortably and glanced at Tuck. "Something is wrong."

"We don't know that."

"She usually answers pretty quickly." Zinnia paced

around the symbol. "If anything happened to her down there, I'll never forgive him."

"Him who?" I was growing anxious just watching Zinnia worry.

"Liesin, the son of Hades." More flower petals fell around her as more nervous magic spilled around her. "He's got a thing for Nova. If something happened to her, I'd put money on the fact it was him."

"Oh." It was the only response I could come up with. "If Nova doesn't show up, then how do we get to the underworld?"

"There's an entrance in an abandoned asylum in Philly, but I'd hate to revisit that little adventure." She continued pacing.

"I second that." Tuck crossed his arms. "Let's just give her a minute before we plan to infiltrate the Underworld to find her."

"Oh I'm planning." Ophelia reached into her satchel of potions on her hip and pulled out a rolled-up piece of parchment. "I've made a list of entry points and places we could easily attack. Also, places we need to avoid."

Everyone paused, staring at her. She returned their blank stares. "What? I had a free afternoon."

Beckett sighed and pinched the bridge of his nose. "Sometimes I worry about your stability."

"Look, I have the ability to stab just fine. You're all lucky I don't." She shoved the paper back into her potions' pouch. "Don't say I never helped you."

While I wanted to stand here and debate ways to get us all to the underworld, I grew anxious. What if we could get there? What if we had to travel farther to get there? I was so used to portaling or traveling by mirror that I never considered the time it would take to go the long way. By the time we got back, if we got back, Titus and Moira might be under attack. We didn't have the luxury of time here. Not when so much was at stake. Just when I was about to suggest we leave and find another way, the markings on the floor glowed even brighter.

The ground cracked into the shape Tabi drew and fell piece by piece through the floor. A man with long white hair rose from the opening. Half his head was shaved, while strands of hair fell over his forehead and into his eyes. The rest of his hair fell almost to his waist. When he peered up at us, his gaze was ice-cold, and his lips were pressed into a thin line. I took a small step back. This was obviously not Nova.

"Thanatos?" Maze's eyes widened.

Thanatos gave a deep, annoyed sigh. He stood before us with one hand pressed behind his back and the other held at his side. His black suit was pressed with clean, crisp lines and matched his shirt, vest, and polished shoes perfectly. "Obviously."

Zinnia looked him up and down. "Where's Nova?"

He rolled his eyes and gave her a bored look. "You summon her like she's still part of your little . . . team." He wrinkled his nose with disdain. "You forget yourselves and the deal she made. Nova is indebted to Hades, and he rules all of the underworld, which is more vast than any of you could possibly fathom. Do you think she can come and go as she pleases? That would be counter-productive to the bargain that was struck."

"Then why are you here?" The words were out of my mouth before I could stop them. "If she's not allowed to come to us, then what brought you here?"

"I am doing this as a favor to Nova." His voice was deep and monotone. "We are *friends* . . . of a sort."

Zinnia pointed at his chest. "So you're going to bring us into the underworld?"

"Unfortunately." He motioned to the hole. "So off we go."

We all stepped forward and Thanatos stepped in front of the hole, stopping us. "This is not a field trip for the class. Make your choices about who is going and be quick about it."

I knew Grayson and I would go, and much to my surprise, I wanted Ophelia with us. But I pressed my lips into a line as Dice got closer to me. She glanced at the floor, then back up at me. "I guess this is where I tap out?"

I didn't want to leave Dice here, but I didn't know what it would be like in the underworld or if a human could even survive down there. "I don't know what we're walking into, and I don't know if we can keep you safe."

"I guess I can understand that." She let out a little huff. "I guess the afterlife will just have to wait."

"For a long, long time." *I hope.*

"When you get back, we'll work on my immortality.

Friends for life." She winked. "Atlas doesn't know what'll hit him."

"Atlas has ears and objects to this plan." He straightened his shoulders. "And I'm going."

"You can't." I shook my head. When he opened his mouth to protest, I cut him off. "War is coming in on all sides of the crown. Titus and Moira need you now. I'll be with the Queens, and Grayson needs a family to come home to."

A growl rumbled deep in Atlas's chest. "I do not enjoy the direction of this plan, but I will be amenable to it. I will watch over The House of Shade as well as Dice, so you and Grayson will have something to return to."

"It's true that I do need someone to keep an eye on me." Dice took a step toward him.

"I'll keep an eye on you." Kylian leaned his back against the bars and crossed his arms over his chest. "All the time."

"Ew, find a well and fall into it." Dice turned back toward me.

"Sure, I'll play Timmy if you play Lassie and come find me."

Dice wrinkled her nose. "Did you just call me a dog?"

"No, I *am* coming!" Tucker's voice rose, cutting off all conversation.

Zinnia placed her hand on his forearm and made her voice gentle. "You're injured. You have to stay here and rest."

"I'm well enough." I'd never heard his voice so harsh and demanding.

Ophelia marched up to him and without warning punched him right in the back—in that very spot where the knife had been embedded.

Tuck dropped to one knee and let out a deep groan. "What the hell?"

"You're injured and will only slow us down." Ophelia stood over him, gazing down at his back. "And now you're bleeding."

"Did you really have to tear his stitches?" Zinnia bent down and wrapped her arm under him, helping him to his feet.

"I barely touched him, which just proves my point."

"Enough of this." Thanatos motioned to the hole. "Decide or I'll leave. Now."

Zinnia held her hands out, silencing us all. "The Queens need to go to make our plan work—"

"See, we've already got an injured Serrina to worry about, we don't nee—"

"O." Zinnia's voice was sharp and cutting. "Enough."

"Fiiinneeee."

"The guardians will stay." She met each of their eyes, giving them a stern look. "And *we* will go with Piper and Grayson."

Maze cleared his throat. "And me. I have knowledge about the Crone and personal dealings with her. You're going to want me."

"I'll give you that," Zinnia grumbled. "But that's it. We're not going to abuse Thanatos's generosity."

His uncanny crystal eyes roamed over the little group we had. "Because six of you is a little group."

His words held a sarcastic edge that I chose to ignore. A few months ago, if he'd walked into the bar with that attitude, I would've given it right back to him. But standing here in his debt, I wanted to remain in his good graces. "Can I please just have one more moment?"

"By all means." Again his words were both monotone and sarcastically sharp at the same time, a talent he must've developed over his multitude of life times. He waved me on. "We have all day."

"Beckett." I turned to face him. "Can you please bring Moira here? I want to give her the chance to say goodbye."

"It'll all work out, Piper," Zinnia tried to reassure me. But we were walking into a world of death. There were no guarantees we'd come back, and if that was the case, I wanted Moira to have the chance to say goodbye to her son.

I closed my eyes for a moment, trying to form the right words. When I opened them, they were all silently waiting for me to speak. "I know it will. But just in case it doesn't, I think she deserves a moment with him. Don't you?"

"Say no more." Beckett opened his hand and his smoky blue magic formed an oval shape that grew until it became a swirling portal. He popped his head through. I could hardly make out his muffled words. When he reached through and took a step back, guiding Moira through the portal and into the dungeon, I nearly lost it.

It wasn't that I didn't have faith in us, but I almost

didn't want to stay to watch a mother let go of her beloved son.

She folded her hands in front of her, and Grayson snarled in her direction. She hardly flinched, hardly. "I see that you're off."

The sadness hung heavy in her eyes as they shimmered with unshed tears. "Moira, I wanted to give you a moment with him . . . the real him."

She shucked in a sharp breath, and I turned to Grayson. He extended his fangs and hissed at me, but I felt no fear of him. I was his and he was mine. The chain between us rattled as I reached for his hand and drew him toward my lips. He froze like a caged animal, yet he was entranced by my movements. I held his wrist to my mouth and let my fangs extend. He had to know what I was going to do, yet he didn't pull back or move away from me. I parted my lip and bit into his wrist. That deep red wine flavor hit my tongue and I wanted to moan at how delicious he was. I took a greedy pull, then another. The lines from his eyes cleared, and they went from the dark bottomless pit to the warm chocolatey color with those mahogany flecks.

"Piper," he whispered my name like a prayer.

I pulled back. "We don't have much time. But we're going to break the curse. The mission is dangerous."

"Then don't do it, little creature. Let me go."

I didn't have time to argue. We were going and that was the end of it. I turned him toward Moira.

She took a step forward and a tear leaked from the corner of her eye. She quickly brushed it away. In an uncharacteristic move, she threw her arms around him and pulled him close. He was so much bigger than her slight frame, but she rested her head on his chest, holding him close. "Oh my boy."

Grayson wrapped his arms around her. "Mother, I'm so sorry . . . for all of this."

"No, it's not your fault." She pulled back and tears ran freely down her cheeks. "You listen to me, this is not your fault nor has it ever been."

"Mother, I—"

"Hush now." She cupped his cheek. "There are things that need to be said. It has been the privilege of my life being your mother. You've brought so much light and joy to my existence."

A single tear fell onto his cheek. "I love you, Mum."

Her breath hitched and a light sob drifted from her chest. "I have always and will always love you. I am so proud of you."

He opened his mouth to speak once more but red lines forked out over his eyes and he sucked in a breath, holding it while the light in his warm eyes died and he turned from vampire to beast once more.

She swiped away her tears as she turned to face me. "You bring him back. You bring my son back to me."

That was a promise I couldn't make. I didn't know if we would make it back or if this would work. "I would love to do that more than anything."

She pressed her lips into a hard line and gave me a nod. Without another word, she marched from the dungeon with her dress billowing around her legs with each step she took.

Thanatos cleared his throat. "Oh, how I love teary goodbyes. Can we go now . . .?"

He waved his hand over the hole in the ground, and it glowed with bright white light once more. Black and blue bolts of lightning flickered in the white light and he motioned to it. Ophelia was the first to stroll up. "So is this how you kill people?"

"Jump in and find out," he grumbled with little emotion.

I didn't want to die, not here and now. We had so much to do, and we were just getting started. But Creator help me, I was going to jump into that damn thing and I was going to drag Grayson with me.

CHAPTER THIRTY-FOUR

KYLIAN

I savored the burn of whiskey as it flowed down my throat and hit my stomach like a hammer. There was something in the smoky oak flavor that reminded me of home. The burn was just a benefit that woke up the senses. I leaned against a thick tree trunk. This close to home, I could smell the clean fresh breeze coming off the mountains surrounding Windelos. I raised my face to the night sky and let the blue light of the moon settle over my skin. I took another swig from the flask, and my lips peeled back from my teeth. As I screwed the lid back on, the liquid quietly swished around within the flask, and I shoved it back into the inside pocket of my jacket.

This time of year, a thick layer of frost clung to the trees, making them look more like ice sculptures than the giant beauties they were. The snow was up over my ankles and soaked into my boots, chilling my feet, yet I hardly perceived the cold thanks to the whiskey. This little reprieve was a welcomed distraction from the castle and the people who currently occupied it. I had yet to figure out what drew me to the little human. Somehow my interest was piqued, though she grated on my nerves like no other.

Heavy footfalls made their way toward me, and I glanced across the small clearing. "For a vampire, you're not very stealthy."

"I figured if you heard me comin', there'd be less chance of you throwing a knife at my head, ya know what I mean?" Lorenzo Romano was an older vampire I'd dealt with from time to time. He didn't much like elves and I didn't much like vampires, yet our past dealings had always been profitable on both ends, to say the least.

"I was surprised to get your call." I pushed away from the tree to meet him halfway. "I didn't realize you took an interest in vampire politics."

He huddled in his long wool coat. "I don't."

"Then why am I here?" I raised my eyebrows at him.

"I didn't realize you were hanging out at the castle." He shoved his hands into his pockets. "Yet when I call, there you were. Care to explain that?"

I'd always found his heavy Staten Island accent somewhat charming. There was something rough yet straightforward about it. Like he didn't have the time or energy to pronounce everything fully, so a person could either get with the program or get moving, which summed up Lorenzo. He had a finger in a lot of different pies, yet he kept them all in line and wasn't afraid to get his hands dirty.

"Not particularly." I wasn't about to admit that a foul-mouthed human brought on a sense of curiosity I hadn't quite figured out yet.

"Fair enough." He glanced around the forest. "Anyways, I appreciate you getting me this meetin'."

I shrugged. "It's an odd call, but I'm intrigued enough to be here."

"You're sure she'll show?" He peeked over his shoulder. "Because I don't see nothing from where I'm standin'."

If the 1920s could produce a perfect gangster, it would be Lorenzo, who stood in the snow in his polished dress shoes and charcoal slacks. He even wore a hat tipped low over his eyes.

I shrugged. "That's because she doesn't want to be seen." I turned toward the forest and called out, "Lyra, someone to see you."

Lyra, the first general of the Windelos army and current traitor, emerged from the darkness like she'd peeled away the shadows. She was all long limbs and graceful movements as she walked toward us. Her flaming red hair was long down her back with braids woven throughout in a wild pattern. The tips of her ears peeked through the waves, and when she looked at the two of us, her gaze was almost feline in nature. The bright-green of her eyes complimented the blue light from the moon shining down on her.

A large grizzly bear walked at a distance behind her, but

I could see the gold chainmail hanging over its chest. It was the same color gold that glinted on Lyra's breastplate. Her sword was strapped to her hip, and I knew she could draw it and take our heads in less than a second. As she approached, she gave me a sideways glance to go along with a cool greeting. "Prince Kylian, you called?"

"I appreciate you coming to this meeting." I had made it a habit not to contact anyone from Windelos, even my closest friend: Victor. It was better for all of us if I remained in the dishonorable shadows where I belonged.

Lyra stopped just in front of me. "I wasn't aware you were in the habit of doing business with vampires."

"I'm in the habit of doing profitable business," I countered. "If it's with vampires, then so be it."

She peered down her nose at Lorenzo. "I see."

"Oh, come on. We aren't that bad." Lorenzo gave her a cocky grin and I could've sworn Lyra did a double take.

Lorenzo was a handsome bastard, and he knew it. He also knew when to turn it on and when to shut it down. Yet I'd never seen him with another female in the years that I'd known him.

Lyra pursed her lips. "Yes, well, state your business."

"I like when we get to the point of things." He spoke with his hands as he gestured between himself and Lyra. "From what I hear, you're havin' a bit of a problem with your Queen."

"And?"

"And it just so happens that I have a King who could use your help. The way I see it, you help him with his problem, and he'll help you with yours in the future." He folded his hands in front of him. "Take a second and think about it."

"You do realize you're speaking of treason?" The bear lumbered closer and stood between Lyra and me.

I tried not to pay him any attention, though it was difficult.

"I've just arranged a meeting. I'm not speaking of anything." If there was anything I was good at, it was keeping my hands dirty and my nose clean.

"This will only work to your advantage." Lorenzo's voice was smooth and soothing. If he'd been human, he could sell anything to anyone. As a vampire, he only grew his holdings and never lost. "*If* you make an alliance with the Vampire King."

Ever the cold shrewd, General Lyra only took a few moments to think the offer over. "What's in it for us?"

Lorenzo shrugged like the subject of war and treason wasn't a big deal, but we'd met in the frozen woods to discuss things that ought never be discussed. "There's a war coming. I know it, they know it. You scratch their backs, and they scratch yours. Don't forget the vampires are now in a strong alliance with the Witch Queens. Now, you can either be in bed with them or face them later. The decision is yours. I'm just a humble messenger."

Kylian scoffed. "Fuckkk. You're good."

"Eh, I dabble." He brushed a snowflake from the lapel of his wool coat. "I like to help people."

Lyra ran her hand over the bear's neck and let her fingers curl into his fur. She peeked over the bear toward me. "Our people are suffering. You know this has to be done. Your mother is playing a dangerous game."

I knew my mother well . . . and her games. There was a time when she was the master and I was the apprentice, now my skills had improved. Whether or not it was enough to outmaneuver her was another question. "As are you."

Her hand froze in place on the bear's neck and her eyes dropped to where her finger lay. "My loyalties are always to Windelos and the elves."

"I don't think there's any doubt about that. But if you want help, and I mean powerful help, you're gonna have to scratch a few backs. Ya know what I mean? The world ain't so big anymore and making friends helps." Lorenzo took a step toward me and caught Lyra's eye. "So what's it going to be?"

She jerked her chin in his direction. "What's in this for you, vampire?"

Lorenzo gave that nonchalance shrug again like none of this mattered either way. "I'm like you . . . making friends. Plus, it's just good business. Who doesn't want to be owed a favor from the King?"

She hopped up onto the back of the bear in a silent and graceful move. "If we do this, then we will need confirmation that the King has accepted the deal, and when we call, he will answer."

Lorenzo smirked, "Yeah, that can be arranged."

"How?" She peered down at him as she shoved her helmet back in place.

"I'm gonna offer him a gift. If he accepts, then we have a deal. If he declines, then you march your army home, and I will be happy to compensate you for your time."

The corner of her lip twitched like she fought a smile. "Then I believe we have a deal."

She gave the bear a little nudge and it turned for the forest, lumbering away. I thought it would leave a trail of destruction in its wake, but as soon as it touched the dark shadows of night, it was gone.

I turned back to Lorenzo. "You're damn good."

"Eh, sometimes. But there's always someone better."

I chuckled. "Let me know when you meet them."

"Oh, Dark Prince, I already have." He winked. "I'll be seeing you soon."

"Undoubtedly." Considering I couldn't help but be drawn back to the castle, back to her . . .

CHAPTER THIRTY-FIVE

ELOURA

"This is a stressful time for the King, and I'm hoping to ease that." These were delicate times full of delicate matters. My loyalty was to the King, but something told me Lorenzo could be the ally we needed.

"Yeah, I know, we're making friends." Lorenzo offered me his arm and my eyes widened as I took it.

We strolled down the long halls of the castle toward the throne room. Lorenzo didn't show the usual curiosity that new visitors did when moving through the halls. He didn't stare at the dark, gothic walls or tapestries hanging in sporadic places. His eyes didn't light with interest as we passed the courtiers in their finery. Nor did he look at me oddly when he saw me in my corseted navy-blue dress. It dragged the floor as we walked, yet he seemed to know what pace to keep so I wouldn't get it caught.

I hesitated. "The King might not trust you."

He gave a warm dark chuckle. "Trust is earned. Isn't that right, Eloura?

The way he said my name made me feel like we were heading toward a rendezvous in a dark corner. It was almost a purr on his lips and I didn't know how to react to that. I gave a light cough to clear my throat. "It is indeed."

Just outside of the throne room, Martin stood waiting for us both. I motioned to him. "Lorenzo, this is Martin. Martin, may I introduce Lorenzo Romano."

"A pleasure, Mr. Romano." Martin extended his hand out to him and Lorenzo quickly took it.

"The pleasure is all mine." Lorenzo's eyes darted up and down the hall, then he lowered his voice, "I've heard . . . things about you."

A grin tugged at Martin's lips. "All good I hope."

"Depends." Lorenzo straightened. "From what I hear, you're the master of information. Is that true?"

Martin ran his hand down the front of his burgundy suit, brushing at a spot just above his midsection. "My skills are adequate."

"Yeah, that's what a guy who's good would say." He gave Martin a side-eye. "It's very nice to meet you, Martin."

We weren't here to make alliances with Martin. "What are you doing?"

"Making friends." He chuckled. "I'm gettin' good at it."

The doors to the throne room creaked open, revealing the King who sat tall and proud on this throne. If he had worries, it did not show in his placid face. Titus was many things at many times but always in control of himself. His long hair flowed perfectly down to his shoulders, and his beard was trimmed neatly on his face. His eyes were sharp as he watched us enter the throne room. His long velvet coat hung loose on his arms as he rested them on his chair, and it flowed to the floor where it pooled at his feet. Under his coat, he wore a pressed white shirt and black trousers. Beside him, Moira stood gracefully still, but there was an unusually heavy sadness about her. More sadness than usual. She too was in her best finery with a long pink dress that cut tight to her body. Gauzy material covered her arms and wound high on her neck. Her hair was pulled into a tight bun at the nape of her neck with braids and twists winding around it.

Lorenzo and I stopped just before the dais. I dropped my hand from his arm and gave them a deep bow just as Lorenzo bent at the hips to give the King a gracious bow. I swept my hand toward Lorenzo. "Your Majesty, may I introduce Mr. Lorenzo Romano."

A deep rumble echoed in Titus's throat. "I've heard much about you, Mr. Romano."

"Lorenzo, please, Your Majesty." He straightened his stance and met the King's eye.

"Very well." Titus sighed and rose to his feet. "Lorenzo it is."

There was an edge to the King, his temper seemed at a short fuse, and the closer I studied him, the more I realized his shoulders were rigid with tension. He marched off the dais and moved over to the sideboard. He plucked up a glass decanter and held it out to Lorenzo. "Care to partake?"

Lorenzo gave me a side-eyed glance. "Of course.

The King poured two glasses. "I know the others will refuse. They've lost the taste for good bourbon."

I wrinkled my nose. "Or never acquired a taste for it to begin with, my lord."

"Or that," the King agreed as he handed the glass to Lorenzo. "I understand you have some interests in the Blood Borns of our society."

"I wouldn't say interests. They're indebted to me." He shrugged. "It's a very simple arrangement."

Titus took a deep drink and nodded. "And you've no interest in growing your status among them?"

"My interests are purely financial. I don't have any use for titles and mostly I like to dabble in business. But the high-class life," he shook his head, "It ain't for me. I prefer to get my hands dirty on occasion."

"How . . . refreshing." Titus raised his glass to him. "You'll forgive me if I don't quite believe or trust you."

"Not for nothin', but if you did believe me, I'd think you were a fool. And guys who are fools only end up in two places in my line of work." He held up two fingers. "Broke or dead, or both, so I prefer you didn't trust me."

"What an interesting outlook on life." Titus chuckled over the brim of his glass. "So, what's in this little arrangement for you?"

"Someone pointed out to me that the favor of a king

would be more beneficial than the debts of the rich." His warm honey eyes met mine and he winked. "I happened to think that's a smart move. Look at it this way, in the future, if you need something done, could be anything really, you'll come to me and I'll handle it. Perhaps there's a small fee or perhaps it'll bring more business to my doorstep."

"I don't fall in with loan sharks," Titus retorted honestly.

"I can see that." Lorenzo took a sip of his drink and his lips peeled back from his teeth. "That is delicious. But what you gotta realize is, I'm in more than just the shark business. I hear you're building a city. You use my guys and everybody is happy. Plus, I've met your Blood Borns, they are a few bagels short of a dozen, if ya know what I mean."

Titus turned back toward the sideboard and poured a small glass of blood wine. When he strolled past us over to Moira, he softened his voice. "Drink. You need it."

Without a word she took it and gave him a nod of thanks. "Thank you, Your Majesty."

I wanted to walk over to her to speak with her and let her worries become my own. Yet I knew I couldn't, not at this crucial time. When Titus turned back to us, all eyes fell on him. "If that is what you're after, then I'm sure that can be arranged. Martin assures me you're in no financial need."

Lorenzo gave a half-snort, half-chuckle. "Yes, I'm sure Martin has."

"Look, I'd be lyin' if I said I wasn't building my own empire. But the way I see it, our operations would co-exist nicely. You be King. I don't want nothin' to do with that. But I do want the business a connection like that would make. I'm not in it for nothing. But at the moment, it seems your needs and my wants align."

"I can assure you neither of you wants for anything," Martin interjected. "I've run the numbers, you both stand to gain heavily from an arrangement such as this."

The King paused. "How do I know your interests won't change in the future?"

Lorenzo finished the contents of his glass in one quick gulp. "What if I can prove my loyalty?"

Titus arched his eyebrows at him. "How?"

"Let's not pull punches here. Your Blood Borns are an advantageous bunch. And when I say advantageous, they want your crown, your castle, and your wealth." He strolled over to the sideboard and placed his glass down on the silver tray.

Titus shrugged as though this were old news. "Yes, well, greed is something the privileged are known for."

Lorenzo paused and licked his full lips. "And murder? Are they known for that too?"

His words brought me up short. The last I'd heard, they were trying to hire an army to fight against Titus and take the throne. There was no mention of murder. "What are you talking about?"

Lorenzo picked up the decanter and examined the contents of the rich, dark liquid. "When their attempt to purchase an army didn't go well, they resorted to other things. More desperate things."

This seemed to pique Titus' interest. There was a sharp glint in his eye as he watched Lorenzo. "Such as?"

"A party. You should get the invitation any day now. When you go to the party, they're going to offer you a bottle of your own personal favorite, a nice blue label blood, if memory serves." He waved his hand in front of the decanter as if saying, *Exhibit A, Your Honor.* "Maybe you don't drink the wine. Maybe you take a glass from the other bottle, then switch the labels and see what happens."

Titus's eyes went round. "They wouldn't."

"They would," Lorenzo countered.

Moira stepped to Titus's side. "And then what happens?"

Lorenzo placed the glass decanter back down on the tray with a little *clink*. "And then we, you and me, form the beginning of a mutually beneficial friendship."

For a vampire who was relatively new to this world, he seemed to be playing chess while the rest of them continued their game of checkers. "Quite the game you're playing."

"I don't play games." He turned to face me fully and I felt the heat in his gaze roam over me. "I win them."

My tongue darted over my lips, and for a moment the flash of his body against mine ran through my mind. I cleared my throat. "Where did they get the poisoned wine?"

A full, broad smile parted his lips. "From me."

Titus chuckled and shook his head. "Then I suppose we'll have to attend a party, Eloura. Won't we?"

"No." Moira's words were hardly louder than a whisper, yet we all heard her perfectly. "I can't bear it if something happened to you t—"

"Nothing will happen," Titus reassured her. "We must protect the crown, not just for us but so Grayson has a home to return to."

Grayson? Where had the Prince gone? I wanted to ask so many questions, but I held my tongue. This was a conversation left for private matters. But the pain in Moira's gaze as she nodded her head told me things weren't going well for her or our young Prince.

Titus turned back to face me. "It seems we will have a party to attend. Won't we, Eloura?"

Lorenzo balked. "Her?"

"Never you mind about me. You might win the games, but I am the master at the rules." I turned my face up toward Titus. "It seems we must."

Martin reached into the inside pocket of his suit coat. "Then it's a happy coincidence that I happen to have this invitation."

Lorenzo chuckled and clapped him on the shoulder, jostling Martin. "I love this guy. You and me, we gotta have a chat sometime."

"Yes." Martin ran his hand over his perfectly combed back hair. "Indeed."

Lorenzo motioned to the pristine white envelope. "Enjoy your dinner."

Titus's fangs extended into a sign of aggression I hadn't seen in some time. It sent a shiver down my spine but made confidence bloom in my chest. He would protect the crown and us all from whatever might come our way. "If your loyalty is proven here, then we will have a deal."

"I have no doubt it will be." Lorenzo gave him a little bow. "Yeah, you'll call me."

CHAPTER THIRTY-SIX

PIPER

I jumped into the bright shining light and felt the tug of the handcuffs around my wrist. They didn't cut or bite into my skin the way the shackles Marius used on me did. It was quick thinking of Astrid to line them with leather and fur. I didn't want to know where that thought process came from on her part, but I wasn't going to question it. Grayson snarled and as we free fell down the hole. Did he know where we were going? Or what we were doing? Or was this all overwhelming to him as much as it was to me?

Black and blue lighting struck around us but never touched our skin. I felt the sizzle of electricity all around me and my hair stood on edge, but it never touched me. I searched for the others in this swirling mess of magic, but they were nowhere to be found. Panic threatened to take over but then I reminded myself I'd been in worse situations fairly recently. The ground rushed up toward us and I braced for impact. At the last second, we slowed to a stop a mere foot off the ground.

I held my arms out to my sides. "Um, hello?"

We plummeted that single foot, and I was so caught off guard I bobbled slightly when my feet hit the ground. Grayson yanked the chain and pulled me toward him, and I collided with his chest. He wrapped his arms around me and began to squeeze. The air was forced from my lungs, and I struggled against his hold. *NO.* I screamed my objection in my mind, and my blood magic exploded from my body in an angry cloud of red and sage. Grayson roared in my face, but his arms dropped their hold, and I took a step back.

Anger flared through my body, and I yanked on the chain, forcing him to stumble forward the way he'd jerked me. When he recovered his balance, he growled in my direction, and I waited for him to attack or swing at me. Instead, he simply hissed in my direction. *Does he know we are here to save him?*

He lashed out with his hand. It was curved into a claw and his nails were sharp and jagged. I leaned back and the swipe missed my face by inches. My instincts kicked in and my arm shot out. My hand cracked across his face and I wagged a finger at him. "No!"

A deep snarl curled his lips, but he didn't try to do anything more. I had to assume he was more animal than man so physical checks might be in order. I could do it for as long as it took. I just had to remind myself this wasn't my Grayson, and the real one would never dare hurt me. I turned from him, trying to figure out where exactly we were.

"Zin?" I called out, only to be answered with silence. "Astrid?" More silence. "Shittttt."

I turned in a half circle and had no idea where we were or even how to get us closer to the others. We were alone and surrounded by tall hedges that loomed around us like giant walls. They were as thick as they were tall. I couldn't see through them or over them. Grayson and I were completely alone and lost in the underworld.

"Alone at last." His words were a threatening growl that would've sent a shiver down my spine only days ago. Now they grated on my nerves. I needed the real Grayson to help me through this. To somehow get us out of here.

"Ugh, shut up." I couldn't even discern the hour of the day when we left. It'd just turned to evening. But when I looked up, there was no sky, or at least I didn't think it was a sky. It was more like a rough cave covered in glowing stalactites. The sound of flapping wings drew my gaze back up, and I tried to make out the creature there. It was too dark and all there was were shadows above us.

I turned to Grayson. "Run."

He planted his feet and gave me a cocky grin, all the while the flapping grew closer. I didn't have time for this shit. He wagged his eyebrows at me, and I wanted to smack that smirk off his face. But I would save my anger for later. Right now, we needed to survive whatever was coming our way. I turned and started running, dragging Grayson behind me. The wings flapped harder above, yet there was no place for us to go or hide.

Grayson cackled and that drew the creature closer to us. We'd never get away like this, not when we were being hunted by some kind of winged creature. Black feathers drifted around us and a light tinkering laugh cut through the air. This thing was entertained by our running. When the giant hedge curved to the left, I followed it and hurried my steps. The creature swooped down, and I pulled Grayson to the side just as two huge talons grabbed at the space where he'd just been. I wrapped my arms around Grayson and dragged him to the ground. We rolled to the side just under the edge of the hedge. My chest heaved, my breaths mixing with Grayson's as he pressed his body on top of mine.

A growl rumbled in his chest, and I felt the vibration against me. He pressed his hands on either side of my body and tried to force himself up. I pulled him back down. "Shhh, they'll find us." He snarled in my face, snapping his teeth inches from my nose. I didn't know how much longer I could keep this up without the others. "Fuck it."

I grabbed his chin and turned his face away from me. I sank my teeth into his neck and let his warm flavor rush into my mouth. I didn't drink much of him, I just needed a moment with my Grayson, the one who knew this world and how to get out of this mess.

A groan slipped past his lips and his body melted into mine. "Piper?"

I pulled back to look him in the eye. "Gray, oh God."

"What the devil is going on?" His warm chocolate eyes took in our little spot under a hedge and then he turned back to me. "I smell death."

"Look, we don't have much time." I sucked in a breath, loving his warm scent and the feel of him against my body. "We're in the underworld."

He froze. "Why the hell are we in the underworld?"

"We're going to make a deal with the Crone to break the curse."

"That's bloody ridiculous." I pressed my fingers over his mouth, silencing him.

"It's already been decided." The flapping stopped and the hedge above us jostled. A prickly branch scratched at my arm. "We are here."

"You came here alone?! Are you daft?"

"You know it would be nice if you said *thank you, Piper, for trying to save my ass*," I whisper-hissed back at him. "We're being chased by a flying thing in the underworld, and I have no idea what to do."

Those forked veins began to appear in his eyes, but I couldn't let him go, not yet. I jerked his head back down to me and nipped his neck. The veins receded, and he shook his head. "Bit handy, that is."

"Gray, how do I get us out of here?" If I knew more about this place, I wouldn't have asked, I would've just kept going, but this was the underworld. It was as vast as it was shrouded in darkness.

"Why are their flowers in your hair?" He ran his fingers

through my long dark locks and let them wrap around his fingers. "You smell different."

Frustration ate at me. Didn't he understand how serious this situation was? "I'll explain later."

I didn't have time to explain that my wayward father was Pan, or that he saved me from dying after what Marius had done. It was too much, there wasn't enough time, and I wasn't ready to talk about any of it. Not yet, not now. He ran his nose over my cheek, breathing me in. "You smell of wildflowers and something else. Something I don't remember."

"We don't have time for this." God, I wanted time for this. I wanted more time for him. "How do I get to the Queens from here? What is the best way to find them?"

He shook his head fighting the curse. "They are here?"

"We got separated." I knew it had to be a mistake, but they could be anywhere.

He sucked in a steadying breath and his body shuddered above mine, his control slowly slipping away. "You must find a river and follow the flow. Do not touch the water or we'll both be lost."

"What? A river?" His words confused me. "Why?"

"They all flow to Hades." The creature above us screeched, and he cocked his head to the side, listening. "Bloody hell . . . Harpies."

My blood raced in my veins, and I went still. "What does that mean?"

"You've done nothing wrong. You have nothing to worry about." His lips hovered only an inch above mine, and I wanted to close that distance between us. The memory of his kisses flashed through my mind and heat ran over my skin.

"What about you?" I lowered my voice.

That cocky grin I knew so well tugged at the corner of his lips. "Questionable, love. Highly questionable."

I wanted to share his grin, wanted to laugh at our circumstances, but in mere moments I would be alone with the monster he would become once more. But this little glimpse of my love was enough to fuel me. We needed this thing with the Crone to work now more than ever. After all the determination and fighting to get us here, it came down to one very simple truth: I missed him. My soul cried out for his and for more moments like this.

His body shuddered once more, and I didn't want to bite him again. Not now, not when I knew the only solution was to run and find a way back to the Queens. The veins around his eyes turned a dark black and ran down his cheeks. Red lines moved in his eyes, and I knew he would be gone in seconds. When a rumble vibrated deep in his chest, my heart sank because I knew our moment was over and I had to move. I shoved him off of me and forced my way closer to the edge of the hedge. The bird thing, or I should say harpy, hovered above us, and I had no choice.

I leapt to my feet and took off running, forcing Grayson to keep in step with me. The squawking grew louder and the sound of flapping wings echoed in my ears. When I glanced over my shoulder, there it was, the harpy. She was both terrifying and glorious with the head and upper body of a breathtaking woman. She had hawk-like legs covered in deep brown feathers and long talons. Thick wings spread across her back and those same brown feathers formed a widow's peak on the top of her head that trailed all the way down her back. Her arms were thin and willowy, but they too were covered in feathers and each of her fingers was tipped with a little black claw. She dipped down toward us with her great talons extended.

I pumped my arms and Grayson let go a wild cackle. He dug his heels into the ground and jerked his wrist back. My body was yanked to a halt by him, and I flew back into his chest. I whirled around ready to strike out at him when that huge talon dug into my shoulder. Each claw shoved into my skin, puncturing it under her grip. With a single flap of her wings, we were airborne. I kicked my legs out. She hadn't grabbed Grayson, only me, and he dangled from my arm. I only prayed my shoulder would stay in its socket. He howled as he dangled there.

The harpy flew higher, soaring over the underworld, and everything came into stark view. Blood trickled from where she held me, and I didn't want to feel this pain. I'd known agony well enough the last few days. First at the hands of Marius, then my father, though one saved me while the other tried to kill me. The power built inside me and hummed through my veins. The wild made me feel these creatures, all creatures big and small. Though this one was particularly large, I felt her intentions like they were my own. Blood magic exploded out of me, forming a sphere around all of us.

The harpy's beating wings faltered, and she threw her head back with an ear splitting squawk. I glared up at her, and at my command, my magic fell over her feathers, seeping into her body. When I knew I'd taken hold, I let my voice ring with the command, "Down. Now."

The harpy tucked its wings into its body, and we began to plummet. My hair flew up from my face and my stomach rose in my throat. She pivoted toward a cliffside high above everything else. At first I thought it might've been a cave and then I realized it was a nest. Her nest. She hovered over it for less than a second, then withdrew her talons from my shoulder and dropped the two of us right into her nest before taking off out of my reach.

Grayson landed first and I followed right on top of him. He kicked me off and I groaned at him but appreciated the fact he didn't take my moment of weakness to attack me. When he eyed the blood trickling from my wound, a pang of guilt overcame me. He had to be thirsty. I knew Atlas had been bringing him blood bags, but I didn't know the last time he actually drank. I didn't want him to starve or feel the pangs of hunger. But high above the underworld, alone in a harpy's nest, how did I figure out how to feed a cursed, mad vampire?

CHAPTER THIRTY-SEVEN

TITUS

*A*nother dinner, another waste of my precious time. We were at war and here I was standing in an estate of vampires who would gladly see me dead. This was the life I was born into. This was the game we all played. Some won, some lost. Tonight there would be losses, but none would be my own. Mirrors were set up just outside the estate, no doubt to force their guests to take in their general splendor. I held my hand out, waiting for Eloura to step through. The moment her hand rested in mine, I stepped forward, guiding her with me.

Large fires were lit in oversized bowls illuminating the whole area. Ice sculptures lined the walkway leading up to the estate. Eloura didn't turn her head as she glanced at them out of the corner of her eye. "For people in debt, they certainly do know how to spend frivolously."

"I couldn't agree more." There were sculptures of lions, tigers, and even bears. None of which were native to

England. Perhaps a field mouse would've been more fitting.

The estate itself was lovely, though farther out in the country than even the castle. The light-colored sandstone nearly blended in with the snowy weather. Three arches sat evenly spaced apart with large columns between each one. A grand staircase with a thick plush carpet drifted from the ground level up toward the front entrance. Large windows were spread across the entire wall, giving views of the grounds.

Once the courtiers spotted us, they all slowly parted, giving a deep bow and allowing us to walk up the stairs unencumbered. Eloura inclined her head at some of them with that perfect smile on her face. I too followed suit with a wave and a smile. "How they lie so easily."

"We're walking into a den of vipers."

It was hard to believe with all of them in their best finery. The ladies all wore the best fashions from their personal tailors. It was a mix of the old world and new world. I'd noticed the steady change in attire since Piper arrived to court. While they were all ballgowns, there was a modern edge to the cut of the dress and choice of fabrics. There was more leather, silk, and chiffon than ever before. The stiff collars were all but forgotten and replaced with open necklines and more skin. For vampires who loathed The House of Shade, they certainly were taking their cues from the younger generation.

The gentleman no longer wore their coattails. Instead they opted for current tuxedos or even suits in some cases.

I lowered my voice to a whisper for Eloura. "What if we have allies here?"

"Let us not forget the Fredrickson's have plotted this entire night based on knowing what's going to happen to you. They would only invite their most staunch supporters." She turned her face up to mine and placed a large, fake smile on her lips. "There is no support for us here."

"Fair point." I guided her up the stairs, and when we reached the top, Waldon Fredrickson and his wife Lordess stood waiting to greet us. Lordess gave us a deep curtsy while Waldon bowed at his hips.

Lordess rose and was the first to speak. "Lady Eloura, what a privilege it is to attend with the King. We were expecting Lady Moira."

"The Lady Moira has taken ill tonight. I was lucky enough Lady Eloura was able to come in her stead." This was no place for Moira. She'd had enough on her mind with Grayson in the underworld. I'd started to worry for her state. She almost seemed to be in mourning already. Moira always held a certain sadness about her. There was a certain beauty to her melancholy, but as of late it was deeper. There was a weariness to the set of her eyes and the way she held her shoulders, like the weight of the world rested on them. I couldn't blame her for it either, her son was fading from this world and she was destined to watch.

Even the thought of Grayson brought a pain so acute to my own chest I could hardly stand to breathe. Yet my faith in the Queens brought about a new wave of hope I had scarcely allowed myself in years prior. They would fight for him, and I would fight for our kingdom so that when he regained his senses, there would be a place for him to come home to. Tonight required all my attention, so I had to force my attention to Eloura as she spoke.

"I consider it my good fortune to be able to accompany the King."

Waldon pressed his hand over his chest. "And how lucky for us you were able to accept our own invitation."

"I was glad to have it. A most welcomed distraction."

He motioned toward the doors. "Please do, Your Majesty."

We fell into step with Lordess and Waldon as they escorted us through the double doors leading to their foyer. It was impressive how far these two dared to reach. Their estate was lovely enough, but they were of little consequence in the vampire world. They held neither fortune nor status. Lordess was no great beauty, in fact she was rather plain-looking with flat brown hair and dull brown eyes. Waldon fit with her easily with his unremarkable looks, beady eyes, hooklike nose, and too full lips. He was no warrior, nor was he that noble. He was what the Americans referred to as new money, which meant he spent most of his time feeling inferior but always wanting to climb the social ladder. Perhaps the death of a king would be the steppingstone they sought.

"The splendor is lovely." Eloura motioned to the candlelit foyer. It was a grand thing. The ceilings were high and unencumbered by too many works of art or pictures.

The walls were warm and beige which matched the white and cream marble flooring. The candles were spread throughout and bathed everything in a warm dreamy light.

Beyond the foyer, music drifted toward us and I found myself pulled toward it. A smaller ballroom was cleared of all the furniture, and in the corner of the room sat a string quartet playing a light pleasant tune. More courtiers lined the walls and milled about. When they spotted us, the dancers turned to face us. They all gave a low bow, and I stood tall, knowing that any of them would put a knife in my back at any moment. "Please do continue."

The music stuck up louder and they began to dance once more. Lordess peered over at me. "Does his majesty intend to dance this evening?"

I gave a hearty chuckle. "No, I fear my dancing days are far behind me."

"What a pity for you," she teased Eloura.

"On the contrary." Eloura motioned to the dance floor with her walking stick. "I much prefer to watch the show."

Waldon pulled a packet of cigarettes from his pocket and offered us both one. I shook my head in a polite decline, but the truth was I detested the foul habit. He slid the packet back into his pocket. "Perhaps you'd like a drink?"

"Of course." A drink was so polite, so innocent, and in this case . . . so deadly.

We walked through the ballroom into a grand dining hall with a table that was at least twenty feet long. It was set with golden cutlery and empty glasses waiting to be filled. Even their show plates were gold. A large chandelier hung in the center of the room that complimented the candelabras spread down the middle of the table. The staff took their time lighting the candles. Waldon motioned for one of them to come over to us.

He was a younger Night Spawn vampire with pale skin and blond hair. Waldon didn't even look at him as he spoke. "Fetch the King his drink."

The vampire's eyes went wide, and he nodded and hurried off. I gave Eloura a small nod and she took the hint. She turned toward Lordess and Waldon. "Tell me, where did you get such fine dining utensils?"

They joined her as she strolled over to the table and picked up a fork, admiring it. She so easily complimented them and asked them questions. The saying *flattery would get us everywhere* was working for us. They strolled down the table at her side while I stayed behind. The waiter hurried to my side with a silver tray and a single glass of wine sitting in the middle of it. I plucked the glass up off the tray, and as I did so I let my blood magic flow into the waiter's face.

His eyes fixed on mine, and I knew my power had a hold over him. The feel of his pulse flowed through my blood, and I lowered my voice. "Whatever wine they have put aside for me, pour to the entire table. Do you understand?"

Red mist swirled around his face and in his eyes. "Yes."

"Tell no one else." I glanced over to Eloura who'd led

Waldon and Lordess even farther away as she pointed out tapestries and anything else she could think of. "Be quick about it, and when it's over, forget we ever spoke of this."

When I flicked my wrist to dismiss him, I knew the wheel was in motion. Once my power took hold of someone, they had no other choice but to obey. The switch was as good as done. When they circled back to me, Eloura gave me a long look and I gave her quick nod. I held the glass as casually as I could have. Had I not gotten Lorenzo's warning, I might have missed the faintest scent of poison. There was a sour note to it, like dead roses. I pretended to take a sip as they approached.

"A lovely vintage." I held my glass up toward them. "I'm hoping it pairs well with the lovely scents wafting from the kitchen."

Waldon gave me a broad, wide grin. *Self-satisfied prick*. "Of course, then dinner must commence, Your Majesty."

He waved a waiter over and again didn't look at them, just barked orders. "Have our guests come through for dinner at the request of the King."

From the corner of my eye, I watched the young vampire I'd enchanted finish pouring the wine at each seat. Lordess took Waldon's arm. "If you'll excuse us, we must greet our guests. But, of course, do take your seat at the head of the table, my King."

She purred the words *my King,* and I couldn't miss the inflection in her voice as if the title was sarcastic or not much longer lived. "I'm looking forward to it."

I offered Eloura my arm and she curled her hand in the crook of my elbow. "I assume all is in place."

"I've arranged it." When I looked back at the young waiter, he stood against the wall looking a bit dazed as though he didn't know how he'd gotten himself there. I stopped at the chair they had reserved on my right and pulled it out for her. "I would refrain from taking a sip."

"Luckily I had the foresight to fill up before we left." She dropped down into her chair and I moved to stand at the head of the table.

Waldon and Lordess took their seats in the center of the table as the other high-ranking Blood Borns all filled in the remaining seats. It was a disappointingly full house of traitors and yet I felt no remorse for what was about to transpire. Once everyone found their seats, I grabbed my glass and held it up toward Waldon.

"A toast to you, my friend. The last few days have been very trying for The House of Shade, and I would like tonight to be a new start for our reign. Moving forward, I want the vampire world to know that with the support of our friends," I waved my glass motioned to the vampires surrounding the table, "we will see a prosperous time. A time of love, loyalty, and mutually beneficial arrangements. It is through your kindness that I am able to make such decisions about the future of all vampires. Waldon, Lordess, thank you for your generosity and for reminding me of the kind of future I'd like to see for us all."

I raised my glass. "Cheers."

"Cheers!" The room all grabbed up their wine glasses and drank deeply.

Waldon rose to his feet, and I took my seat at the head of the table. "Your Majesty, it is my honor to have you with us this evening. And to a happy, bright future for all vampires."

He took another drink, and I sat back in the armchair waiting. If Lorenzo was wrong, then dinner would commence without a hitch. I would eat and be merry knowing my own people hadn't tried to poison me. Yet the sour scent still lingered in my glass, and I dared not hope for such a turn of events. Eloura tilted her head to the side, watching as the first course came from the kitchen in a flurry of activity. The movement was almost coordinated in the way each waiter stopped beside the table and placed the plates in front of the guests.

The first sign of distress started when Lordess had the slightest cough. Waldon narrowed his eyes at her, as though she had the audacity to cough during his dinner where he was poised to triumph over the King. I let my hands rest on the arms of the chair as more coughing joined her. A fine mist of blood sprayed from their lips, and when they started to dab it with their napkins, panic set in. They started with deep wet coughing and then the screams of terror and confusion started. No doubt they expected these symptoms to affect me and not them.

The waiters around the room all began to step back from the table with wide, panicked eyes. I waved my hand

and let my blood magic run over them. "You are dismissed. Lock all the doors."

They hurried out of the room, and one by one the doors leading to the dining hall slammed shut with a loud bang of finality. I rose to my feet and slowly strolled around the table. The coughs grew more constant and blood dripped from the corners of their mouths. It sweated from their pores, ruining their clothing with large stains that started to spread. Several of them jumped from the table and ran for the doors. They begged and screamed to be let out, but no one would answer their cries.

"You think to kill me?" my voice boomed over their panicked cries.

They began to flop to the floor, their bodies convulsing wildly as they scratched at their throats, clawing for breath. Blood tears streamed from their eyes and were joined by rivets streaming from their mouths and ears. I stopped as Lordess dropped to her knees in front of me.

"Please." Blood sprayed from her mouth as she held her throat. She pawed at the sleeves of my coat. "Please. Mercy."

"Mercy?" I looked up to Eloura, whose face was as smooth and as impassive as one could be while others all perished around us. "Was I granted the same mercy?"

Lordess dropped onto her back and her body convulsed at my feet. I took a step over her to where Waldon sat stone still in his chair. I wrapped my hand around his throat and jerked him to his feet. Blood had started to trickle from his eyes, yet the effects seemed slower moving in him. His beady eyes widened. "Please, Your Majesty."

I shook him and his legs and arms flopped about like a limp rag. "Where is Clive?"

"He . . ." Waldon choked, and his eyes rolled into the back of his head. I loosened my grip, and with my other hand, I slapped him across the face. The strike stung my fingers and traveled up my arm. Waldon's eyes widened. "He is with the other families."

"Who?" I threw him to the floor to lay at my feet like the maggot he was. When Waldon hesitated, I bent down, hovering over him. "I have the antidote. For the right kind of information, I'm willing to give it to you."

More bodies dropped around us, and the screams were nearly deafening. Blood coated the floor at my feet and more bodies fell over the table in the final throes of death. I motioned to the carnage around me, the exact death they had planned for me. "What's it to be?"

"He's with the Mavrick's, Peterson's, and Blackstone's," he choked out and blood began to trickle from the corner of his mouth.

"Doing what?"

"Once you were dead, they were to kill Lorenzo Romano as quickly as possible." A crimson stain spread over the white of his shirt, and I knew he would soon die.

"Why?" I wanted to reach down and choke the life from him, but the blood misting from his pores was enough to stop me.

"To erase our debts." A shudder wracked him from head

to toe. "When an army could not be bought, we decided a quick death would be in best order."

I motioned to the sight around us, to the bodies lying around us with wide, unseeing eyes, with blood covering them and their screams echoing in our ears, though they were starting to quiet now and the banging on the doors had stopped all together. Not a single vampire stood living besides me and Eloura. It had worked better than I thought.

"You call this quick?"

"Please." He reached for me with a pathetic swipe of his hand. "I've told you all that I know. Please! The antidote! I will serve you well."

"The only person you've ever served is yourself." My lip curled with disdain and disgust. I rose to my feet and glared down at him as he lay dying. "May your death come slow."

I turned for the door and Eloura fell into step with me. She held her head high and there wasn't an ounce of remorse in her features. I'd always appreciated her candor, but on this night, she'd earned her place at my side for years to come. "Tell Lorenzo we have a deal and give him the names to look into. I have business to attend to."

Eloura's cane tapped on the marble with a bit of a sticky sound to it. "Business?"

Tonight, I would clean up the entire vampire kingdom. I'd gotten news from Prisha earlier that I would be sure to handle as only I knew how: head on. "Another party to attend."

I planted my foot and kicked the double doors wide open, breaking the lock and shattering the wood to pieces. The wait staff, along with the entertainment, all stood there gaping at us with wide eyes and slacked jaws. I turned toward them. "Go from this house and let them know what happens when you betray your King."

When they didn't move, I waved my hand, and my blood magic flowed over them. "Go. Now."

I continued toward the front doors, and Eloura stayed with me. "Busy night for you, my lord. May your hunting be as fruitful as this."

We walked down the front steps, and I relished the cool air in my lungs after the foul odor of death. "I have no doubts it will be."

Eloura paused at the bottom of the stairs. "What would you like me to do with the bodies?"

I tilted my head back, looking up at the great estate, knowing the horrors I left lying within. "Burn it down . . . Burn it all down."

I scrambled back from Grayson and took in our new surroundings. I grabbed a scrap of fabric and threw it in his face. "Very freaking helpful. You couldn't just keep your mouth shut, or I don't know, keep running?"

I knew it wasn't Grayson, not really. My Grayson wouldn't have done anything to jeopardize this mission. He growled in my direction, and I yanked on the chain, forcing him to sit beside me. "I'm not afraid of you."

Pain shot through my arm where the harpy had skewered me. Three perfectly round holes were punctured into my skin. I leaned back in the nest and let my head rest on a pile of fabric scraps. The nest was made of scraps of all kinds of different fabrics mixed with some dried flowers and a long bit of tapestry that looked like it'd been ripped from a wall somewhere. Nothing about this nest was cohesive. There was even an odd couch cushion covered in little pink flowers. Yet somehow, I could see why the harpy might find this comfortable. It was soft and thick over the rocky cliffside.

When I peeked over the edge of the nest, I was shocked by how high up we actually were. Below us was an entire view of the underworld. It reminded me of being at the top of the Empire State Building where the world moved below us, but up here it was quiet and untouched. In the distance was the lava-like glow of what I could only assume was Tartarus. Closer to us were golden, shimmering fields that looked like wheat blowing in the breeze. With my vampire senses, I could pick up a light tune that hummed in the air coming from those fields. Farther away, there was a large area that appeared grey and desolate with a heavy fog settling over it. I didn't have any idea of what these places were, Greek Mythology wasn't my thing, but I knew once this curse was broken, I was going to brush up on my history lessons.

Several rivers flowed through all these lands, and at the center of it all was a huge castle. The one place where I knew we had to be. It was tall and imposing with a black exterior that was like a shadow looming over everything. The roof line wasn't symmetrical in the least, instead it had multiple turrets jutting up toward the sky. I imagined each one would be considered a wing of its own. Firelight flickered through the open windows and all manner of flying creatures circled the castle, which included the harpies and what I thought might be furies with giant bat wings. But I couldn't be sure. Their shrieks could be heard over the dim hum of souls crying out.

I crawled and rested my chin on the edge of the nest. The moment I looked down, I knew it was a mistake. We were so high up that even some fog lingered below us, and I could hardly see the ground. How the hell were we supposed to get down from here? If it were just me, I would try to climb, but Grayson was unpredictable at best and homicidal at his worst. He might decide to jump halfway through our climb and take me down with him. I wasn't sure if even immortal vampires could survive a fall like that, so I scrambled back into the nest, hoping I'd freaked out the harpy enough with my power that she wouldn't be back for some time.

I tugged the sleeve of my shirt down to look at my wounds. The more I bled, the more my pearl began to turn pink. It didn't matter that I'd fed only a day ago. An injury would make the need to feed even more dire. I just didn't know how long I could hold off until I needed Grayson's blood. When I eyed the pulse in his neck, he turned his face away from me.

"No. She's not here," he spoke to someone who wasn't there, no doubt hearing Lucifer in his mind. "I am close."

"Don't tell him that." But my words had no effect on him. "Gray, don't."

"Yes, yes, I will get her." He sounded so sincere, his words more like an oath than just a promise.

I had to stop this. If Lucifer found out exactly where we were, there would be literal hell to pay. I had to break the connection, and there was only one way I knew how. I dove for him, and he tried to fight me off. We tumbled over each other, wrestling for the upper hand. He snapped his teeth at me, and I felt guilty for doing this, but I had no other choice. The connection had to be severed. I flipped him onto his back and straddled his hips. I shoved my hands to his shoulders and pinned him down. That delicious vein was exposed for the barest moment, and I struck hard and fast.

My teeth pierced his skin, and his blood flooded my mouth. Power and energy flowed through me and the pain in my shoulder already began to ease. His hands went from pushing me away to pulling me closer to him. I pulled back and ran my tongue over the little punctures I'd made.

"Hmmm," he rumbled. "I might have to get cursed more often if that's how I wake."

I sat up but didn't move off him. "That's not funny."

He sat up and rested his hands behind him. "Come now, little creature. Waking up with your fangs in my neck and your little tongue on my skin is the best thing a dying man could ask for."

"You're not dying. I won't let you." The words were hard to say even as I knew the others were fighting to save him. Because, deep down, I knew what we were about to do was difficult, more difficult than anything else we might ever face.

A sad smile tugged at his lips. "You don't know that, love."

I threw my arms around his shoulders and pulled him

close. Our lips smashed together, and for one brief moment, time stopped. There was nothing else but me and him and this stolen second. My memories of his lips did not do them justice, they were both firm and soft at the same time, and when his lips parted I knew he felt the same fire between us as I did. Our tongues wound together, and I savored the flavor of him. Strong arms wrapped around me, pulling me closer, and he hardened underneath me. I wanted to stay like this forever, perched above the world and trapped together.

He pulled back slightly and turned his head, taking in our surroundings. "Are we in a harpy's nest?"

"Um, yes?" I didn't let him go, not when we were this close for the first time in a while.

"Right." He set back into kissing me, and I knew when his body began to shudder that I would lose him again.

"No, it's too soon." I held him tighter. "I need you."

"Bite me again." He turned his head to the other side. "Keep me with you. Bite me again." I didn't hesitate. I needed these stolen moments with him. Not just to figure out how to get away, but to have him near me. I sank my fangs into him, not taking too much but just enough to keep him here with me. "Ahhh, you're so sweet when you do the dirty things to me."

"Stop playing around. This is serious." I tried to keep the smile out of my voice.

He ran his finger over the vines at my temple and down my neck. "What's this then? What's happened?"

"It's too much to explain now." He trailed his finger

down between my breasts and I arched my back into his touch.

He ran his hand up under my shirt and cupped me while running his thumb over the tight peeks. "Try."

"Shouldn't we be trying to figure out how to escape or something?" He slowed his circles, and my eyes rolled into the back of my head. His touch felt so good that I nearly forgot about everything we were facing: the curse, the wars, the fact I'd probably died . . . again. All I wanted was his hands on me and for the world to fall away.

He twisted his hips, and in one smooth move, he had me under him with my knees on either side of his hips. His eyes sparkled with fun, and I'd almost forgotten the playful nature that attracted me to him in the first place. "Or I could spend my last moments of sanity wrapped up in you."

"We're in a nest."

"There's cushion and I'll be oh so gentle."

This was crazy, but I wanted him, wanted this moment. I groaned. "You're being ridiculous."

"Am I or do I make complete sense?" He leaned down and kissed one of the flower petals surrounding my neck while his hand skimmed over my skin, leaving feather-light touches. My sweater began to rise over my stomach, and I let him continue to tug it up higher.

The balmy air breezed over my skin as he pulled my shirt off and tossed it aside. He extended his claw and sliced it through the center of my bra. I fought the need to cover myself and let him look his fill. His eyes filled with sadness, and his lips turned down. "Oh, love."

He traced his finger over the vines covering me and the raised scars under each one where the wild knitted my skin back together. "Piper, I —"

"No." I wrapped my hand in his hair and fisted the strands, pulling him down to me. "Don't apologize. I'm still here."

"But . . ." He closed his eyes, and those lines began to re-form. I didn't hesitate. I bent my head down and nipped his chest. Blood welled and I licked at it. He shook his head and came back to me. "But I should've been here."

It wasn't his fault. I wanted to tell him that if he'd been there none of this would've happened. But Grayson didn't leave on purpose. This curse took him from me, and I was going to take any time I was offered. I kissed the little teeth marks all the way up to his neck. I ran my hand over the muscles rippling over his stomach. He reached down between us and the top button of my jeans loosened. I shimmied out of them and found myself bare to him. "I've missed you."

"I love you." Our kisses turned frantic as I shoved his pants down his legs, and he fell into my hands. I wrapped my fingers around him and stroked. A low hiss slipped through his teeth, and it sent goosebumps over my skin.

"I love you." The second the words were out of my mouth, his body began to change, the curse pulling him down even harder.

I flipped him onto his back and kept my hips poised

above him while I grabbed his wrist and brought it to my mouth. As much as I wanted to linger in his touch, we didn't have the time. I lowered myself down on him at the same time I bit down on his wrist. My body parted around him, and I moaned. I'd waited for him for so long I didn't realize my body would respond to him so wildly. My muscle stretched around with each inch I took of him.

"Piper." My name was a whispered prayer on his lip.

When I began to move over him, something in me snapped and I couldn't stop even if I'd wanted to. A growl ripped through him, and he flipped me onto my back, pressing one of my knees up into his shoulder. He hooked my other leg around his hip and drove into me. My body took over, and I wanted him rougher, deeper. I wanted every bit of him. The connection sizzled between us, and my magic started to seep from me. Red and sage mist surrounded us, and his own power rose to meet mine. They twisted together all around us, and my magic seeped into his skin.

Lights exploded behind my eyes, and his pleasure was my own. Every touch, every kiss was like fire sparking between us. I loved the way his body rippled against mine and the feel of skin on skin. There was nothing like our breaths mingling together and his fingers pressing into my skin. I wanted this, I wanted him, I wanted the life we could have together. He traced this thumb over my bottom lip as he drove harder and faster. The lines forked out over his eyes, and I nearly stopped, but he shook his head.

"I got this." But even as we moved together, his body

grew bigger and his muscles more rigid. He'd always been the monster who owned me down to my soul, but moving beneath him now, I could see how tight his control had been and how hard he tried just for me.

I grabbed his other wrist and shoved my fangs into his skin. He threw his head back with a deep moan. "Don't let me go."

Never. I'd never let Grayson go as long as there was breath in my lungs. I gave a gentle pull, and he was back with me. I was lost in his eyes, the feel of his body and how we moved so perfectly together. He wrapped his arm around my back and flipped me onto my stomach, bending me over the side of the nest. He pressed his hand to my lower back, and I instantly arched for him. With one swift movement, he was inside me, and I sucked in a sharp breath. Our skin smacked together, and pleasure drove my body to the brink.

I pressed my chest down into the soft fabrics and spread my knees wider, taking as much of him as I could. I couldn't fight off the slow build of pleasure that began to rush through my body. His hand wrapped around my body and cupped me, giving me an extra shot of desire that drove me even higher. A moan escaped my lips, and he ground into me. "That's it, love. Let go."

His smooth accent shot me straight into ecstasy. Pleasure rocked my body, and my magic sparked all around the two of us. Grayson's hands pressed into my hips, guiding me to move harder and faster. His hips smacked into me one last time and he stilled, finding his own pleasure as his body pulsed inside mine. A guttural yell broke free of him and he collapsed over me. We toppled to the side, and I ended up with his body curled around mine. I sank back into his warmth and never wanted this to end.

Silence hung between us, and he curled his arm around my ribs and let his fingers lie against the leaves and scars. He pressed a kiss to my shoulder, and I felt his warm breath fan across my skin. "What happened? Did I do . . ."

"No, of course not." I squeezed my eyes shut, not wanting to ruin what might be the last time I was with him like this. I wanted to hold on to this time with Grayson for as long as I could. His claws splayed across my chest and dark lines ran up his forearm. I leaned into him.

"Don't let me go." He tightened his grip. "Just a bit longer."

"Just a bit longer." I turned my head to the side and let my fangs nip his forearm.

CHAPTER THIRTY-NINE

SANCHITA

"*T*his feels like the worst idea we've had yet," Jester mumbled from right beside me. "We're too out in the open, too exposed. I don't like it."

I let my arm brush against his as we sat in an auditorium full of Night Spawn. It was much like the one we'd been in before. Here, Marius was out in the open, not skulking around in tunnels that none of us had ever seen before. We were back in the regular Night Spawn headquarters. I knew I shouldn't find comfort in that, but this was my home, and we were surrounded by Night Spawn vampires who had not yet fallen under Marius's spell. Even so, Jester forced us to stay at the back near the doors just in case we needed to fight our way out. Before we left the castle, he forced Prisha and me to strap knives under our shirts. What he thought I was going to do with a knife was beyond me. "I don't bloody well like it either, but here we are."

Prisha turned to face us and moved in closer, leaning over me so Jester could hear us. "We've sort of figured out what's happening to the vampires and now we need to see what else he has to say. I feel like we're missing something, like how far into his operation he really is."

"Fair enough, but I still don't like it." He sat so stiffly that the two of us couldn't get closer. He wrapped his arm around the back of my chair, draping it across the back of my chair and resting it on Prisha's. It was as though he were shielding our bodies with his own. He glanced over his shoulder toward the door and his face went pale.

Prisha and I turned to follow his gaze, and I felt the blood drain from my face. "What is he doing here?"

"I have no idea." My face mirrored the horror on my sister's face. "I told him about everything we'd seen and heard, including this meeting, but I never thought he'd show up . . ."

Jester rose to his feet and offered me his hand. "He's the King. He does whatever the fuck he wants."

The other doors slowly slid shut as the meeting was about to begin, but I'd be damned if the King didn't have some allies here. We slid out the last door and stopped short just behind him. Jester yanked us to the side to hide in a little alcove in the wall. I sucked in a sharp breath. There was King Titus all tall and imposing standing in the middle of the hall just as Marius appeared.

"This ought to be good," Jester mumbled and pulled a knife from his boot. When my eyes went wide, he shrugged. "Just in case."

Marius slowed his steps to stand before the King. He spread his arms wide like he was giving the King a warm welcome. "Titus, what brings you to our humble neck of the woods?"

"You should know," the King snapped at him, and the smile dropped from Marius's face. "What happened to us? We used to be the best of friends."

Any warmth in Marius's face dropped, and in its place was a mask of anger. His eyebrows drew low over his eyes, and his lips curled into a sneer. "Friends? Do friends abandon each other to live in hovels? Do friends take away a life without asking?"

"I have no idea what you speak of." The King shook his head. "This discord between us must stop. Lives are at stake now."

"Is that what brought you down here?" Marius glared at him. "Lives are at stake? What happened to my life? The life you lot stole from me?"

"Stole your life?" The King's voice slipped to a low rumble. "We gave you a life, a home, a position of power. And you thank us by abusing it."

"Thank you?" Marius took a step back like he'd been struck. "I have lost everything! The magic I used to wield, the power I held in the palms of my hands. I was turned into this *thing*. Left to skulk about in the night never to see the daylight once more. We truly are Night Spawn, the walking dead, because we all might as well be dead."

The King clenched his hand into a fist. "I should kill you where you stand."

Marius spread his arms wide. "I welcome you to. It'll only make the Night Spawn rise up faster."

"I find this disappointing. I've done everything in my power to make life better for the Night Spawn and you throw it back in my face. Why? What happened?" He softened his voice. "Why such discord between someone I used to call friend?"

Marius jabbed a finger toward the King. "You happened. What have you taken from the fae, witches, shifters? They lost a part of themselves when they were turned. You're under the impression that being a vampire is the best thing when they've lost a piece of who they are at their core."

Prisha crept over to the auditorium door and pulled it open just enough that their voice would carry in for the others to all hear the King. "We have tried every way to make life better here. I'm building an entire new underground city with funds from my own pocket. I want the Night Spawn to have a home where they can live and dream. I can't help how any of you came to be, but I can make life better. The city is nearly complete. We didn't have the means before but human technology over the last fifty years has given us the chance to finally build underground like we always wanted. It could have been done faster with the witches but you of all people know that Alataris' rule made that impossible. It's been Grayson, Moira, and me supporting this endeavor from the start, financially and socially. I've given you Martin's dedicated services. If anything, the Blood Borns should be cross with me because all my attention has gone to the Night Spawn and making this world better for us all. Can you not see we are doing everything? And you, what is your plan for them once you take my crown?"

"To rule," Marius spat. "Better than you ever have."

The other door to the auditorium creaked open, and the Night Spawn began to exit after hearing this little tiff. I gave Prisha a tiny thumbs-up and pulled my phone from my pocket and opened a text threat to Martin. This high up, our phones would finally work. I quickly typed my text.

The King is here, and we might need help with a quick exit. Not everyone here is sold on Marius's plan.'

Martin's response was immediate. *'On it.'*

Marius's eyes widened as he peered behind Titus, watching Night Spawn vampires leaving their meeting. His face heated and a pissed-off red color bloomed in his cheeks. His voice rose with anger. "I lost a piece of my soul in being turned! How would you like that?"

"I'm sorry you feel that way. That was not our intention. We didn't want our friend to die. I'm sure Moira thought any life would be better than mourning your death. Perhaps she was wrong." The King didn't turn away or let him speak. "I heard Clive offered to join forces. Were you planning to force me to fall to the curse?"

There were so many things spoken of that I wasn't sure I was following. Was Moira Marius's sire? What curse would befall our King?

Before I could think more on it, Marius gave a harsh,

loud scoff. "Please! As if I need that waste of space. You Blood Borns are all the same. You think you're so much better. I was only too happy to decline, but he might try on his own and let me just tell you that I won't save you from this curse again."

The King's head snapped toward him. "What do you mean again? I've never fallen to the curse."

Marius took a step toward him and lowered his voice. "Your whole life is a lie, and you don't even know it. If you have questions, perhaps you should ask your offspring. Oh, wait, you can't because he's a breath away from falling to his own madness."

Jester's grip tightened on his knife, and I placed my hand over his. "Don't. Marius is right. You'll only make him a martyr. His supporters will rise up and there will be chaos. We can't do that."

Jester gave me a single nod and I turned my attention back toward the King. Marius gave a dark chuckle and walked past the King, leaving him there. Titus turned and followed him with his gaze. His face was a mask of confusion, and I knew how he felt. So much was said but so much more was left unsaid. I let the door to the auditorium fall shut and hurried to the King with Prisha and Jester right behind me.

"Your Majesty, what are you doing here alone?"

The King gave his head a shake and turned to me with a shell-shocked look in his eyes. "I thought I might be able to reason with him to stop this. I didn't want more death for our people."

"There is no reasoning with him, I'm afraid." I'd seen the worst of Marius, as had Prisha, and we knew there was only one outcome for him.

"Yes, I see that now. My old friend is gone." Sadness filled his eyes, and a weariness fell over his face. "Long gone."

I took a step toward him and placed my hand on his forearm. "My King, you are not safe here anymore. Not now. You need to leave right now. Marius wants you dead and he will not stop. Martin has arranged a quick exit. We must go."

The King gave me a light nod, and I knew his mind was somewhere else entirely. Marius's words had shaken him to his core, and I wished I could help. The King patted my hand in a warm, fatherly way. "You're right. Let us depart."

CHAPTER FORTY

MARIUS

he very audacity of him coming here to confront me. The sheer obliviousness he had in regard to the life I'd lost spoke to the selfishness he exhibited on a daily basis. And now I'd lost my audience full of new recruits to his false, emotional words. They'd fallen for his dredged-up sincerity and exited like the cowards they were. I had the opportunity to give them more of this life, more of what they used to be. Unless they were human, then their deaths would be terrible yet swift. But still little more than humans-turned-vampires deserved.

I turned for the auditorium that'd been set up and marched down the hall away from Titus and his fabricated ignorance. It'd taken every ounce of me to fight the hold Moira's command held. As my sire she asked only one thing of me. As her progeny I wanted her to piss off. Yet I was able to allude to enough of the truth to wreck Titus's day. With any luck that bit of knowledge would unravel him and force him to fall to the curse. Once fallen there would be nothing anyone could do, witch friends or not. If I hadn't been powerful enough to break it, then not even those Queens would be. I was sure of it.

At the end of the hall, a group of mirrors was set up for vampire travel, and I stepped into one. It wasn't impossible to follow another vampire through the mirrors, but it would be damned difficult, so I was confident he wouldn't be behind me. There were things that needed to be attended to, most pressing things. I marched down the end of the hallway toward that white light and stepped through into a much darker space—a space very few others knew about. But it had to be done. Titus's words would spread through the Night Spawn like wildfire and I needed it to stop the sympathy for the King in its tracks. It'd taken me years to gain the influence over them, and with one little speech about friends and trying to make things better, he swayed them to his side. How could they be so bloody daft when my intentions were clearly the best path for the Night Spawn? Their stupidity fueled the anger burning through my veins.

I marched down another hall, and Kendra stood there waiting for me with her clipboard in hand and a cup of steaming blood. She handed the cup over to me without a word. What a practical little weapon she'd become for me. Ever obedient, ever useful. I took a deep sip and marched through the double doors behind her. "Explain to me how no one knew he was coming?"

My words were sharp and harsh as they should have

been for their oversight. The busy din of the room came to a halt as they all stopped to look at me. At the center of it stood a large round wooden table with chairs spread all around it. A map of England was spread over the surface. On the other side of the room were tables lined up with monitors of each of my holding tunnels where our newly turned vampires dwelled and trained. From here I could see my whole underground world. From here they should've been able to monitor arrivals and notify me the King had arrived. Five of my soldiers faced me, and not one of them had an answer. I slammed the door shut behind me and threw the cup of blood to the floor. It smashed to pieces, leaving a sticky pool spattered there.

Anger and frustration warred within my veins. "I ask a question, yet no one dares speak?"

The youngest of my soldiers cleared her throat, drawing my attention to her. She'd only been a vampire for less than five years, which showed in her smooth, ageless skin, light-blue eyes, and ginger hair braided into a crown around her head. She wore black pants, a royal blue sweater, and boots. It was the attire required to be part of my service. They were all made to blend in and not stand out in any way. They'd gone undetected by the Night Spawn and Blood Borns alike. It was easy to get lost in the headquarters, and I'd made sure each of them was good and lost to the public eye.

I arched my eyebrows at her. "Something to say, Samantha?"

"Sir, all intel pointed to the King attending a dinner

tonight with the rest of the Blood Born vampires. Our contact reported that he'd entered the party."

I walked up to the table, surveying the map. "Then why did we not get confirmation of his leaving?"

They all exchanged awkward glances, and I turned to an older vampire whom I'd known for fifty years. He'd been changed slightly later in life, but it hadn't affected his dark good looks or the way he held himself. In fact, his age at the time of his change contributed to how he held himself with a maturity I'd only seen in very old vampires. "Care to enlighten us, Jonathan?"

"Sir, our contact went dark after they entered the party," he hesitated, "and according to our interrogations of the staff at that party . . . they're all dead."

There was no way that an entire house of Blood Born vampires was dead. It was unheard of. A most outrageous rumor at best. "I'm sorry. Who exactly is dead?"

"Every Blood Born vampire in attendance at that party was killed and the manor burned to ash." His face turned stone cold. "Only the staff survived."

I threw my head back, letting a cackle rack my body. How absolutely divine. He was slaughtering his allies. "My, my, our King did act swiftly and harshly. Did he not?"

Samantha pointed to Fredrickson manor on the map. "From what we've gathered, it was a bloody, gruesome death."

"Well, that's good, very good indeed." I placed my hand on the map. "It shows all of our work until this moment is paying off, except for the fact that the bloody King showed up here! Where were you all during that little interruption? I do not favor those who fail at their jobs." They flinched back, stepping away from the table. I slammed my fist down. "I have done my role and my duty to you all. I've been in the spotlight. I've been followed by his little spying rats. I've acted my part beautifully. I've even held Clive Christianson in my hand and crushed him according to all our plans. And yet on the evening when we are supposed to recruit our last few hundred soldiers, the King is at my door asking if we can be *friends* of all things."

Sergei, a wily vampire from Siberia, moved to stand at the table across from me. His hair had a constantly wind-blown look, giving his face a severe look complete with high cheekbones and thin lips. "Then it would appear things are working."

His deep Russian accent rumbled around the words and drew them together. I tried for patience and failed. "Not if we do not know where the King is at every moment. I prefer not to be ambushed in my own territory."

"Technically speaking, it's still his territory." I snapped my gaze toward Samantha and ground my teeth together. She lowered her gaze back to the map, "I mean, technically until the crown is yours that is, sir."

"That's right. The crown is as good as mine." My hand curled into a fist and I dug my nails into my palms, tearing at the skin there. The sharp sting brought my focus to attention. I didn't wish to speak of this any longer, lest I snatch one of their heads from their bodies in a fit of rage. "Tell me where we are with our plans."

Kendra stepped up beside me and pointed to five different points surrounding The House of Shade. Each one was marked by a little red flag. "Our transportation routes have been set up and are ready to be used at any point in time. The elemental units—fire, water, earth, and air—are well prepared now, and we've weeded out any potential weaknesses among them."

Weeded out? "Meaning?"

"We euthanized them." Her features were impassive as she so casually talked of killing. Not even a hint of a twitch around her eyes or those ruby-red lips. "As you say, better to put down an animal that is no longer of use."

At least she was taking my word seriously. I wasn't so sure the others were as devoted as she was. "I do say that, don't I?"

"Indeed." She glanced down at her clipboard, making a note of something, then turned back to me. "The blood supplies are ready for our army, so they won't go without sustenance before, during, or after. We've also provided them with the apparel you've requested."

There was nothing like a show of force moving as one, that force being my own army of course. "There is a possibility our schedule has changed. We no longer have the luxury of time, and I feel we must move sooner rather than later."

Kendra gave me a stiff nod and jotted more notes down. "We will be ready, sir."

"I'm almost pleased." All the pieces of my plan were slowly clicking into place after years of planning. Our numbers outranked theirs, our powers out-measured theirs, and our leadership, my leadership, was not prone to madness.

"Then what can we do to please you, sir?" The others all stepped closer, listening intently to my words.

I slammed my fist down on the table, smashing it beneath my fingers. "Don't lose the bloody King!"

CHAPTER FORTY-ONE

NOVA

$\mathcal{T}$here were days when being trapped in the underworld was less like a punishment and more like a privilege. I loved the dark, the cool feel of death, and its constant sounds. There were wails of pain coming from Tartarus, gentle music from the Elysian fields, and silence from Asphodel. Rivers rushed around the castle, each one filling the air with their trickling sounds as the water hurried over rocks and dips. I never was at home in the world of the living, but here in the underworld I was comfortable, at ease for the most part. Even in the halls of Hades' castle, nothing frightened me. Death was peaceful, death was certain, death was almost . . . fun. A ghost drifted into my path, and I stopped short.

"Stanley, how many times do I have to tell you?" I pointed toward the corner where this hallway intersected with the next. The castle halls were nearly pitch black . . . nearly. Reflections of the torches on the wall lit my way and I could see myself in the gleaming onyx floors. Gargoyle-like sculptures were etched high into the tops of the walls. "You have to lurk around corners if you want to startle people."

Stanley, I'd learned, died during the Great Depression while working as a clown at a traveling circus. He stood before me in oversized pants with thick red stripes, a white thermal undershirt, and shoes that were way too big for his feet. I was sure his red nose would've looked much brighter had he not been completely translucent. But for some odd reason, Hades had a thing for the sad clown, and so he lingered around the castle. He pulled a ghostly flower from behind his ear and tried to hand it to me. When he dropped it into my palms, it went right through my fingers and dropped to the floor.

His mouth dropped into a dramatic O shape and his shoulders shook soundlessly as he laughed and then slinked back into the wall. I sighed and shook my head, trying to forget that my only friends should be on their way to me at this very moment. I was forbidden from going topside, but that didn't mean I couldn't ask someone else to do it. I hurried down the hall and through the grand ballroom where music played twenty-four hours a day, seven days a week. The organ masked the laughter and fun, but I ducked my head, knowing if I stayed, I'd be here for days. There would be another time, another moment to celebrate with them, to join in the deathly waltz.

I went right out the ballroom doors and made my way down another hall that led to the front entrance of the castle. I'd hoped that Thanatos would drop them off to me instead of taking them straight to Hades. I had yet to warn Hades, but I'd hoped if he saw the Queens, he'd be willing to help us. But given our last interaction had gotten me trapped here, I wasn't exactly excited at the prospect of asking Hades for help. I pushed through the front doors and walked down the grand stairs that led up to the castle. When I reached the bottom, I strolled to the thick dark banister and let my magic flow from my palms. Purple sparks fired from my fingertips and leapt on the ground and a skeletal hand popped up. It cupped its hand, and I stepped right into it. The hand shot up, hoisting me higher, and I hopped up on the end of the banister where the marble flattened out. It was thick and even, which made it the perfect place for me to perch myself.

"You know he hates surprises." Liesin appeared out of nowhere, the way he usually did in his typically annoying fashion. He was always around, always beside me, and always looking at me with that cocky smirk on his face.

I moved to the edge of my perch and let my leg hang down while I tucked the other close to my body. "Go away."

"Aw, you say the nicest things."

I couldn't pinpoint the exact moment I decided to hate Liesin, it just came as second nature to me. He was too pretty with his inky black hair that fell in wild, loose waves down to his chin, and his lips were too full and his eyes too purple.

He was too agitating beautiful for his own good. I tried not to look at him. "I'm busy."

"Yes, I know." He strolled to my side in a casual prowl, and even though I sat higher on the banister, he was face to face with me. "Your friends like to ask you for help where they shouldn't."

"Before I was a prisoner, I was a Queen. You forget that a little too often." I knew I'd struck a bargain, one that worked to my advantage most of the time, but I still had responsibilities as a Witch Queen.

That stupid dimple appeared just at the corner of his mouth when he smirked up at me. "I don't forget a thing about you, dead girl."

"I think you mean Queen of Death, dead boy." I looked over the rivers flowing in front of the castle and watched the ferryman moving souls from one place to the other. I found the rivers peaceful, though sometimes one of them burst into random flames. I loved the soft glow of Tartarus, despite the torture I knew was there.

He stepped in closer and white light wrapped around me. "I remember everything about you well enough."

It was warm and welcoming. Had it not been from Liesin, I might've enjoyed it. I opened my own hand, and purple sparks flew to the ground. More skeletal hands shot from the ground, wrapping around his ankles holding him in place. The white light dropped from around me and I returned his smirk with my own. "Maybe you should start forgetting me then."

"Never." He glared and jerked his leg, trying to break free from the skeleton holding him.

I waved him away with the flick of my finger. "Do the words *give up* mean anything to you?"

"Not really, no."

"Nova!" My head snapped up at the sound of my name.

Zinnia strolled up the hill toward the castle with Astrid, Tabi, Serrina, and Ophelia flanking her sides. Their power rolled out before them, and for a split second I longed to be walking among them. Behind them Maze shoved his hand into a backpack he had slung over one shoulder. He pulled out a small white bag and forced the crumpled top open. He pulled out a powdered covered donut and took a huge bite. White powder covered his lips and rained down on his black shirt.

I glared at Liesin for a second longer before I leapt off the banister and headed down to meet them. "Hey!"

Ophelia marched right up to me and held her fist out toward me. "Fist bump because hugs are awkward."

"Umm." The fist bump felt awkward as hell, but I went with it. "Okay."

The others took their time greeting me, and while I was comfortable down here, I missed them. I missed them more than I cared to admit. Thanatos floated down next to us on a dark cloud with bolts of blue and black lightning. White-blond hair floated around him until he landed just across from me. Then the long strands fell perfectly into place.

"The other two got lost," he said in that matter of fact tone he always used with me.

"Got lost?" I glanced around, looking for the others. "What do you mean, *got lost?*"

He shrugged, "You asked me to bring them to the underworld, not bring them right to you."

"Are you kidding me?" Astrid shoved her hands on her hips and golden, sparkling magic fell from her hips like drops of rain. "They're the whole reason we're here."

Thanatos stood as still as death. "So?"

"So, we need them." Tabi crossed her arms, and her wild curls bobbed around her face.

"Okay, hold up." I put my hand out, stopping them all from talking. "Thanatos, how could you just lose them? I asked you to help me. They don't ask for me to help them unless it's absolutely necessary. It's important."

"I am death. It's my job to ferry souls into the afterlife." His chest heaved with a heavy sigh. "I am not a carpool driver."

I'd pulled his ass out of the fire on more than one occasion, though I dared not bring that up in front of the others. But my anger flared, and purple sparks bounced all around me. The ground rumbled and more skeletons shot up around us. I groaned and stomped my foot, forcing them back down. "One day you're going to need my help, and if I don't help you, you're going to be so screwed."

Thanatos rolled his eyes. "What could I possibly need your help with?"

Oh, how easily he forgot our past. I glared at him. "The world is a complicated place. You never know."

"Death isn't complicated." Before he could say another word, he disappeared in a flurry of white light and black lightning.

"I hate it when he does that." I turned to Zinnia. "Any idea where he might've lost them?"

Zinnia shook her head, "The whole ride was kind of . . . blinding. But we need them to face the Crone. Especially if we plan on winning."

I stilled. Hades was going to kill them for wanting to go to Tartarus. That whole place was off limits to *everyone*. "The Crone? Are you out of your minds?"

"Yes." Maze's eyes turned milky-white as he gazed at me in that uncanny way that made me feel like he was looking right into my soul. "We are."

I couldn't think of a worse idea than one that involved the Crone. If it involved the Crone, then it really involved Hades, and if it involved Hades, then he'd be even more pissed with me than he usually was. "Well, shit."

Liesin appeared by my side, completely free of my skeleton friends. "You know you could always ask for my help to find your friends."

Liesin knew the underworld better than anyone, probably even better than his father. But I didn't want his help, even though I knew I needed it. "I loathe you."

CHAPTER FORTY-TWO

TITUS

My offspring? Marius knew good and well I didn't have children. Why would he say such a thing? And why would he imply that it was Grayson? His words shook me to my very core. I didn't know why I would trust the words of a traitor who clearly had no regrets about doing so, but there was something in the way he said it, something in the smug set to his shoulders and his direct gaze that made me feel like he spoke the truth. Or the truth as he thought it to be.

There was only one place I could find solace in a moment like this. The same place I always went when I struggled in times past: to see my brother. The trek through the castle and up to his tower was as familiar to me as it was for me to walk to my own quarters. The hum of the castle fell away the higher I climbed the winding staircase. It was blessedly free of the courtiers that normally roamed the castle. The halls were respectfully empty. The guards were only stationed at the entrance to this wing, giving way to a stillness that I only experienced when visiting Graymont. A single crimson carpet stretched out before me and cushioned each of my steps as I drew closer to his door. I let a heavy breath fill my chest as I pushed the door open and his glass coffin came into view.

I strolled up to it and placed my hand on the cover just over his heart. "It's been too long, Brother."

Each time I came here it became more difficult to accept the loss of someone so dear to me. Perhaps it was a mistake to acquire a glass coffin to preserve him in death, but I couldn't bear the thought of his body cold in the ground, decaying. He was my baby brother. It was my job to protect him and keep him safe. I'd failed miserably and lost not only a brother but my best friend.

"I'm so sorry I failed you, Brother." Each time I came to visit it reminded me how even an immortal like me was not immune to the touch of death. On occasion it was easier to picture myself lying there in endless sleep than him. Our similar looks made the thought of my own death that much more real. While I'd always been a touch bulkier, we were nearly the same height. His hair flowed back from his face and was the same sandy brown as my own. His cheekbones were a touch higher but not much. We had the same set to our mouths, and though my eyes were closer to honey-colored than his, our mother had still gotten us confused on more than one occasion.

"I had to come here. Sometimes this is the only place I can think. If only I could hear your easy voice again doling out useless advice. But this time I know not what to say. Marius suggested Grayson was my son and not yours. It's impossible, isn't it? What I meant to say is . . . I would never make a cuckold of my own brother."

I paused, trying to think of any other possibilities as to why Marius's words might strike me in such a way that made it difficult to dismiss him. "Moira is lovely in every way, but she was your wife. I'd never take your wife from under you. And Moira isn't the sort to do that to you or me. No, she is an honorable woman as I am an honorable man. Have my memories failed me?"

I strolled around the room and ran my fingers over the delicate rose petals of the roses piled into vases around the room. They were soft to the touch and reminded me so much of Moira's skin. "This can't be right. Marius is fussing about with more of his games. It's a manipulation to get in my head. If you were here brother, you would tell me to calm myself with that easy smile. Yet I'm finding it impossible to find a peace I once held so easily. I've got a taste for blood now, and I want his. I should not let his words affect me so."

I turned away from the flowers and back toward Graymont. "It's impossible for me to be Grayson's father. He reminds me so much of you."

I paused, pondering everything about Grayson. He shared our good looks and easy sense of humor. But he too had an edge where his patience waned and his temper took over, which was more suited toward me than Graymont, who never lost his cool. Though . . . Graymont held the power to control others emotional states while Grayson and I shared the blood magic to control their bodies and actions. I hesitated, the similarities between the three of us could all be summed up to family genetics.

"You know I would be proud to call him son." I smirked to myself, picturing Grayson at a young age and the way he raised hell around the castle. "I know he's yours, but it's been the privilege of my life to step up as his uncle. You'd be proud of him, Brother. He forges alliances, he didn't run in fear from the curse, he's loyal. Honestly, Brother, he's a credit to our family."

A light chuckle rumbled in my chest. "Stubborn too. Like you wouldn't believe. You would've been proud to be his father."

I curled my hands into fists on top of the glass. "We might lose him to this bloody curse, and I feel as though my hands are tied. He's everything the future should be, Brother. And I can't . . ." I coughed around the ball in my throat. "I can't imagine this world without him. He is our future."

Grayson was everything The House of Shade should be. He made me a better vampire, a better King. "I wish you were here to meet him, Brother. You'd be able to help see through Marius's lies and all would be well. You wouldn't have lost your temper as I have or even doubted for one second."

But now it was stuck in my mind. How could there be doubt as to who his father was. I remembered his birth . . . vaguely. Visions of Moira screaming at me, the joy, the excitement. Then everything just went . . . black. I tried to remember other things, things that were my own memories—not things I'd been told or overheard over the years but something I honestly remembered. Where there should have been a wedding, there was nothing. Where there should've been my brother's death, there was . . . nothing. No memory at all.

But how could that be? Was Marius right? Was my life a lie? Was Grayson actually mine? But why would everyone have lied for this long? Why would Moira? No, this wasn't right. None of it was correct. Something scratched at the tip of my brain, something out of reach, protected by a red haze I could not see through. There had to be a way to settle this once and for all. To ease my mind. I pulled the small dagger I kept on me from behind my back. With my other hand, I gently pulled the corner of the coffin up, exposing Graymont's body.

"Apologies, Brother. But I cannot let this sit in my mind any longer." I ran the tip of the blade over his hand. A small drop of blood slipped onto the blade. It was all I was going to get from him. Had he still been alive, he would've bled more, but I was able to get this small drop in his deathly state because of the magic that preserved him in the coffin. One was all I needed. One was more than enough. "We're gonna settle this right now."

CHAPTER FORTY-THREE

MOIRA

*J*f I didn't exhaust myself soon, I would go mad with worry. I stood over Claire, letting my healing magic gently drift over her. I couldn't cure whatever Marius had done, but I could ease her turmoil. It was the least I could do. If I was not to find my own comfort, then it was better that I helped her find some. She peeked her eyes open at me and I dropped my hands.

"Hello there, dear." She was so delicate I worried for her survival.

History showed that many of these vampires did not survive whatever had been done to them. Even now we housed so many of the affected in the lab just outside her doors, their cries of pain and madness occasionally breaking the silence of the lab. They were yet to recover and may not ever. The techs did the best they could to ease their suffering but there was naught to be done for them.

Some were too delicate, like Claire, and they hadn't survived.

Claire was so petite I worried she'd go quickly. But the last few days proved she was a fighter. I hated seeing how this illness affected them all, or I should say how the things Marius was doing to them affected them. The more I looked at her, the more endearing I found her features. They were almost elven in nature but not quite. She had a small pert noise and full lips, and her bright eyes were a touch too big for her face, but when she peered up at me, my motherly instincts took over and I wanted nothing more than to help and protect her.

Theon sat up straighter and brushed a light touch over the hair by her temple. "There you are."

"Theon?" Her voice sounded as though she'd been in a deep slumber for days on end.

"You remember me?" Theon was a bit of a disaster. His hair was tangled around his head and deep sleep lines creased the side of his face. He'd hardly left her side since she'd been brought here. It reminded me of those early days after Titus had fallen to the curse when he'd woken with no memory and assumed Graymont was the love that I'd lost rather than him.

My sorrow grew so deep in those early days that it nearly drowned me. At every turn Titus was there trying to comfort me for the loss of his brother, my supposed husband. It was a difficult thing grieving a love who stood before me each day. Yet I found solace in raising Grayson and giving my love to him. Each day with him made the pain worth it. But now even he was gone, and the sorrow could no longer be held at bay. It consumed me, and no matter what I attempted, it colored my days and nights, keeping such a hold on me I could hardly draw a breath.

Try as I might to force the sorrow away, to keep it back, it overwhelmed me. All I could do now was live with it for as long as possible and then when I could no longer take it . . . actions would need to be taken. I wanted to believe in the Queens and Piper, but years of failure told me this bloody curse was nearly impossible to break, so I turned back to what I thought might distract me. I ran my hand beside Claire's face and a fine pink mist danced between my palm and her skin.

"Umm, yeah?" A warm blush returned to her cheeks, giving her face a nice warm color. She blinked harder and I knew my gentle help was working. She glanced around, confusion riddled her features. "Why am I here?"

Theon fisted the bed sheet, and I could see the anger flash in his eyes. "Marius. He—"

"Hurt me?" Her eyebrows drew low over her big eyes as though she struggled to remember. She bit her bottom lip and shook her head, pulling the crisp white covers higher over her body. I waited patiently for her to settle down and speak once more. "I remember walking into a room with him. He told me I was going to join him, and I thought . . . I thought I might find you."

Theon's face paled. "You were looking for me?"

"It'd been a long time since I'd seen you." She hesitated, and her gaze dipped down to the sheets where she pushed the creases around making little shapes with the tip of her finger. "I remember being so lonely."

"I should've never left you." He took her hand in his. "I thought I was keeping you safe."

"Safe?" She let her head fall back on the pillow as she gave a sad smile up at the ceiling. Tears leapt from the corners of her eyes and fell onto the bed. Each one hit the pillowcase with a dim pang that wretched my heart even more. How could Marius be so cruel?

Claire sniffled and ran the back of her hand over her nose. "Bit late for that, isn't it?"

"It seems crazy now, stupid even, but I promise I was only trying to do what I thought best for you." His words were almost pleading, and deep down I knew his plight. I'd been in that same position for two hundred years. Always doing what was right for Titus and the crown, no matter the cost to myself. To keep my loved ones safe, I would do anything.

She cleared her throat and tilted her head to the side to face him. "Perhaps you let me have a say in what's best for me."

The objects in the room all began floating up from the surfaces around us, and I took a step back from a cup of blood moving in my direction. Claire's eyes went wide and darted around the room. Her breaths came in nervous pants as sweat beaded on her forehead. "What's happening?"

Theon jumped to his feet and pulled her hand close to

his chest. He leaned over her, resting his arm just by her pillow. "Look at me, Claire."

When her eyes turned to his, her breaths slowed. Theon's lips pulled up and he spoke to her in a soft tone. "You have some new powers now, but it's nothing to worry about. Do you hear me?"

She gave him a nod and her throat bobbed as she swallowed. "I hear you."

"Everything is fine." He kept holding her gaze. "Deep breath. I'm here and I'm not going anywhere."

Claire sucked in a deep breath and the objects in the room all fell to the floor. That one moment of support of knowing he was here for her was more than enough to make her feel better. They didn't look away from each other, and I feared I'd intruded on an intimate moment they both so clearly needed. I gave a polite cough into my hand, and when they both turned toward me, I excused myself. "I'll be just outside if you require anything else."

Before I left the room, Claire called after me. "I-I think I remember hearing you here with me . . . I thank you. Your words, they helped me."

"Of course." I pressed my lips together and ducked my head as I hurried out of the room.

It wasn't that I begrudged them their budding love, but I preferred not to remind myself of the constant ache in my chest, so I turned away from her room to go through the lab and into the next room. I was three steps toward my next patient, a young woman who exploded into puddles of water at random, when Titus came flying into the lab. The last I'd heard he'd gone to pay his respects to Graymont, and now he was moving through here with a knife in hand that held the tiniest bit of blood on the tip.

I froze, knowing in my gut something was amiss. It was easy to blend in among the busy movement of the lab. I'd become a staple in this lab, helping the sick and injured, so it was easy for me to drift around the table and tuck myself into an empty room next to the one that Titus had gone in. I tried to focus only on his words as I stood next to the rough wall between us.

"Get me a sample of the Prince's blood," he barked at a lab tech. I knew they'd had plenty of it since Piper arrived. Even if she'd drank the entire supply he'd left for her, we would still have a drop or two for the doctor to analyze when Piper became his progeny.

"Yes, Your Majesty." The tech hurried out of the room. It would only take moments for him to return, too quickly for me to intervene. Panic and doubt flowed through my body. Was I going to let this happen? Was I going to let Titus run a test I knew would tell him the truth? Would it change anything between us? He still didn't have his memories because if he had gotten them back, I would've known, he would've come to me. Our love had been a fiery timeless one.

But I didn't know if I wanted to intervene, something was happening here. The constant exhaustion I felt deep in my bones wanted to stop fighting and give up this charade. My heart hammered in my chest and my hands shook. After two hundred years, why would he question

Grayson's genetics now? Sweat broke out over my body, and I wanted to go to him and ask what he was doing, but fear held me in place.

The tech returned faster than I anticipated and stood there frozen, unable and unwilling to stop what was about to happen. Titus's voice boomed through the wall. "I want you to compare these three samples and tell me what you see."

"Of course, Your Majesty. But would you prefer the doctor to go over them and report to you when you get the results?" I could tell from the timbre of his voice the tech was nervous to be in the presence of the King. Titus had that kind of effect on others, all but me. I'd been comfortable with him from the start.

"No, I want the results now." I could picture him motioning to the lab equipment. "Do it. Now."

I could stop this, but I wouldn't. There was only one thing he could be doing after visiting with Graymont. He'd gotten samples of his blood, along with Grayson's and his own. My breath hitched and my hand quivered as I placed it on the wall between us. Tears threatened to spill, and a ball formed in the pit of my stomach. The sound of my own heartbeat nearly drowned out the words as the lab worked on comparing the samples one after another. I let the rough wall scratching on my skin keep me in the present. I scraped the tip of my finger over it, focusing on the feel of the cool rock under my touch.

"Hurry up about it." Titus snapped and something clattered onto the metal table.

"Ye-yes of course." The tech drew in a breath, trying to calm himself. "I'd just like to double check."

"You've already double checked. Tell me," Titus commanded, and I knew he'd used his power on the tech. "With complete honesty."

"Th-these two are uncle and nephew." He hesitated, his words stammering out of his mouth slowly, "And these two are father and son, Your Majesty."

My breath hitched and a small sob escaped my lips. I hurried out of the room only to nearly crash right into Titus's chest. I froze, unable to speak but needing to say something so badly. How did he know? What made him suspect? Did someone tell him? A tear slid down my cheek and I swiped it away. His entire body vibrated with tension, but he didn't take a step toward me. We just stared at each other, neither of us speaking but the tension so thick I could cut it with a knife.

I licked my lips and forced myself to say something, anything. "You know?"

"I know." His honey eyes bore into mine and the swirling mist of his blood magic pooled on the floor around his feet. His hands clenched and unclenched. Noises from the lab drifted down the hall toward us and he lowered his voice. "It's . . . what I mean to say is . . . is it true? Is he mine?"

For two hundred years I'd dreamt of this conversation. For two hundred years I wanted my family back together, to have my husband with me the way so many others were afforded their own soulmates. For two hundred years I wanted my son to know he had a father. I wanted to hug him, to hold him close, to cry two hundred years' worth of tears into his chest and give him the two hundred years' worth of love that was stolen from us. But he looked as he always had for the last two hundred years. There was no love or recognition in his eyes. The curse was still intact and the fear that I would lose him to it for good made me hold two hundred years' worth of secrets.

"My lord, I know not what to say." I folded my hands in front of me and clenched them so tightly I swore I was going to break my own bones.

Titus's honey eyes shimmered, and he shifted from one foot to the other. He took a step closer to me and I took a small step back. If he touched me, I would lose that tight control over myself. He pressed his lips together and lowered his voice, "My memories have failed me. Speak the truth. He is mine and you're my soul—"

No! I couldn't let him go there. Not now, not while the curse still stood. If he didn't remember a thing, that meant he only suspected because of something someone said, not because they'd broken the curse. I had to stop him. It was uncharacteristic for me to be so rude, but I cut him off. "Do not speak the words to me. The curse is still very much alive, and I do not wish to live that hell again."

He sucked in a sharp breath and looked like I could push him over with a feather. He pressed his hand to his chest and tried to speak several times. I wanted to comfort him through this and give myself a moment of happiness with him. But there was no joy to be had. He knew

Grayson was his, but he knew not of our love, or how any of this came to be. I would not be the one to confirm his suspicions. I knew Titus better than he knew himself. If I told him, he'd take responsibility so quickly and the curse would surely ruin him. Like father, like son.

"I refuse to live it again," I said quietly.

"Again?" His shoulders hunched and he hung his head. We stood like that for a long moment with him taking the time he needed and me fighting the urge to wrap my arms around his waist and bury my face in his chest the way I used to.

I was too scared to even speak or breathe. He straightened and the muscle in his jaw ticked as his gaze bore into mine. "Our . . ." he cleared his throat, "our *son* needs me. And upon my return, we will speak of this . . . in great detail."

Before I could say a word, he turned from me and stormed away. My stomach turned and I couldn't breathe, couldn't think. I ran past the lab techs staring at me, past the holding cells for the sick, and right out into the hall. I was up one flight of stairs and through the castle in an instant. My panic and pain had me climbing the stairs to the tower where Graymont lay. There was no one I could talk to, no one to comfort me. No one to offer me a shoulder. I'd been alone for two hundred years and even now I was still entirely alone.

I threw myself through the door and onto Graymont's coffin. I placed my hands on the lid and leaned over, resting my cheek on the cold glass. Tears spilled over my cheeks and pooled under my face. I let the racking sobs take me, my breaths barely filling my chest before I wept them out. I didn't know how long I stayed there just letting my tears flow, but it was as though a dam had been broken and now I could not stop. Graymont would've known how to fix this or stop this or what to say to Titus, but I was at a loss now more than ever.

"He's figuring it out just as we're about to lose our son." I lifted my head to look down at Graymont. Still as beautiful in death as he ever was. "And when he asks me, how am I to tell him he killed you? He's about to find out all, and your death would have been in vain."

I could hardly stand the thought. I never believed this day would come but it was steadily closing in. And now he'd gone with the others to face the witch who did this to us. I scarcely believed they would return alive. Just as I was about to get him back, I would lose them all. "Titus will join you in the afterlife and you all will leave me. If I lose them both, I will have no choice but to soon follow. I swear it. One way or another, we will be reunited."

CHAPTER FORTY-FOUR

PIPER

*M*y wrist jerked, rousing me from my sleep. It'd been so long since I'd had Grayson's arms around me. Even in the underworld I found his touch soothing. The chains jerked once more, and my eyes shot wide open. I scrambled to sit up and looked over at Grayson. He crouched there like an animal, staring me down. I suddenly felt beyond exposed, lying naked in a harpy's nest with scraps of fabric draped over my hips. I glanced around hoping to find my clothing. When he yanked the cuffs once more, my eyes caught on my sweater, which dangled from the chain connecting the cuffs. I shoved my arm forward and pulled the sweater over my arm and head.

Grayson hissed in my direction, and I rolled my eyes at him. "Yeah, yeah, you like me naked. I know."

"Well, this is . . . interesting," a female voice purred. My head snapped up to a woman who stood over the nest.

There was a hint of amusement in her voice as she smirked down at us. She was petite and willowy with a thinner stature, pale skin, and white hair that went down to her hips.

I scrambled for my pants when she picked them up from just outside the nest and tossed them to me. "Yours I presume."

"Thanks." Embarrassment flooded my body and heat filled my cheeks. "Can you turn around?"

"She will but I might not." A guy who was slightly taller than Grayson stood across from us. He chuckled as he ran his hand through his dark, wild waves. They went out of his face for a moment, then fell right back into place around his face and to his chin. His vivid purple eyes freaked me out and my magic rose around me.

"You're an ass," the woman snapped at him. "Turn around before she makes you."

"Fine," he muttered with a heavy sigh. "Not the one I want to see naked anyways." He turned and gave me his back just as the woman had.

"Pig." She shot at him over her shoulder.

I hurried to my feet and pulled my pants on quickly, buttoning them. It only took me another second to locate my boots and shove my feet into them. I glared at Grayson who apparently had gotten his pants up before we'd had visitors. Though he still remained shirtless, and those dark veins were back with a vengeance, his body was still amazing, with all his toned, lean muscles and towering stature.

He even had his stupid shoes on . . . or had he never taken them off? "You could've said something."

He growled at me, and I wanted to slap the curse out of him. Illogical, but true. I turned to face the woman. "Who are you?"

She peeked at me over her shoulder. When she saw I was fully dressed, she spun back around. She didn't exactly smile, but her lips turned up a bit. She pressed her hand over her chest. "I'm Nova. It's nice to meet you."

"Nova! The Queen of death?" I recognized the name instantly. The Queens had spoken so highly of her I almost felt like I knew her already. "It's nice to finally meet you."

I offered her my hand in greeting.

She held her hands up and shook her head. "I don't shake hands."

Though she had on elbow length gloves she still didn't want to shake my hand? What was up with that? I awkwardly pulled it back. "Okay, cool."

She looked over my shoulder. "Sup, Gray?"

He snarled a greeting, and I yanked on the chain, pulling him closer before he could attack either one of them. "He's not himself."

"So I've heard." She pursed her ruby-red lips. "Not a good look for him."

"Tell me about it." I was so relieved that someone had found us that I was ready to just go with them without question. The view of the underworld was still spectacular with the glow from Tartarus and running rivers. Even the onyx castle was breathtaking. Yet I knew danger lurked around every corner down here, and I had no idea how to navigate that. It was a relief to have her with me, even if she just caught me naked in a harpy nest.

"How did you find us?"

Nova motioned to the cliff's edge and my eyes widened. Crows, so many crows surrounded the nest. Some flew above us in a giant circle while others hopped along the cliff edge and pecked at the fabric overflowing from the nest. Oily feathers littered the entire area, and their little *caws* filled the silence. There were so many they nearly blocked out the castle. My jaw dropped. "Um, that's my bad."

"It made you entirely too easy to find." The guy behind us crossed his arms. "I was hoping it'd take a bit longer."

"Sorry to disappoint you." I hiked my thumb at him as I faced Nova. "Who is this guy?"

Her chest heaved with a heavy sigh. "His name is Liesin, son of Hades. I find it best to ignore him."

"Oh, you couldn't ignore me if you tried." He snickered.

Nova held up one perfectly gloved finger. "You want to be useful and get us out of here or are you going to be yourself?"

"I do love the way we banter." He winked at her. "Like foreplay."

Nova pinched the bridge of her nose and groaned. "I'll do it myself then."

A burst of laughter forced its way from my chest and I pressed my hand over my mouth. "I'm sorry."

"Something funny?" Liesin raised his eyebrows at me.

"Well, I mean, you said it was like foreplay." I motioned between the two of them. "And she said she'd rather do it by herself. If ever there was a rejection, that was it."

Nova chuckled. "I meant get us to Hades, but both ways apply in this case."

Liesin gave a deep rumbling laugh and tipped his head toward me. "I'll give you that one. And of course I will take you to my father. But only because Nova asked me so nicely."

He stomped on the ground, and it opened up right in front of him. Each piece fell away like breaking apart a puzzle until there was nothing but a hole with white light glinting from it. Liesin motioned to the opening. "Everyone down the hole."

"Not again." I hated jumping into holes and falling forever. It's how I ended up being chased by a harpy.

"Problem?" Nova stepped up to the edge.

I didn't want to jump down another one of those things and end up someplace worse . . . again. Looking back at Grayson, I knew I was left with no other choice. The curse was worsening, and now he cocked his head in all different directions as if more than one person was talking to him. I couldn't bear to see him like this any longer. That one night with him was nowhere near enough. I wanted a lifetime of nights like that.

"No problem. Let's go." I stepped up behind her, dragging Grayson with me.

The chain rattled and he jerked on it. I stumbled back and nearly crashed into him. I turned and held my hand over his chest. The well deep inside me rose at my request and crimson mist mixed with sage fluttered from my fingertips and spread over his skin. His body quieted but his inner turmoil rolled through him. With my power simmering in his veins, it gave me a front row seat to his pain. "Relax, we're almost there."

He shook his head with a sharp, quick, jarring movement. Yet his eyes never cleared, and his body still thrummed with turmoil. But my magic calmed him enough for me to pull him forward. We neared the edge, and he stiffened. Nova took one look at him, then she dropped into the hole. I wrapped my hand around his upper arm and tugged him with me as I too dropped right into it. My stomach rose to my throat, and I twisted along with this blinding tunnel. It was like riding a slide into madness. My grip tightened on Grayson and my nerves began to fray as this ride seemed to never end.

Then as suddenly as that twisting descent started, it stopped, and I staggered into a huge throne room with Grayson right behind me. I tripped to a stop and put my hands on my knees, sucking in a hard breath. This room was a far cry from Titus's throne room. These walls were a shining black, like someone had coated them in oil. It was almost reflective yet not. When I moved, it appeared like the walls moved with me. Torches burned every few feet, sending their flames high against the wall and lighting the room in warm, flickering light. The ceiling was vaulted up to a sharp point. When I followed the architecture with my eyes, I stopped at the swirling vortex of ghosts drifting in a slow circle around a grand chandelier.

"Piper!" My head snapped around at the sound of my name. Relief washed over me as I spotted Zinnia marching through the center set of doors along with the other Queens. There were several sets of black double doors, and I could only imagine where each of them led.

"Zinnia, thank goodness we found you." This mission was enough of a mess already without having the Queens by my side. Seeing them brought a sharp relief.

Ophelia walked into the room with a battle axe draped over her shoulder. Her wide onyx eyes bounced every-where else but at me. "It's not like we'd leave you here. We'd find you."

"Oh, would you?" a deep rumbling voice boomed and echoed all around the room.

I froze, as did the Queens. A man as tall as The Fallen appeared in the center of the room. I could see the resem-blance between him and Liesin—both of them with wild dark hair, chiseled jawlines, and perfectly sculpted bodies, though Hades was much more muscular and his eyes were a few shades lighter. He wasn't what I expected a ruler of the underworld would look like. His clothing was casual, with a fitted black V-neck T-shirt, black dress pants, and matching black shoes along with a belt that showcased his trim waist. He was beautiful, and yet I knew if he wanted my soul, he could yank it from my body at his leisure.

He spread his arms out wide and walked in a slow

circle. "You little witches have a bad habit of thinking you can just waltz in and out of the underworld."

Tabi stepped forward with a sweet look on her face as she beamed at him. She folded her hands in front of her looking poised and diplomatic. "I assure we d—"

"I'm sorry, did I say it was your turn to speak?" He wagged his finger at us. "And now you're back in my kingdom to fuck more things up. Tell me, how many of you shall I trap down here this time?"

My pulse raced and I had no words. I didn't think talking to Hades would be the difficult part, but here we were. Something told me that even if we snuck into Tartarus, he'd know and we'd be in even deeper shit. He turned away from us and strolled over to a huge throne. It wasn't like anything I'd ever seen before. It too was inky black and towering. The back stuck out from the wall but also seemed to melt into it at the same time. He dropped down into the seat and rested his forearms on the arms of the chair. Somehow, he seemed to fill up the whole chair even though it was huge and towering.

Silence fell heavily in the room, and I took a few steps closer to the Queens. I didn't know how well their power would work against a god like Hades, but if I was going to stand a chance here, it would only be with them.

Liesin cleared his throat, and Hades' gaze snapped toward him. "Father, perhaps just hear them out?"

"Hear them out?" He glared at his son. "It would be even more convenient if they would hear me when I say they are not welcome here."

Liesin's gaze slid toward Nova, and though she didn't even look at him, her back stiffened like she knew his gaze was on her. That one look was less than a second, but enough to tell me he wasn't faking his interest in her. He continued on, "It could be worth your while."

Hades waved his hand in that regal way that told us to plead our case. "In that case, please make it worth my while. Let's be clear: make it quick and it better intrigue me."

When no one spoke, Zinnia nodded her head in his direction, encouraging me. I swallowed. "The House of Shade has been cursed for a thousand years."

He made that impatient waving motion for me to hurry it up. "Tell me something I don't know."

"The Crone is the one who cursed them, and we've come here to trick her into breaking the curse and freeing The House of Shade."

He sat forward on the throne. "Let me get this straight, you've come here to go into Tartarus to try and trick a being who, by all accounts, is hundreds or possibly thousands of years old? And you think that's going to work?"

I motioned to Grayson and the state of madness he was growing deeper and deeper into. "What other choice do we have? I can't leave him like this. Would you leave your soulmate in such a state?"

"Why is it always life and death with you people?" When none of us said anything, he gave an annoyed groan. "If you're going to do this, then you need an expert in negotiations because the Crone sure as shit isn't going to talk to you. You're far too young and far too naive."

"Okay, who did you have in mind?" I didn't want a stranger trying to help us. An unknown element would only cause problems, and we had one shot at this. One shot to save Grayson and The House. *No pressure.*

Hades waved to a second set of doors and they flew open. My eyes widened and I sucked in a sharp breath. "Holy shit."

"Is that anyway to greet your King?" Titus strolled through the doors, and I couldn't put my finger on it, but the second I saw him I knew this was going to work. Titus commanded a room just by being in it. He himself was tall, imposing, and ancient. He winked in my direction, and I offered him the warmest smile I could, given our circumstances.

"What I mean to say is . . . um . . . Your Majesty, what are you doing here?"

Astrid held her hand up. "I'm wondering the same thing. Though I will admit it is lovely to see you, Your Highness."

"I can hardly stay behind when my . . . when Grayson needs me. I am here and I will make this happen." The muscle in his jaw ticked as a mask of determination overcame his features. "If this is to work, the Crone needs to think she has the upper hand and we need to give her the one thing she wants most of all."

After all that we'd learned and all that we knew, it was obvious who she wanted. "Her sister? But I thought they'd pledged themselves to Lucifer, which means if they die their souls go to him, right?"

Hades gave a dark chuckle as he slumped deeper into his throne. "In theory, *orrrr* I enjoy pissing Lucifer off whenever I can, and when she died, I may or may not have intercepted her soul before it reached him."

"That is brilliant. Yo, death god, do me a favor and when I go, you just go ahead and snatch my soul, will you?" Ophelia dropped her battle axe on the ground next to her and it landed with a harsh bang. "Because I'm pretty sure my dad might've given my soul away to Lucifer at some point."

Everyone turned shocked faces in her direction. Hades didn't bat an eyelash. "Consider it done if you leave my battle axe alone. I'm rather fond of that one."

Ophelia ran her hand lovingly over the handle. "I don't know. It's pretty greatttt."

"O!" we all yelled at her at the same time.

"I wasn't going to keep it." She peeked up at us. "I just wanted to borrow it . . . until I was dead."

Hades rolled his eyes but said nothing. The rest of us turned back toward Titus.

I wanted to run up and hug him, though he always struck me as the *do not touch* type. "I'm really glad you're here, Your Majesty."

"We can thank Hades, my old friend." Titus gave a little bow of his head.

"Tha—" I started to give him my thanks.

Hades held his hands up, cutting off my words. "You

cannot let her out. You cannot under any circumstances give her Danna. You cannot fuck this up in any way, shape, or form. And I'll need one more thing."

Zinnia's face paled. "And what is that?"

"A favor." A sinister smile tugged at his lips while he flicked an invisible speck of dirt from his clothing. "Of my choosing, to be given at a time also of my choosing."

"Done." I didn't even give the others a chance to respond. We would all pay any price for Grayson. I was sure of it. We were so close, and I wanted this taken care of now.

"Wait! Before we go." We all looked toward Ophelia as she pulled six pieces of paper from her potion pouch on her hip then gave one to each of the Queens. "We're gonna need this to trap her."

Astrid took the paper, and when she looked down at it, confusion riddled her features. She flipped the paper over and held it out toward Ophelia. "It's in a different language."

Ophelia shrugged. "So?"

"So, we can't read it, O," Serrina snapped at her. "How is this supposed to work?"

"I wrote it phonetically . . . sound it out, duh." She lowered her voice to a mutter, "Always making things more complicated than they have to be."

Titus cleared his throat. "Are we ready then?"

Zinnia gave a stiff nod. "We're ready."

Hades gave me a devilish look. "Then let's go to Tartarus."

CHAPTER FORTY-FIVE

KYLIAN

Suffering fools was not part of my job description. Yet I found myself uncharacteristically doing just that. It was almost too easy, which made the situation very tedious. The only thing more predictable than a fool doing foolish things was a desperate fool doing desperate things. So here I sat perched on a barstool at the edge of a seedy vampire bar in one of the shadiest parts of London. Here the humans skulked about in alleyways looking for their next fix. They had that nervous way about them, with the itching and the ticking. Their addiction was clear in the parlor of their skin and the distinct odor of toxins in the blood.

The vampire bar was not much better. This was a place where they came to get lost, where no one asked questions and sampling the toxic humans would get them a high that made them junkies as well. They were what they ate. The bar itself ran the length of the wall and was made of shabby sticky wood, a juke box played offbeat tunes from the corner of the room, and the bartender was an older vampire turned in his late sixties with a balding head and too round belly. It was as though he'd gone from human to vampire and not a thing had changed about him—not his job, not what he ate, nor even his lack of life's ambition.

As I sipped at my drink far too early in the day, I absently wondered what it would be like to be content to just exist. There were a few regulars spread throughout the small room, yet no one spoke to each other. They were too lost in drowning their own sorrows to acknowledge anyone else. The bell above the door gave a little tinkering sound and a vampire in a hooded cloak hurried through the door and walked straight to my side.

He kept his shoulders hunched as he clambered up onto the stool next to mine. With a little wave, he signaled the bartender for a drink and made a show of flashing a wad of cash when he paid, then the man lowered his voice, "I take it you know who I am?"

I gave a light chuckle over the rim of my drink. "Clive Christiano."

"Shhhhh." He glanced over his shoulder. "I'm a wanted vampire."

"Hate to break it to you, but no one here gives a shit who you are." I motioned to the few vampires who huddled to themselves.

"Of course they do." He straightened his shoulders yet never let the hood fall back from his face. "I'm the Ambassador to the Blood Born vampires."

"You mean you *were*." Last night there had been a swift, harsh move from Titus. I couldn't say I disagreed with his tactics. Evermore was a *kill or be killed* kind of place at times. With one bloody dinner he'd earned my respect and then some. "I think you've been fired."

"Perhaps, but it matters not." He sipped at his drink. "I've got a price on my head. I'm sure of it."

"If there were a price on your head, I would've claimed it already." It was easy to tell him the truth of his situation . . . and mine. It was no secret I operated for profit. Usually.

He froze and slid a sideways glance at me. "I have a proposition for you to avoid just that."

This ought to be good. "I'm listening."

"I've heard you have full access to the castle." He lowered his voice. "It would work to your advantage for the job I'll hire you for."

"Depends on which one you're talking about. I'm a Prince. I have access to a lot of castles." This asshole was doing the exact opposite of what would help him survive.

More of that head darting around and hunched over posture. I could almost feel his heart hammering in his chest. Beads of sweat gathered on his brow and he brushed them away with a jerky, sharp movement. His hands shook as he took another sip. "Don't be daft, you know which castle I'm talking about."

"Let's say I do." I knew exactly what castle he was talking about. "What do you want with me?"

"I heard you're for hire. No matter the job."

"True." *It wasn't true.* Was I for hire? Most times. Did I

take every job? Not even close. I took the jobs that intrigued me, the jobs no one else wanted, the jobs that would gain me some kind of connection or experience. I had plenty of money and whatever else I desired.

He pulled the crumpled wad of money from his pocket and shoved it toward me. The bills were all folded together in a messy bundle, like he'd grabbed them in a hurry, and I was sure he had after the bloody dinner and subsequent bonfire afterwards. He glanced at me from under his hood. "That should do it."

I took the money and thumbed through the bills. "Do what?"

He slammed his fist down on the bar and no one looked in our direction. He shot forward, getting a little too close to my face. Rancid breath fanned over my nose, and I sat back away from the stench of him. "To bloody assassinate the bastard murdering King Titus."

This was what I hated about well . . . everyone. They assumed because I was banished, been in prison a few times, maybe stolen a thing or two, and might have had killed a person or two, that I was willing to do any shitting thing they could dream up. I shoved the money into my pocket. "That's half, where's my other half?"

"Other half?" He growled and the glass shattered in his hand. His drink spilled over his hand along with shards of glass. "Bloody greedy git."

"Careful." I turned and wrapped my hand around the fabric just under his neck. I jerked him forward so we were almost nose to nose. "Don't forget who you're speaking to."

Any ounce of bravado or anger he had evaporated as his eyes widened and his body shook. "You're quite right. Apologies."

I eased my grip and shoved him away. He tipped back on the barstool and then reached out, grabbing onto the bar, scrambling to keep his balance. I waved him away. "Fuck off. You're not worth my time."

"I have more." His words rushed from his mouth.

"How much more?" I turned back toward my drink and grabbed it up.

"A whole house full." He swung his arm as though presenting me with a brand-new car. "You can take your pick."

"You're going to take me to your house and let me pick whatever I'd like?" How pathetic could this guy get? It was almost sad how desperate he was . . . almost.

He rose from the stool. "I'll take you right now."

Sucker. "I'll see if you have anything worthwhile."

I made a show of slowly rising to my feet and following him to the restrooms. Clive hopped up on the sink and placed his hand on the mirror there. When it rippled under his touch, he crooked his finger at me. "Just this way."

It was a rare occasion that I found myself traveling via mirror with a vampire, so I took the opportunity to take my time. When we stepped through the mirror, it slid across my skin like cool slime, though it didn't leave a damp trail in its wake. We stood in what could only be described as a long white hallway. The sound of my boots echoed back at me with each step I took. It wasn't as remarkable as traveling through a portal with Beckett or Ophelia, but it was different enough to keep my interest until we reached the other end. He placed his hand on another mirror, and when we stepped out I was in Clive Christiano's gaudy-ass house. The guy literally had crap everywhere.

The mirror was set up in the foyer just beside the door. The house was dark and there was no sign of life to be found. A thick tiger-skin carpet sat under our feet, and I pointed to it. "Is that real?"

"Shot it myself."

Prick deserves to die.

I stepped around it, not daring to further desecrate the poor animal. Roman-style columns went from the floor to the ceiling, though I didn't find the ceilings that high. They were painted a bright gold and blocked the general flow of the home. Vases stood in random places all around the foyer and in the room beyond. I was growing tired of this game. I walked right past Clive and down the hall. "What's in here?"

I bypassed the kitchen, sitting rooms, and even the movie screening room, though I was sure I was going to take some of it later. Soto, one of my most trusted friends, wanted a flat screen to sit across from her bed and I promised I'd get her one. I shoved through the doubled doors at the end of the hall and let them smack into the walls. When the doors hit the walls with a loud bang, I knew I was going to leave dents.

Good. Fucker. A deer head was mounted on the wall, and I was ready to end this little game I was playing with him. Cruel bastard spent his days harming innocent animals. He earned nothing less than what he was about to get.

Clive hurried behind me. "This is just the dining room. There's more in the other parts of the ho . . ."

His words trailed off as he took in the scene before him. He turned to run for the door, but I darted around him, blocking his path. *Run, little rabbit. Run.* I wrapped my hand around his throat and walked him back until his back pressed against the wall. I pulled a dagger from behind my back and held the point close to his eye. "I should plant this dagger right in your eye, you pathetic fuck."

"I-I'm sorry."

I wasn't in the mood to accept apologies. "How dare you think I would even take a moment to consider murdering Titus—a King who is ten times the vampire you'll ever be. You sniveling pile of greedy piss."

"N-no." His body quaked and I wanted to shove my dagger through his eye and into his head. It would be a pleasure to take this garbage out of this world for good.

"I'm an elf. You think the dead carcasses around your house are impressive? Animals are sacred." I leaned in closer. He scratched at my arm, but his attempts were useless. He might have super vampire strength, but I was a Prince of Elves, and we came with our own tricks.

His face turned a deep crimson as I squeezed. "I-I apologize."

"You're a fucking barbarian. I should skin you alive and mount your hide to my wall." I wanted to do it, to kill him where he stood.

The sound of a throat being cleared drew me back and I eased my grip. "You're lucky."

I stepped back and turned from Clive toward the open doors. I shoved them closed, and when I placed my hand on the metal doorknobs, I let my magic flow over them. Dark-burgundy smoke seeped around them, and they melted together, locking us in. I turned back to face him and motioned toward the twenty-foot dining table towards the silent party he hadn't noticed because he was too busy watching me and what I might take from him.

"Please do join our little dinner party."

He looked from me to the table and back again. His body quivered from head to toe, and he froze there. I groaned, knowing I'd have to force him. I walked back over to him and fisted my hand into his hair, pulling the strands. I jerked his head forward and forced him to walk to the head of the table. I yanked the chair out and shoved him down into it, then strolled to the other side of the table and took a seat.

"I believe you know my friend, Lorenzo."

Lorenzo leaned back in his chair and crossed his ankle over his knee. One of his arms rested on the chair while the other rested on the table. He was the very picture of cold indifference. "We've met."

Clive had yet to look at him. His eyes were locked on our other guests, and if he'd been human, I was sure he'd piss himself. There was still a possibility of him vomiting judging by the green pallor to his skin. He sank down in the chair seeming to finally grasp the gravity of the situation he got himself into.

"Haven't we, Clive?" Lorenzo spread his fingers on the table like a spider. When Clive didn't answer and just stared at the others, Lorenzo snapped his fingers. Clive's eyes snapped to attention. Lorenzo cleared his throat. "I said, haven't we?"

Clive broke down into heavy sobs. His shoulders rocked and he hunched over like the pathetic piece of turd he was. "Oh please. Don't kill me."

Lorenzo tilted his head, staring him down with that cold calculation. "Have you met our guests? I believe you already know them from the families you joined with: the Mavricks, Petersons, and Blackstones."

I chuckled as Clive continued to sob. Sitting in the chairs lining the far side of the table were each of the men who were responsible for their families. They were propped up to sit straight, with each one of their disembodied heads sitting on the plates in front of them. Their bodies occupied the chairs. Their wrists and elbows were tied to the arms of the chairs while the stubs of their necks were in full view. Their spines had been severed, and I could easily see the muscles and tendons in their necks surrounding the bones. Each one of their heads faced in Clive's direction. Their skin had begun to droop in odd ways with their eyes open and unseeing. Their mouths hung wide as though they'd died screaming. A big brown duffle bag sat open and empty in the middle of the table.

Clive turned his head to the side and vomited on the floor beside his chair. "I-I'm so sorry. I—"

Lorenzo held his hand up, cutting him off. "Let's not make this emotional. I'm not an emotional man, Clive. I can be unemotional about the money you owe me. Well, you and all these other families that I'll never recoup from. That I can forgive."

"P-please, L-lorenzo." He was a stammering mess, and I relished every moment of it. This fuck who dared to challenge a King, this weakling who dared to hire me to do so, this useless piece of garbage who deserved to die just for hunting innocent animals was falling apart like the little bitch he was.

"I wasn't finished speaking." Lorenzo's face was all cold hard planes. This was the Lorenzo I knew, this was the gangster who owned half of New York and allowed the other half to exist out of the kindness of his heart. "I thought we were friends. I like to make friends."

"We are friends." Tears ran down Clive's face, mixing with the sweat already coating his skin.

I stabbed my knife into the table with a loud thump. "It's still not your turn."

He tried to press his lips shut but his sobs continued to escape as his body shook. Lorenzo cleared his throat. "As I was saying. I'm not emotional about the money, but what I am emotional about is the plot against my life. Now, from what my understanding is, friends don't try to kill their friends. Isn't that right, Kylian?"

"That's right." I tightened my grip on the knife, and my knuckles turned white.

Clive whimpered. "We can be friends. I swear it."

Lorenzo shook his head. "No, we're not friends no more. Though we have some things to discuss. I believe this conversation is necessary between all of us."

He motioned toward me and the headless bodies across from us. Clive pressed his hands over his face and a wailing sob wracked his body. "Oh, Creator save me!"

Lorenzo rose to his feet and held his hand out toward me. I yanked the dagger free of the table and handed it over to him. He ran his thumb over the blade, checking to see how sharp it was. A smirk tugged at his lips as he turned toward Clive. "Save your prayers. The Creator ain't here tonight."

CHAPTER FORTY-SIX

MOIRA

*M*y dearest love,

It has been ages since I've had the privilege of admitting my devoted love out loud, or as it stands now, in writing. It is my wish that when you look back on our time together, you will see that all I am and all I have been was for us, and of course for our beloved son. Two hundred years of being a breath away from you yet unable to speak these words was a torture I would not wish upon our greatest enemy. Oftentimes my mind travels back to the days and many nights we've spent together. I held them close to me like an oath to you and the day that you could fully return to me. I believed our love would survive this. I believed in us. I believed love would conquer all. But seeing our son fall to this curse that has crushed our family has taken a part of me I didn't know I held on to. And now, now I dare not hope that either of you will come back from this. For if this mission fails, I know you will be forced to do your duty and remove our son from this world, and I cannot bear to watch any more of our family fall to death. It is my wish that *The House of Shade* leaves this world as a family. As you have gone to join our son, I have decided to face my progeny, a progeny I never should have made. I saw him into this world, and now I will see him out of it. It is with greatest hope that I will join you both in the after-life. If by some miracle you are able to read this, then know I am leaving our son in your hands and my love will eternally be yours, my dearest and greatest joy of my life.

Forever your Queen,

Moira

I scribbled my name across the bottom of the page before I could lose my nerve. Never before had I been so bold as to make a move like this. But it was what my honor demanded of me. Titus and Grayson went to face their demons. It was high time I faced mine. I dropped the letter onto the desktop of my sitting table. If Titus returned, this would be the first place he'd look for me. Instead of finding me, he'd find my letter. With that in mind, I rose and crossed to my closet.

I rarely wore trousers, but on this night I would out of necessity. I slowly removed the court regalia that I'd grown so used to, taking my time to loosen the laces of my dress and letting my gown fall to the floor around my feet. I stepped out of it and left it sitting there as I moved to my closets and grabbed a pair of slim-fitting jeans. I wasn't used to the material as it molded around my legs while I zipped them up, but the ability to move freely was a most welcome one. I slipped my arms into a cream-colored sweater and pulled it over my head. I finished the outfit off with a pair of boots and a lightweight blazer. Years ago, Titus had given me a small dagger with a golden hilt that had rubies encrusted into it. I shoved that into the top of my boot like I'd seen so many of the warriors do all these years. It wasn't going to be a blade that killed Marius, and I wasn't sure why I brought it, it just set me at ease knowing it was there.

My room was so still and quiet as I moved to my door. I refused to look back at the plush opulence of it. Knowing I was leaving my home might unnerve me, and my mind was settled on this course of action. I couldn't let this sorrow drown me any longer. I had to make use of myself. I crept out of my room and let the door silently fall shut behind me. When I moved through the halls, no one stopped me to talk. They barely even noticed me. It was as though taking off the dress had turned me into someone no one knew. Perhaps it turned me into someone I, myself, didn't know.

The mirrors stood at the end of the hall, and I peeked around ensuring that no guards would try to stop me. Just as I was about to go place my hand over one of the mirrors, a guard appeared at my side. He was a soldier that'd been in the castle for years yet remained very benign. He had a pleasant enough face with dark skin, lighter eyes, and dark hair cut close to his head. When he smiled at me, it was slightly dazzling. "Can I help, my lady?"

Though his face was impassive, he looked me up and down, no doubt taking in my casual attire. I shook my head. "No, thank you, Benjamin. I'm well enough on my own."

"I feel I should escort you, my lady. Times have been odd around here as of late."

I placed my hand on his forearm. "Oh, come now, dear. I'm just going to tea with the Lady Eloura. It would be eternally boring for you to listen to us discussing flower arrangements. A fine soldier like yourself is needed here, especially after the attacks."

He hesitated and his head dipped shyly. "Thank you, my lady."

"I'll return shortly. Nothing to fret about." I dropped my hand from his arm and reached for the mirror before he could think on it any longer than necessary and decide to come along. "I do thank you for your concern though."

"Of course, my lady." He gave me a small bow of the head and turned away to march back down the hallway.

The mirror rippled under my touch, and I was through it in an instant. It'd been decades since I'd taken this route, but I remembered it well. I used to spend much of my time checking on my wayward progeny, and I knew my memory would serve me well as I stepped out on the other end. I stood in the middle of a small room with a single mirror in it. It had a thick gold frame and even wider legs holding it up. A gift I'd given to him. Two wall sconces were dimly lit with flickering flames soaking the room in gentle lighting. A plush purple carpet sat under the mirror and filled the whole room. Off to the side were two leather armchairs with a single table between them.

Little had changed since the last time I'd been to Marius's quarters. I pushed through the door leading to the hall and began the long walk to his sitting room. Marius had taken his time digging this space out for himself. I remembered taking the time to help him plan out the layout and decor. The halls were all arched and formed of the rough, rocky terrain. It was almost cave-like and yet I found it aesthetically intriguing. I remembered each room perfectly.

As I approached his sitting room, I let my power swirl within me and rush to my hands. I grabbed the doorknob and shoved it wide open. The room was much larger than I remembered, with plush furniture and thick carpeting. It was tastefully done with cozy sitting areas gathered throughout the room. Marius sat on a large leather sofa.

When he spied me, he slowly rose to his feet. A sly smile spread over his lips, and he folded his hands behind his back. "Moira, how lovely to see you."

I marched into the room and slammed the door shut behind me. "What the devil is wrong with you?"

He glided around his couch with that easy walk of his that made me want to slap him. He straightened the lapels of his coat and pressed his hand over his torso, looking like I'd been the one to offend him. When in truth, everything he'd done to me, to my family, was the real insult.

"I beg your pardon. You've come into my home, not the other way around."

"Oh, I bloody well beg to differ," I shot back. His eyebrows shot high at my use of the foul language. It wasn't something I did often, but rage had brought me to this point. "Or was that someone else who sent an army to attack my home."

"I'd hardly call *that* an army. More like a unit. A minor tiff if you will." He moved closer to me. "Yes, of course *your* home. It's always been yours, and no one else is welcome."

My hands curled into fists at my sides. "What are you on about? This is about you feeling left out?"

"It is not!" He raised his voice at me like some kind of petulant child. "You all sat there ruling the vampires, looking down your noses at us."

"I feel like your inferiority complex is . . . How do they say it? A *you* problem!" I snapped back. "Not once have you been not welcome in our home, and this is how you repay us? After we built a new city, appointed you ambassador, and raised you up to fulfill your ambitions. And what, it's not enough?"

"A *me* problem? I will not be so easily dismis—"

I marched up to him and cracked him across the cheek with a bone-jarring slap. "No one has dismissed you. No one has excluded you. No one has intentionally hurt you. And this is what you do? You are my biggest disappointment."

He pressed his hand to his cheek and hissed in a breath. "Oh, mother, come to scold me? How trivial."

"Scold you? I could kill you for what you've done."

"You? Kill me?" He scoffed. "Right. Too bad you weren't more involved. I could've taught you something."

I crossed my arms. "Like how to betray your closest friends."

"My closest friends abandoned me in this world, forced me to be lesser than, and treated me as such. Not to mention you stole a life from me, a life I dearly loved."

"Oh, yes, running and cowering from Alataris is a life. You hid here among us, and we welcomed you! Protected you when he would hunt you down and steal your magic!" I threw my arms up. "I saved you. I could've left you for dead. I *should* have left you for dead."

"You might as well have. You vampires—"

"You are a vampire, and yet you sit here and think about all the things you do not have rather than thinking about everything you do." I was sick of this. Sick of his role in playing the victim. "I know you lost your magic, but you would have died. I tried to save you . . . my friend."

"A positive mindset? Is that it then? Mother has come here to give me an attitude adjustment."

The mocking tone he used with me made me even more resolute in my decision to kill him. I ground my teeth together and took a step toward him. Pain suddenly rocked the side of my face, and my body levitated off the floor. I crashed into a small wooden side table and it splintered under me. My cheek burned from the strike, and I shook the hit off. Marius stood over me while rubbing at the back of his hand. I scrambled back from him, and he slowly followed me as I crawled across the floor.

"Much better." His fangs extended, and I didn't like the

look in his eye. He wanted me dead just as much as *I* wanted to kill *him*.

My elbows scraped on the fragments of broken table, and he bent down low and grabbed my ankle, dragging me across the floor toward him. "Are you happy you came here? Because I am, sweet Moira."

"I hate you, bastard." I kicked my leg out, connecting with his chest.

Marius soared back and smacked into the wall. But it was a short-lived reprieve as he darted back toward me. I hopped to my feet and he was there with his hand around my throat. The air cut off from my lungs as his fingers dug into my skin. He shoved me back until I was pressed against the rough, rocky wall. He pressed his body into mine, holding me there, and whispered in my ear, "You're a disappointment to me too."

I jerked my knee up, connecting right with his balls. He sucked in a sharp breath and hunched over. With both hands, I shoved him back from me. "Arsehole."

He bent down low and dug his hands into my thighs, yanking my legs out from under me. My head smacked into the wall, and I crashed to the ground. Warm blood trickled down the back of my head and pain exploded over my body. He leapt on top of me, straddling my hips and pinning me to the ground. He wrapped both of his hands around my neck and squeezed once more, cutting off the air to my lungs. My throat and lungs burned as I wrapped my hands around his wrists, trying to pull his grip free.

"I will kill you for what you've done to me." His eyes

were wild and every muscle in his body strained. "You took my life! My magic, my power!"

I called on my blood magic, that part of myself that I used to help others, to heal, to save. I'd used my magic for only good . . . until now. I let my anger, sadness, and loss flow into it, taking my power to a place I always knew I could go but never dared to. As much as I could mend someone, I could un-mend. Pink mist spread from my hands to drift across his skin, tearing his jacket to shreds and exposing his skin. A deep cut opened under my touch. It ran from his wrist to the middle of his forearm. Another opened on the other arm, and he bellowed in agony.

His grip loosened on my throat, and when he tried to jerk back, I kept my hold on his wrists. I forced more of my power to creep up his arms, and the skin ripped open farther up his arms, covering his biceps. He tried to pull away, but I kept my hold on him, digging my nails into his skin. More cuts opened over his neck and he threw his head back, bellowing toward the ceiling. He dropped to his knees, and I kept on pushing my power over him. If I could make him, then I could unmake him just as quickly.

"I brought you into this world. Now I will take you out of it." My pink mist swirled around the two of us, and I wanted to rip him apart from the inside out. Blood dripped from his cuts and a larger gash started across his forehead.

"No!" His eyes bulged as I drove my magic deeper.

His skull showed through the flaps of skin, but it wasn't enough, not near enough for what he'd done to us. The plotting, the betrayal, it was all premeditated and he deserved this . . . to be ripped apart piece by piece. A hair-line fracture started on his skull, and he cringed back, throwing himself down on the floor and trying to roll away from me. But I went with it, letting him drag me around with him. I didn't care what happened to me so long as I took him down too.

I could feel his body starting to falter.

The door flew open with a startling bang and a black cloud swarmed the room. It flew between us and wrapped around me. My body went airborne and my hands were pried from him. No! I needed this to keep my family safe, to end this stupid war that was brewing. The cloud glowed with a touch of sparkling light and it threw me across the room. I tried to crawl toward the door, but I had no idea which direction to move. The black cloud swarmed my vision and I collapsed to the floor. I'd used the full strength of my power on Marius and now I was drained. Lighthead-edness sent black dots through my vision. My strength seeped away and every muscle in my body gave out all at once. I crumpled to the floor and flipped to my back as the swirling black cloud closed in around me.

CHAPTER FORTY-SEVEN

PIPER

*H*ades brought us right to the hills overlooking Tartarus. The sight was something to see. Before us was a huge metal gate with no beginning and no end. There was no top, and the bottom seemed embedded deep into the earth. A set of ornate double doors was planted squarely in the middle. The thick metal seemed to wind around itself in intricate patterns that I couldn't quite make out. Gears, wheels, and cranks filled the entire door like a lock that held anything and everything.

Above the door, the gate was made of a million jagged sets of teeth that would snap shut and rip anyone to pieces. They varied in size from big to small, one more terrifying than the next. Random bursts of fire exploded from between the teeth gates. Screams and groans of pain came from behind that wall, and I didn't want to go near it or see in. I could see why this part of the underworld was made for punishment.

Just a few feet away from where we stood on top of the hill, my eyes were drawn to a set of hulking black wings. I took a small step back and bumped right into Grayson. He growled deep in his chest, and I took a step forward, still unable to take my eyes off the fallen angel before me. His eyes darted toward us, and he gave a heavy sigh. He looked back to the bars and I saw the figure of a beautiful woman lurking just inside the gates. She was backlit by the burning fires and kept herself in shadows, but she almost seemed to know he was there watching her.

He barely dragged his gaze away from her as he approached us. No one dared move or even ask what he was doing here. It was none of our business, but something told me it had something to do with that woman. He towered over us and the fragrant scent of blood and chocolate stung my nose. I found myself wanting to drift closer to him.

Titus extended his hand out toward him. "Tristen, good to see you."

Tristen just looked at Titus's hand before his gaze landed on each of us. "Isn't this quite the little power group."

I cleared my throat, nervous to even dare speak. He was one of The Fallen, and I knew they ruled the world the way Titus ruled the vampires. There was a swift harshness in the things they did. In my limited time in this world, I'd grown a healthy, respectful fear of them. "We've come to—"

"He knows why we're here," Maze cut me off as he moved to my side. "I told him."

Why the hell would Maze call one of The Fallen down upon us? Yet when I looked at the sadness that riddled Tristen's features, I appreciated Maze's foresight.

"Do what you must." Tristen faced Zinnia and there was a flash of pain behind those blue eyes. "And when you're through return home to Evermore Academy."

Return home? They couldn't go, we needed them. "But the vampire world—"

"The vampires are more than capable of handling their own problems." He turned toward Titus. "Aren't they?"

Titus straightened and met his eye. "Of course."

He took one last look toward the gates and hung his head. "Then be done with it."

"We will." Zinnia's tone sounded like a solemn promise.

Tristen turned and walked away from us. After a few steps, he froze and glanced at her over his shoulder. "Take your leave from the vampires and prepare for the battles to come. You are not yet ready."

Battles to come? His words sent a shiver down my spine. They were the most powerful witches in the world and Tristen believed they weren't ready for whatever was next. I didn't even want to think about his warning. It was almost too much. Before I could ask what the hell he meant, he was gone, leaving us all there.

Ophelia clapped her hands together. "Noice. More

training, more battles. Keeps life interesting. I hate being bored."

"O." Astrid sighed and shook her head. "How can you be so . . . actually, never mind. That tracks. No panic, just happy to have something to fight."

"You know I get destructive if I don't have something to occupy my time. Like a dog left alone too long, you might come home and find your couch destroyed." She skipped to the edge of the hill and looked down at the gate. "Like this. This is fun. Your couches would totally be safe."

Her glee did nothing to bolster my nerves. Titus gave a low groan. "Let's get this over with before anything else happens."

"But did you hear what he said?" I couldn't imagine what more was to come.

Hades groaned. "We have other things to attend to. Focus."

Maze gave a light nod to the Queens. "You all stay out of sight."

"Not a problem." Astrid opened her hands and golden magic poured over the Queens. One by one they disappeared from sight, leaving only me, Titus, Grayson, Hades, and Maze.

Maze's eyes switched from green to milky-white. "You will have only one shot at this. If it doesn't work, then The House of Shade will be no more."

"Comforting." My stomach was twisted into knots, my hands shook, and a light sheen of sweat ran down the small of my back. Yet I traversed the rocky hill while dragging

Grayson behind me. It helped that Titus was here shoving him along with his strength. All the while, Grayson hissed and thrashed against us. The chain rattled and my wrist was jerked around, but there was no stopping us now.

The rocks crunched under our steps, and no one said a thing as we descended toward the gate. It grew progressively hotter with each step I took toward the gates and even more sweat slicked my body. When we were just about twenty feet away, Hades held his hand out. "That's close enough."

Grayson hunched over, pressing his hands to the sides of his head. "No! No! I won't do it!"

Hades narrowed his eyes at him. "We'd better get this done or there'll be nothing left of his mind."

"We're ready," Titus growled and narrowed his eyes at the gate. "Open it."

Hades waved his hand and sparkling black magic drifted from him toward the doors. The moment it touched those mechanical cranks, the mechanisms began to move. It was so loud. It was what I imagined it would be like standing inside a giant clock. Everything twisted and moved with a noisy grinding and clicking sound. The doors peeled back, folding in on themselves as the metal pieces twisted away and opened at the center, forming a little half-circle around a shadowy figure. Three of those razor-sharp bars remained in front of her, almost like she was in a holding pen.

I didn't know what to expect or if this Crone would even be there waiting for us. Yet there she was. Smoke billowed out from Tartarus behind her and drifted all around her body. This was not what I expected the Crone to look like. I thought she'd be old and unsightly with wrinkles and gray stringy hair. But this woman was beyond beautiful with long silvery hair and huge striking blue eyes. Her skin was pale but seemed to glow from within. Her nose was small and pert while the rest of her body was full and curvy. A wide smile spread across her face, and she ran her hands through her hair, lifting it above her head as she gave a cat-like stretch.

"Well, well. This was not what I was expecting. But I'm intrigued nonetheless." Her bright eyes roamed over all of us, and instantly I knew she was sizing us up. Her gaze landed on Grayson and her smile broadened. "Well, now that is a shame. Isn't it, King Titus?"

There wasn't an ounce of regret in her face, and she seemed very pleased with her handy work. Titus stiffened. "Hello, Dracinda."

"Hmm, It's been a long time since I've heard that name." She grabbed a piece of her hair and wound it around her fingers, toying with it as she spoke.

"I see you've kept well in there." Maze stepped forward and neon smoke poured from his hand to pool on the floor around his feet.

Dracinda took a small step toward him with a look I could only describe as covetous on her face. Her eyes widened and she curled her fingers as though she could grab him from there. "Such power you have. We would've made a dazzling team, you and I." Those razor-like bars snapped in front of her. She chuckled and took a small step back. "Testy."

"It seems you've already made a few allies in there." Maze motioned to her. "You're looking replenished. I must say I miss the old crusty version of yourself. It was much creepier."

"There are a lot of deals to be made behind the walls of Tartarus. We all might be trapped here, but there's power to be had. The deals keep me young, you know?" This whole interaction was not what I expected. I thought I'd see an old woman desperate to leave, not one who was comfortable and thriving in a hellish place. She turned her wide eyes on me. "And I do so love a good deal. Tell me, little vampire halfling, what is it you seek from me?"

"Then make me one," Titus cut in, his deep voice rumbling from right beside me, drawing Dracinda's attention back to him.

The smile dropped from her face and all pretense of fun left her. Her lip curled in a snarl and she crossed her arms. "I have no deals to offer the likes of you."

Titus kept his stance relaxed with his arms loose at his sides. His voice was calm and impassive. "What if I can give you what you most desire?"

"You had the opportunity to do so, remember? And now you'll suffer the same fate I have. Just like you made me do all those years ago, you stand by watching as your family suffers and dies before your eyes." She took a step to the side and leaned against the gate. "Tell me how it feels knowing there is nothing you can do?"

"Perhaps I was foolish not to take your offer all those years ago," Titus hedged, and I didn't know how he was keeping his cool when I was so on edge.

"Indeed, you were foolish, and now you have nothing I want." She turned toward Grayson and me. "Not when I get such pleasure seeing how well my spell took hold of your bloodline."

I wanted to leap across the gate and beat her into submission. My hands curled into fists and my power rose to the forefront. Yet I held myself back, vibrating with the need to maim her. My fangs extended of their own accord, and in the distance a large dog howled while crows began to circle over my head in a black swirl. I fought to keep my voice calm and even. "There must be something you want? Something of value to you?"

That playful smile spread over her face once more and she pushed away from the wall she leaned against. "And what manner of creature are you, little halfling?"

I glanced to Titus, and he gave me a single nod. I lifted my chin. "Half-vampire, half-Greek God."

Her eyes flashed wide, and I felt like a bug under a microscope . "What manner of Greek? Come on, dear, tell me . . . who's your daddy?"

"Ew." I wrinkled my nose. "I am not why we're here."

She waved a dismissive hand at my words. "You're the only thing of interest to me here."

"How about this?" Titus turned back toward Hades. "Hades, if you please."

Hades gave a wave of his hand and a large golden plate

stood between us and Dracinda. It was about six feet tall and five feet wide. The impression of a young woman who had the same gorgeous features as Dracinda was frozen within the gold plates. Her mouth was pressed together, showing her full lips, and her hand reached out to something unseen. The sight of the woman trapped within the gold was bone-chilling, yet I found no pity for either of them.

The breath rushed from Dracinda's lips. "Danna."

"That's right." Titus motioned toward Danna. "Your beloved sister."

"Impossible." Dracinda shook her head. "You lie. We are pledged to Lucifer. She would've been sitting at his side all this time."

Hades gave a dark chuckle. "You think I'm not powerful enough to take a soul? How . . . surprisingly naive of you."

"Lies!" she snapped. "We are pledged to Lucifer. Her soul is with him."

"You've been dealing in my realm." Hades sauntered around the golden block holding Danna. "I know he siphons power through you and you've been taking it while in Tartarus."

Dracinda lifted her shoulders and dropped them in a nonchalant shrug. "Lucifer and I have been intertwined for ages. The deal is simple: I take the power and we split it. I get to live forever, and he uses it for whatever he pleases. It's mutually beneficial."

"And yet you're stuck in here," I countered. "Forever."

"Oh, child, nothing is forever." She chuckled as she turned to Titus. "Isn't that right, King?"

"Hades." Titus waved toward the golden box that held Danna frozen.

Hades flicked his wrist, and the gold began to melt down. It ran in streams from the top and slowly peeled off Danna's body. I watched as she went from a statue to life. At first she was frozen in that position with her hand lifted, but the second the last bit of gold left her body, she staggered forward. A curtain of midnight hair fell in straight lines from her head down to her hips. Her eyes were a pale green nearly as pale as Dracinda's blue eyes. She sucked in a sharp breath and staggered toward her sister, holding the cloak that danced around her body.

"Dracinda?"

Dracinda's face paled, and she tried to take a step toward her sister, but those gates snapped like teeth right in front of her. "Danna, it cannot be you?"

Danna seemed just as dazed as she examined her hands and the white shift dress she wore under her cloak. I'd seen many of the souls in the underworld in that exact same simple dress. "What am I doing in the underworld? I should be with Lucifer . . . He promised."

"I'll fix it, Sister." Dracinda reached out toward her. "Just stay. Please."

Hades snapped his fingers and glittering black magic wrapped around Danna, freezing her in place. "I suggest you deal with the King, or I will send your sister's soul where you will never see her again."

Dracinda pivoted toward Titus. "What is it you want?"

"Break the curse and you'll be reunited with your sister." Titus opened his arms. "It's that simple."

She arched an eyebrow at him. "That simple? I am the queen of contracts, and I will have a deal that benefits us both. I will break your curse—"

"The entire curse," he interrupted. "For the entire bloodline. Not just me."

Her lip twitched as though fighting a smile. "Fine. But I want to be united with my sister outside of Tartarus. She's too delicate for this place."

"Done," Titus countered. "But first break the curse."

"It's only done when he agrees." She motioned to Hades. "Our captor."

Hades gave her a bored look. "Done."

"Swear it." She tried to stay calm, but her body thrummed with anticipation. Her eyes glittered with unshed tears and even her hands curled toward Danna unconsciously.

I almost pitied her and the desire to be with the only person she loved. I was, after all, in the same boat as she was. I only wanted Grayson back with me. The desire to be with him was so acute it nearly hurt. We were so close to a deal I dared not speak or even move a muscle for fear she'd back out.

Hades rolled his eyes. "I grow bored with this, Titus."

"Be done with it then," Titus countered.

"Fine, I swear you shall be reunited with your sister outside of Tartarus." Hades sighed.

Dracinda's eyes locked on Danna just as Grayson fell to the ground and wailed in pain. Blood trickled from his ears and ran down the sides of his face. I dropped to the ground and pulled him into my lap. "Gray! Come on, Gray. Hold on."

"It seems you came just in time." Dracinda chuckled. "My how the tables have turned. I should let him die before you."

"His death means the deal is off and you can rot," Titus snarled. "So either be done with it or Hades will send you both back."

She held her hands up in surrender. "Fine, fine. Deal. Now free me and I shall break the curse."

"The curse first, then your sister," Titus clarified.

"Yes, of course." She winked. "What a lovely piece of magic that is to destroy."

I held my breath and clutched Grayson as he thrashed in my arms. Convulsions racked his body, and those black lines spread even farther over his skin. Adrenaline raced through me and panic set in. "Are we going to keep talking about it or are we going to be about it?"

"Such desperation from someone so young. I do look forward to our future dealings."

"There won't be a future." Maze knelt down beside me and hissed under his breath. He placed a card over Grayson's chest and red ribbons wrapped around his body, forcing him to instantly still. "Eight of swords. He's bound in his own mind for now."

"Hades," Titus warned. "Let her out."

"Very well, but you owe me for this." Hades waved his hand and more of that black magic drifted over the gate. The claw-like razor slid apart with a loud *clank*, allowing Dracinda her freedom.

She glanced down at her feet, then gave a sly smile as she took one step out of Tartarus . . . then another.

Titus held his hand up. "That's quite far enough."

Dracinda froze. "I think I want my sister first."

"No."

"I'll let him die," she snapped.

"And I'll kill you faster, your sister be damned," I growled in her direction. "Try me, witch."

"I like you." She gave me a little wave. "So much potential."

"Do we have a deal or not?" Titus interjected. "I grow tired of these games."

"Yes, you were always impatient." She clapped her hands together and magic rippled around her.

When she closed her eyes, I felt an invisible power wrap around me. It was familiar and strong, and I knew the feel of the Queens' power protecting us under their invisible disguise. Magic crackled around Dracinda, and her smoky indigo power seeped from her. She didn't move but her power filled the space around us like a creeping fog. Her magic slithered over the ground like two snakes slithering toward us. They wrapped around us, then shot straight into the air before diving back down right at Grayson's chest. His back bowed as he sucked in a sharp, gasping breath. His eyes shot wide and he lifted up off my lap, hovering in the air above our heads with limp limbs hanging from his body. Maze's card burned to ash on his chest, and with it so did those ribbons holding Grayson bound. Grayson threw his head back and bellowed in agony.

I shot to my feet just as another set of snake-like power jumped off the ground and shot right into Titus's chest. He patted his hand over the spot as though he were trying to put out a fire, but there was nothing there. The muscles in his neck strained, and his face turned a dark shade of red. His body too rose off the ground and the two of them hovered in the air. Her power swirled around them as she lifted her arms and they both rose higher. Bolts of lightning appeared from nowhere and fired right into both of them. Their bodies jerked and panic filled me. They were both dying, I was sure of it.

I took a step to grab her or do something when Maze placed his hand on my arm. "Don't. Just watch."

"The House of Shade has come to bow, so take my vow and break it now." Her voice boomed as though she spoke into a microphone.

Black and indigo mist shot from their bodies and swirled around them. Dracinda threw her arms out to her sides and the mist shot away from them. The moment it stopped touching Grayson, those black lines disappeared from his body. His stature returned to his normal beautiful size and the blood trickling from his ears disappeared. They drifted back down to the ground. Titus landed on his feet just as Grayson was laid on the ground before me.

I dropped down to my knees and brushed his hair back from his face. He peeked open his eyes, and they were so clear I could see those perfect mahogany flecks. "Hey."

"I would say I'm rather disappointed not to wake up with your little fangs in my body, but it's good to see you, my love." And when the word love brushed past his lips, he didn't react. There was no shudder, no pain in his eyes, no magic to mark the curse.

I bent down low and threw my arms around him, feeling free for the first time since I came into this world. His arms circled around me, hugging me back, and tears prickled my eyes. He was back. My love was back. My heart nearly burst open then and there while his warm scent surrounded me.

A gagging sound came from behind us and I froze, suddenly remembering that this wasn't over yet. Dracinda rolled her eyes and gagged again. "Reminds me why I cursed love in the first place. I've held up my end. Now you hold up yours."

Her power drifted around her in long tendrils that snaked over the ground and up in the air around her. Grayson shot to his feet and pulled me up with him. His eyes shot wide when he spied Dracinda and Titus facing each other in some kind of silent standoff. "I've clearly missed a lot."

His hand wrapped around mine and our fingers intertwined. I lowered my voice to mutter, "You have no idea."

"The Crone? That's the bloody Crone, love."

"Yeaaaaa." I squeezed his hand, pulling him closer to me. "It's been an interesting ride."

"Hades." Titus motioned to him. "A deal is a deal."

Hades snapped his fingers and Danna unfroze right before us. Grayson's head snapped in her direction. "Who the devil is that?"

"Shh. Just go with it. I'll explain later."

He gave me that cocky smile that I loved so much. "You always were an impressive little creature. I'll go with it, love."

Danna ran the distance between her and Dracinda. When she got to her sister, they crashed into each other, throwing their arms around one another. Dracinda pulled back for a moment, just staring at her sister like she was trying to remember her face. Danna's eyes filled with tears. "You did it, Sister. For I am better."

Dracinda's face fell. "Sister, it has been an age since that night. The night you perished."

Danna turned from her to take in her surroundings. "The underworld, but how, Sister . . . We—"

"Shh." Dracinda pulled her in for another hug and I couldn't make out the rest of her words as she whispered to her sister. But a light of panic flickered in Danna's eyes. In a flash, they ripped apart and magic exploded from Danna like a firecracker. It was bright and flaring, burning white at first then turning red. Dracinda's own power joined her and fired at the rest of us in a wave of an explosion.

I took a step back and the explosion came up against an

invisible barrier. One by one the Queens revealed themselves, each of them standing in a semi-circle between the Crone and the rest of us. They held their hands up and their magic flowed together to make a half-moon that trapped Dracinda and Danna in.

Hades clapped his hands together. "Hot damn."

"Treachery!" Dracinda bellowed over the crashing of their powers. "You said you'd release us!"

"I said *outside of Tartarus*." Titus motioned to the gate. "And indeed you *are* outside of it."

"Queens!" Danna's eyes flared and she turned toward her sister. "Queens?"

"Hold tight, Sister. Our power will win over." More of the indigo magic shot from Dracinda and now multiple tentacles fired from her to shoot out toward the Queens, trying to strike at them.

"Move them back toward the gate!" Hades barked over the roar of the power colliding.

Danna and Dracinda took a step forward, and the barrier shook, sounding like thunder rocking the earth. I dropped Grayson's hand and opened my fingers, letting my blood magic pour out of me and head right toward them. When it seeped around their feet, mixing with the fog from Tartarus, I felt my hold on them begin to solidify.

"Back," I commanded, and my power poured into them. The crows above our heads screeched and dove lower, flying into their faces and pecking at them. Scratches formed over their cheeks and around their eyes as the birds flew at them relentlessly.

"Magnificent creature." Grayson moved to my other side and his power joined mine. He yelled over the magic. "Back, witch!"

Maze stood just on the perimeter with his cards swirling over his head. One after another he fired them at the sisters, calling them out as he did. "Eight or swords! Three of cups!"

I wasn't sure what each of them meant, but his neon-green magic grew brighter each time he threw one. Then he turned to our own side and threw more cards at the Queens. "Chariot, strength, sun."

Each time a card hit them, their magic grew stronger and brighter. When he smacked me with the empress, I felt my magic expand and shoot out of me so fast it was nearly painful. Titus moved to stand beside Grayson, and for the life of me I didn't know how no one saw it before, but there they were: father and son fighting for their family, fighting for each other, fighting for life. When Titus unleashed his magic, a wave of power flowed over us all and I felt my own power growing stronger. When it hit the sisters, he snarled at them. "Back, witches!"

"NOW!" Ophelia called out to the others, and they began to chant the spell she'd given them. I couldn't make out the words, but their power grew, rising up like a tidal wave. At the center was Zinnia's silver glitter, then Astrid's gold on one side and Ophelia's grey smoke on the other. Tabi's yellow ribbons tumbled over themselves on the flank, and on their other flank was Serrina's red ribbons.

All the while, Nova stood strong with her purple sparks bouncing over the ground.

Skeletal hands jumped from the earth and shoved the sisters across the entrance to Tartarus. The gates began to close, and Danna looked to her sister. "Sister, help!"

A single tear streaked down Dracinda's cheek. That one tear was a sign of their impending defeat. With the Queens, we were unstoppable. With the Queens, we were united as one and the sisters would not win. Dracinda dropped her power and dove for her sister, pulling her into a hug just as Danna did the same. They closed their eyes tight as Hades snapped his fingers. Melted gold rose up around them, covering their feet at first and then drifting up toward their head. They didn't move or fight it. They just held each other tighter, two sisters bound together for eternity. They were frozen into gold statues with their eyes squeezed tight and their arms around each other. When the gold solidified, we all dropped our power. The crows lifted back up to their great height and drifted in lazy circles over us.

Hades snapped his fingers again and the gates of Tartarus slammed shut around them like a shark swallowing its prey. The cranks all turned in unison and the gate wove together, trapping them in. When it was all done, silence lingered around us and I focused on my heaving breaths. Rose petals were all around my feet.

Ophelia leapt into the air. "Now *that's* how you bind a witch bitch! Whooo! Hell yes."

Grayson wrapped his arms around me and his lips

crashed over mine so warm and firm that I lost myself. His fingers dug into my hair and I kissed him back with everything I was. Tears streamed from my eyes and fell over my cheeks. When he pulled back, he pressed his forehead to mine and locked his gaze on me. "I love you. Don't ever forget that. I love you."

"Nice that you can say that without turning into a monster." I sniffled. I didn't even know what to do. My insides were shot. Everything I'd worked for came to this moment with him. I'd dreamt of it, envisioned it, but never dared hope. I didn't want to let him go. Not now. Not ever. The curse was finally broken. After all this time, he was finally mine and I was his. "I love you too. So much."

"She truly is the blessing for the whole family." Titus's voice was gentle from just beside us.

I pulled back from Grayson, and when we turned to face him, Titus's eyes swam with unshed tears. He placed his hand on Grayson's shoulder and ran the other over the top of his head, messing up the chocolate locks. The muscle in his jaw ticked and he couldn't stop staring.

Grayson cleared his throat. "Thank you, Uncle."

Titus pressed his lips together and his chest bowed. "I- I would do anything for you, my son."

Gray's eyebrows drew low over his eyes. "Son? Apologies, did you say *son*?"

Titus nodded. "I- I didn't know. I didn't remember. But you are my son. Mine."

CHAPTER FORTY-EIGHT

DIANA

I am nothing and everything at the same time. My existence was a life without a body forever formless and forever alone. All but for Marius, who helped me at every turn. I existed because of him. My debt could never be repaid, yet I tried to help him with each of his friends that I freed. It was only a touch to unlock their powers, but I brought them great strength and helped Marius. I hovered over the beautiful, delicate woman on the floor. I couldn't understand why she'd want to hurt him. Curiosity forced me to want to dig deeper.

I dove over her, letting my smoky form seep into her body the way I did the others. But her magic was there, a powerful and untapped well that protected her from me. I couldn't change her. She'd heal just as fast as I could try to unleash more of her inner power. But I could delve into her memories and know why she harbored such anger for the friend who saved me. The moment I touched her mind, so much pain and sorrow flew from her that I nearly retreated from all that sadness. I remember feeling my own sadness . . . the loss, the helplessness, the depression was deep enough to bury me.

Images flashed through her mind, and I began to recognize her from my previous life. She was Moira, Queen of the Vampires. But as I dug deeper, I saw so much more: a curse falling over her family and the night it overtook her greatest love. In one night, she'd gained a son and lost a husband. I knew loss well, more than any mother should know. Then the death of a friend, Graymont, one of my dearest friends in a life that'd long since passed me by. He was beautiful and lovely but then his death came . . . She'd watched him sacrifice himself for his brother. Her guilt was nearly overwhelming, and I felt it as though it were my own. There were more memories, so many more that showed her devotion and how she saved Marius. He'd died and she brought him back. Yet when I saw him through her eyes, he held only hate and contempt for them. Why? I dug deeper and she screamed, crying out in pain. But I couldn't stop. I had to see more. She lost consciousness, but I pushed just a fraction farther. Flashes of names and faces flickered in rapid succession. Some I did not know, but then there was one. He was everything: tall, handsome, and powerful, with dark hair that used to match my own and the same odd eyes that were hazel in the middle and blue on the outside. She called him . . . Atlas.

I pulled away from her, leaving her on the ground and turning toward Marius. I made a noise of anger at him.

How and why had he done this to her? He held his hand out. "No, Diana, stop!"

But how could I stop? He told me Atlas was dead. He told me he was at peace. He told me lies . . . so many lies. I dove forward, wrapping him up in my smoky black form. He never wanted me to touch him before and I'd allowed for his wishes, no matter how much it hurt me to stay away from any sort of touch. Now I would know everything once and for all. I forced myself upon him and seeped into his skin. There was nothing gentle about this, but I had to know. I saw him . . . my Atlas.

Marius thrashed around, swinging his arms wildly, but I was nothing but smoke and power. His hands went right through me. I refused to let him back away. I delved into his memories, starting with the most recent. Marius stood before the vampires I'd helped, watching as some of them turned to puddles of water and died on the spot while others died only moments after I'd touched them. He pulled the bodies and dragged them along like they were garbage. No, I couldn't bear it. How could this be? He told me I helped them unlock the magic of who they were. He told me they were happier as themselves. He told so many, many lies. Anger and sadness ripped through me. I never would have . . . If I had tears to cry, they'd flow from the depths. All pretense of being gentle was left aside as I tore through him, not caring that he cried out in pain. After the things he'd persuaded me to do under the guise of helping others, he deserved my wrath and his pain.

What of the pain he caused for those innocent

vampires? Pain *we* caused. I shoved deeper into his memories and there I was taken to the past, a past I tried to forget and sometimes, when I let myself fall into the misty form, was lost to me. Sometimes I was only the smoke, but tonight I was vengeance. His mind whirled but I kept hold of that memory, the memory of the night we met. Suddenly it wasn't just a memory I was watching. I was sucked into where his mind and mine fused together.

I lay on the floor of a dirty hut, my stomach round with child. Pain ripped me in two and I knew the babe would come this night. I pressed my hand over my stomach as I breathed through the contraction and the midwife ducked down between my legs. After it passed, my head fell back, sweat-soaked and red.

"Rest for a moment." She rose to her feet and walked over to Marius.

I saw myself in the background, laboring so hard that sweat matted my dark hair and smoky black blood magic seeped from me. I remembered being blinded by the pain and not hearing this conversation between these two. But I was in Marius's memory. Marius ducked his head, listening to her.

"I fear she will not survive the birth."

He lowered his voice. "And the child?"

The midwife shook her head. "It struggles even now."

In his mind I felt the way he looked at my power, a power I didn't even know I had. The way his eyes took it all in was covetous, greedy. He wanted to save me but for all the wrong reasons. "Get the child out. I'll see to the rest."

The midwife moved back toward me, and I shoved the memory of the delivery away, pushing past it until that moment, the moment that changed my life forever. Marius moved to my side and dropped to his knees, taking my hand. "I'm sorry, Diana. The child did not survive."

A wailing cry escaped my lips, and I threw my head back, letting the racking sobs take me. Blood flowed from my body, and my only comfort was knowing I would soon join him, the child I'd just lost. Marius squeezed my hand. "Let me help you. I don't want you to die on this night."

I remembered wanting to die but Marius wanted anything but that. Without waiting for me to consent, he wove his magic over me. Green light flowed over my skin and through my body. He closed his eyes and chanted some words I couldn't understand. Even in his memories the words didn't make sense, though I knew he tried to save me, all of me. When his power flowed through my body, something went wrong. It awoke something deep and ancient in my blood, something no one suspected would be there. His magic touched it, and my body couldn't take it. I was too weak, too injured, had lost too much blood. The pain was a distant memory, but I could see in his memories Marius had real panic when my body started to disintegrate. He never intended to kill me, only save me. Yet he'd lost the battle, and my body died that night. All that was left was this thing I'd become.

He offered me a home, and I flowed into a small jar that he'd taken from my pantry. He took me back to his home and that's where I remained, but the memory continued to a place I didn't recognize. My knowledge ended with that jar and his home. But the night hadn't ended for Marius. He skulked outside to the back where a woman waited with a bundle in her arms. She rocked back and forth, waiting for Marius.

"Is that the babe?" Marius approached her, holding his arms out.

"It is." The midwife handed him over. I didn't blame the woman for trying to help the baby. She wasn't from any sort of means and was incredibly plain-looking. "Will you see to him?"

"I will." Marius turned from her and hurried into the night, running across fields for hours until he happened upon a great estate. The building was made of the finest stone with large columns around it. The property was extensive, with no one else around and grounds that stretched for a great distance. He knocked on the back door, a servant's door, and a Blood Born lady answered it. She was clearly well-off with a fine nightdress, dark hair, and eyes. But there was no kindness behind her eyes, and when she pulled back the blanket from his face, she only pursed her lips. "He'll do."

Marius handed the child over and my heart simultaneously both broke and leapt. He was alive . . . my baby was alive!

The door flew open, and I was jarred from the memory.

There he was. My Atlas. Large and imposing, with health and vitality shining in his skin. We shared the same hair and eye color. I pulled back from Marius, freeing my hold of him. But when Marius spotted Atlas, he pulled a dagger from behind his back and charged toward him. I forced myself into a wall, blocking Marius from taking a swipe at him. I couldn't bear it. I wouldn't lose him again. Not now, not ever. Not my son!

CHAPTER FORTY-NINE

GRAYSON

"Come again?" My ears were not hearing this correctly. "Did you say you're my father?"

Titus shifted uncomfortably but never looked away. He drew himself up, holding his shoulders back and his chest out, the way he always did when he was preparing himself for news. But I was too shocked to even know how or what to say. My father had always been Graymont, who was more of a figment of my imagination. But Titus, Titus had always been here for me. I might not have called him father, but he'd always acted like one to me.

"Grayson, I am your father. I know it's a shock but . . . you need to know. I have always loved you as a son. Always."

I didn't know what to say, but he was right. Titus had always been my dad. "So, you and my mother? What about my fath . . . Graymont?"

"He was never married to your mother. I was." He

pressed his hand over his chest and his words were choked by emotions. "She was my soulmate, and I . . . I love her so bloody much. I fell to the curse after trying not to. Graymont . . . he died trying to save me."

Titus' swiped his hand over his eye and sniffed. "When I fell to the curse you were but a babe. Marius, Graymont, and Moira tried to save me by casting a spell to cleanse the curse from my blood. But it didn't work. My brother died for me and I'd forgotten because of a spell that backfired on all of us."

I sucked in a sharp breath and glanced toward Piper. All my life I'd loved Graymont and believed he was my father, a great man who loved my mother so much it tortured him to death. Instead, my father was a great man who stood by us even when he didn't know who we were to him. Emotions rolled within my chest, so many it was difficult to even name them. Doubt and confusion riddled my body. The only anger I felt was at the time I'd lost not knowing Titus was my father. My real father. How could this be?

Piper took a step closer to me. "It's all true."

"You know?" Titus's eyebrows shot high. "How?"

"Moira told us." Piper motioned toward the Queens. "We had to know to help save Grayson. She held back all these years because she loved you, Titus. She didn't want to see you fall again."

"I know that." His hand curled into a fist. "She stood by us all and I . . . I didn't love her enough these last two hundred years. I didn't do enough for you, my son."

I shook my head, thinking of all the time he'd spent

with me. Even as a child I was forever following in his shadow, clinging to his coattails. He'd been there for my first steps, my first school lesson, my first training, and for my first love. There wasn't a period in my life when Titus hadn't been there for me. If I really thought about it, he'd been my father all along, even in the times when he chided me, even when we didn't see eye to eye. It was always the father and son relationship. "How can you say that? You've always been a father to me."

"I could've been more, my son. From now on, I will be more." Titus's body shook as he took a step closer to me. I wanted to hug him. My real father. So much pride burst in my chest. My father was no longer an imaginary figure whom I heard stories about. My father was a great King, a great man, and a great dad. Titus yanked me to his chest, hugging me so tight I nearly lost my breath. I didn't know I was missing a father until he was standing right in front of me. He's always been the man I'd hope to become one day: strong, devoted, fair. I threw my arms around him, pulling him close.

"You don't have to be more." I pulled back and smirked up at him. "I've always found you to be quite a lot as my uncle, and now I know why, Father."

He pulled back and a single tear streaked down his cheek. "My boy."

"Fuck all. I did miss a lot." I chuckled as my emotions overwhelmed me, but I was so bloody elated to be rid of the curse and back with Piper and my real father that I didn't care. "I don't know what else to say."

"That's a first," Piper muttered, and I threw my arm over her shoulder, pulling her into my side.

"There will be more times for this, and we have a lot to discuss but right now we need to get home to your mother. I've just remembered a few things I need to say to her." He shook his head. "There is so much I remember now, so much to say, so much to do. She needs us. She deserves to have us."

My mother, the woman who silently stood by the love of her life because she loved him too much to leave. She stayed so I would have my father even if we both didn't know it. My mother was the glue that held us all together when none of us knew it. "We need to go home."

My father turned back to Hades. "I can't thank you enough, friend."

"My favors are never free, *friend*." He winked and turned to Nova. "I assume you'll see them out."

"My pleasure." She beamed at us all and gave me a wink. "Good to see you back, Gray."

"Oh, and Nova," Hades called for her attention, "do stop torturing my son."

"Not any time soon." She gave him a little wave, and with a heavy sigh he disappeared.

"Did you guys see that?" Ophelia ran up to us. "They were all *boom* magic, and we were all *surprise*, bitches, we have more. I mean, I didn't get to stab anyone, but like that's a close second. Nine out of ten recommend."

"Now *that* I'm familiar with." I pointed at O as I turned toward my friends. The people who put their lives on the line to save my own, even when I didn't want to be saved. "I can't thank you all enough."

Zinnia shrugged and then marched up to me and gave me a little hug. "It's what we do for each other."

I didn't dare let go of Piper as they all hugged her one by one. "You all have my eternal thanks, my Queens," she said.

"Ew. Stop that." Astrid wrinkled her nose and smacked Piper's shoulder. "You're one of us."

"Yeah, so get used to us." Serrina walked up and bumped Piper with her shoulder.

"Just not now. Tristen was clear we must return to Evermore." Zinnia met each of our eyes. "I am not going against The Fallen. I feel like we've pissed them off enough for the last few weeks. Maybe we should give it a rest for a while."

Ophelia crossed her arms and pouted. "Just when we were gonna play in a vampire war. I was excited about that."

"WAR!" My voice rose. Had things gotten that bad with Clive and Marius? Were we on the brink of war? I didn't want war for my people. How long had I been out? What happened? I ran my finger over the vines and scars around Piper's neck and plucked at the roses in her hair. "You lot have a lot of explaining to do."

She squeezed me tightly to her and pressed her cheek to my bare chest. "When I'm done explaining, I don't think you're going to object to what needs to happen to Marius and the rest of the vampires."

"Explain it to me." I didn't want her to hold back anything from me. There'd been enough of that between us to last a bloody lifetime, no matter how awful I suspected it to be. "You can trust me, love."

"Oh, I do. I'll explain on the way back. I think the King has some things he needs to take care of." She nodded her head toward my father and the way he seemed almost antsy to get back. I could understand why.

"The curse is broken and I . . ." he looked almost frazzled, "I-I remember *everything*."

"I'll get you guys home." Nova walked up to us and wiggled her fingers.

The ground rumbled under our feet, and my eyes darted toward her. "Are you doing that?"

"No!"

A huge dog with three heads leapt over the hill and crashed to the ground a few feet away. The ground shook as he ran right at us. I pushed Piper behind me, wanting to protect her. The dog looked like a mix between a Black Lab and a Rottweiler only three times the size with three more heads. I tipped my head back, looking up and up and up as he stood over us.

"Cerberus, what the hell?" Nova called out to the dog.

One by one the three heads dropped big round red balls in front of Piper. They were covered in slime and twice the size of her. When I just gaped at them, the dog leaned down on his front legs while keeping his butt in the air. His tale wagged, making wind kick up around us.

"Aww. Bigggg stretch!" the Queens along with Piper yelled at the same time.

She motioned to the balls that were so much bigger than her. "Yeah, I don't know what to do with this."

"You want to tell me why you have crows flying over our heads and a massive underworld dog serving at your feet?" I eyed her closely. She looked different and even her scent was a little different. But she was who she'd always been. I felt her deep in my soul.

"That's more of the story and more to explain." She gave a heavy sigh. "It's been . . . interesting."

Nova chuckled. "Let's just get you home. I'll take care of the rest."

"Yes. I need to return," my father said but the look in his eyes was haunted, almost distracted.

"I'll tell the others to go back once we get there," Piper called over to Zinnia.

"No need. I've told them already." She winked and held her hand up with a note in it. It caught fire and disappeared into thin air. "They'll be gone by the time you get back. So, good luck."

I knew a lot had happened, but with Piper and my father by my side, everything would get sorted as it should be, even if war brewed on the horizon and my friends had been sent home. With Piper's newfound powers, my returned abilities, and my father at full power there would be no stopping us now. "Thanks to you lot, we don't need luck. I think we've got this."

Piper chuckled and shook her head. "And he's back."

"Now it's time for me to get you all back." Nova wiggled her fingers and purple sparks fired from her palms. The ground opened up beneath us, but the descent was slow and steady.

I turned toward Piper as Nova's magic carried us home. "Tell me everything?"

She drew in a deep breath and the words flowed from her lips as though they'd been pulled out bit by bit. The torture, her subsequent death, the way her father saved her, and everything else. With each passing moment, the tension in my body coiled tighter. I'd missed so much, done so much to her. I didn't deserve her, and she didn't deserve anything that'd happened to her. "This is my fault."

"No." She shook her head. "You tried not to fall to the curse and none of what happened to me could be helped. It's what we do from here on out that counts."

"I will kill him." Marius might've pissed me off before, but now that I was back, he was going to suffer for what he'd done to her. Suffer in ways he could not imagine.

"Yes . . . we will," my father growled. "His sins cannot go unanswered. Friend or not."

Once we were back in the castle, I grabbed Piper's hand and pulled her through the castle toward my mother's quarters. Titus was far ahead of us, and we hurried to keep up. I wanted to see my mother, to thank her for all that she'd done for all of us. As I turned the corner and her door came into view, I stopped short just behind Titus. He hadn't walked through, and his shoulders bunched with tension. "What's happened?"

There on the door with a dagger stabbed through the top of it was a note in my mother's handwriting. I couldn't believe my eyes as I read each of her lines. She'd kept this family together and protected us all this time and now she was doing it again. But there at the bottom was different handwriting, clearly added after she'd left the letter.

I've gone after her.

-Atlas

CHAPTER FIFTY

GRAYSON

*M*y stomach dropped as Titus grabbed the paper and crumpled it in his fist. Atlas would find her, I was sure of it, but I wasn't going to leave it to him. We weren't going to sit around and wait for him to come back. I refused. I grabbed it from his hand and threw it to the floor. "Let's go get my mother."

Blood magic swirled around Titus and his eyes blazed red. "I will rain down death if he touched a hair on her head."

We hurried to the mirrors and leapt through. My heart hammered and anger shot through my body. Marius had tortured and nearly killed Piper, and now my mother, my delicate mother, went to face him. She wasn't a warrior. She was lovely. We were through the mirrors and deep in the Night Spawn territory. Titus, my father, moved down the hallways as though he knew exactly where to go.

His power rolled out before him in a wave of red magical mist consuming anyone in his path. "MOIRA!"

His voice shook the walls and blood magic surged around him in panicked waves. Piper and I stayed in his wake. I thought we'd take on anyone who got by him or came up behind us, but he was everywhere and nowhere all at the same time. His magic was an extension of himself. Innocent Night Spawn were knocked unconscious. But anyone this deep in the headquarters was devoted to Marius. The only reason they'd be there was to try to guard him, and those loyalists were dispatched with a vicious quickness I'd never seen from my . . . father.

Though Piper's face seemed more shocked at his behavior than anything else, there was a light smile playing on her lips, like she was happy he was doing this. I didn't want to leave her side, not after she'd filled me in on everything that'd happened while I was gone. I could understand Titus's anger and his reaction to my mother coming here. Even now I craved Marius's blood. My father stopped before a door that seemed to stand by itself in this long hallway.

"MOIRA!" He slammed his fists into the door and it exploded into the dwelling. Splinters of wood snapped under his boots as he marched deeper into the place.

"Where are we?" I called out to him.

"Marius's bloody hovel." He stalked forward and I followed as he turned down another hallway.

The sound of screams drifted to us, and we moved impossibly faster. Titus rounded the corner and darted into a room to the right. I leapt in behind him, not caring what we were facing. There before us was a giant wall of black smoke, sparks of light fired within it and Atlas stood before it with both swords drawn. The wind kicked up and blew his hair out of his face.

"Atlas!" I grabbed a dagger from the thigh holster Piper wore and leapt to his side.

"Get her out of here!" He pointed toward my mother who lay unconscious on the floor.

Titus dove for my mother and scooped her up into his arms. Piper jumped in front of them and held her hands out. Blood magic poured from her. "What is that?"

"I have no bloody idea," Atlas bellowed.

The smoke peeled back, and my eyes landed on Marius pressed up against the opposite wall. His body was frozen there as the inky smoke seeped from his eyes and mouth out onto the floor. He hunched over, choking out the last bit of smoke. When he stood straight, an evil smile spread over his face. The deep furrows on his face slowly knit back together and he threw off the tatters of his coat.

"My, my. Look at the whole royal family descended upon my humble dwelling. Even Piper . . . How shocking. I could've sworn you were dead." He held his hand out to the side and a tiny spark of brown power fired between his fingers. A wild cackle racked his body. "Oh, Diana, we should've done this a lot sooner. You have my thanks for unleashing my power. I'm healed and I am whole. Oh, how I love the feel of magic in my veins. But what timing, the whole family in one shot."

"I will bathe in your blood." I held my knife up, pointing it at his chest.

He lifted his hands and brown streams of power flowed from them. Every piece of furniture in the room rose off the floor and broke into a thousand different jagged pieces. My father tucked my mother under him, covering her tiny frame with his huge body. "Marius, don't!"

Marius threw his arms forward. A mix of power and jagged pieces flew at us. I leapt in front of Piper just as a wall of black smoke shot straight up between us. Every place those jagged pieces smacked into the smoke wall it flared with light. Atlas moved to my father's side. He wrapped his hand around his upper arm and yanked him to his feet. "Get her out of here!"

"I can't—" He looked toward me. "I can't leave you."

"GO!" I wasn't going to let Marius get away. Not now. Not when he was so close. I was going to rip him apart from the inside out.

The smoke faltered against the onslaught of Marius's renewed power, and I got the sudden feeling it was alive as its own entity. It started to shrink back down as his power waned. It made a sad, pitiful mewling sound and Marius stopped long enough for Atlas to shove me toward the door. "Go."

"Never." Atlas was my family too and I'd be damned if we left him. I planted my feet and stuck by his side.

The black smoke wrapped around Atlas, twisting around him in a wild tornado. He swung his arm out, slicing through it. But there was nothing to fight, nothing to slice. The smoke turned into a long plume that jutted from his chest. His sword seeped back into his forearm and a bellow ripped from his throat. The muscles of his body strained as the magic poured onto his skin.

"Atlas!" Piper leapt for him, but the smoke twisted to the side, knocking her back.

I jumped to the side and wrapped my arms around her, catching her before she slammed into the wall. The smoke continued toward Altas, shrinking down until there was barely anything left. His back arched painfully, and the front of his shirt ripped wide open. The smoke drifted down to his skin, embedding itself there on his chest. Power flowed from within him and black smoke seeped around his arms, a level of power I'd never seen him use before. Sweat gathered over his body, and he threw his arms forward. Two tendrils of power shot forward, connecting right with Marius's chest. He shot off the ground so fast his body went right through the wall behind him. Rocks and dust crumbled from the opening he'd flown through.

The smoke cut off and Atlas hunched over, sucking in heaving breaths. I jumped up and pulled Piper with me. I motioned toward Atlas. "Watch him."

"Gray, don't!" She reached for me, but I had to get to Marius.

I darted toward the hole in the wall where Marius had flown through, ready to finish whatever was left of him. I leapt through the hole and there, just on the other side, was a mirror rippling like he'd just passed through it. "Bloody hell."

"Gray!" Piper called out. "We have to go."

Footsteps sounded just down the corridor and my father hurried back into the room with my mother tucked close in his arms. "There is a time to fight and a time to regroup, Son."

Piper pulled Atlas to his feet and threw his arm over her shoulders. "He's right."

We weren't at full power, my mother needed help, and I had no idea what happened to Atlas. We were so close to ending this once and for all, and now Marius had gotten away with some kind of freaky power. There was only one choice to make. The smarter choice. I glanced back toward the mirror, knowing we had a way out. I didn't want to give up, but I wouldn't put my family in any more danger. Not when I'd just gotten them back.

"Let's go home."

CHAPTER FIFTY-ONE

PIPER

I rushed behind Titus as we flew through the mirrors and came out in the lab. The madness had died down, and when we walked in, they all froze for half a second before leaping into action. Titus kept Moira in his arms as he walked into the biggest exam room. He gently laid her on the bed, taking care to place her head down and brush the hair out of her face. He ran his hands over the back of her head where she bled the most. When he pulled his fingers away, the tips were covered in crimson.

"Doctor!" he bellowed, and the doctor hurried into the room. I was beginning to think he lived in this lab and never left, even though his lab coat was pristine and not a single hair was out of place on his head.

"Good lord, Moira." The doctor shoved in next to Titus, practically elbowing the King to the side so he could get a view of her injuries. "Turn her on her side."

Titus moved to the head of the bed while Grayson hurried to her side. Ever so delicately they rolled her. Titus held her head perfectly straight while Grayson held her slim shoulders. The doctor shoved his glasses up his nose and bent down low over Moira. He took his time probing the wound, then gave a sigh of relief. "It's not too deep."

"Then why does she not wake?" Titus snapped at him.

"She's got a nasty bump on the head." He grabbed a few packs of gauze and placed them on the back of her head. "You can turn her back now."

They did so and Grayson slowly backed away to stand next to Atlas and me. Atlas dropped his arm from my shoulders and leaned himself against the doorframe while Grayson moved to stand between us.

Grayson's eyes were wide and almost dazed as he stared at her. "That's my mum."

"Mine too." Atlas mumbled and that cloud of smoke danced across his skin from one pectoral to the other. Atlas placed his hand over it, and it seemed to move around his fingers.

"What if . . ." Grayson's words choked off, and I knew he was expecting the worst. After the last few weeks, I'd be lying if I said I too wasn't expecting the worst. It seemed to be how our lives were going lately.

"Don't think that way." Atlas's voice was laced with worry and a touch of sadness I could hardly bear to hear. This family deserved to be complete. They deserved to be happy. Fate was fickle but she was also glorious. The

House of Shade deserved glory. "I know. Moira is strong, she'll be okay."

I reached out and took his hand in mine. All we could do now was watch as the doctor hunched over her and examined her from head to toe. It seemed like the moment took forever. She was an integral part of this family, and no one wanted to lose her.

Titus ran a shaky hand over his face as he looked on the verge of tears while he waited. "How is she? Tell me. Now."

"Just a moment, Your Majesty." The doctor held his finger up as he leaned down over her, listening to her heart. He ran his hands over every inch of her, checking for breaks, any scratches, even the slightest thing. When he stood straight and looked up, a deep sigh left his chest. "The Queen will recover."

Grayson's eyebrows shot high. "You know? You know she's the Queen?"

We all froze, and the doctor gave us a wide, tear-filled smile. "Oh yes, I remember. We all do. Whatever spell had fallen over all of us is somehow broken. All these years. Her devotion to you and our people will never be forgotten. I daresay you will find the vampires will be as loyal to her as they are to you, Your Majesty."

"Are . . . are you certain?" Titus took up her hand and held it over his chest. "She will be all right?"

"I am certain of it." The doctor motioned toward her head. "She's got a nasty bump and a deep gash, but her blood magic is already healing her. Even now the wound knits back together. It shouldn't take long for her to wake."

Grayson staggered back into us as if the relief almost took too much out of him. I wrapped my arms around his hip and held him to me. "She's going to be all right."

He placed his hand over mine. "Thank the Creator."

My arm slipped off his waist as he turned toward Atlas and threw his arms around his shoulders, pulling him in for a hug. Atlas stiffened, then returned the sentiment after an awkward pause on his part. "This is not how I envisioned this moment occurring."

Grayson pulled back from him and clapped him on the shoulder. "I owe you my thanks for not killing me."

"It wasn't for lack of trying." Atlas shot a look toward me. "She was very determined to keep you alive."

Grayson pressed a kiss to my temple. "'I couldn't be luckier."

Titus took a few steps from Moira and motioned for us to follow him out into the hallway. He gave a heavy sigh. His eyes looked haunted as he stared through the doorway at her slight form. "I don't know how I could've gone so long without knowing she'd always been mine. I have much to atone for."

"You mustn't blame yourself, Your Majesty." Atlas shook his head. "It was a very powerful magic. Not one of us knew you were soulmates until she told us."

"All this time, how lonely she must've been." He ran his hand over his hair. "I can't bear the thought of it."

"You've got a lifetime to make it up to her." I lowered my voice in case the others were listening. She was their Queen now and I could hear the buzz throughout the lab.

It was full of both shock and excitement as they spoke of their lovely, devoted Queen. "You can't blame yourself over this. Not when you had no knowledge or control over it."

"If only it were that simple." Titus only dragged his eyes away from her long enough to look at Atlas. "I'm glad you were there for her."

Atlas pressed his hand over his chest and that smoke moved over his skin around his fingers. "A pleasure, my King."

Titus narrowed his eyes at the smoke that seemed more like a tattoo now on Atlas's skin. "And what shall we do about that?"

"Are you in any pain?" It didn't look particularly painful, but it was scary to think that thing was now embedded in him.

"None at all. I must admit that burst of power didn't feel like my own and I was quite knackered afterwards, but I'm feeling much more myself now." He dropped his hand from his chest and that smoke moved back to settle on his pec. It transformed into a smoky female form. Her face was small and delicate with her hair standing up from her head in smoky tendrils. The rest of her body was also just strips of inky blackness.

Titus tilted his head to the side studying it. "There is something oddly familiar about it. We will have to examine it further very soon."

Atlas glanced down at himself. "At least she's done me the courtesy to blend it with the rest of my tattoos."

It was true she fit in perfectly with the swords tattooed

on his arms and the hooded figure on his back. There was a tattoo I couldn't make out that sat lower on his stomach just above the waistband of his pants.

Grayson scoffed. "Indeed it does."

"And what do we have happening down here?" Kylian strolled toward us through the lab like he owned it. Dice was by his side. He held an apple in hand and took a big bite of it before he spoke again. "Are we all going shirtless now?"

He glanced from Grayson to Atlas. Dice's eyes locked on Atlas's chest. "If it's not a trend, then it really should be."

I chuckled and let my eyes linger over Grayson. "I couldn't agree more."

"Keep your lust to yourself, woman. No one wants to see that." Kylian stared down at Dice.

"Oh, you mean you only want to see it when it's directed at you?" She clicked her tongue at him. "Jealousy is not a good look for you."

Kylian shrugged. "I don't mind trying it on for a while."

Dice ignored his words and turned toward us. Her eyes darted from me to Grayson and back again. "You good?"

"Yeah, I'm more than good." I would take all the time in the world with her later to explain things. When I winked, she knew exactly what I meant. It was an unspoken communication between us. I was gonna tell her everything. There were no secrets between besties, and there never would be again.

"So, we're all spilling secrets now?" Kylian finished his

apple and shoved the core into his pocket. "I'd love to be a fly on the wall for that conversation."

Titus groaned. "What are you doing here, Dark Prince? I thought The Fallen made their orders clear."

Kylian glanced over his shoulder, watching the lab technicians flutter about. "They ordered the witches back home along with their guardians. I am neither a witch nor a guardian. Besides, business has been booming since I arrived. You want me to stay. Trust me."

Dice slapped his arm. "So full of yourself."

"Someone had to keep an eye on you." He jabbed a finger in Atlas's direction. "Not everyone just runs off at the drop of a hat."

"Liar," Dice snapped at him. "You were gone as much as they were."

He shrugged. "Business is business. Besides, we came down here to find you, Your Majesty."

"What could you possibly have to do with me?" Titus crossed his arms. "I'm not leaving Moira's side."

Kylian glanced over the King's shoulder, looking into the room. "It seems the doctors have this well in hand, and you're going to want to see what I have to show you."

"You are going to want to see this, Your Majesty." Dice met his eye. "As a matter of fact, you all will."

My brow furrowed but Dice never lied about anything. "I would go, Your Highness."

Titus took one last look at Moira, then turned back toward Kylian. "Do not make me regret this, elf."

"Oh, I promise you won't." Kylian turned away from us and started walking out of the lab.

We silently followed in his wake, making our way through the castle and up the stairs towards the King's quarters. Martin stood in the hall just outside the door with his tablet in hand. He blocked the door and stopped us all from entering. A wide smile spread across his face when he saw me hand in hand with Grayson. He gave the King a deep bow.

"Your Majesty." Then he turned to the rest of us. "I'm pleased to see you all alive and well and no longer cursed."

I gave him a quick hug with my one free arm. "Happy to see you too."

He motioned to Grayson and Atlas's state of undress. "Is this a choice or are we in need of clothing?"

"If you would, please." Grayson ran a hand over the back of his neck. "It's been a long few days."

"Right away." He paused as he turned his face up toward the King. "If I may, Your Majesty. Please do brace yourself. It's been quite a shock for us all."

"I really hate prefacing. Open the door, you posh bastard." Kylian motioned to the door.

Martin looked him up and down with his nose wrinkled. "I'd rather be posh than whatever this is."

He grabbed the door and shoved it wide open. There before us stood something I'd never thought I'd see. He was strikingly familiar in the sense that the men of The House of Shade shared the same devastating good looks, dark sandy hair, and striking eyes. He faced the TV hung on the wall and stared at it with a perplexed look on his face. "What the devil is that?"

"Graymont?" Titus choked out as he staggered into the room. His face paled and his hands shook.

Graymont threw his hands up into the air. "Brother! You did it! Took you long enough. I was starting to get worried there for a moment."

I gasped. "Holy shit."

"Right." Kylian chuckled. "Told you you'd want to see this."

Titus nearly tripped over himself as he hurried to get closer to Graymont. "Brother? Is it . . . is it truly you?"

"It's me. In the flesh. Though why you preserved me in a coffin for that long is questionable." He walked up to Titus and pulled him in for a hug. "Bit creepy that was."

Shock had Titus frozen in place as Graymont clapped him on the back. When he pulled away from Titus, he kept his hand on his shoulder as he pointed toward Grayson. "Is this him? Is this the little lad?"

Grayson swallowed and I could feel his nervousness as though it were my own. The shock was nearly too much, and he blinked at him a few times before taking a hard swallow and offering him his hand. "It's nice to meet you, Uncle. But, um, you're dead?"

"Not anymore! Isn't it grand?" Graymont stepped away from Titus and shook Grayson's hand. "Do you go by Gray? I used to go by Gray. But I'm going to let you have it. I can take Monty. Yes, that's the right of it, call me Monty."

"Um, yes? I do go by Gray." Grayson looked at me with

wide eyes, and I had no idea how to help him through this. I had yet to come to terms with my own father . . . Pan. But holy hell, Graymont was alive!

Graymont pointed toward Grayson and Atlas. "Is this how they dress these days?"

He pulled his old linen shirt over his head and threw it onto the couch across the room.

Dice chuckled. "Imma love living here."

I elbowed her. "Not the time."

"Can you blame me?" She shrugged. "I mean, would you look at him."

She wasn't wrong. Graymont was just as lovely in form as Grayson and Titus. With strong broad shoulders, long lean muscles, and thick strong legs. He now stood before us in a pair of pants that tied in the front and black boots that went just up to his knees. He put his hands on his hips and looked to his brother. "So, how's the rest of our family? Beatrice?"

"She, um, she died." Titus sucked in a sharp breath and tears streamed down his face. His shoulders shook as he openly wept. "The . . . the curse."

"Oh, man, that was a bloody bad one." Graymont shook his head. "How about Collin? Dead too?"

Titus could only nod as his breaths came in hard pants and he tried to swipe the tears from his face. Graymont stood there for an awkward moment before he placed his hand on his brother's shoulder and gave it a little squeeze. "You know what, I'm going to give you a minute."

He turned to the rest of us and his face was bright with

excitement. He extended his hand out toward me. "Hello, I'm Graymont of The House of Shade. Pleased to meet you."

I took his hand and just stared at him. "I'm Piper. It's nice to meet you."

He glanced down at my wrist, then at Grayson's. "Oh. Soulmates. Bet that got a bit dicey with the curse and all. Or I should be thanking you for breaking it? I couldn't come back until you did. Deals with Hades and all that."

"Is this what it's like dealing with me?" Grayson leaned in close to me and whispered, "Feels like a lot."

"You're more," I muttered back.

Titus still hadn't stopped sobbing, and Grayson moved to his side to pat him on the back. "It's all right, Father. It's all right."

"Eh, he does that. Don't fret about it." Graymont waved his hand at his brother once more, then he clapped his hands together and rubbed them back and forth. "Who's next?"

He turned toward Atlas and pointed his finger at his chest. "You look familiar. Have we met before?"

"I don't believe we have. No." Atlas extended his hand toward him. "I'm Atlas Savage."

"Well, that's quite a name you've got. But I do love it." He shook his hand and turned to Dice. "And who are you? Aren't you lovely? They really didn't make them like you back in my day."

"Why yes, yes I am lovely." She tucked a strand of hair behind her ear. As she was about to step closer to him to offer him her hand, Kylian and Atlas stepped in front of her just enough to block her from making a move but enough where she could still see between them.

Graymont chuckled and pointed to both of them. "Right then, okay. That's a bit complicated, isn't it?"

Just when he was about to turn back to Titus, a circle appeared in the floor like the one we'd used to get to the underworld. It opened piece by piece and Liesin slowly began to rise up in the center of us all. He glanced around the room, sending those dark strands of hair around his face.

Graymont threw his hands up in greeting. "Liesin!"

I motioned between the two of them. "You know Liesin?"

"Of course. Who doesn't? So, can I call you my niece? It seems fitting."

"Oh, um, sure?" There was so much energy and excitement pouring from Graymont I didn't know what to say or how to act. It seemed the two hundred years he'd spent dead hadn't taken an ounce of his joy.

"Liesin, have you met my niece, Piper?" He motioned between us.

I'd never been called niece before, or daughter, or anything that would have a family title. It was odd to me that Graymont just accepted me right away. No questions asked. Yet here he was introducing us as though we were old friends.

I shook my head. "I'm still confused on how you two know each other."

"You'd be surprised how many people we know." Liesin chuckled and turned back to Graymont. "Dad thought you might be a bit lost up here and he sent me to check on you."

"I'm great. Aren't we, Brother?" Graymont pointed to Titus. But when Titus couldn't catch his breath to speak, Graymont shrugged. "Yeah, we're all fine. He just still needs a moment."

Liesin gestured to the room and our shocked faces. "Listen, Uncle Graymont, give them all a moment. They didn't know you were coming back."

"I'm actually quite pleased with the welcome." Graymont beamed.

Liesin shook his head with a little chuckle, then turned toward Grayson and me. "He's been around my father for two hundred years, so good luck with that."

How had he been with Hades? Also, why? How did he manage to come back from death itself when Hades never let anyone go? Before any of my questions could be answered, Liesin stepped back into his hole and disappeared.

Graymont moved back toward Titus. "Oh, come now, Brother. All is well and will be well from now on."

Titus leapt at him and pulled him into a tight hug. He gave heaping slaps on his back as he rocked him from side to side. "I missed you."

"And I you." Graymont's face lit with a gentle smile, and I instantly liked him for it. Such joy and merriment came from him so easily. He closed his eyes, embracing his brother. "I was a bit worried you'd never break the damn thing."

"I'm so sorry, Brother. I . . . I killed you." Titus looked him dead in the eye. "Can you ever forgive me?"

"You did no such thing. The curse did that. So come on then." He patted Titus. "Let's go see my sister-in-law. Where is she? The lovely Moira? I've missed her sharp tongue and sassy wit."

The Moira we all knew was gentle, lovely, delicate. But I looked forward to getting a glimpse of this sass and wit from her.

Grayson cleared his throat and tried to shake himself. "She's in the infirmary, Uncle."

"She always loved to help others. It was one of the things we had in common." He motioned to the door. "Let's be off then. I've longed to see her."

"She's not helping others, Brother." Titus cleared his throat and swiped at his tear-stained face. "She's been injured."

Graymont's face fell for the first time since we'd arrived, and I wanted to do anything I could to bring it back. This man who clearly was full of enthusiasm and happiness . . . I wanted to soften the blow. "But the doctor says she'll make a full recovery."

"Then let's see to it. We can't all leave her alone. I think she's had quite enough of that." He headed toward the door. "Is it still this way?"

I could imagine that so much had changed since the night he'd passed away, but it almost seemed cruel to tell him that when he was just happy to be here. Grayson stepped in front of him. "Let me show you the way."

Grayson grabbed my hand, and I tightened my grip around his fingers as he opened the door to the hallway. "I'm gobsmacked, love."

"You're not kidding." Even I was surprised, and I'd only heard stories of Graymont.

As we walked back through the halls, the courtiers openly stopped and stared at him. But Graymont was unphased by it. He waved and smiled at them as though he were in a parade. "Elena, good to see you. Haven't changed that hair in two hundred years I see. Oh, Darien, you still owe me fifty gold pieces. I haven't forgotten. Marcus, have you switched wives yet? Whoops, no, there she is. Apologies, Lauren."

They all stared at him with their jaws hanging and their eyes wide. Graymont turned back to Titus. "Perhaps we should've made it less of a surprise?"

"There is no amount of preparing for this." Titus sniffed.

"You're doing all right." Graymont dropped back and patted him on the back. "Look, you've stopped weeping and everything."

"Can you blame me?"

"Bit of an overreaction I'd say," he teased.

Grayson chuckled. "I think I'm going to like my uncle."

"I think I'm worried about the two of you together." We made our way down the stairs and into the lab. The moment Graymont was through the doors, he froze. His jaw dropped. "My word, how marvelous. Fascinating, this is the technology Liesin has tried to explain. I must admit he wasn't very good at painting a picture of things in the world of the living. I must see it all and learn how it works."

Titus waved his arm toward the lab. "And you shall, dear brother, you shall see it all."

He guided him toward Moira's room, and we all grew silent as Graymont approached her bed. He grabbed a stool and pulled it close to her bedside, taking up her hand. "Hello, darling."

Titus moved to his side, and they both stared down at her. "You can't imagine what she's endured."

"For you, I would imagine she endured much, Brother." Graymont smirked up at him. "She's always loved you and you her. It is the way."

He held his hands over Moira and a mist of blood magic flowed from him to her.

Grayson moved in closer. "What are you doing?"

"Graymont has the power to control others' emotions," Titus whispered. "He's very soothing to those who are injured."

"It's my gift." Graymont dropped his hand and let it lay on the bed next to Moira. "I think I need to stay here for some time, Brother. She needs me. There is much . . . sadness in her heart."

"Then you must stay. She needs you." Titus squeezed his shoulder. "We all have."

I didn't know how long we all stood there silently

watching the rise and fall of Moira's chest as she took deep breaths. I took comfort in just being able to stand next to Grayson with no secrets between us and only our future ahead. Did we have some shit to work out? Yes, we did. But our love for each other was strong and it would see us through. The way it had for Titus and Moira. I just wanted to see them together. For them to have their moment along with us.

I leaned on Grayson and let my head fall onto his shoulder, loving how close we were. Just as I got comfortable and my body sagged into his, a loud bang came from outside and an instant later the castle walls shook.

Graymont's eyes shot toward the ceiling. "What was that?"

"Marius," we all replied at the same time.

"Is he still around? Shall I go say hello?" Graymont looked to Titus.

"Oh, the things you've missed." Titus sighed. "He's no friend to us."

Graymont's face went deadly serious. "I know, Brother, I've heard much in the underworld. Now go and do what needs to be done for us all."

The castle rocked again, and dust rained down.

Martin hurried up to Grayson and Atlas. He threw black sweaters at each of them as well as long leather coats. "You'll need these."

Grayson yanked it over his head. "Do you happen to have—"

Two vampires ran up behind Martin with a large silver

box. They dropped it on the ground and flipped the lid open revealing a load of swords, knives, and other weapons.

Martin turned toward Grayson. "Oh, and these were some of your favorites. I remembered."

"Throwing stars." Grayson shoved his hands into the arms of his jacket, then took them. "You're getting a raise."

"Already gave myself one six months ago." Martin turned toward me. "This is for you."

He tossed me a leather jacket. I hurried to put it on. "Thanks."

Dice marched over to the chest of weapons and started to load herself up. I grabbed her arm and pulled her to stand next to me. "What are you doing?"

"If you're fighting, I'm fighting."

I didn't want to tell her no, that a mere human couldn't compare to a vampire, but she couldn't. She'd be dead within minutes. I shook my head. "I need you to stay and protect Moira."

"What? No." She threw her hair out of her face. "I can fight."

"I know you can. That's why I'm asking you to stay here with her."

Graymont tilted his head at her. "I'm also staying. I'm not quite ready to spill blood, even though it's necessary."

"Oh, this is for you." Martin threw a soft blue sweater at Graymont. "I think you shirtless is a bit much for the court."

"It always has been." He winked as he pulled the sweater over his head.

"Fine. I will keep an eye on her." Dice rolled her eyes and marched into the room as Titus stomped out toward us.

He stopped in front of Grayson, Atlas, and me. The muscle in his jaw flexed. "We end this tonight."

We nodded in agreement and turned for the door. Theon ran out of a room off to the side and walked in our wake. "Mind if I join you?"

"You betray us for even half a second and I'll see your head on the ground at my feet." Atlas shoved the door open.

"I would expect nothing less." Theon chuckled and fell into step behind us.

Grayson glanced toward me. "Let's end this."

My heart hammered in my chest as I nodded at him. "Once and for all."

CHAPTER FIFTY-TWO

PIPER

J stepped out onto the top of the wall surrounding the castle and rage instantly filled my veins. Night had fallen and the castle was surrounded by a legion of Night Spawn vampires. Huge bonfires lit up the surrounding areas and Marius's army writhed around the walls like a flood of cockroaches covering the ground. Within the foggy forest there was the distinct glare coming from multiple mirrors. My hand curled into a fist and my power rose to the forefront. Sage and crimson mixed as it swirled around me.

Grayson moved to my side and gazed out over the armies gathered at our doorstep. "Bloody hell."

"We can handle this." Even as I spoke the words, I didn't know how this would turn out.

The soldiers protecting the castle were nowhere near strong enough to face these forces alone. It would take a lot of power to fend off all these vampires, and I knew the odds were not in our favor.

A deep growl rumbled in Titus's chest. "I was not aware that so many vampires wanted to join an army united against us."

"If it makes you feel any better, I don't think some of them rightly know what they're doing. Mind you, I said some of them, not all, because some of them are just bastards." Theon kept his voice low. "The vampires in the lab don't know who they are. They're rather mindless."

Titus grumbled a slight agreement. "I'll keep that in mind for the future . . . if they survive."

"You don't need an army. I'm quite sufficient." Atlas stood with one foot on the wall while holding his sword in the other hand. The wind whipped his hair back from his face and his eyes nearly glowed under the moonlight. Black smoke drifted up from his hands in thin plumes.

"He always did talk a big game." Kylian sauntered through the doorway with another vampire I'd never met by his side. "But I brought one who actually has big game."

"I would wager I'd kill more of them than you lot." Atlas pressed his hand between his shoulder blades and that hooded figure tattooed on his back slid up and over his shoulders in a veil of black smoke. The hood settled around his face, covering him in shadow that blended in with the night and billowed out behind him.

Kylian pursed his lips and nodded. "I'll take that wager."

The vampire next to Kylian was nearly the same size as

him but sleeker looking. He had light-brown curly hair cut neat to his head and warm olive skin. His eyes were a deep honey-color with flecks of yellow in them. His pinstriped suit was pressed and fell neatly over his body as he carried a large brown duffel bag slung over his shoulder. When he approached us, he gave a warm smile to the King.

"I trust your dinner went well, Your Majesty."

"Lorenzo." Titus offered him his hand. "Good to see you."

Instead of shaking his hand, he dropped the straps of the duffel bag onto Titus's palm. "If you accept my offer, then I consider our deal done."

Titus chuckled as he bent down and unzipped the bag. Grayson looked over his shoulder and his eyes went wide. "Is that . . . is that Clive Christiano's head?"

"I would say he'd think twice before crossing me, but he can't exactly do that with no head. Ya know what I mean?" Lorenzo chuckled.

"I think I've got the right of it." Grayson looked him up and down. "I think I like the way you work. Bloody hell, Uncle. I mean, Father. You certainly have been handling things lately."

"Eh, the punk got what he deserved." Lorenzo shrugged. "So, tell me, Your Majesty, do we have a deal?"

Titus threw the bag over the wall and the heads inside soared into the crowd below. Screams echoed up toward us, and I couldn't say I wouldn't have the same reaction to a head falling on me. Titus rose to his feet. "We have a deal."

Lorenzo pulled two daggers from the inside of his suit coat. He turned toward the wall and waved his arm high up in the air.

Grayson moved closer to him. "I think I rather like you."

"Don't get any ideas. I got this woman in mind." He shrugged and motioned toward me. "You understand."

I'm not sure what I understood about this guy aside from his Staten Island accent. But I was happy he was on our side. At his signal, the ground rumbled and the sound of an army marching forward filled the air. There, in a rolling field just past Marius's army, a large army of elves melted from the forest shrouded in fog. Their armor gleamed under the bright blue moonlight. Their chainmail glittered and moved with each of their steps. Long, light-green cloaks fell from their shoulders and whispered over the frozen ground as they walked. A woman with bright-red hair straddling a huge brown bear was at the center of them all, and they appeared to move on her command. Their approach was slow and methodical as she rode toward the castle.

Kylian motioned toward the army. "My army. Does their body count go to my tally?"

Atlas scoffed. "If you think you need the assistance, be my guest."

At the sight of them, a loud, strange bellow broke the night and drifted toward us. My eyes quickly landed on Marius standing behind all of his vampires. Of course the coward would be toward the back of his troops. The front lines would be cannon fodder for a man like Marius. A growl rumbled in my chest, and I wanted nothing more than to jump down off this wall and kill him with my bare hands. My blood magic seeped over the side of the castle.

Titus pointed toward one wall. "Atlas, be free. Kylian, will you be joining us?"

Kylian placed his hand on the ground and his burgundy smoke spread around him. The stone beneath his feet rose up to meet his palm, and as he slowly stood, it twisted and turned until a dark stone sword sat perfectly within his grip. "I can't let that pretty boy vampire win, now can I?"

He walked to the opposite wall from where Atlas stood and called over his shoulder. "Game on."

Titus motioned to the courtyard and dozens of vampires flooded from inside the castle, all in uniform. They scurried up the walls to take their places all around the castle. Archers were spread through the walls and turrets of the castle. He turned toward us. "I'll take the front of the castle to the north. Grayson to the south. Piper, if you can, to the west. The elves look like they've got the east covered."

"And me, Your Majesty?" Theon piped up.

"You know how Marius thinks the best, you'll be with me."

"Put a bit of thought into this, have you?" Grayson smirked at his father as he pulled his throwing stars from his pocket.

"You can thank your friends, the Queens, for that. The last time Marius attempted to attack the castle the Queens gave me the idea." He turned and strutted toward the front of the castle. "Remind me to thank them later."

Grayson turned toward me. His hand shot out and he wrapped it around the back of my neck and then yanked me toward him, crashing our lips together in a desperate kiss. Fire sparked between us and wolves howled in the distance. It was over too soon, and he turned from me. "Be seeing you, little creature."

"Happy hunting," Atlas called out and then leapt over the side of the wall into the fray. Screams followed and the wet sound of a sword cutting through flesh filled the air.

Marius bellowed something and a volley of fireballs surged up toward the castle from the army below. The soldiers scrambled around the walls switching positions to allow the vampires with water power to step forward. A second later the Blood Born vampire soldiers all fired their water powers, stopping the volley of fire midair with spouts of water shooting like geysers toward them. Titus bellowed a command, and the archers stepped to the wall and loosed their arrows. They were like a dark cloud blocking out the moon as they soared down toward Marius's army.

All hell broke loose. Fire, water, stones, and wind flew up at us from every direction. The castle rocked beneath my feet, and I staggered forward, dodging them as best I could. Rocks pelted my body and water soaked my hair. The heat of the flames licked across my skin. I turned to face out toward the army and nearly faltered when their sheer numbers came into view. I lifted my arms and called on my power, digging deep into that well within my stomach and letting it all go free. My anger rose and I threw my arms out. My blood magic poured over the side of the wall like a tidal wave into the swarm below.

I'd never tried to control more than one person at a time with my power. But the wild in me forced it to grow and move in directions I couldn't imagine. My intention was clear, and I let every ounce of my power ring out in my voice. "Turn on each other."

One moment they were aimed at me, the next they started firing at each other. Fire-throwers turned and burned the vampires next to them, turning them to ash. Water-wielding vampires tried to drown the others all the while the ones who could manipulate the earth opened giant crevasses that forced their comrades to plummet to their deaths. Even with the power of air, they were helpless in falling to their deaths.

It wasn't enough, not nearly enough. Dark shadows flooded the night sky, their wings blocking out the moon. Crows of all shapes and sizes flew toward the castle and dove down into the army surrounding the castle. Their *caws* were nearly deafening and were only overshadowed by the call of wolves. The wolves flowed from the forest surrounding the castle and ran into the army, attacking them like K9 police dogs running down a suspect, except these were bigger, meaner, and I by no means controlled them. My power only attracted them to me. What they decided to do from there was up to them. But I found solace in their snarls and growls as they attacked.

A large brown bear barreled for the army on my side of the castle, it's giant paws taking one vampire down after another. He ripped at their heads and tossed them to the side. His thick fur was covered in blood, yet the bear continued to wreak havoc. I turned toward the east wall where our soldiers stood against the army with the elves in support. Huge boulders hovered over their heads, and if they crashed down onto the wall, there would be a giant hole in the castle for Marius' troops to flood into. I refused to let that happen. I darted to the side and shot my magic into the crowd. Before it even touched the offending vampires, a dark shadow moved through them like the plague. There was a swath of death as it moved and twisted in different directions.

"Atlas," I breathed just as he reached the vampire wielding the stones. The first one lost its head and the stones dropped just outside the castle wall, crushing the front line of the army. They rolled back into the forces, crushing all those in their wake. Another head fell to the ground as did the giant boulder. I smirked to myself. "He really is like death."

The elf army was like a wave of golden power plowing down the vampires with quick ease. They dispatched the vampire army like they'd been training with their swords for years on end and their blades were an extension of themselves. All Marius had was sheer numbers and untrained magic. The elves moved with a quiet efficiency that sent a chill down my spine. Their swords bathed the ground in blood and body parts. I spotted Kylian leaping over lines of vampires with his stone sword. He dropped in on them and spun in a circle, cutting them down in one move. He moved like the soldiers of the elven army but there was more of an edge to his fighting style. "I've killed more, vampire!"

"Prick!" Atlas bellowed from some unknown shadow.

Flashes of bright brown magic drew my attention from where I stood toward the north. "Titus."

I pumped my arms, running toward him. There on the other side of the wall Marius wielded his magic like he'd had it all his life. Brown tendrils of power shot from him, grabbing whomever and whatever he could to hurl at Titus, though the rest of the army around him lay at his feet with their bodies snapped in precarious ways as though death had taken them in one shot as he stood there resisting Titus's power. A huge boulder launched up at the King from the side and I didn't know if Titus saw it, but I couldn't chance it. I ran at him headlong and dove for him, knocking him to the ground just as the boulder soared by and crashed into one of the turrets of the castle.

The stone walls of the turret cracked, then the turret started to crumble in on itself. The cylindrical turret toppled to the side, falling away from the castle and damaging it as it slid and toppled over. Rock smashed into rock as dust and debris crumbled. I leapt off Titus and turned to face where Marius stood.

A shit-eating grin spread across his face, and I wanted nothing more than to jump from the castle walls and stab him in his smug ass. When he looked up at me, he winked. "I'll make sure I finish the job this time!"

Titus rose to his feet and threw his arms out wide. Crimson blood magic shot out to the sides and flowed down the wall and over the armies there. All at once they turned toward Marius and fired their magic in his direction. Fire, water, and massive stones flew at him all at once.

Grayson ran to Titus's other side and snickered. "Bloody brilliant."

Marius launched himself straight up into the air, using his magic to propel himself higher. He arched in midair and shot toward the center of the castle. Like a bomb, he dropped into the middle of the courtyard and looked up at the three of us.

I took a step toward him and Titus held his arm out to stop me. "I should do this."

"He owes me a life." I would have my vengeance here and now. Nothing was going to take that from me.

"Father," Grayson called his attention. "We've got this. See to the rest of the army."

Titus dropped his arm and took a lasting look at Marius. "Make it hurt, Son."

"I swear it." Grayson glanced toward me. "Together, love?"

"Together." In unison we stepped off the walls and dropped down into the courtyard across from Marius.

"Well, look who survived." Marius held his arms out and those brown tendrils of magic flared from him. They blended with the shadows as he strolled slowly to the side. "Looking much better than I remembered."

Grayson and I stood side-by-side, our own blood magic pouring from us and seeping over the ground toward him.

Memories of the way he bit me over and over again flashed through my mind. The way he'd beaten me mercilessly and how after he was done, he disposed of me like I was little more than trash. "Look your fill. I'll be the last thing you see."

"I could say the same." He took a step forward into the mist swirling at his feet, and with everything I had, I thought the word *freeze*.

He smirked at me and took another step. "Apparently I've got a new bag of tricks."

"Go!" Grayson dove to one side as I dove to the other.

I rolled to my feet and popped up on the other side of Marius. A brown tendril of his magic shot right at me, and I ran to the side and slid over the floor as it shot over my head. I yanked the dagger from my boot and charged toward him at the same time that Grayson leapt right for his head. At the last second, I dropped to one knee and sliced my dagger across the side of his thigh while Grayson's blade sliced across his cheek. Marius screamed and clutched at his leg. I jumped to my feet and sprinted away, but something wrapped around my ankle and yanked me off my feet.

I flipped upside down and hung there. Grayson swung his sword at Marius's neck, and he ducked under the blow, twisting to the side and taking me with him. My body was flung from side to side. Dizziness swarmed my vision. Magic poured from my hands just as Marius turned and flung me over the castle wall out toward the army. I twisted midair and tried to right myself before I crashed to the ground. The sound of beating wings filled my ears and tiny claws dug into my skin. I stopped flailing as the crows caught me. I dipped down, and when their wings beat together, they lifted me higher and flew me back toward the castle. "Holy shit. Um, can you drop me in the courtyard?"

They pumped their wings and soared right toward the castle. When we got close enough, they dropped me back into the courtyard. As he battled Grayson I landed just behind Marius and shoved my dagger toward his back. He twisted around and caught my wrist. He threw me in front of Gray as he tried to stab Marius in the chest. At the last second, Gray pulled back and Marius threw me into him. We sailed across the courtyard and crashed into the wall. Grayson tucked me under him as stones caved in on us. The air whooshed from his lungs, and I felt every hit he took. I rolled to the side, forcing the stones off us, and kicked my legs out, sending them flying. Grayson staggered to his feet and faced Marius just as I rose to mine.

"You think you'll beat me? Not with my magic and not as a vampire." He opened his arms wide and brown magic shot between us, knocking us to the sides.

My body crashed into the wall and pain shot through my side, a pain I was familiar with. Broken ribs. I sucked in a deep breath, feeling the sharp ache. But I couldn't stop, wouldn't stop.

Grayson called out to me. "You all right?"

"Yeah." I felt like we were getting our asses kicked, and I couldn't take it.

"Not for long." Marius cackled.

I threw my arms up, calling on the wild. My power shot straight up into the air and a tornado of birds answered my call. They dropped down on Marius, and I dusted myself off as I rose once more. He spun around, swinging his arms out, trying to stop them from pecking and scratching at his skin. I locked eyes with Grayson, and he gave me a single nod. I charged forward and dove into the birds. They made a little opening and I leapt at Marius and drove my knife into his side, stabbing him quickly.

He pressed his hand over his ribs as he spun and kept swinging at the birds. Grayson leapt into the swarm and slashed for his throat. Marius arched his back at the last second and the tip of the sword sliced his other cheek open. The scent of his blood drifted on the air. Brown magic shot from him like an explosion, sending my birds scattering away from him. Grayson flew back toward me, and I braced for impact, taking the brunt of his hit on my chest as I tried to catch him. He planted his feet and we both slid back from the force of the blow.

"Nice catch, love."

"This isn't working."

"We need the same intention . . . together." He held my hand and extended it out toward Marius.

Our blood magic flowed together in a twisted mess of power. It shot right into Marius's chest. He froze on the spot, and we began to circle him. Grayson swung his sword first and Marius unfroze for the barest of second, just long enough to throw up his magic to block the blow. But we had it now. He could fight us off alone but together the blood magic was enough to freeze him for precious seconds.

Outside the palace walls, the sounds of war began to slow, and I knew it was coming to an end. Just as I came to that conclusion, Marius tilted his head to the side. "No matter. I can just make more."

I threw my knife at him, and he turned to the side, catching the hilt and then throwing it back in my direction. I twisted to the side, and it embedded itself in the wall next to my head. "Fucking hell."

"Marius!" a familiar voice screamed over the hum of battle.

There in the courtyard stood Moira, and she nearly took my breath away. Pink mist swirled around her, and when he turned to face her, her power shot into his face, and the side of his neck split wide open. He pressed his hand over the cut, and when he took it away, his own blood coated his fingers.

"You bitc—"

She struck out again, and this time deep furrows ran down his arms. Brown power gathered around him, but I couldn't allow it. I called on my own magic at the same time as Grayson, and we slammed our power into him and he froze. Moira pulled her arms down and more cuts sliced over his shoulders and across his chest. Grayson surged forward and drove his sword up through Marius's ribs and into his chest. Marius staggered and I shoved my dagger into his other side.

Blood and magic flowed from him, seeping to the ground around him in dark pools. "I'll kill you all. I swear it."

I gripped the back of his neck and kicked out his knee, shoving him to the ground. I closed my eyes for a moment, calling the wild I knew would come. The resounding growl told me my call was answered. There was a bang on the doors, then a scraping against the wall where the turret had fallen. A bear climbed down from the rubble where the castle wall had been. Rubble crunched under his feet as he prowled toward us. Blood dripped from him, turning his brown fur into a dark crimson. His teeth were covered in gore, and when he rolled back his lips, he roared in Marius's face.

"No, please," Marius begged with a shaky voice. But I had no pity for him, nor could I find the mercy. When I glanced toward Grayson, he gave me a nod and I knew exactly what I wanted to do. He tried to fight my grip, but his injuries seeped any kind of strength he had left. "This will haunt you. I will haunt you."

"The world will forget you. I will forget you. And your death will only be a caution to others." I bent down low to whisper in his ear the way he'd done to me when he held me captive. "The House of Shade will always stand."

He gritted his teeth as blood trickled from his mouth. "I would see it fall."

"It will never fall." Grayson pulled his sword free from Marius's ribs and more blood poured to the ground at our feet.

"Welcome to the wild." I threw him at the bear and the animal leapt on him without hesitation. His mouth surrounded his head, tearing into the skin around Marius's neck. The bear shook his neck and head from side-to-side, ripping Marius's head clean off his shoulders and spitting it on the ground at my feet.

Grayson stumbled to my side and threw his arms around my shoulders. He pressed his forehead against mine. "It's done. We did it. It's done."

I sucked in a sharp breath and pain shot through my side. I winced but kept still with my skin pressed against his. "Thank fuck."

The sounds of the outside war died down and Moira ran toward us. Her long hair streamed out behind her as she threw herself at Grayson. She wrapped her arms around his neck and pulled him down to her. "My boy! You're alive."

He pulled her in close. "Was there ever any doubt I wouldn't be, Mum?"

She pulled back, then pressed a kiss to his cheek. "Oh, darling, I could scarcely have hope."

"Not with my Piper." His eyes drifted to mine. "She saw to it, didn't she?"

"She most certainly did." She turned toward me and

with her one free arm she pulled me into her too, hugging me so tightly. "How can I ever repay you for giving me back my son?"

I was at a loss for words. I didn't want anything from her, just her acceptance. All I could do was hug her back. "I'm glad you showed up when you did."

"Moira!" Titus's voice boomed over everything else.

Her head snapped up ,and when he looked at her, it was all there so plain on his face. How much he loved her, how he needed her, and a lifetime worth of regret. He leapt off the wall and dropped down in front of her. She let us go to face him while Gray and I took a step back.

Titus took a step toward her. "You're alive."

She drew in a sharp breath and her eyes went round. "You're . . . you."

"Two hundred years." He took another step toward her. "I have two hundred years to give back to you."

She shook her head and tears sprang to her eyes. "It can't be. You can't know."

"I know." He wrapped his arm around her back and pulled her in closer. With his other hand, he brushed the locks of her hair from her face. "I know *everything*."

A sob broke past her lips and he leaned down ever so gently and pressed his lips to hers. Moira cupped his face with her tiny hands and tears streamed down her cheeks. She pulled back. "You remember?"

"I remember it all." He couldn't keep his hands from exploring her face, her hair. His eyes never left her delicate features. "I'm so sorry."

"No, don't apologize." She shook her head. "We've been together this whole time."

"And yet a million miles apart." He pressed his lips to hers once more. "No longer, love. No longer."

She closed her eyes and pressed her forehead to his. "Say it again."

"My love," he whispered, and I felt we were intruding on a moment they needed alone. But seeing them together after two hundred years of being so close yet so far was sweetly satisfying. As if this whole journey was worth it to bring them back together.

"Don't ever leave me again," she breathed against his lips.

"Never."

"Right, I've had about enough of that." Grayson threw his arm over my shoulder and pulled me toward the front of the castle. "Something's not right about watching your parents have a snog right in front of you."

"I think it's sweet."

I glanced over my shoulder as Titus pulled her so tight and Moira returned his embrace. She rested her head on his chest and her eyes slid shut as a deep breath left her. Silent tears trickled down her face as he cupped the back of her head, holding her to him.

The corner of her lip pulled up in a half-smile. "Finally."

CHAPTER FIFTY-THREE

GRAYSON

"*B*ut explain to me why we must wash him in here, love."

Piper stood on her tiptoes with her hair balled into a wild knot on top of her head. Those rosebuds were still there, and I'd grown to love the vines over her skin, though they were evidence of the scars of her torture she seemed to love them despite what'd happened. Her sleeves were rolled up to her elbows and white suds floated around the room. Her pants and shirt were soaked as she held a giant sponge. "Because Winston needs a bath. Because he's the goodest boy and deserves one."

"Winston? How can you name a creature like that Winston?"

Piper had brought the huge damn bear into the castle, and because there was no bathroom large enough for him, my father had given her full access to the King's chambers, and now there was a bear sitting in his bathtub while my soulmate and her best friend tried to give him a proper washing.

Piper scrubbed just under the bear's chin. He tilted his head up and I could've sworn a smile spread across his face when she got to his cheeks. "He likes the name Winston."

"I really don't think there's any arguing this point." Dice chuckled as she grabbed a large scrub brush and ran it over the bear's back.

"Who's arguing?" I hopped on the countertop next to the sink and sat there watching these two treat a bear who only beheaded someone days ago like a house pet. "I only thought he needed something more fitting, you know? Like Galdious the warrior King."

"Galdious?" She chuckled and shook her head. "No, he's a Winston. Aren't you, buddy?"

When she scratched his ear, he tilted his head to the side, leaning into her touch. How this creature could so easily be tamed was not a mystery to me. She was everything all at once—a lover, a killer, so strong, yet not afraid to give me her heart—and for that I was eternally grateful. "Very well. Winston it is."

Atlas strode through the door with a tray of fish and sat it down in front of the bear. I gave him a sideways look. "Not you too."

"I dare say that Winston is . . . How did you put it? The goodest of good boys and deserves a bit of a snack." He took a step back and leaned on the counter next to me.

"Are you sure you aren't a witch, love? It seems you've cast a spell on the whole castle." I wasn't wrong. There were crows littering the roofs of the castle and wolves running about the halls. Yet no one seemed to mind a single bit. Three little mice had taken to following her around and even now sat a few feet away on the sink with a hunk of cheese and a bit of crackers to snack on.

"Nah, I like being a vampire." She filled a bucket of water and dumped it over Winston's back, rinsing blood and soap off his thick brown fur.

"She's got full Disney princess status now. All the little critters love her." Dice chuckled. "I'm jealous, but I won't be for long."

Her bestie was determined to make the change to vampire, even though I could see the hesitation in Piper's eyes. I wasn't quite sure why, but I knew she'd come around at some point to it. I think deep down she was terrified that the catalyst to becoming a vampire was death, and she didn't want to see that for her friend.

Atlas cleared his throat. "You're in such a hurry to die."

Dice shrugged. "You volunteering to help with that?"

Before he could answer, Prisha and Sanchita sauntered into the room with two wolves lumbering behind them. The wolves were enormous, one white and one black, both nearly as tall as Atlas and me.

Sanchita gave a heavy sigh. "Piper, tell them they need a good brushing. They're shedding all over the castle and my leggings are covered in fur."

Piper chuckled. "You know I'm not an animal tamer. They just kind of do what they want and go where they want. They just like hanging around me."

"Who wouldn't, love?" She'd brought life back into the castle and so much love.

She giggled in my direction. "You're biased."

"Undoubtedly." It was a relief to openly love her the way I so desperately wanted to and in the way she deserved.

"The wedding is only a few days away. They need it. We can't have guests flooding the castle and mangy wolves roaming around. It's not respectable." Prisha turned to look at the black wolf. "You need it, Harold. I'm telling you."

"Harold? What is with the old man names?" She'd gone around the castle giving all the lingering animals names, some of which I did not understand but still loved.

Piper put her hands on her hips and water sloshed from her hands down her pants. "They're distinguished names. Very respectable."

She turned to the wolves. "Harold, Edith, will you please let them brush you? You do have those little fluffy things flying out of you." With a heavy sigh and a bit of growling, they moved over to the corner of the bathroom and lay down. Piper motioned toward them. "I think that's an okay. Just don't brush Harold's ears. He doesn't like it."

Prisha and Sanchita hurried over to them and dove in. They lay over the wolves as if they were pillows, cuddling with them as they worked. I still couldn't believe there were wolves and bears in England. Piper thought they were a gift from her father. I thought nothing could resist her and so naturally they'd appeared.

My mother hurried into the bathroom with a small

cardinal in her hands. She rushed up to Piper. "Darling, I think it's injured."

Piper dropped her sponge into the tub and moved to Moira's side. "Oh no. He's hurt his wing."

"Honestly, dear, I think he's a bit daft. He keeps flying into the windows of the castle repeatedly. It does make this god-awful thumping sound." My mother had never looked so well. Gone were the uptight dresses and in their place were modern dresses that hung from her body and didn't require a corset. On occasion, I spotted her in a sweater and even jeans. A smile blessed her face daily, and she'd taken to walking in the forest with Piper. My mother adored all the animals as much as Piper did.

Piper chuckled. "Why do they do that? They're gluttons for punishment."

"I was thinking perhaps we need to take him farther from the castle and release him into the forest? It might help him get some freedom." Moira opened her hands and showed the little bird to Piper.

"I think you're right. Just let me finish giving Winston his bath and we can take a ride if you like."

My mother nodded. "I'd love nothing more. That'll give me time to heal his wing." Each day they rode their horses out into the forest and were gone for hours. Of course, my father and I stood watching the door for the return, all the while pretending we weren't sad, lovesick sacks. My mother turned to the huge bear. "Hello, Winston, you're looking quite fetching."

"Moira? Moira, where are you off to?" My father sauntered into the bathroom and took one look around his personal chamber with wide eyes. "You really did put a bear in my bathtub."

"Your bathtub is more like a pool." Dice chuckled.

"I hope you don't mind." Piper looked at my father with a sheepish smile.

"Not at all, dear." He motioned to the vanity I sat on. "There's more soap in there if you need it."

"Is that really the King we grew up with?" Atlas muttered under his breath. "I remember he'd give us a right proper flogging for frogs in the kitchen and now he's got a bloody bear in his bathroom."

I smirked to myself with satisfaction flowing through my body. My family was finally happy. Martin stepped into the room with his tablet in hand. His eyes widened at the mess in the bathroom, and he punched something into the screen. "No, absolutely not. I'll have it set to rights as soon as the zoo moves on, Your Majesty."

Piper blew a fistful of suds at him. "Don't be a party pooper, Martin."

"Speaking of." Martin walked up to my parents and held the tablet up for them to see. "The table settings are complete, as well as the music, catering, and location. Now I had some ideas—"

"Martin dear, whatever you decide will be fantastic." My mother didn't look at him. She just stared at my father. "What are your thoughts, darling?"

"If you're pleased, then I'm pleased." My father practically went gooey each time he looked at her.

"I'd be disgusted if I wasn't so bloody thrilled for them," I whispered to Atlas.

He chuckled under his breath. "Bet you never thought this would be your life."

"Not in a million years." I shook my head.

"It's bloody grand, isn't it?"

"Wouldn't change it for the world."

CHAPTER FIFTY-FOUR

PIPER

Later

*L*ight music drifted all around us as we sat at a table located just off the dance floor. Titus and Moira whirled around at the center of it all. They swayed in unison as though they'd never been apart. She rested her head against his chest as he held her close, and they swayed together as though there was nothing else in the world but them.

"Your parents look happy."

Grayson rested his hand on my thigh and gave it a little squeeze. "Sickeningly so. I don't think I've ever seen either of them so elated."

"Don't take this the wrong way, but your mom is hot." Dice dropped down in the seat next to him. A wide smile spread over her face as she placed her champagne flute on the table in front of her. She wore a simple black silky dress that she'd taken from my closet and piled her hair high on her head.

"I'm going to take that as a compliment to my own genetics." Grayson winked at her. "But my mother does look lovely as ever."

Moira wore a long silky white dress that hugged her body and pooled on the floor around her feet. The back was cut low, exposing all of her pale skin while the front dipped low across her chest. Soft pieces of lace trimmed the back and across the neckline in the front. It was simple but beautifully delicate. Her thick chocolate hair flowed from her head in loose waves all around her body and nearly to her hips.

"Yeah, your dad isn't bad either." Dice teased with a light chuckle. But she wasn't wrong. Titus opted to forego his usual floor-length crimson coat for a white one that matched Moira's silky dress. Under his coat he wore a black button-down shirt along with matching pants. It was simple yet stylish.

"I think you have your hands full at the moment. Don't you?" Grayson motioned to Atlas and Kylian who sat on opposite sides of the table.

Dice rolled her eyes at him. "Oh please, as if either one of them could handle this."

"She's not wrong." I chuckled and laid my hand over Grayson's.

Theon stopped by our table with Claire by his side. Silence fell over us, but Grayson was comfortable in any situation. "Theon, you're looking well."

"Listen, I," he glanced down at Claire and she gave him an encouraging smile, "I just wanted to say thank you for giving me the chance to help with the Night Spawn again."

Grayson gave him a slow, easy smile. "It's a pleasure, and you've done well with the opening of the city and getting it ready. My father also tells me you've been invaluable with information regarding the Night Spawn."

"I'm grateful that the King and Queen decided to hold their vow renewal here. In our new city." Theon glanced around at the party. "It's an honor."

"Any news about Kendra?" Grayson inquired.

"We're still searching." Theon lowered his head to meet Grayson's eye. "We will find her."

"Excellent, we don't want the likes of her loose for long." He winked. "In any case I'm quite pleased with how everything turned out with in the city."

The city did look amazing. With the help of Lorenzo and his construction crew, the city had been ready in days. It was gorgeous. The buildings were built of beautiful stone that'd been carved into intricate designs and shapes. It was a mix of the beauty of an ancient Roman design with all the modern touches of twisted metal, carved stone, and pristine roadways. There were apartment buildings that looked more like a luxury resort. A makeshift river flowed around the city. It filled the area with the sound of running water, and many of the balconies overlooked it. Other buildings that had pointed steeples were spread through the city, and tiny shops were at the ground level with big windows to peek into. At the center of it all was a beautiful park filled with night-blooming flowers.

Grayson stood and shook his hand. "Perhaps we might become friends yet."

"Don't push it too far." Atlas narrowed his eyes at Theon. "He's a right pain in the arse."

"So you're saying you have a problem with my personality and not who my sire is?"

Atlas picked up a glass of champagne and took a deep sip. "I didn't realize hating you because of Marius was an option. I just thought you were a daft prick."

"You know, I'll take that." Theon took Claire's hand and guided her toward the dance floor.

"I think Theon has got the right of it." Grayson rose to his feet and offered me his hand. "Shall we dance?"

I took his hand and let him pull me to my feet. We walked out onto the dance floor. Grayson wrapped his arm around me and his hand splayed across my lower back. This close, his warm chocolate scent enveloped me, and I could feel his heartbeat through his clothing. He swayed to the beat, and I followed his lead. "This will be us someday, with a grand royal wedding."

"Someday." I tilted my head back, looking up at him. "Maybe."

"Are you putting me off then?" He chuckled. "We are soulmates after all."

I chuckled. "So you plan on following me around to pester me until I say yes?"

He pressed his hand into me and our bodies were flush

against each other. His eyes bore into mine and I was lost in those mahogany flecks and the soft way his lips curved. Grayson Shade had always been intoxicating, but now as his soulmate I found him devastatingly beautiful. His chest rumbled with a deep sultry chuckle. "Oh, you know how it goes, little creature. Where you go, I will follow."

WANT to find out what Graymont and Hades were up to in the Underworld? Click the link below and join my FB group Megan Montero's Wicked Readers for a fun free scene!

Click here to join the Wicked Readers

WHAT IS NEXT FOR THE ROYALS??? Welcome to the Underworld in my next book WICKED DEATH in my new series The Royals: Hades' Court.

https://mybook.to/wickeddeath

DON'T MISS OUT ON THIS FREE BOOK!

THIS POWER CHOSE *ME...*

Within the supernatural world of Evermore everyone prays their child will be born with the Mark of the Guardian for they have unparalleled strength, intelligence, and *power*...but they have no idea what it's actually like. I didn't wish for this *gift* and I definitely don't want it. I was born a prince, I already had it all. This Mark on my neck stole all of it from me and forced me into a dangerous life I'd gladly trade away if I could...

But now the Witch Queens have ascended and it's time to try and defeat the evil King once and for all. For over a thousand years his cruelty has spared no one as his torturous power grows stronger. He must be stopped now, before his reign destroys everything and anything in his way. So I must push aside my dreams of returning home to the family that cast me out. I must step up and claim the power that chose me. I *must* enter the Trials and become a Knight in the Witch's Court.

There's only one way to prevent the tyrannical king from destroying everything I love...I must become the one thing he can't beat.

Click here to get your FREE book now!

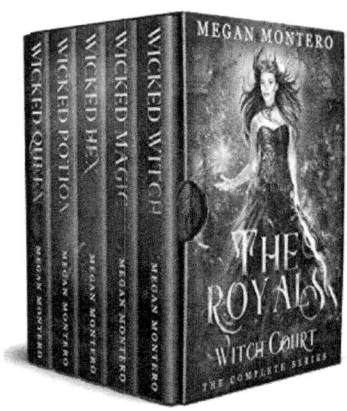

INCASE YOU MISSED the first season of The Royals: Witch Court check it out now!

CLICK HERE TO GET YOUR WITCH COURT BOXSET

It's time to claim my power...

ALL MY LIFE I've lived under lock and key, always following the strict rules my mother set for me. A week before my sixteenth birthday I sneak out of my house and discover why. Turns out I am not just a normal teenager. I'm a witch blessed with a gift someone wants to steal from me.

And not just anyone...the evil King Alataris.

For a thousand years the people of Evermore have suffered under his tyranny. The Mark on my shoulder says I am the Siphon Witch, one of five Witch Queens fated to come together and finally destroy him. The only thing keeping Evermore safe is the Stone that shields the witch kingdoms from Alataris's magic…and now he's found a way to steal it. Suddenly, I'm sent on a quest to find the ancient spell to protect the Stone. My only hope for surviving is through my strikingly beautiful and immensely powerful Guardian, Tucker. The laws of Evermore state that love between us is strictly forbidden, and it appears I'm the only one willing to give in to the attraction…

When the quest turns more dangerous than expected I realize I have absolutely no idea what I'm doing. I was raised human. But I have to learn my magic fast because If King Alataris gets his hands on me he'll steal my magic and my life…but if he gets his hands on that Stone we all die.

THE MAGIC CONTINUES in the second season of The Royals: Warlock Court Now in this completely set!

CLICK HERE TO GET WARLOCK COURT

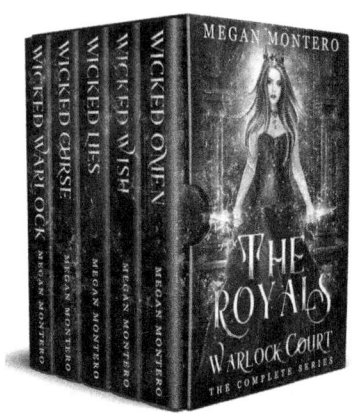

THERE'S **no such thing as magical powers. . .**

All my life the only kind of magic I'd ever seen was the sparkling jewels on fifth avenue. On the night of my sixteenth birthday all hell breaks loose, and by hell I mean me! I never felt power like this, so dark, so tempting, so out of my control! No one is safe around me. And now I'm being thrown into Warwick Academy.

An academy for the darker side of magic. . .the warlock side.

My captor, my savior, and the bane of my existence, Beckett Dust insists on keeping me here even though we can't stand each other. I don't care how drop dead gorgeous he is or that he rules the school like he owns it, I need to stay as far away from him as I can. His deepest desire is to turn me into a weapon in the great war to come. My deepest desire is . . . him. There's a thin line between love and hate and right now I'm walking it.

IF YOU'RE all caught up on The Royals don't worry there's more to come. In the mean time check out The Night Realm: Magic Marked my awesome co-written series with Chandelle LaVaun.

CLICK HERE TO GET MAGIC MARKED

He put a spell on me...

Or at least he *must* have, because none of this makes any sense. None of this can be *real*. I'm not a mage with magical powers...I'm just *me*. Ellie Sutton. Your average, everyday seventeen-year-old high school *human* student. My biggest concerns are bullies, failed exams, and missing the express subway twice in one day.

Magic is something I read about in comic books, it's not real. People don't move things with their minds or summon lightning with their hands. I don't care what Stellan Wentworth says. It doesn't matter that he's breathtakingly beautiful or that his eyes sparkled when I challenge him. He's the kind of hero found in romance novels, not my real life. I'm dreaming, I have to be.

Because if I'm not, then what he's telling me is true. This gorgeous, terrifying world is in turmoil...and if I don't learn how to use my magic overnight...they'll all die.

The Night Realm (Co-Write With Chandelle LaVaun)

Magic Marked

Midnight Mage

Marvel Mage

Master Mage

Court Marked

Fatal Fae

Fiery Fae

Final Fae (Coming Soon)

Christmas Marked

Bite Me, Santa

Jingle My Bells

Trim My Tree

Ride My Sleigh

Stuff My Stocking

Halloween Marked

Trick My Treat

Hocus My Pocus

Carve My Pumpkin

Published by Leo Press

Cover Design by Lori Grundy @ Cover Reveal Designs

Artwork by Samaiya Beaumont @ Samaiya Beaumont Art

❀ Created with Vellum

For Gigi

ABOUT THE AUTHOR

Megan Montero was born and raised as sassy Jersey girl. After devouring series like the Immortals After Dark, the Arcana Chronicles, Harry Potter and Mortal Instruments she decided then and there that she would write her own series. When she's not putting pen to paper you can find her cuddled up under a thick blanket (even in the summer) with a book in her hands. When she's not reading or writing you can find her playing with her dogs, watching movies, listening to music or moving the furniture around her house...again. She loves finding magic in all aspects of her life and that's why she writes Urban Fantasy and Paranormal.

Learn about Megan and her books by visiting her website at:

Www.meganmontero.com

Printed in Great Britain
by Amazon

61638304R00316